About the Author

Monty Bassett has made numerous Natural History documentary films for Discovery Channel, National Geographic and Knowledge Network. His first film, "Life on the Vertical" won a "Gemini", a "Finalist Award" at the New York Film Festival and was chosen to represent Canada at the Cannes Film Festival.

His first book, "Slim the Guide" focused on the conflict between industrial mining, logging, the loss of the wilderness and the Indigenous people caught in the middle.

Acknowledgements:

First, I would especially like to acknowledge Lynnda McDougall, Lori Widen, Debby Meissner, and my lovely wife Nicole for making me appear literate.

Most of all, I want to recognize the wonderful people of Nevis, especially the villagers of Hard Times, Rawlins Village, Mollybon and Stoney Hill for the stories and lessons of how humans should act in times of extreme crisis.

Table of Contents

Preface:

"Mangoes by the Bushel"

On a small Island in the Leeward chain of the Caribbean, on the end of a high volcanic ridge that shoulders off a jungled mountain, sat an ancient mango tree. Squat and round like a Buddha, its stubby limbs intertwined in arthritic angles around its trunk, then pruned and sculpted by the winds off both the Caribbean and Atlantic seas. The mango tree's age was marked in hundreds of years, and like the green mantle of the volcano that surrounded it, the tree had become its own eco-system teeming with life.

Lacing through the lattice of limbs, great boa constrictor philodendrons looped and drooped in thick, fat serpentine coils, punctuated intermittently with floppy elephant-ear leaves, each a calypso of yellows and greens. In the shelter of the foliage, even delicate life like bromeliads and feather-thin orchids found purchase and refuge amongst the vine-snakes encircling the trunk. The tree sang with life, as insects hummed and buzzed for food and shelter to lay their larvae. Termites built complex tunnel cities in the soft parts of the mango's bark, bees and hornets made paper-thin palaces high in the canopy for their queens.

Flycatchers fed on the maturing larvae. Mourning doves cooed their message "Moses speaks the word of God... Moses speaks the word of God." Broad-winged hawks and kestrels soared overhead studying the foliage for geckos as the lizards in turn stalked dragonflies unaware of their own peril from above. Egrets, motionless statues, perched in the mango tree snapping forward their necks with lightning speed at a bug or lounging lizard.

Periodically, a circus of chattering, gamboling, vagabond monkeys trouped through the tree. They came for sport and play, but not for food, for there was none. The fertility of the tree, once virile and fruit-bearing; like an old woman, had dried out and only when passing boys struck the mango's trunk with their cutlasses did the tree grudgingly produce one or two mangoes each year.

Its first seeds were brought from India, while its neighbours came with the Arawak Indians from the Orinoco River of South America, who established villages on the escarpment sandwiched between the bounty of the ocean and the lush abundance of the jungle. They were followed by Carib Indians from the lands surrounding the Caribbean. Christopher Columbus sailed passed the Island. Soon great marine battles were fought between the Spanish, French, and English off its coasts.

Inca gold sailed across the horizon to the treasuries of Europe, though many ships were plundered and sunk in the blue Caribbean Sea. It was a time of global trade as routes opened East to West. Fruits of the original trees were harvested by monkeys from Africa. Settlers came from the Old World, and with them they brought slaves to cultivate the rich volcanic soil until eventually it became bleached and sickly from crop after crop of sugar cane.

Emancipation brought the end of the slavery but not the end of the once enslaved African people who persisted like the mango -- even when the era of plantations perished. Finally, cruise ships replaced pirate galleons, sunbathers replaced green sea turtles coming ashore to lay their eggs. Yet, through it all, the mango tree flourished.

And then one day, in the year 1989, the wind began to swell. It was a clear day, not quite the full moon rose above the distant Island of Antigua. Yet, there was something that forewarned that the gentle fragrant breezes which shifted from the West to the Southeast were forerunners of a violence never known on the Island. Finally, late in the night of September 18th, hurricane winds from the "Storm of the Century" struck the Island and hit the mango tree full-force, ripping the surrounding jungle apart, striking the mango tree head on! And, for thirty-six hours the storm pounded the tree with 100 mph to 130mph, and gusts reaching 150 mph.

Vegetation was the first to go, and soon the sheltering elephant-ears and delicate bromeliads adorning the mango tree were shredded, their boa coils torn from their hold and fell in a slurry that saturated the air.

Insect life vanished early, leaf-miners were mulched with the leaves they once mined. Colonies of termites with their cardboard-thin nest collapsed causing limbs to be torn from the tree. The birds followed the plight of the insects, seeking shelter further down the tree's trunk until finally there was no shelter except the protection of the ravines, called "ghauts'. But that too was futile, and the moment they rose into the wind their wings were torn off and their featherless bodies ground into the earth. Species by species were devoured by the storm until finally there was only the wind!

When it was over the mango tree high on the volcanic ridge was reduced to a stump resembling a human torso, be-headed, de-armed of all its appendages except a few sap-bleeding stubs. Around the tree the carnage was complete. Where once the jungle was a painter's pallet of colour, now a monochrome brown covered the land. In the heavy humidity, rot came quickly and soon the torrential rains began stripping the battered landscape of the dead and dying, exposing raw and open lacerations, and craters where uprooted breadfruit and mahogany trees once stood, now pocketed the earth. The soil succumbed to fatigue and released its grip, sending tons of erosion cascading down the waterways, cutting in its wake new, even greater scars in the jungle shroud.

Death held the Island as though life had never flourished upon it. And so it was with the ancient mango tree, as the effort to live became too much and its will to survive seemingly passed with the destruction of its body. The tree bled openly and a silence of despair blanketed the land-locked purgatory punctuated in the absence of sound; the land was paralysed in a state of systemic shock.

8

****

When, all hope was gone that life would never come again, a miracle happened.

The first tendrils of *elan vital,* a life force as primitive as the first protein chains growing from a primordial sludge, emerged defying the laws of bio-physics. The mango's scarred and calloused hide turned a pale green-sheen with mould and algae. From its amputation-wounds, small shoots began to bud.

From the shelter of the ghaut the few creatures that had survived deep in its recesses crawled out. The primitive insects were the first to return, but often they were strange, new species carried by the storm from Africa. Timidly birds made cautious sojourns from deep in the ravine feeding on the exotic new bugs. Joining them, from pits in the ground, lizards and frogs crept across the corpses of devastation. Mongoose soon followed the reptiles. Monkeys, awestruck by the destruction, ventured forth, their bewildered eyes and empty bellies sharp to any sign of food.

In the following months, the jungle floor -- opened for the first time in centuries to direct light and the heat of the sun, awoke it from its exhaustion and the Island slowly with a vitality spawned by a second chance at life, emerged. And once again the will to live out-measured the force to die.

But, something was different. Free of the hold of age and time, decay and ambivalence; the mango tree, like the Island itself -- its fertility so long atrophied and dormant by age, grew with a vitality stronger than it had known since youth, and slowly the Buddha tree bore flowers then fruit, until finally it bore mangoes by the bushel.

Chapter I

The Message

"Goats! Don't vex me up!" Sueky yelled, but her words lacked energy and authority, tumbling from her like round stones rolling over each other in the surf. Noise without consequence. "Move on roight smartly o' Youse be sorry das Youse fuss me up," she muttered to herself hoping the goats were paying attention. Raising her walking staff she slapped it against the rubble-stone wall separating path from pasture. But neither words nor threats with the stick conveyed that this command was any different from the usual rain-on-tin prattle that followed Sueky like a constant traveling companion. But there was something strange in the air, something ominous and it upset her that she could not give it a name. The goats were her target for her frustration.

" Dis no be d'time fo Youse foolishness."

Defiantly, one goat, a brown and white pinto billy, reared up on his hind legs as far as he could reach and began eating the topmost hibiscus blossoms from a bush growing on the other side of the wall.

"Goat!," muttered again the cusha-thin old woman. "Dis's not de day no' de place to be pestering me. Now move! And does so smartly 'cus me won't serve Youse no second warning." But the pinto billy merely glanced back defiantly and arrogant, his lips "Jamaican Night"-red with Miss Sutton's hibiscus blossoms.

Carefully leaning her stick against the stone wall, she reached up for the bundle of grass on her head and deposited it on the top of the wall. As she hobbled into the center of the path, her hand slipped into the apron pocket of her frail, faded dress, the old fingers sorting through the nest of stones she carried there. She found one, a fat one she imagined would cause the goat as much disgust as he caused her. With great labor, she drew back her arm wooden-plank-straight and stiff as high behind her as she could reach behind, and let it swing with the force of gravity.

Then just as her hand started down the crescent of the pendulum arch, the ancient fingers releasing the stone, sending it in a lob-shot trajectory which she directed towards her target by sheer will alone… of which she had plenty.

And suddenly the billy sprang off Miss Sutton's wall, spitting hibiscus petals as the stone shattered beside him. When he landed, it was at a full run which spooked the rest of the herd. Again, Sueky's hand disappeared momentarily into her pocket, and a second egg-sized rock followed the goats, but it lacked conviction and fell far short of the mark — no match for the goats' speed when they allowed their imagination to direct their feet.

"See dat, Mister Goat, ye does misreads me patience," Sueky cackled at him. "Ye churely does, fo' chure, fo' chure." It was the Caribbean, heat and humidity plus years of working the land by hand that had welded Sueky's joints with arthritis, and before she could pick up her walking stick, she had to rub her hands and her throwing shoulder to ease the spasms of pain that followed the two pitches.

Finally, she stopped rubbing, drew a deep breath, re-positioned the bundle of grass on her head and took up her walking stick. Rocking forward onto it, she sighed a "Lobetojesus" without any particular reason except to clear the path before her.

Sueky walked like a feeding crane, bent over at the hip, advancing her head and walking-stick first, then moving the rest of her body up to them with stilted, brittle, measured strides. White coils of her hair escaped from the tattered, floppy felt hat that sheltered her from the sun and cushioned the load on her head. The grass, the hat, the hair framed a portrait face. Had Rembrandt painted in blues and blacks and deep lavenders and in the West Indies, Sueky would be his most famous model.

It was her eyes, great ebony eyes, full of expression; and, like her running discourse with the ether, whatever she felt in her heart at that moment was written in the eyes. They were owl's-eyes wise, and when they were young, they were hawk-eyed sharp, but since her cataracts, her sight had diminishing rapidly. Her skin had pulled taut across her cheekbones. Causing her great round eyes to ride high on them, crowding the bridge of her narrow, elegant nose. Her mouth was mostly full of teeth that radiated when she smiled, which was often. Her lips were muscular and equally expressive, messaging each word lightly before it flowed from her.

Sueky never wasted much time reflecting on the content of her dialogue, believing that she was just an intermediary, a conduit, and if her heart was pure, her words could not be otherwise. Consequently, her thoughts flowed fresh from the spring into the current of continual dialogue without obstruction or the restraint of studying them. Nor was the presence of a listener requisite; she needed no other audience than herself... and of course... the Lord, whom she assumed was continually listening. Her accent had a Scottish edge, as did her idioms: when things went poorly she'd be "vexed up", and when things went well it was "boony".

Her neck was a cypress trunk with sinewy roots disappearing into the floral-print dress, fatigued by experiences well beyond its life-expectancy, that hung limply on her coat-hanger frame. Without benefit of protective cartilage, her bones rubbed painfully on each other; her joints had no flex. Also, Sueky was shrinking and her sandals slapped the polished path with the double-time beat of footwear too large for the foot. Once the sandals had fit, when her feet were full and supple and she danced the calypso of youth beneath a tropical moon, but now she was withering and petrifying.

Already the bottoms of her feet had turned to polished marble from a lifetime of walking pumice paths. Her feet had become black granite hard, that now wore troughs into the cobblestone paths as she traveled back and forth. Her knees — which she talked to continually about their numbness — had

12

become knobby knots of obsidian, and her fingers long shafts of black coral, each joint an angular twist in the colony. One day, if the process continued, all that would be left of Sueky would be the pure essence of the human spirit distilled into a single crystal, a flawless black diamond. "Sueky is living testament," the Anglican priest had said about her in church on her eighty-seventh birthday, "living testament to just how little shelter it takes to house the Holy Spirit!"

"Amen!" the congregation had shouted to the heavens.

At the crossroads of Pasture Path and the Uptee Doon Road, the lead goat turned down towards the sea to the pen beside Sueky's house. The grass Sueky carried on her head was their supper and breakfast. The Uptee Doon Road was just that, the road that snaked up the mountain and straight down to the sea. There was only one road circling the island, and Sueky could never understand how strangers from off-island, or even the other side of Nevis, could get lost. The "Uptee" led up, to the emerald volcano — "El *Montoya de un mil verdes,*" as Spanish sailors called the mountain of a thousand greens. Even from afar, Sueky knew the many faces of the peak. She could read the jungle by its colour: a bright splash of yellow green was a bamboo patch, rusted-red/chocolate-green were pods on the cocoa tree. The deep, dark violet-greens that pulled in light like black holes in the universe were great mahogany trees trapping the sun before it hit the forest floor.

Sueky could go straight to a mango tree, a breadfruit or coconut palm without seeing it up close just by its distinct color of green. In her head she carried a map of the jungle that was as detailed as a street map of New York. She could also read the wind by the jungle's colour. The "umbrella tree" living high near the peak, for example: Its large platter-sized leaves are green on the sun-side face. Like a broken umbrella in a gale, the leaf folds over, showing the white side, when the wind blows hard.

13

Just this simple observation gave Sueky advance notice — direction and intensity about when a squall was coming. Everyone in upper Poppy gave her respect for her bush skills. She knew root-teas, potions and jumbie names for the winds on moonless nights when her grands were afraid to venture out. And, they said, she knew all of the voodoo rites of the Obeah.

During the dry season, water for her animals was a problem and Sueky daily had to move her small herd to a pasture far from her cottage. But she preferred living near the sea and at the edge of the rainforest. It was quiet and slow there, exactly as it had been since her mother Em was alive; even her great-great-grand Ella, and before her the granddaughter of Naomi all lived upon that parcel of land. It was still quiet, and when she wasn't talking to the Lord she was talking without shouting with her ancestors. The road was rough by her yard and only the brave or kind church van ventured down to take her to church. Not like the Uptee stretch of the Uptee Doon Road beginning at the boundary and running straight up towards the peak. Even worse for the mayhem of motorised traffic was the Ring Road that belted the Island and crossed the Uptee Doon Road halfway. It was the main road, encircling the island's midriff, and around it, the island commerce flowed from the country to the main town, Portstown. One and a half lanes of two way traffic , rendered "flowing" impossible and worked because of custom and courtesy.

The Ring Road confused Sueky. Too much noise and movement. The "tap-taps", the small passenger vans with painted names she didn't understand, like "Rambo" and "Dem-say", passed her so fast going to and coming from Portstown that she wondered if they ever picked up and discharged passengers. She seldom saw who was inside, and if she did, they were strangers from the other side of the island. The big trucks shook the ground, their bunks so high above her that Sueky wondered if they carried anything at all, or if they were merely there to frighten old people. Even the occasional tourist in a Mini-moke from the Hotel Lemon bewildered Sueky, although they were always friendly — that was the point, they were always friendly, and never seemed to have a care in the world except taking photographs.

In truth, St Augustine. sat far back in the backwaters of the Caribbean, but from Sueky's perspective it still traveled "by de fast-clock" towards the edge of the galaxy. It was the end of the twentieth century and St. Augustine's Ring Road had only just been paved two years before. Prior to that, what cars there were on-island ventured into the country for sport, or challenge more than commerce — often having to be towed home by a donkey. The situation was that the island lay in one of those temporal tidal eddies out of the flow of time, and therefore pursued a future that looked very much like the past of a hundred years earlier. It was a simple mistake: Somewhere around the beginning of the Industrial Revolution, when the rest of the world took a turn towards mechanisation, St. Augustine, quietly unaware in her peaceful self-sufficiency, kept going straight. Sueky, like most of her generation, knew well by stories the era of cane and slavery; not by personal memory but by inheritance of the vivid tales passed down from people like her grandmother's grandmother, Ella.

Sueky's view of on-island life wasn't so different from Ella's, she suspected, only the sap that sustained the plantations was gone. Ella had worked in the big house when the Rutherford family lived there. "Dey drank up deys rum just fine, but don't tend to d'source," Sueky's grand, used to say.

There were stories told of shiny carriages, and serving grand banquets in the manor house where the table was so long you could hardly see the far end. Her grandfather, she said, was clear, a Scots stone mason. "But me skin be me mother's skin, and she skin be she's mother's, 'til it reaches all de way back ta de soil from de 'odder place'." Even in Sueky's time, elders still spoke longingly of the A-free-ca. "We hear it calling not width da ears, it's our hearts dats we know dey stories be true about 'A-free-ca'."

15

Married by their isolation on the island to sugar cane and slavery, both Scot and African transformed the jungled lava rock into great stone structures; manor houses, windmills, boilers and chimneys for the rum industry. The wealth of a plantation was measured by the strength of the mill towers that caught the wind on canvas sails and converted its force to drive giant iron rollers that crushed the cane into juice. "Back den," Ella had said, "cane was king over everything and rum, dey use't say, be he 'dusty maiden'," then she'd laugh, "cus he make she be queen, as he does width slaves, and he take she freely da same as he take da slave."

The fertile coastal-apron forest of the island was cleared first and became fields divided by rubble-stone walls, impounding orchards of breadfruit, bananas, palm and papaya. The cane grew so high that, by its fourth month, it swallowed a human from sight. "Da Rutherfords always treats Ella right and she does respect dem accordingly, but times dey were changing."

When Ella was very young, the fever of emancipation swept through the Caribbean like a cane fire, finally reaching St. Augustine. Colonised by the English in the 16th century, in the early 1800s, when freedom's ring finally was heard in St. Kitts, the British empire had lost its majesty and in turn had perfect its skills of abandoning their holdings in the West Indies. Consequently unlike the end of the Spanish and French colonialism in the Caribbean, the transition was peaceful and orderly.

At first, the landowners of the island believed that the abolition was of little consequence. But the great wealth they'd enjoyed for generations was not solely the product of the wind and cane; the pivotal ingredient was slavery!

There were brief attempts to industrialise with steam mills and swathers for cutting cane, but they only intensified the demands upon the exhausted land, until eventually the once-deep, black volcanic soil turned pale and sickly; baked hard by the sun and leached yellow by two hundred years of a single crop. And slowly St Augustine had slipped from the mainstream of trade and commerce into the quiet solitude of self-sufficiency.

Obsolescence ate away at the great stone fortresses, as fine tendrils of the "lub vine" and delusions of self-importance worked against the colonialists. By the end of the 19th century, only a few owners remained on their plantations and most of those were addicted to the product they produced — their children went to school in Europe and the United States, never to return.

Finally, all that remained of the great cane era was an empty armchair on a vine-choked veranda, surrounded by hollow ruins that beat with life only twice a day as the bats left in the evenings and returned at dawn. And the cane industry that had bought and sold souls, changing the destiny of tens of thousands of lives, died a silent death as goats denuded the last stubble of the crop and erosion took what was left of the topsoil, leaving rubble-stone walls of the plantations standing out like skeletal ribs.

A protectorate of the English monarchy, St. Augustine benefited with schools, a legal system complete with robes, wigs and English law, and huge churches full of shadows and mystery — shelters from both heat and hurricanes. Though free to do work of their choosing, the freemen were still prisoners, trapped on the island more by tradition than by inability to escape. The "odder place A-free-ca" now had a location on the map, but no one returned there. And as small parcels of land were traded for work and loyalty, the people of the "odder-place" accepted that the Island was now their place, their home, their destiny. Moving away from the plantations, villages sprang up around pockets of rich soil and ancient fruit trees: places with names like Deputy, Poppy Dawn, Hard Times, Paradise,, Jumbe Hallow, Jumbe Holler, Zion, Hope, Beyond Hope.

******

"Lobetojesus," Sueky grumbled, her gaze fixed on the trail without focus. She didn't need to see the path, she could walk it

17

blind for she had history with each stone and the sequence of steps to master each.

Instead, her mind tried to corner the cloudy thoughts that had been evading her like frightened chickens all morning. They were shadowy thoughts, memories of a time gone by when she was very young. But the more she chased them, the farther they scattered. Elusive, they still made her anxious with a sense of dread. Were they memories of real events or merely some nightmare that she'd once held so vividly that it seemed real?

She wanted to believe that the thick haze that began settling onto the ocean was only "Sahara-dust", the flour-fine mist that swept through the Caribbean during the fall doldrums when the sea was glass-smooth and the air vacuum-void. Or maybe it was when the air was so pregnant under the weight of a low-pressure blanket that only the meanest of winds could drive it away. The Christmas winds of December would lead it out, but they were still months away.

She looked close at the ocean, "Sheep comes thick on da water dis day," Sueky muttered, watching the white, woolly waves on the pewter sea. But though the "flocks" had force and swell, there was no surface wind.

"It's da moon," she told herself. In two days it would be full for the second time that month. "Da land she not so accustomed so soon to da light. Das what she-be." Sueky sighed, content that she had found the reason for the unsettling weather.

Suddenly, something came upon her without warning. She could not breathe against the pressure in her chest. One hand grasped at the pain, the other desperately clutched her walking stick for balance. She swayed, her eyes clinched tight, but the more she struggled against the seizure, the stronger its griped her until finally the old hand slipped from her breast to her side, and she crumpled against the trunk of a giant gum tree and laid round her stick, like a pile of rags.

18

She waited in the dark for the seizure to overcome her. She was helpless, she knew there was no escape. Finally, needle-thin shafts of light seeped into the void, a lantern light behind a closed door. When she was young, she had opened the door freely, and the light would explode upon her and she joyously welcomed whatever was asked. "It is a blessing of two edges," counselled, Grand Em, who also had "the gift".

"She be a gift and a burden. But Youse be picked and groomed, Youse privileged, and Youse must do dey's bidding."

Once she'd overcome her youthful fears, she surrendered to the power that the trance gave her. She felt as though she'd been with a lover, but like no man she'd known, and throughout her years she carried with her the glow of one who has known the pure essence of love, not just its samples. Of course, she never told anyone besides Em about the trances, or the things that happened to her during them.

Sometimes she was a channel, an earthly voice for someone else's message, sometimes there were tasks... how to perform the rituals for assisting Grand Em when she performed the Obe'.

And sometimes, there were messages for her alone. Her only counsel was her great-grandmother Ella, who was the granddaughter of Naomi. Each woman carried the knowledge:.. "Keepers of da light." It had been a long time since the last visitation and Sueky had thought she was too old. Myah, her granddaughter, had the gift, Sueky guessed, and the young woman would take up the knowledge in due course. The next time the light came to Sueky, she believed, it would come to take her with it. Before, when she was full of youth and fire, she welcomed the visitations, but that was back before petrification made even the slightest task laboured and painful.

Maybe, this <u>was</u> the time she would pass on. Sueky relaxed and let it come over her easily, folding herself into the contours of the gum tree, opening herself to its comforting caress.

She approached the door without reserve then stopped. Written words appeared slowly, clearly, one at a time before her. Sueky whispered each of them in turn and only when no more came did she study them together. " KEEP THE DEAD SO"

But their meaning evaded her! She became frustrated, then desperate, fearing that she would lose the message. She didn't have to understand the words, only remember them.

Finally the phrase became a chant that she repeated again and again like waves upon the beach so her memory might never lose them. At last she reached for the door. It would not open!

Just as suddenly as the trance had possessed her, it passed and her eyes flew open like shutters flung wide after a storm. She blinked but lay still beneath the gum tree, exactly as she had fallen. The "Light" had not taken her with it. The miracle had passed.

She rubbed her eyes with disbelief. After so many years of peering through clouded cataract-veils, her sight was suddenly fresh and sharp! She lay looking up through the gum tree, spellbound by the textures and colours as shafts of sunlight streamed through the silver and satin leaves.

Tears of joy ran down her cheeks, the ancient dried-out ducting flowing with the same ease as the day she mourned Em's passing. Slowly she moved her legs from beneath her. But they too felt strange and straightened without help. She stood without pain, her legs steady and without hesitation, her back straightened without the deformity. She felt twenty years a younger woman.

"Praise b'ta Lord Jesus," she whispered in disbelief, fearful that the miracle would be but a dream, gone upon awakening. But there was no need for concern, she truly had shed the mantle of the last two decades. More confident, she stood erect and lifted her face to the sky... then, suddenly, renewed joy and abandonment possessed her and she shouted, "Praise b'ta d'Lord!" her voice strong and full. Again and again she gave thanks. But then abruptly she stopped. She'd forgotten it. The message had no substance except that there had been one! The words were gone.

"Let not d' heart be troubled," Em used to say about her own fleeting memory. "What goes away freely, comes back da same."

Sueky was unsure how long she'd lain there in the trance, but the goats hadn't wandered far. And judging by the sun's position, there was still a few hours of daylight left. The goats, unaware of the change in Sueky, continued to ignore her when she told them to move out smartly. She smiled, letting her hand slip into her dress pocket once again, but this time the rock flew flat and straight and carried authority and mass, striking the same pinto billy hard on the rump. The herd didn't stop running until they'd reached Sueky's wooden gate and the entrance to their brush pen beside the old woman's tiny chattel house.

Sueky didn't know why, but she felt the goats should stay down at the sugar-mill for a while. "Youse b'taking better lodging tonight den you's accustomed to... or probably deserves!" Her laugh was strong. "Ok..." She moved towards the goats, picking up her cutlass just inside the gate. "Down da road width Youse, to d'mill-pasture Youse go," she said pointing with her cutlass down the Uptee Doon Road.

A side trail branched off to the right of the Doon Road just before it pitched over the escarpment and out onto the Government Farm and the island's flat apron to the sea. A hundred yards along the lane, it emptied into a clearing with great iron rollers and cogwheels sticking out of the earth like toys in a child giant's sand box.

Brown and pitted with rust, they were once the internal organs of the windmill: the gears and wheels, the rollers, boilers and great copper basins that converted the mill, the wind and cane into wealth. In the center of the pasture stood a large circular stone tower, a hundred feet across at the base and thirty to forty feet in height. A working sugar-mill was like a landlocked ship, but where a sailboat turned the wind into motion, the mill sails turned it into rum. Its walls were three feet thick and tapered in slightly as they rose to

21

carry the great bulwark of axis-beams, blade-beams, and a main drive shaft of lignum vitae from Guyana. The drive shafts were themselves huge, two feet square and thirty feet long, weighing tons. The shaft, the complex of cross-beams that held it vertical, the giant hub that carried the wind part of the windmill... the sails... all had disappeared from fire, rot and, of late, scavengers, who'd turn them into lawn ornaments, pieces of furniture, and the hard wood into deep-sea fishing rods or anchors. Gone now were the blades that held the sails to the wind. The roof, too, was gone; the goats would have to find what shelter they could. But Sueky didn't expect vertical rain, though she didn't know what to expect.

The goats grazed on the meadow grass, the pinto billy keeping close watch on Sueky. But Sueky gave them no notice as she walked up the ramp leading into the mill and dropped her bundle of grass just inside the door. A tree had taken root in the mixture of Sahara-dust, bat droppings and goat dung. It reached through the top-opening, spilling over the upper lip of the ancient mill like a botanical head on a beer glass. It was good, she thought; the tree would give the goats some shelter if the rains did come straight down. She returned to the outside. Standing high above the pasture on the walkway encircling the mill, she studied the surrounding thicket. "I thought so," she smiled, recognising the colour of the "bullo" bush a goat aphrodisiac amongst the thorny cucha.

She was amazed at herself. She cut the tough bush so easily and pulled it out of the spiny thicket without a scratch. She would never have even considered doing that yesterday. It was a miracle, nothing less. "You must have something special planned for Sueky, Mistah."

Partway up the ramp into the sugar-mill, Sueky called to the goats, then snapped a few twigs from the bush and let the breeze carry their pungent aroma over the meadow. Dropping a trail of crushed bullo leaves where the goats would see them, she then dragged the bush into the mill's inner chamber and threw it on the floor against the trunk of the tree in the centre of the vault so the goats would have to come all the way in to reach it.

"Thanks given..." Sueky smiled as the goats came running without hesitation up the ramp and into the windmill. "Youse do sometimes give me ease," she said it to the heavens, but not letting the Lord off completely, she added, "but jus' sometimes!" She moved around the goats to the entrance and spread the grass around the chamber floor. A giant old copper kettle, too heavy to be disturbed, was full of rainwater and tadpoles. The goats wouldn't go thirsty and goats aren't particular about tastes, even tadpoles.

A set of rusted metal bed springs leaned against the wall inside the door. Normally she'd need help from one of the youths to tip the springs across the entrance, but this time she turned them on edge with ease and, backing out the entrance, she pulled them against the door, making a gate that even frightened goats couldn't break or jump. Taking up a thick iron staff from the yard, she propped it across the outside of the entrance and lashed it to the springs with the rope she'd used to bundle the grass. The bar, caught on either side of the doorway, pulled the springs hard against the windmill inside walls. They would remain that way until the knot was untied upon her return. And when would that be, she wondered.

"Now, don't pester dat none," she warned the goats, tying off the ends of the lash to an iron cleat anchored deep in the outside face stones.

"It wants for a full roof, I knows, but me feels da time come soon dat Youse give praise jus' for dease good solid walls." She started to walk away but turned back. "And you study me words, you's little stick house at Sueky's ain't gonna serve a'tall... not a'tall.

"Youse a long measure better here den dere" She pushed and pulled one more time on the gate, testing it. Satisfied, she moved along the walkway circling the mill tower and into its shade. Leaning back against the cool stone, she looked from her perch out to the sea.

She wondered what had made her bring the goats to the mill. She wondered how long they would have to stay there. Then something on the ocean caught her attention. "Deys mak'n lambs," she said to the Lord, nodding to the rapidly swelling flocks of whitecaps. But they were no longer white. The foam water in the wave's wake was ashen and murky.

Resting her head on the cool wall, Sueky opened her mouth and extended her leather tongue, tasting the air, massaging it against her gums, chewing it with her lips. It had substance and tasted of fungus, fine tendrils of decay.

She curled up her lip, her nostrils flared and she sniffed, pursuing another edge to the air — it was a smell Sueky knew! It came from a long time back, sharp like rotting seaweed, or eggs; sulfur, and salt, and vinegar.

Horse sweat! That was the smell! All of her senses rushed back to that moment when they ran the racehorses up to the mountain to the sheltered paddocks of the Lough Plantation. The horses charged up the track, their hooves electrifying the earth, the air and the raced from the pending storm. They were crazy with fear, the whites of their eyes revealed their terror as they raced up the trail in front of her mother's house. She was in the garden and huddled behind a cabbage. What was it Em had said that day? "When dat smell be on d'horses, d'Devil not far behind!"

"OH LORD!" she gasped, pushing her head back hard against the stone wall. "Dats what Youse got in mind?" Her breathing was quick and short. "Is dat what Youse planned for us?" she cried. "Youse set a hurricane upon us?! Ohhh my… oh my… and it's big one too!" she realised, one that would challenge all.... but the already dead.

Now Sueky understood. The color of the sea would soon be black and it would be a long time before blue would come again.

August 30th, 1914: she would never forget the date of the hurricane that had destroyed Saint Augustine and much of the West Indies. Then, just as now, the sky was grey and charged, the air thick with anticipation and the smell of the horses pulling the "Devil's Chariot".

It was Justinella's fifth birthday. Sueky had to take Justinella to Auntie Liburd for a party. But Sueky couldn't stay, she remembered. Instead, she had to go with Grand Em to the graveyard, following behind as her grandmother passed from corner post to corner post, making the sign of the cross on each with a foul-smelling white paste that glowed in the dark. That day was the last time she saw Justinella.

Often Sueky thought about the two days of that hurricane, how they'd so changed her life. She would carry that time to the grave. Thirteen. Thirteen years of innocence and shelter, then, within just two days, she'd know death so intimately that she would never again forget its presence in every act of living. After that, there was nothing more death could do; she had gone beyond fearing it and sometime in those nights she became a voyeur of what death could do. And as the storm beat her Island she knew that it too would die as she knew it. Yet in that moment of acceptance that death was omnipresent, she tasted too the first thin roots of life for *it* too is omnipresent. Memories of the storm rattle even forgotten memories of the dead from their sleep and she did something she hadn't done in a long, long time: she wept for Justinella and Auntie Liburd.

"Keep da dead so!" Sueky suddenly said aloud, remembering the words before the door. "KEEP DA DEAD BE SO!" That was the message in the visitation. The words still meant nothing, but she held them now fresh as they'd first come to her and she laughed, repeating the phrase again and again so that it would not slip away once more.

Whatever it meant, she must keep her own counsel, at least until she knew for sure. She would understand when the time was right.   Oh, how she wished Em were still alive.   She wished Justinella and Auntie Liburd were still alive.

But she could not let herself dally on wishes.   There was a hurricane coming; everyone must prepare! The Devil was coming, and she must tell people to be ready.

"Me does what me can and prays lobetojesus das enough." She arched back slightly, pushing off the stone mill tower. "I does what I can... but not what I can't." She turned her face skyward. "Does Youse hear?!" she yelled.

"And goats," she said as she passed the entrance to the mill, "me knows now why me takes da precautions, Youse' in for a hurricane. But fear not, likes de Lordbeto Jesus, I'll come again."

****

Sueky took the long path back to her house, walking along the edge of the ghaut and the beginning of her orchard. She had to think it through before she saw anyone; she must have a plan. She studied the orchard trees to see what they'd require. At the young banana slips she'd planted a few months before, Sueky bent down and pulled sharply on each stalk. They'd rooted well, they'd bunch big next year this time... if they lived so long.

The ground around the mature plants was littered with half-eaten fruit. She'd have to tie the dog out there to keep the monkeys away until one of the youths could harvest the ripe bunches and put bags over the rest.   With her cutlass, she flicked a rotting banana peel out of her way.

"Me does give all God's kin something, each and every one."   She spoke to the jungle down in the ghaut where the monkeys lived. "But you mistah' monks! You does want all! Well, not dis time, mistahs!"

There were still a few mangos left on the big tree in from the edge of the ghaut, and Sueky took up a long bamboo pole which leaned against the gumtree by the orchard's corner bounds. A small knife blade was wedged in a split in the thin end of the pole then lashed in place with a leather thong. Sueky positioned herself above the base of the mango tree and slowly extended the pole through the limbs, her head moving back and forth with the concentration of a snake. At last, the blade came in contact with the stem of a ripe mango. Bracing her feet, she jammed the pole forward, then jerked it back. The blade sliced the mango stem and the fruit fell, tumbling down through the maze of foliage. Sueky leaned the pole against the trunk and tracked the mango's course until it dropped from the tree. She noted where it lay.

Again, and again her head swayed back and forth, following the knife blade, until, finally satisfied that the tree had no more fruit, she stopped. Sueky picked up the fruit, her long bony fingers caressing each, squeezing it, separating her take from what she'd leave for the monkeys. "Thanks be given to all He creatures," she muttered each time she left one.

Sueky would get the youths to harvest all the papaya, even the green ones, for soon they would be no good to anyone anyway. There was one late, withered breadfruit, its surface milk turned to thick glue and black with trapped insects. Normally Sueky wouldn't bother, but the time was coming when even it would be a feast.

Finally, when she'd passed through all of her orchard, she returned the pole to the gumtree and surveyed the piles of produce once more, reminding herself of what was where. Taking up her cutlass and walking stick, she followed the path along to her garden.

The picket gate at the garden plot sagged and she had to lift it to get around. She went first to the potato plants and, with the end of her cutlass, began probing beneath them. Finding a nest, she pried the potatoes to the surface. "Thanks be given... and received," she mumbled as she moved to the next colony. Onions, carrots, everything must come out. She'd have the youths come immediately after school and fetch everything back to the house. She wouldn't need much for herself but there would be many others to feed. When the time was full, she would send it up to the church.

Sueky's house was set back on her land. Nestled beneath a giant white cedar, it looked like a shrine tucked into the grotto of deep forest greens. Now the tiny pasture house was faded, but when her son Eldon came from England two years before, he'd painted it a bright flamingo pink, the trim and the ornamental gingerbread eaves a deep Caribbean blue. It was the comment of all who passed.

A dull muddy border had formed along the sides of the building, just the height of her hog's back where the animal rubbed as it passed. The door and shutters drooped with fatigue, and the roof of galvanized tin had weathered red with rust. But the foundation of the wood structure was concrete.

Eldon had bought the land for her, and the foundation had been laid by her neighbours. As was their friendship, it was solid, permanent, not like the chattel houses of those who did not own their land. They had to balance their dwellings on loose stones in case they might one day have to move the houses. Not that anyone would have been evicted. Not on St, Augustine where people gave respect to people's rights even more than they did the law... should the two come up against each other.

In contrast to the surrounding tangled jungle, Sueky's yard was bare dirt, pecked over by chickens and swept clean by a dog chain, though Sueky didn't have a dog. People tied their dogs on the end of the chain when they came to linger with Sueky. When she needed one, she borrowed it. Halfway between the mountain and the beach, Sueky's house was an oasis to all who passed. She listened, not just to what they said, but to what they meant. And her insights were butter-thick interpretations of Scripture to meet the problems according to their weight.

"Da bible say da youths does carry da future on dey backs," she'd say as youths carried water pails balanced on their heads from the government cistern along the main trail in front of her land.

In the absence of a formal village government, order and social justice were maintained by the "Council", ..."the Wise Ones" she called them. Sueky was a member of this august tribunal, and her opinion was sought on matters related to the community.

Her nine children had been conceived and born in her two-room house. Four had died there, as had her husband. When her surviving children moved to their own homes and land, Sueky tended to her grands and great-grands, watching over them as she did her goats and sheep. But age had slowly changed the roles, and now the youths came to Sueky to tend to the things she could no longer do herself.

But somehow now, as Sueky stood in the yard, looking at her quiet chattel house, the adjacent cook-shed and the outhouse behind; the familiarity of her home failed to reassure her and she wondered if the buildings would stand the test put before them. She remembered how Grand Em's little house exploded and took flight. Only foolish people, who had never smelled the horses' sweat or heard the drumbeat of their charge, would actually say they wanted to know a hurricane.

Chapter 2

Bueno and Sueky

"De first be de last," said Bueno as he pulled the last concrete cinder-block across the deck to the edge of the flatbed truck. He positioned himself, feet spread, weight straight up and down, then dragged the block over the lip. As it fell, he effortlessly transferred its downward momentum into a pendulum-arced swing that brought the block shoulder-height to the next man in the human chain.

"And de last be de last," he said to the man, who caught the block as it stalled in space.

"De first be last," the man repeated as he swung the block to the next in line, and so forth until it reached a great stack of blocks beside the half-finished building, each block seemingly propelled along only by the initial energy of loading it onto the truck down at the harbor.

"Yes, yes!" Bueno exclaimed, arching backwards to address the October sun hanging honey-thick in the strange humidity. "Mister Sun, you do no more ta me for dis day. Dis man is free of d'likes of you." He rolled his shoulders forwards, releasing the tension in his muscles, then bent forwards, stretching his back and calves. He looked at the cement and block building; the week was over and they'd got a lot done. They'd finished all the forming and had capped the cisterns. Next week, they'd put up the walls with the concrete blocks they'd just unloaded. In two weeks, they should be able to form in the corners. And if all went well, and the rain held back, they'd be able to cast the ring beam and start the rafters within the month. Satisfied, Bueno began moving around the construction site picking up his masonry tools. "Who takes me hammer up?"

"Dere, by de mixer," pointed one of the younger boys who came after school on Friday to help clean the site. "You be's de thief what takes she up," he laughed. As Bueno reached down for the hammer, a skiff of dust swept across a spent cement bag, whipping dust into his eyes. The Christmas winds were building early for the year two months early, he thought. The sooner they got the roof on, the better. When the Christmas winds rushed into the Caribbean, they brought all forms of havoc. Besides, Christmas was a month-long holiday on St. Augustine and it would be impossible to hold his crew once it began.

Like tired workhorses at day's end, the men trudged up the hill, with heavy feet and bowed heads, towards the cistern that held the water they used for making the concrete and mortar. It was an old stone cistern, just waist deep, and Bueno flopped his torso over its wall and drove his head into the cool green water. The cold engulfed him, soothing the heat of the day that still harboured in his aching muscles. It was delicious. Ecstasy. Baptism for both body and soul, extinguishing every burn, soothing every cut, rekindling the spirit. Ah, to fill one's day with such pleasure, he thought.

The surface of the cistern lay quiet, undisturbed by the man half beneath its glaze. A water bug skimmed the glass; an egret eased cautiously to the edge of the cistern, watching the insect. Suddenly Bueno exploded out of the water, bellowing with the last thrust of breath in his lungs. The egret screeched and startled into flight, landing on the adjacent ancient mango tree -- glaring at the man.

"Buyo!" Bueno called to one of the labourers, a young muscular man who had run the wheelbarrows when they poured the cistern cap. "Bring some sours."

The lad nodded and disappeared into the trees edging the site. Bueno turned again to the tank and, cupping his hands, drew water from it and slopped it onto his chest, under his arms, scrubbing at the cement tracks with his large, coarse hands. Again he plunged into the pool, but this time did not linger beneath its surface.

Bueno was a tall man. His hair, cut close to his head that had skiffs of white salting his pepper-black sideburns, giving his presence the distinction of a statesman.

He was a handsome man who was accustomed, ever since his teens, to women approaching him to make babies. His eyes were

31

gentle and when he laughed, his grin was full of white teeth and his voice devoid of concern. He was a man habituated to smiling and on the rare occasion when something did disturb him, his face went through great contortions to capture the illness of his mood.

Women wanted gentle children who frowned little and laughed lots. He was a smart man, the youngest of the village's "Wise Ones". But more than that, they wanted a legacy of Bueno's peaceful soul. And they watched and waited for him as he walked the long hill to the Methodist Church on Sundays in his white shirt with his Bible lost in his great hands. For unlike other "baby-making" prospects in the village, who wrestled with demon hangovers and tried to remember what they did and forget what they remembered from the night before, Bueno was a man without addiction. Bueno walked alone and ladies went to great lengths to "chance" upon him en route. And to his dismay, they walked with him as if it were he who initiated the stroll. Still, for all the requests for Bueno to make babies with them, he had only one woman.

With buckets of water filled from the cistern, two men on Bueno's crew washed out the turning barrel of the cement mixer. They spun the pitch wheel and turned the tub upside down, where it banged and clanged joyously, spitting out the last of the concrete mix onto the ground. One of the men went to the diesel engine mounted on the side of the machine and, lifting the cover, pulled the throttle lever backward, cutting off the fuel. The mixer had been running non-stop since an hour before dawn and it gave an exhausted cough, then a sputter which sent each heart racing for fear it would start again. But it fell silent.

"Eighty six," called a boy who had been counting empty cement bags and throwing them into a pile to be burned. It had been a big pour and in twelve hours, from 4:00 a.m. to 4:00 p.m., the crew of ten men had mixed two truckloads of sand, three large piles of "pong", crushed rocks, and two cisterns of water. The job was vastly labor-intensive… most of all, the amount of labor in making pong. Just one pong mound occupied a family of six for two months of beating boulders collected from the site into domes of aggregate five feet high. That day the crew had consumed two months of three families' work.

Because St. Augustine was small and for the most part steep from cone to coast. The island had no active riverbeds. As a consequence, the aggregate necessary for the concrete had to be crushed by hand, beating boulders down into lime-sized lumps, the "pong". It was a practice that had evolved from the forced labor of slaves into a secondary income by choice. If you had some time on your hands, you ponged stone. Every family had a mound of pong in its front yard. It was an asset, banked for the future, either to sell or to use themselves for the foundations of a family's new house. Each pile was a family effort.

With a heavy sledge, the family member with the most muscles and patience would stand upon a boulder, swinging the hammer with unerring piston-like repetition hour after hour. Days, sometimes weeks, of the same dull cadence with no noticeable effect. Then, suddenly, the sound of the sledge hitting the rock would change. The sledge man would feel it, a slight sigh. On hands and knees he'd study the boulder, searching for the fracture reaching through to the other side. The trained eye would map the hairline crack radiating from the point of impact. A wedge and water into the crack and more beating, and suddenly the rock would release a final sigh — split out of exhaustion, submitting to the man's relentless will.

Then the ponging began from the big pieces, reducing them to soccer-ball chunks, which the children lifted onto their heads and carried them to the pong pile. It was a game: "I can carry one bigger dem you." "Not so, I can carry one bigger dem both us." Everyone who wasn't a beater or a packer was a ponger. Usually it was the women and the older children big enough to wield the heavy two-pound hammers. They were the night crew. They came onto the site when the construction day crew had finished — ponging, visiting, laughing in the quiet peace of the receding day. Their prattle was gentle music in comparison to the barks and boasts and bantering of the day crew arguing over cricketers, bowlers and test matches involving the West Indies and the rest of the World.

"Me still says Ambrose de better bowler be," said Spoon emphatically as he approached the cistern. He had been saying it all day and it was only when he put his head beneath the water that he stopped.

Cinnamon-buyo, the young labourer Bueno had sent to fetch the sours, returned, carrying in his shirt half a dozen large oranges.

"Me still say Ambrose, but he can't bat no more."

"Mon, you'd be best speak'n o' t'ings Youse knows. Bet Ambrose's own mother don't t'ink bout him as much as you."

Out of his pack, Bueno took a knife, its blade ground thin from years of sharpening. He drove the tip of the blade into a sour orange and drew it around until he'd cut the fruit in half. Taking one half, he began running its open face over his hands and forearms, scrubbing the juice into the skin bleached white by the cement. The acid in the lime burned into each crack, but it neutralized the caustic cement, stopping it momentarily from drying out and splitting his skin. Then from inside his day-bag he drew out a bottle of lotion and rubbed it into his hands. Combing his hair, he repacked his tool bag

While the crew washed and rubbed sours on their limbs, Bueno strolled around the job site picking up cement bags strewn by the wind during the pour and throwing them into the burn pile. He broke two dry fronds off a jelly palm and lay them over the pile of bags to keep the wind from spreading the sparks. Finally, he lit them and watched momentarily to see that the fire caught.

He rooted around in his bag and drew out a pack of ten small brown envelopes, each the size of a playing card. Printed on each envelope was the name of a crew member, his wage, deductions, and the sum of his pay for the week.

"Cinnamon," he called, handing the boy his envelope. "Bullo." A large man with blue-black skin came forward. He was Bueno's foreman. "She come good today," said Bueno. Bullo nodded and

34

walked away to the lee of a palm tree before opening his envelope. A smile came over the foreman's face. Sunday was the christening of Bullo's first child, but he'd earned the bonus too. Bueno got good work from his men, keeping them to the task while having a fine time as they'd rattle on about whatever topic made its way into the conversation.

The men approached one at a time to collect their pay and discuss it with Bueno if necessary. "Delbert" called Bueno finally, and a tall man with a thick brow came forward, hunched over in a laboured gait that made his hands precede his body.

"Delbert Ain't Crazy, You Know," Bullo had assured Bueno when he first brought the man on site. "Jus' cuz most others say it, don't make she-so. Chure he talks in circles, and sometimes in tongues cuz of de jumbies ... and chure me once see'd him only make animal sounds for an entire day... but he's still de best mixer-mon on-island".

The mixer-man was responsible for the ratio of gravel, sand and cement. He was the one who made the buildings strong. "She need for more bite," meant more cement had to be added. "Too slick", meant more sand. No one corrected Delbert's mix — not out of fear, for there was nothing violent in Delbert's nature, but because it was always right. He wasn't part of the main crew but was brought on when they had a big pour. The rest of the time he laboured in Portstown keeping the town clean, and her people entertained.

Three men got into the front of Bullo's pickup and seven in the back, causing the tires to bulge and the springs, exposed by rusted-out fenders, to bow backwards like a coconut palm in a storm.

"Dis trans-she waits for no mon, mon!" Bullo called to Bueno.

"Den let she wait no more," Bueno laughed. "I'll walk it off. But you remember," he called to the men, "d'sun comes same time on Mondays as any other work-day."

"Yea, yea", they yelled back as the pickup lumbered off the construction site and up the hill, a wisp of dark blue smoke chasing its exhaust pipe.

"Afternoon, Miss Easter." Bueno walked over to the woman positioning her ponging rock... her anvil on the ground, where before it had ridden high on a pile of pong.

"And... all the little Easters," he said to the children around her.

Easter and her family were already beginning a new pile after a weeks' worth of their labour having vanished in the day's pour.

Bueno gave her an envelope, "Seventy-five barrows."

"Seventy-five?" Easter looked at the littlest child, a boy whose job it was to count each wheelbarrow by dropping a pebble in a bucket each time a wheelbarrow load of pong passed him. The boy, though only five, studied the seven piles of ten laid out on the ground and counted again the number of pebbles. With great round eyes, he looked only at his mother, and shyly nodded.

"Then seventy-five she-be, for a bonus!"

Easter smiled and reached out for the envelope.

"You going to spend it all on a fling in Puerto Rico?" Bueno teased the next youngest. The little girl bounced her head affirmatively, and grinned when everyone laughed.

"Dis money will sleep with de rest 'til de day come she be need'n it," Easter said to the children.

"Maybe den you'll be hiring me," Bueno smiled and slung his tool bag over his shoulder. Near the property bounds, he picked up a bundle of pigweed he'd collected during lunch. "Until!" He called out.

"Until!" The smallest yelled the loudest.

*****

The air beneath the jungle canopy was dense with the day's heat and the intoxicating bloom of wild jasmine. Periodically, the trail passed artery trails lined with walls of stone and white cedar blossoms leading to brightly coloured chattel houses set back on the property. Many were freshly painted for the coming holidays. The houses were like Christmas presents tucked under the trees. Lime greens with maroon shutters, canary yellow and royal blue. Soon the poinsettia leaves would turn to red velvet, and the hibiscus would

36

explode with their own lace delicacy, and even the cottages would be lost in their splendor.

As Bueno came to the clearing where the Hard Times Estate mill stood, his nose quickened to the bite of fresh goat dung, which was strange since no one had penned animals there in years. When he came to Sueky's, the pen, which he'd often thought stood more out of respect for the old woman than from strength of structure, was empty. He looked beyond to Sueky's house.

"Sueky!" Bueno called out to the woman sitting on the stoop, but she did not answer, though her donkey, tied to a cusha limb, began to bray. "Sueky," he called again as he approached.

"What's to be done width Youse, till dis t'ing pass?" Sueky spoke to the cluster of chicks that scurried about her feet fighting over a mango pit.

"What thing dat be, Sueky?" Bueno spoke loudly as he approached the porch.

"Lobetojesus!" The old woman's hands flew to her breast as though stopping her heart from leaping through her paper chest. Then seeing it was Bueno, she laughed at her fright.

"Bueno-boy, you gives dis ol' woman such a start." She beckoned for him to come forward. "Ye knows, Bueno," Sueky cocked her head seriously to one side, "me does tell you sometin' true... either folks be getting more quiet and spooking about like jumbies... or," and she smiled sheepishly, "or ol' Sueky-she be growing deaf."

"It's not you, Sueky," Bueno yelled louder than he knew to be necessary, "It's me, me's spook'n and jumbie'n around."

Sukey's laugh was rich, "Dat's a good joke, Bueno, but me knows de truth, I churely does." She thought about telling him about the miracle and the message and that she did hear him well and was merely preoccupied when he called out. But she decided not to, at least for now.

Still, Bueno realised there was something different about Sueky. He couldn't tell what maybe her laugh was freer, she sat more erect, her hands were more attentive to their tasks. "Sueky, you decide to grow younger for a while?"

She eyed him cautiously. "Jus' de same ol' Sueky, alroight."

"Who was you talking to when me come spook'n up?"

"Jus' me alone talk'n ta de animals and course de Lord-amighty." This time Sueky's laugh was brittle and crackled like dry sticks in an open fire, though still it started her animals to clucking and grunting at her merriment. The pig, not knowing when to stop, continued his bivalve snorts long after Sueky and the others had stopped.

"Hoag!" Sueky yelled, "Stops dat disgusting noise and stands up fo' de company." The huge black pig lying in the shade of the house didn't move, only grunted louder, happy to have her attention.

"Come along now, pig." Sueky leaned towards him. "Show de company how big Youse be." She prodded the pig with her walking stick, then began scratching the hog's belly with its tip. But instead of getting up, the pig flopped onto its back with a sigh of ecstasy.

"Hoag! Don't you too be vexing me," she growled... but continued to scratch.

"So how you be for de day?" Bueno asked. "Where you's goats?"

"What's you mean?!" she exclaimed. "Dey's where deys supposed to be, in dey's pen. Unless..." eying Bueno suspiciously, "somebody thieved dem up." Noticing Bueno wasn't falling for it, she confessed, "No, dey deserves lodging at de mill 'til dis t'ing passes."

"Why's de donkey tied to de cusha tree?" Bueno asked. "Sueky, you been feeding him cusha bark?"

"Damn dat miserable creature," Sueky cursed with disgust. "He does act de fool all day, running hither and yond while me's away to pasture... he's just trying to perturb me with his lowly ways. Well, when me does catch he up, me's so mad, ah does tie him roight to dat spot, and dats jus' where he be now... maybe forever if he don't change his foolish manners!'

Donkey!" Sueky yelled at the animal. "Say good afternoon to me friend, you miserable t'ing."

The donkey gave a forlorn, repentant bray, but Sueky was not touched. Her anger had passed, but not her need to give the beast a lesson.

"So why Youse goats at de mill?"

"Dey's safe dere 'til after de trouble."

"What trouble?" Bueno prodded.

She pursed her lips. "Bueno… me wants dat you study me well and spread de word ta all." She stopped scratching the pig and looked at Bueno. Then, waving her hand, scattering the chicks towards their house, she said, "Look around, Bueno. Look around good and hold what you see in Youse heart, cus soon nothing gonna be de same! After de Mon comes, nothing, not even <u>you</u> will be de same."

She paused, letting the words sink in. "Bueno," she looked hard at him. Dere's a hurricane coming, and a big one!" She followed his face, determining if he perceived the urgency of her warning.

"And study me dis, you must take precautions immediately." Her voice was grave. "And don't ask me no more how me know, cus I don'ts know meself… only fo' chure dis will come to pass."

Bueno studied Sueky. He believed in her powers and respected that she saw events ahead of their occurrence. She'd been right about his mother. She'd seen the sinking of the ferry, though in her vision it was the *Flora Gail* barge.

"What man is coming? De Lord?" Bueno's voice danced lightly with the woman, beckoning her to join him. "Is de Lord coming?" But Sueky would have none of it.

"Bueno, don't be testing-me-up dis day. De Lord, <u>and</u> de Devil, de night, and de day." She turned to her chicks with anxious eyes. "De Power and de g'lory, Bueno," Her eyes burned back to him. "De Power and de Glory! Both gonna pass."

"I hear talk the wind's giving Guadeloupe some licks," Bueno said, "but it's not coming here, according to the Anglican, he says St. Augustine is protected by d' Lord."

"Den he be de fool! Sometimes me's jus not chure how things gonna be." She frowned. "Usually dis headset," she touched her forehead, "don't serve me so good no more. But dis time me does see what He's about and you must tell de people to prepare. Find shelter for all, collect everything what grows in de gardens and trees cus dey's soon be gone."

There was silence, Bueno finally realising the seriousness of what she was saying. "De air she's not roight."

"Sueky, I go to come back." He touched her shoulder and started towards the path.

"Until!" She called out. Bending over, she spit a mango pit out on the ground. The chicks immediately scampered for it, pecking at it and each other in the frenzy. "Until de power and de glory does pass.

"Oh! Bueno," she called again, " me does ask one boon of you. If Youse see de youths what calls me "Grand", tell dem dey must come-so quick. Dere's much fo dem to do.

"And mark me words, befo' Youse pass again, Youse gonna know'd de Devil's wrath!" She spoke as much to herself as she did to her visitor.

Chapter 3

Garth Arrives

The inner-island ferry from to St. Augustine rolled heavily to starboard as it came around Nag's head into a gale blowing from the west down the channel, while the Atlantic current running between the Sister Islands pushed the keel east. Garth grasped the rail on the upper deck and looked quickly around to measure the severity of the starboard list by the reaction of his fellow passengers. If there was any at all, it was subtle. The domino game on the open deck below continued without interruption, the ivory cubes snapping on the tabletop, followed by exclamations of delight or disgust in a language unrecognisable to Garth. A large black mother on the wooden bench beside him nursed her child without concern for the ship's heaving or the immodesty of her large, clearly exposed breast.

"Julia!" she called to a little girl maybe eight years of age who was standing on the sea rail feeding popcorn to the gulls, "Come-so, look sharp. Taks dis bag to Senora Lopez below. Tell she *es ua regato por* she from she Auntie Jermaine." The little girl took the bag and danced down the stairs to the lower deck, the bag bouncing merrily on the steps behind. By sound alone, Garth guessed that the present for Senora Lopez had once been breakable and now was broken. With the ease of one slinging a grain bag from one shoulder to the other, the mother transferred the baby to the other breast, leaving the first breast still partially exposed.

"Never see that on the Rez," Garth mused to himself, thinking how modest Indian women were on the Shoshone Reservation. Babies were breastfed in public, but only if the child was buried beneath layers of shawls and blankets. In fact, as he looked around, he could find no similarity with anything from his past life.

"Ticket, mon?" asked a tall, lean man wearing a pale blue t-shirt with "Caribbean Queen" so faded it was barely readable. Garth undid his waist belt and drew out his passport, looking to the man to see if identification was necessary. No, he indicated, though Garth still had to open the document to remove the ticket carefully folded between the blank pages.

"Fus time come ta de Leewards?" the man asked.

Garth nodded.

"Indian?" He asked.

Astonished, Garth again nodded, surprised by the man's perceptiveness.

Still, Garth was unmistakably an Indian, his features classic: dark eyes, high cheekbones, skin drawn drum-taut across a stoic face. His nose, except where it had been broken by his cousin, was ruler straight, turning neither up nor down. He could be from the Amazon, the Andes or the great North American prairies, or even Inuit, judging by his eyelids that hung like half-open sash-blinds.

His hair was raven black, normally long and straight, it had recently been cut severely short like an army recruit's or a shoe salesman's. His hair roots, accustomed to bending over with their weight when his hair was long, now they shot out in all directions like unruly wheat sprouts refusing to comply to the rules of gravity until they would again grow long -- which Garth sincerely hoped would be soon as he found the standard issue Peace Corps "brush cut" humiliating.

He was a tall man with wide shoulders and chest. His hips slender giving his physique a wedge shape. But his posture was not that of a wedge nor the "noble savage", for he carried himself more like a cowboy than an Indian in that he leaned against things — pickups, saddle-sheds, whatever vertical surface offered itself. He slouched, he sat in chairs backwards, he sauntered with his hands in his pockets when discussing matters of ranching, weather or politics. When the conversation turned to women, he carved half-circles in the dust with the toes of his boots.

"Me does take-in de Car-ni-val dere once," the ticket man said to Garth. "And mon, whas a'time me does 'ave... whas width de

42

rum and dem pretty gals, and dat music! Oowee! Dat music so sweet she makes me dance all night!" He chuckled.

"What?"

"Trinidad, mon! Das where you's from, ain't she?"

"No," Garth laughed. "Wyoming." But he could see that this information meant nothing to the ticket man. "Wyoming, it's a state in the western United States. I'm an Indian, a western Indian, like cowboys and Indians."

"Oh," the man said, losing interest.

Garth turned his attention back to the open water and the small island growing on the horizon. So, it was finally happening. After all the anguish of what to do with his life after he'd graduated from the Wyoming State Agricultural College, he was finally about to make the first footfall. The endless orientation meetings had been the hardest part of his initial few weeks in the Peace Corps. First in Washington, D.C., where over two hundred volunteers sat in a lecture hall off Connecticut Avenue and listened as the Director of the Peace Corps, then the Assistant Director and finally Assistant to the Assistant, conveyed the same message. What a great opportunity and adventure the volunteers were about to undertake, for themselves, for the communities of their assignments, for the countries, and even for the Free World. They all sounded like political speeches of wanna-be John F. Kennedys dazzling the troops with their rhetoric.

"Peace Corps volunteers are America's ambassadors, and your conduct will be your credentials. Many of you will go on to be great leaders and your performance in the Peace Corps will stand out like medals of honour." The message would not have been so inspirational, Garth suspected, were it not delivered in full view of the National memorials, Lincoln, Washington, Jefferson and Vietnam.

Finally, they received their assignments. Garth had requested Chad in northern Africa, where he wanted to work with solar pumps and drip-irrigation systems. He'd done a lot of study in that field and had even collaborated with one of his professors on a resulting project and a paper detailing how to adapt the technology to the Third World. But for reasons unfathomable, maybe thinking that the black people of Chad were no different from the black people of the Caribbean, or maybe that there was no essential difference between the desert and the tropics, the Peace Corps had assigned him instead to the Caribees, where it rains with some regularity. Specifically, to a tiny island midway up the Leeward chain that relinquished little information to the Library of Congress, or even the Island's own tourist bureau.

Leaving the States via Miami, his next orientation was in Barbados. The group of volunteers had been "regionalised" and their numbers shrunk to twenty-five, each headed for a different placement across the Caribbean Island chain. There, the inspirational messages from the Peace Corps directors were distilled down to "Reality in the Overview" … specifically, what behaviour would get you thrown off-island. Garth had the feeling that his exit from the service was more important to the Peace Corps than his accomplishments.

"Don't piss-off the government, don't piss off the locals, don't cheat, steal from or fuck the locals, or engage in any other improprieties the Corps deems not in keeping with its Charter. Keep your nose clean, stay out of politics, report all incidents to your Peace Corps supervisor immediately, be they rape or physical harassment."

Garth wanted to "keep his nose clean" in the Peace Corps, but he wasn't completely sure he'd report it if some lady seduced him.

Fortunately, reggae music was not one of evils on the "avoid" list. And while he was in Barbados, Garth discovered Bob Marley and the Wailers, and Jimmy Cliff busking on the dock and selling tapes, which Garth bought.

As the ferry slipped out of the grip of the channel and righted itself in the lee of St. Augustine, the sun was in the first throes of setting on the starboard side, bathing the approaching island in low, lateral light. There was a halo of tall cumulus clouds-- their tops burning like hot lava, garlanding the peak of the main volcano which formed the Island. There were greens of a thousand shades, each a different plant colony, he suspected. Garth wondered if one day he'd be able to pick out specific trees in the forest by their colour. Accustomed to the deserts of Idaho and the near monoculture of its mountainous forests, Garth was in awe at the abundance and variety of vegetation that carpeted St. Augustine.

The island was formed by one central volcanic cone, the north side of which had been eaten away by erosion or maybe blown out by some ancient eruption. Numerous ridges ran down from the peak to the sea, creating deep indigo slices locally called "ghauts" — a Dutch word for a canyon or ravine, he'd read in a book about the Caribbean.

He was startled at how quickly darkness came. Out west, dusk was long and lingering — a sentence whispered without haste from the horizon, bathing the front porch of the ranch house in twilight. Here, sunset was a single sharp command: "Dark!" And a black backdrop fell like a splitting maul. But just as immediately, the lights of the Capital, which was apparently a town of only a few thousand, twinkled and danced like a carnival of fireflies along the harbour.

He had been in correspondence with a young farmer named Caraja who wrote a lot about cattle and crops but made no mention of more pragmatic things like currency exchange rates, whether the water was safe to drink, or even what kind of clothes to bring. In fact, the only piece of advice that stuck with Garth from the man's letters was, "Everything you need to know about the Island, you'll learn in your first few hours ashore."

As the motors of the ferry shifted into reverse, easing towards the wooden dock, the first smells to greet Garth were diesel, then mildew, then phosphates from laundry water, and dead fish that had been left in the sun too long. But Garth also caught the scent of jasmine and honeysuckle. This was the Caribbean he'd wanted.

And while the other passengers crowded towards the rail to depart, Garth lingered, inhaling the perfume, drinking in the moment.

The bulwarked town was made of 18th century stone buildings... or rather stone fortresses, for their walls were a meter thick to withstand sieges or hurricanes. The most prominent structure was the Treasury Building that sat at the end of Wharf Street. It was the first building encountered when ships landed. Great stone steps led to an impressive single-gable structure lined with bright shutters and open windows to inhale the sea breeze. For three hundred years it had been the hub for the proceedings of an English colony once called the "Gem of the Caribbean". From brigantines to bareboat charters, buccaneers to bikini-clad tourists. At one time or another, everyone and all commerce passed through the portals of the Treasury Building.

Further along the streets, Garth could easily locate the town's municipal establishments by their distinctive signs in large pastel lettering, often illuminated by bare incandescent bulbs: the Island Courthouse, the St. Augustine Library, the old cotton gin and the Police Station with its round white glass balls on either side of the entrance, each with "Police" written on it. Many of the shops and small businesses were sandwiched into the ancient stone structures, selling everything from tourist gifts to plumbing parts. There were also clusters of brightly painted wooden houses lining side streets leading away from the capital's centre, each accentuated with bright gingerbread trim and complimenting color shutters.

There was also an abundance of sounds new to Garth's ears. Crickets and tree frogs blended easily with barking dogs and chickens to form a background chorus to the "Hallelujahs" rolling down the street from the Wesleyan Holiness Church. "One Love", Bob Marley and the Wailers' sang the unofficial anthem of the Caribbean; the call to solidarity of humanity that floated up from the dock and the people waiting for ferry passengers. Slowly, however, as night descended, the melee of exotic sounds faded into the gentle murmur of the evening as the tranquility of Island's contentment absorbed the noise of the day's commerce.

As the departing passengers prepared to leave, moving towards the port rail, two old men-- line handlers, sat on the dock on their respective mooring posts waiting for the bow and stern lines.

"Wha Youse say now, mon!" called one of them to the stevedore on the ferry.

"No, mon, es-Youse wha say! Now stands ye straight, look sharp," he yelled back and slung the end loop of a rope as thick as a man's arm towards the dock, feeding out line as it flew.

Deftly, one of the old men leapt to his feet and caught it with both hands, then with one quick, fluid movement, turned, dropped it over the lanyard, took up slack and cleated-off the ferry line around the post with two quick half-hitches.

"Three seconds flat!" Garth laughed to himself — a rodeo roper couldn't catch and tie a calf any faster.

When the boat was finally tied tight against the rubber-tire curbs wedged between the ferry and the dock, Garth went downstairs to the main deck.

"Everything you need to know about the Island, you'll learn in the first few hours," he remembered reading. The first thing he realised was that except for a couple of European backpackers, his fellow passengers were all black. Their dress covered an astonishing range from dockhands in rags and kids in bright school uniforms to satin Dior knock-off dresses, homemade from photos in fashion magazines. Garth suspected that the designs had never looked so beautiful on the Paris models as they did on these black women. Businessmen in ties and briefcases, market vendors bearing great baskets of vegetables that Garth couldn't identify, balanced effortlessly on their heads without assistance from their hands.

But the thing that most immediately stood out to Garth was the conduct of the people. Unlike Barbados, where everyone pushed and shoved to exit or enter, or even remain where they were, the people of St. Augustine were orderly, respectful and patient.

47

"Wash you's feet," said the ticket man, taking Garth's elbow as he stepped over the short gap between dock and ferry.

"What?" Garth asked as he landed on the pier, but the crewman had turned to the next departing passenger. "Wash you's feet!"

Watch your step! Garth realised he was saying.

He was finally there! He felt like Christopher Columbus must have felt on finding land at the end of an interminable trip. After all the orientations and travel, he had finally arrived at his home for the next two years. Garth remembered smiling to himself at that moment, amused by the incongruity of an Indian boy from a remote ranch in Wyoming settling here in the West Indies. He had crossed a temporal watershed of not just space and time, but history, culture, even cosmology. Before him, on the metaphorical mountain divide, was a land full of promise... and he saw no pitfalls. He slung his pack onto one shoulder and picked up his duffle with the other arm.

"What ya sell'n, brother?" came a belligerent voice from behind him. Garth turned to find a stocky black man in his mid-twenties. His hair was cut prison-short, his face was hard, his eyes were mocking, betraying the insincerity of his question. He wore a Chicago Bulls t-shirt cut open at the throat, and round his neck he wore a gold "Leo" medallion. Garth assumed it was his astrological sign, his name or his personality. His hands were laden with as much gold as his arms could carry.

The man stepped forward, close to Garth's face, definitely inside an Indian's space. Back in Wyoming that alone would have been sufficient provocation.

"I said what you selling? Religion, anthropology, or maybe politics?" He studied Garth's face. "That's it, you've come here to teach us pickannies about emancipation."

"Agriculture," Garth said without inflection or elaboration, looking the black man directly in the eye.

"Come to teach the dumb nigger farmers how to use tractors instead of donkeys? You're all alike," the man said with disgust.

"You all got that 'White Savior Syndrome' don't you? Come to dazzle and enlighten us, did you?" He glared at Garth. "Maybe you shouldn't be ask'n what ya can teach de niggers but ask yourself what you's running away from."

"Garth Longgrass?" asked a man quietly from the crowd. He wore dark blue pants with yellow stripes down the outsides of the legs, topped with the white shirt of the Port Authority.

Garth nodded.

"My name is Sutton's.." He extended his hand. Come with me, there's a taxi here to fetch you up."

Garth turned back to the man of gold. "Friend, we're gonna continue this conversation at a later time." This time his words were full of intent. "And you can <u>count</u> on that. What's your name so I know who to ask for?"

"Bushroot Messiah!" the man said, raising his arms as if he were the Pope bestowing a blessing, the gold on his hands caught the harbour lights. Garth smiled. He was tempted to respond physically, but that certainly wouldn't do on his first official day as a Peace Corps ambassador.

"He-name be Settee," said the officer, obviously embarrassed by Settee.

"Settee, like the couch?" Garth asked.

The government man laughed. "Exactly."

"And what's yours, *friend*?" Settee started to place a hand on Garth's shoulder but thought twice about it.

"You can call me Geronimo!"

Garth recalled, too, the first night that he lay on his bed in the small wooden frame house that the Peace Corps had secured for him behind the Methodist Church. He had never felt so alone and for the first time, he longed for home, for his family, his girlfriend and, most of all, his saddle horse. The horse was more than a horse, it was his access into a vast wilderness. When this is over, he'd thought to himself, I'm saddling Bolero and going straight for the mountains.

49

He thought of a special lake known only to him, his horse and a band of bighorn sheep. It was a cirque lake, high above timberline. He had discovered it by following mountain sheep up through a breach in the surrounding cliffs. They were the guides, he believed, sent by his ancestors to show him the route to this sacred place on top of the world. Across the cloud-mirroring lake was a wall of spirit peaks that echoed his chants, and sometimes sent their own messages back in the form of wind-whispers and dreams.

"Find your place," his great-grandmother had told him. "We each have a special place."

"A 'place in the plan of things 'place', or a 'place on earth' place?" he'd asked.

"Both. For once you've found one, you've found the other. Go there with an open heart and understanding will come as you can handle it." Certainly the lake of clouds was his place, he thought.

He remembered the last thing the old woman so sculpted by the elements of <u>her</u> chosen place, said to him as he got on the bus to Salt Lake City where he'd catch the plane to Washington: "Your ancestors are never far away."

When he graduated from the Stoney Creek High School, then to the Wyoming Agricultural College, he had choices. Too many, he thought. Though it was never spoken, Garth knew that his father secretly hoped his son would stay on the ranch, expand the operation.

His mother wanted an education for him. She spoke of college and urged him to apply for admission and the scholarships which the federal government made available to Indians. Garth did well academically. And part of him liked the idea of applying his new sciences to making the land more productive, but the studies that interested him had no practical application. Strange esoteric subjects like philosophy, and one summer while driving swather, he'd read *Plato's Republic*.

"Too much time on your hands," his father warned him the first time Garth tried to explain what the book was about. "You should find a girlfriend." It was around that time that he met Jodenne. She was white, blonde, a cheerleader and very keen on him. Garth was the football team's quarterback and when they won the regional championships in Pocatello, Jodenne made it clear that she was willing to part with her virginity. But Garth, for reasons he couldn't explain to her, felt in his gut rather than his brain, that he wanted to wait.

When he graduated from college, the wealth of realistic options — aside from staying home and marrying Jodenne or going on to graduate school — had shrunk to only two, thanks to the impending draft and Vietnam. He could go into the military or the Peace Corps. Garth had a cousin, Arnie from Driggs, who had joined the Marines. He said it was okay, but there wasn't a war at the time; now there was. It was a hard call for Garth. He had killed often, as one does living on a ranch, but that was pragmatic, for food or protection, not out of idealism. Garth felt <u>no</u> allegiance to the United States for taking his ancestors' land and confining them to worthless reservations.

Also, Garth had realised early that he was not a "man's man" in that he'd never hung out with his buddies, preferring instead the company of the mountains and his saddle horse. And while he played sports, he couldn't abide spending his free time sitting around watching sports on television. It was the difference between watching a rodeo and being in it. No, hanging out in barracks, or a war-zone firebase, smoking dope and trying to prove your manhood to a bunch of guys who are equally terrified, seemed closer to hell than being scalped alive. Also, Garth was ready for an adventure. Free flying while you're learning how to do it. So, by default and intrigue, he chose the Peace Corps.

******

Garth had finally fallen asleep to the chorus of tree frogs and didn't wake until he heard a knock at his door.

"Garth Longgrass, it's Mister Swanson from the Ministry of Agriculture." Garth quickly dressed and opened the door to a short

51

man dressed in a white Panama shirt, pressed slacks and polished shoes... a bureaucrat, not a farmer, Garth suspected. "I've been asked to show you around the island, and later this afternoon we have a meeting with the Minister himself."

Far from the backwards, poverty-stricken island he had expected, Garth was amazed at the abundance of small, fastidiously maintained farm plots and the thick black volcanic soil that he saw as they drove around the volcano on a single, though double lane road that circumvented the Island.

Along the apron towards the sea, the government had appropriated a large tract of noncommercial land, denuded, explained Swanson, by countless crops of sugar cane and by wild goat herds and donkeys. Through slow, diligent farming, the soil had been brought back with cattle and silage crops turned under again and again, until finally the government had been able to reclaim the land known simply as the "Government Farm". Garth was intrigued with the prospect of working there and learning how they'd done it.

At the cattle corral, a shirtless black man worked a herd of Santa Gertruda cows, crowding them into a long chute. One cow with a calf had slipped the herder's notice and as soon as her calf let out a bawl, she lowered her head and charged the unsuspecting man. Garth saw what was happening even before the cow dropped her head. Reading her intentions, he ran toward the corral, and grabbed up an empty burlap feedbag on the ground, he scrambled over the fence and dropped in front of her charge.

Waving the sack in the cow's face, he diverted her away from the herder and then, showing off a little, he did a quick matador sidestep, drawing her past him and out into the center of the corral. The black man moved quickly to the fence.

Surprised that she hadn't hit her target, the cow spun around and started at Garth again, this time at a full charge! Again, Garth shook the burlap bag and again easily sidestepped her, swatting her on the butt with his left hand as she charged past.

52

Then, before she'd got too far away, the Indian ran in close and, with the bag, started leading the cow in tighter and tighter circles until finally she stood dazed, dead still-- head down, swaying from side to side with dizziness.

It was more than Garth could resist. Running at her from behind, he placed two hands on the cow's hips and leap-frogged onto her back... then swung off her before she could respond. Again, he couldn't resist; he scooped up the bag again and gave a brief bow to the government agent and the black man.

"I ain't seen 'nudden' like das befo in me whole life," stammered the government agent. The black herder was hysterical with laughter as they drove the confused cow into the chutes, dropping the gate behind her.

T'anks, mon!" said the black man, wiping his hand on his pants before extending it to Garth. "I'm Caraja."

"I guessed as much." Garth shook his hand. "Garth Longgrass."

"I guessed as much." Caraja began to bellow with laughter in great expansive huffs.

"I'd be careful around that one," warned the agent from the Agriculture Department later. "Those Rastas are a bad lot."

"Then why do you keep him around?"

"Too good a farmer to let go. In fact, likely the best on-island. But just don't get in too thick with him. Won't go good on your record."

Chapter 4

Making Plans

As he walked up the trail to the Main Ring Road, Bueno studied the volcano through breaks in the thick forest. Though the air was heavy and stagnant, the soft gentle clouds that usually laced around the summit high above, were quietly being stripped by upper winds, making a great cloud banner that unfurled far out into the Caribbean towards Puerto Rico.

He frowned, for it added fuel to the dark shadow of Sueky's warning. A storm now would be inconvenient timing, for he had other plans: the house he was building in his spare time for his brother in England was way behind schedule and Christmas holidays would be starting soon.

He knew it would be hard to hold a crew during the long Christmas break. Also, Raymond, his oldest son, would be auditioning that night for one of the positions recently vacated by two unexpected deaths in the Masquerader Troupe. If the storm hit, who knew if the troupe would even perform that Season. It was a trivial matter but still an inconvenience. Maybe they would be spared, he hoped, but in his heart he knew Sueky was right for she had more than science on her side, she had "informed" intuitions — in fact some said she heard the voices of the past who knew the future.

"Da day slides smooth for Mistah Bueno?" The greeting startled him. He turned to face a small man coming up a side path leading to Fluteman's small fruit orchard. The stocky man approached, carrying a stalk of bananas on his head, balancing it with one hand while the other carried a bag of breadfruit slips and a cutlass polished bright from care and use.

Fluteman had a presence that was easily recognised, even beneath his baggy pants and loose-hanging shirt. He walked smoothly to a rhythm of his own making, his stride that of a dancer.

54

He was the head gardener at Hotel Lemon. But his avocation was leader of the Hornets, a village "thump and strump" string band. His eyes had a perpetual twinkle. His soul was pure music and he possessed the gift of taking raw energy from the air and changing it through his flute into both melody and motion — dancing feet, clapping hands, swinging hips… taking the rhythm from soul to sole.

Beneath the load of bananas, Fluteman wore a fedora hat which he never seemed to remove throughout the day except to punch it back into shape when he'd discharge his load. His white hair grew in a contoured wave that formed around the hat's rim. Moreover, he was married to a woman who wore an identical felt hat that she, too, took off infrequently. She was Fluteman's mirror, a short woman, whose step was lively even when she was tired. She did not go to Fluteman's dances anymore, she'd had enough of his children to know the consequence: She'd have to satisfy him at home where he could dance to her music. Their four children, all boys, were grown and had moved out of the house and into lives of their own. And like most parents, it was only when they had grands that they had time to learn what they'd missed raising children. There was one son in particular, named Fife., who continually made them marvel and laugh.

All his life, Fluteman had been a "Sweet Boy", as the girls called the handsome boys with sultry eyes and gentle hearts; and he was still, even in his late fifties, sweet. Women sought out Fluteman to make babies, for he carried in him the spirit of the sunrise, a joyful song to the new day.

His face was round with coffee eyes, a wide honest nose and a smile that pushed up his cheeks into dark furrows the color of planting-soil. Even as a youth, they were musician's eyes, impatiently waiting for future notes while the present ones played out. When Fluteman played, it took more energy not to dance than it did to dance, so one might as well give in from the start. Everyone said it, and even those who didn't dance tapped their toes or slapped their thighs instead. "He takes you's soul to the soil and plants de music deep down inside, cus dat's de way he be." Only Fluteman knew how many children he'd sired.

Fluteman was the giver of life to a rumpled band that ranged in talent from great musicians to village idiots, sometimes the same title applying to the same person depending on the time of night and his rum consumption. Pulling life out of thin air and pumping it through his flute in doses big enough for everyone!

His dream as a young man was to entertain the whole world. Now, with age, he was satisfied to give pleasure and thanks on his island. The band, "The Hornets", was composed of three regular, legitimate musicians who knew how to move notes into recognisable tunes. The balance of the band accompanied him on the scratch (metal washboard), the toot (a length of 3/4 inch plumbing pipe), the triangle or any other object that could be plunked or thumped. Still, they traveled with the band faithfully to play in the villages, the capital… and most recently Toronto, Canada.

"So, I hear so you travels some since I sees Youse last?" Bueno smiled at Fluteman, then studied him closely, "But can't say Youse looks da worse for it."

"Oh mon, Toronto!" The musician waved his hand in a grand arch. "No other place like She, das fo chure! We'n has such a fine time," he laughed. "We surely did. Dem folks dere jus goes crazy over our music. Plays twice at Carnival in de Park, den dey ups and asks us to play in dey's "Music Hall" for da last night's festivities!" He shook his head without disturbing his load. "It was soooo sweet. And de people we meets comes from all over de world and dey say dey's never hear music so sweet... like honey, dey say!"

Even as a youth, Fluteman was one of the elders of Poppy Dawn, one of the "Council", the "Smart People" of the village, the un-appointed, un-elected court whose opinion was sought whenever a clear head and a sharp eye were required for a judgment on community matters.

Fluteman had, as the others, clear insight into Human Nature and the nature of the humans he'd known since. But he was also a "no-problem-mon" man, even when there <u>was</u> a problem, which was to say he could be calm in times of crisis. Still, his greatest asset was his flute, for it calmed the hysterical, uplifted the forlorn, and, for the guests of Hotel Le Lemon, created the romance of the West Indian tropics for which, (along with sun and rum) they paid large sums for large doses. He was, for them, a one-man Caribbean.

Bueno waited for him to join him.

"How goes de day?" Bueno repeated Fluteman's question to himself. "De day pass without occasion and now dat de devil cement mixer sleeps for de weekend... can't ask for more. And you?" he nodded to the trail leading up the mountain. "Go so?"

"Go so," Fluteman affirmed, and walked in stride beside the builder.

Fluteman was silent for a few minutes, selecting his words, checking his delivery so that he wouldn't sound alarmed, even though he was. "Dere's a storm to de South," he said almost casually.

Bueno nodded.

"Some of de guests at de Hotel been listening to de radio, and de storm sounds like he might be a big one," Fluteman said. Class five and growing, dey say. Dey's even given he a name... 'Hugo'. 'Hurricane of de Century' dey's calling he."

"What's Gage doing?"

"We's taking precautions... preparing for maybe a direct hit just in case. Cutt'n back de trees round de buildings, treating de water. Tying down everyt'ing what loose to take flight." He looked at Bueno. "How's you hear so?"

"Sueky."

Fluteman stopped in mid-stride, his face tightening as he considered the implications of Bueno's words. "Den we too gots to make plans as soon as we can," he said finally more to himself than to his companion. "And do so without alarming de people," he added quietly. "Don't mention whas Sueky say to nobody 'til we talks width de Elders, and den tonight at de tryouts we'll give de people some direction."

"I does study dat me-same-self," Bueno agreed.

Fluteman would be at the Perch anyway. On Friday nights it was the meeting place for the village, plus he'd be playing there that night, accompaniment for the Masqueraders, a dance troupe that had been formed in a recent rush-to-the-past movement that was catching the Island in a frenzy to rekindle its cultural traditions, especially with the passing of two of the old guard.

Of course, Bueno would be there. Raymond wanted to be a Masquerader even more than he wanted to be a cricket hero, and Bueno thought he'd be good at it, for the boy was a natural dancer, everyone said so. But he was still young and Bueno wasn't sure there would even be a Masquerade that Christmas; maybe they'd pass that year out of respect for those in the troupe who'd gone to dance for "The Maker".

Usually, only the older men danced, which suited the young boys, who were normally more interested in playing cricket or dominos or watching Maple Leaf Wrestling from Toronto. But of late, with rekindled interest in their culture <u>before</u> slavery, a number of youths wanted to be involved. Besides, the girls gave more attention to dancers than cricketeers.

According to Bueno, Raymond got his gift of dance from his mother, Sally, since Bueno claimed that he knew only three steps... "start, stumble and fall"!

But since he never took off his heavy concrete-encased work boots, who knew what his feet might do if bared to the world? Even as a baby, when other infants screamed in fear of the masqueraders' whips snapping and cracking above their heads, and the shrill whistles and shrieking cries as the whirling masked demons in feathered headdresses and multi-colored, long-tendrilled capes orbited in great high-stepping circles to the Zulu-cadenced beat -- Raymond's eyes sparkled as he bounced and cried in ecstasy.

58

Though Bueno was tired from his day's labors, he definitely didn't want to disappoint Raymond and if his son didn't make the troupe this year, Bueno wanted to be there to support him. Besides, like Fluteman, Bueno was a member of the "Council" and would attend the gathering of the "Smart Ones" to discuss the pending storm.

For a while Fluteman and Bueno walked in silence, absorbed in their thoughts, until they came to the point where the trail intersected the Main Ring Road, and the back wall of the Secondary School.

Bueno saw Raymond out in the school-ground playing cricket with some upper-grade boys. Their bats were homemade and the balls were tennis balls found outside the wire of the Hotel Lemon's tennis courts.

"Boyo," yelled Bueno when the play reached an ebb. One of the fielders near the wall looked up and saw him.

"Paca!" the player yelled towards the wicket. "You's fadder calls." Raymond looked up, waved, and hurried to collect his books. He gave one of the girls in the yard a playful push and ran towards the front of the school where the wall met the road, swinging his school bag in great windmill loops.

"Well, boyo?" Bueno smiled with pride. "How goes it for de day?" He handed the boy his lunch kit.

"Fi... ne," Raymond smiled. Centering his school bag on top of his head and placing the lunch kit on top of it, he balanced the load so it would ride steady without hands to hold it.

"Does de Masqueraders start practice at de shop tonight?" he asked Fluteman, even though he knew the answer and had thought of nothing else for the past few days. He pranced with excitement, even under his load. "We gonna go, Doddy?"

"Chure," said Bueno absently as his attention fell upon the young Peace Corps volunteer coming out of the High School -- a small band of students following him like chicks around a hen. At the school-ground's gate, they separated, and Garth started up the

Uptee Doon Road towards Poppy Dawn. Bueno waited for Garth to join them. "Going up so?" Bueno asked.

"Going up so," Garth repeated with an end-of-the-day sigh. Bueno didn't know much about him except that he was an American, an Indian, Shoshone, he'd heard. And a Peace Corps volunteer working at the Government Farm, plus teaching an English writing class and coaching soccer after school.

Though his skin had color, his innocent attitude and sincerity were flour-white — but Bueno liked him anyway. Garth didn't seem to suffer from the "White Saviour Syndrome"" of trying to make the world into his own mold. A tall, gangly man with long black hair and a brick-solid face, ...according to Raymond, he was a real Indian, from a place called Wyoming. Bueno didn't remember if it was east or west Wyoming. East Indians from India, Bueno knew, but this one didn't fit the mold.

"I heard mention from my son here you are going home to the States soon," said Bueno in his best English.

"You heard right, four days and I'm homeward bound."

"Do you want to go?"

"It's time," Garth said without hesitation.

"You go to come back?"

"Probably not. I'll likely have to go to work out in the oil patch and earn some money to pay off my Dad for my volunteer time down here."

"Maybe, if you come back, I'll give you work cutting stones with me," Bueno teased as though he hadn't heard Garth. "Put some fat on those bones. I'm Bueno, by the way."

"Garth Longrass." The two men shook hands.

Bueno was surprised at just how much strength there was in the Indian's grip. His hands were hard and callused without a hint of fat or flab. "Mon, you shoulda…" then he caught himself. "*Should have* taken a woman while you were here. Someone to feed you up and make you contented like a happy he-pig," Bueno teased. "When a man doesn't have a woman he gets anxious. And a nervous pig what's being vexed won't put on pounds, no matter how much government grain you pour into him."

Garth thought for a moment about "Stomp", the Official controller of his exit permit. and his experience earlier that afternoon with her. He shook his head smilingly. He liked Bueno. "Next time," Garth said for the benefit of all, "When I go to come back to cut stone for you, you must find me a woman to calm the anxious pig."

Everyone laughed, pleased with the Indian's comeback and that he might come back to the island. Only recently had Garth learned to enjoy the Islanders' rich, dry humour, mainly because it was only of late that he understood enough of the language and idioms to participate without offending.

"Mister Garth, this is my friend Fluteman," Bueno introduced the musican.

They walked in silence, enjoying the comfortableness of each other's company. Raymond wanted to speak up but he was too shy to breach the silence — until finally he could contain himself no longer. "Are you going to de Masquerade practice at de Perch tonight?" He suddenly blurted.

"We are. Someday I's gonna be a dancer. Already I know'd most d'steps, and I can do ever call, every beat dere is," he said with pride. "And snap de whip too!"

"Can't be there tonight," said Garth. "I'm going up the mountain with a friend of mine for a couple of days' camping."

"Dots all you need, more lean eat'n," Bueno grunted. "Best pack a sandwich 'less your friend knows he way around de bush."

"I think he does. You know the man — Caraja?"

"De rasta mon?! Mon... best you be careful how you deals width de Rasta. Dey's slick and t'ings gets very slippery when dey's around." Bueno stopped and looked at him. "One time a Rasta mon what lived near Fey Ghaut done asks me to grow some herb for him. Says I could make some good change."

"Which herb?" asked Garth naively.

Bueno studied him to see if the teacher was teasing him or was really that innocent. "De herb, de 'ganga' herb, de weed, bush tea... marijuana."

Finally, Garth nodded with recognition. Bueno studied him for a while before starting again. "Now understands me, only de Rasta and me know'd where de crop-she be, and don't Youse know da night b'fore I was fix'n to cut she down for curing, the whole crop disappeared! De Rasta say de monkeys done it, but unless dey be wearing running shoes and using a cutlass, me thinks he be de one."

"So what did you do?"

Bueno glanced to Raymond and Fluteman and spoke softly. "Me calls de police a reports de Rasta for possession of ganga. Dey go dere to he house and what you 'pose dey find? Forty herb plants hanging upside-down curing from de ceiling of a pig shack." Bueno's smile spread into a keyboard of ivory. "Forty, das just how many plants was t'ieved from me."

Garth stopped walking and looked at Bueno. "I can't believe Caraja would do that."

"Naw, not Caraja, he's a good man, was anodder mon. But dey's all de same."

"That's like saying all Christians are the same." Garth had Bueno there, and he had to laugh — "or argue that all Christians were the same!"

"Well, maybe you's right, but study he friends closely and be in a watchful way."

"I'm one of his friends," Garth rose to the bait.

"My point exactly!" roared Bueno, clapping Garth on the back. "I hopes to see you around before you leave, I can think of a couple ladies might fatten you up some before you get on de plane." He shook Garth's hand.

Garth saw a bus approaching. "That's my trans." He said nodding to Josiah's van coming up the road from Charlestown.

"Until." Bueno patted the Peace Corps on the back.

"Until," Garth repeated, nodding to Fluteman and Raymond, then as he got into the bus beside the driver. He smiled to himself as looked back at his companions, wondering just how much he'd missed while he was here.

"Das de trouble with Peace Corps, or the VSO," Flute remarked as he watched Garth leave, "'bout de time we get dem trained, dey goes back home and forgets it all." Then his gaze fell upon a brilliant patch of green running down the path from the primary school. It was his youngest son Fife. He was still wearing his school's soccer uniform, bright lime-green shirt and tan shorts.

"Footmon!" the little boy called, suddenly seeing his father. He began running harder, waving his arms while his dog ran beside, snapping at his shoelaces.

"Boyo," Fluteman laughed. "One day dat dog gonna get you's laces, den you be in a fix."

Fife came running up, out of breath. He held his hands behind his back. Fluteman pointed to the right and Fife brought it around, grinning as wide as his cheeks would stand. In his hand, he held Fluteman's flute. It was a nightly ritual. Fluteman took it, balancing his package of plant-starts on his head, he brought the instrument to his lips. Then, without warning, three quick, sharp notes danced out it, then more rolled down the scale. A pause of equal duration, then seven notes cascaded out, leading one into the next. And though Fife heard them every evening about that time, there was magic and awe in his eyes.

"Doesn't seem that you done it any harm in my absence," his father said, then noticed something in the boy's face.

"She won't sing sweet for me." Fife's eyes grew large and concerned. Fluteman looked long and seriously at the boy. "Well, I'll tell you what, suppose I talks with Miss Flute and tells she dat she's got two masters now, you and me, and she gots to sing for both."

Fife's face burst into an astonished, sun-through-a-rain-cloud grin. "You means so?" He looked up to see if Fluteman understood what he was saying, then he looked down at his feet. "Dat would be good, cuz Miss Flute doesn't really sing a-tall fo me, to tell the truth."

"That's because she hasn't showed you yet how she likes to be caressed. You can't just push air through she. You gots to give she you's soul. Dat's what music is, somebody's soul dat's been twisted through an instrument." The little boy didn't understand his grandfather at all.

Fluteman saw this and gently poked two fingers into Fife's chest and gave them a twist, then a tickle. "You want to be a music-mon, you got to talk to she from right dere. Das how to swoon a womon."

Fluteman reached up and adjusted his load, then, taking the flute to his lips, he started up the trail again with the opening note of "Yellow Bird". It was his calling card. The hotel guests loved it; it fit their preconception of the Caribbean. Fife loved it; it was his first lullaby. And Fluteman never tired of it, for he never played the song the same way twice. Sometimes he'd draw out the "Yel..." of "Yellow" like an unending note, and you knew its neighbours were coming but you didn't know when, and anticipation built.

Then, when you marveled that a human could extend his breath so long, the "...low" note fell into line and a rapid-fire Gatling-gun jazz variation followed.

Sometimes the song would take a Latin twist, a hip-jigging rumba or a neck-snapping tango. And sometimes he would simply play "Yellow Bird" like a love song to a yellow bird "... high up in banana tree", sweeping the listener in a flight that reached beyond the jungle canopy up to the heavens themselves.

The village marked time by Fluteman's evening passings as his bird of notes flew through the window on the breeze, circling around the knot of people under the mango, and people cleaning fish, and no open window was safe from the bird. Conversations paused as the bird flew past. They were a parade of two, Fluteman with the box on his head, playing the flute, the boy in the bright green shirt marching, swaying back and forth to the music his grandfather created.

"No guessing about which block dat chip flew off-a," Bueno laughed at the sight of Fluteman walking down the path ahead of him, playing the flute with Fife coming right behind in lockstep.

"Fluteman," he called out, and waved him to wait. "There's much to discuss." Bueno stepped close to Fluteman. "We agree, de elders' council should gather dis evening before de masquerade practice. I'll tell Aunt Josey when we pass she's domain."

"See you there," Fluteman nodded, then turned to Raymond. "Tonight you just listen to me and dance accordingly, mon. Youse'll do jus fine."

He and Fife turned onto the upper crossover road. It wasn't the most direct route to his house, but it led to the crest of a stone cliff where they stopped and looked south towards Montserrat and beyond towards Guadeloupe. He hadn't been too concerned at what he'd heard from the guests talking about a hurricane, but Sueky' was a different authority. If Sueky said there was going to be a problem, then he was certain they must prepare. Still, as he looked at the dark clouds forming around Montserrat, it didn't seem as if the storm was real, and even if it was, it was detached, removed, another man's problem. But maybe in a day or two it would be his problem.

"Fodder, if'n I make de Masquerader Troupe tonight, I 'ave a boon ta asks of you," Raymond said as he and Bueno continued toward the Main Ring Road.

"What boon dat be?" Bueno smiled, anticipating it had something to do with coming of age, which Raymond was continually querying of late. "You's ready to settle down, make babies?"

Raymond frowned to think that his father was making light of something so important. "Naw, das never gonna happen!" He stopped walking and looked very seriously at his father. "Fodder, I wants for you and Mudder to stop calling me 'Raymond'".

"What?! Youse prefer 'Hey you?' Or maybe 'Lordship'"

"Naw, I wants to be called 'Paca', das my name at school and das what I wants for people to know me as."

"And how is Mistah Paca different from Mistah Raymond?"

"We's both de same be, but Paca fits me better when I becomes a great footballer, or a Masquerader."

"Paca... not Poco, or Loco?" Bueno teased in a way that made it clear that Paca was fine with him. "But it's up to your grandmother Priscilla. Raymond was her father."

"Grand will understand when she reads my name in the *London Times*. Paca, just plain 'Paca', be fine." He smiled at Bueno. "Will you grants me dis boon?"

"Mistah Paca, dance tonight like Youse does it for a living."

Aunt Josey didn't see them until Bueno and Paca were just a meter away from her as she stooped, feeding her chickens, she sang a Christmas carol the choir had begun to practice in anticipation of the season.

"Merry Christmas, Aunt Josey," Bueno said loudly.

"Oh de Lord Jesus!" Josey startled, her hands flying to her chest as though containing her heart from leaping through her rice-paper-thin frame. Then, recognising Bueno, she laughed. "Oh, Mr. Bueno, you does gives me soul such a fright!"

"I'm sorry." He reached out and laid a hand on a thin shoulder. "I do apologise. How does de day find you otherwise?" Asked Fluteman

"To be alive is enough," she beamed with a great, open smile uninterrupted by teeth.

"Aunt Josey, does you remember my son Paca?"

"No, only de one named Raymond. Dis one much more handsome!" Paca grinned and looked down at his feet. What a difference a name made.

Aunt Josey and Sueky were best friends, sisters by choice, not necessity. And like Sueky, Josey's purpose in life was to dispense wisdom and contentment "with what you's got, and not what Youse

66

don't. Me t'anks de Lord for all I got, and don't trouble Him for what me aint."

Age had distilled Josey, like Sueky, to pure Spirit. And where Sueky was turning to stone and God, Josey was an old mahogany tree. Her skin was a rich cocoa color, withered to an ironwood trunk and bone-dry limbs. Like Sueky, her roots reached back through generations to the slave era, while her leafy branches of children, grands and great-grands extended around the world. By both honor and blood, she was everyone's "Aunt Josey" — one of the Island's "Smart People". And if someone had a problem that either age or wisdom could solve, it was taken to Aunt Josey first.

However, *except* for age and wisdom and a huge family, Josey had nothing. She cooked her pigeon-pea soup on an outside charcoal fire in a pot made of red terra-cotta clay from her backyard. She washed her clothes in a pail of water carried from a cistern far up a steep and stony hill. She lived in a dilapidated wood-frame house that sagged like a dying mushroom.

And because she did not own the land beneath her shanty, it was balanced on loosely stacked cornerstones for easy removal, though it was inconceivable that anyone would even consider evicting Josey. Still the shack rested on ill-fitting rocks and, just as a pendulum is only plumb for an instant in each swing, the floor of her house was level only in passing. More importantly, the structure was so latticed with termite nests that the roof was supported solely by wild vines and the will of God. Hornet nests, hummingbird nests, a mongoose and sundry cats and piglets... she shared title to her home with many creatures.

In her lifetime, she had been rattled by enough earthquakes to "shake de teeth outa de corpse". And had endured, for decades, a goiter on her neck the size and shape of an eggplant. "Me bump," she called it. "Some does carry dey's burdens on dey's hearts. But me heart is free of cares cuz me carries me toil where de Lord can see it. It be me pass-boat to heaven. By me bump, de Lord knows Josey." But what she remembered most of the nine decades of her life was the hurricane named Helen, one of the worst storms recorded to date.

"Twice she comes to visit. First she comes straight on and wreaks all sorts of havoc, den jus as we's getting our senses back, she come again two days later for an encore dat destroyed all dat she missed the first time. Dere was not a tree, not a house dat remained on dis side. Many died and many moved away."

"Aunt Josey," Bueno said somberly, reaching down and taking her hands in his. "Sueky feels dis island is gonna be hit by a very bad hurricane, one dey calls Hugo."

The old woman looked into his face. "Me knows dat, I feels he in me bump. We must make plans early."

"Aunt Josey, how you get so wise?"

"By breathing in and out for ninety years, das all." She smiled, though her eyes betrayed frightening memories of that disaster so many years ago. "Tell Busman to fetch me to de Perch tonight. Das where we's gathering, yes?"

Chapter 5

Go to Come back

Jonathan Douglas woke well before dawn, turned on the reading light on the table beside his bed, and lay there. His eyes wandered the room. From the matching colonial furniture to the curtain valences, coordinated with the colors and pattern to the bed-skirting, the hand of Mallory was everywhere in their upstate, colonial home

His sighed with resignation. It was time. When he returned from St. Augustine, he would have an interior decorator come in and make the changes. He had resisted, fearing somehow that to remove this last signature of his wife would remove her from his memory — even though he knew that was not possible. But first he would deal with the house in St. Augustine.

Quickly he made an inventory of what remained to be done before leaving, but in keeping with his meticulous habits, there was nothing beyond shaving and getting dressed; his bags were packed and by the front door.

As he stood in front of the mirror with the razor, the man before him looked very different from the one he used to know. He was still a large man, six feet four inches, late fifties, a full head of dark hair, though strands of grey hair etched his short sideburns. It was a protean face. Since his wife's death, he filled his time with work and working out at the gym. Even now that his children were grown, he jogged, played tennis and, in the Winter, went skiing with Jonathan Junior's — JJ's — family at Stowe.

What was different about his face, he decided, were the eyes. They seemed beyond tired, they were… well… bored. In fact, they were beyond boredom, they were resigned, for they lacked the will and imagination to find something that might rekindle his interest.

Jonathan hadn't always been a workaholic. There was a lost summer in his late teens working with the migrant grape pickers and

Cesar Chaves in Delano County, California. It was a singular adventure which landed him with broken ribs and a short time in jail, and experiences for him to fill a dozen notebooks. But the free spirit ended when his father bailed him out, and soon Jonathan became, at his father's insistence, serious about his future and interned for the next two summers at the law firm where he would later article, and where he was now one of the senior partners. But now he was tired of it.

Downstairs, the marble floor in the kitchen was warm from the radiant heating system. It was great on fall and winter mornings. The layout of the kitchen was logical, efficient. In fact, the entire house had been designed to be lived in. Again, it was Mallory. And yet, of late, he dreaded coming home even to a warm floor.

Jonathan made coffee, called his office with last-minute instructions for his secretary when she came in, then called the airport. There was an early fall storm coming in from the north, some delays due to de-icing, but all the carriers were flying. He was a little disappointed. The trip seemed unnecessary: surely Simeon, his on-island lawyer, could handle the details of selling the property. But the Honourable Simeon Williams, former Minister of Tourism for St. Augustine and the senior partner in a St. Augustine law firm, assured him that his presence would be <u>absolutely</u> necessary. Simeon had said that the last time and all he did was direct his local contractor to fix a few minor problems. Well, that wasn't quite all he had done; he had also met Danielle. And though nothing could ever materialise from it because any relationship would fall short of the one he had had with Mallory, and, because he was twice Danielle's age, still it was the bright moment in the previous trip.

No. With any luck, he'd be back to that very kitchen before the weekend and he could go into his Manhattan office on Saturday and finish the work necessary for probating the Tennyson estate, and prepare for the annual Board of Directors' meeting.

With his bag in the SUV, he locked the front door of the house and set the alarm system. As he backed his Toyota out of the driveway, he stopped midway, his lights shining on the colonial mansion that had once radiated with so much life when his family was young. Now it was dark and foreboding except for the occasional blink of a burglar alarm warning light. Not even a porch light to scare off thieves; the alarm system did it all, turning on lights whenever anyone approached, alerting the police if they tried to enter.

Oh, how he missed those mornings of mayhem when the family used to fly down to St. Augustine for holidays in the winter. Getting the kids out of school was always a struggle with the administration, even though the children always returned far ahead of their classes in their assignments. Then the dogs. What to do with two Saint Bernards? Who has the passports? You do! No, you do... no wait! The passports are still in the house! Give me the keys! Hurry, we are going to miss our plane." And always there was a storm and a traffic jam between Mill Oaks, Connecticut, and Kennedy International Airport, but they never missed a flight.

Jonathan liked the thought that, somewhere on the planet, the sun blazed with impunity upon ad-agency-cliché white-sand beaches and turquoise-blue water. In six hours, he would be there. For all the times he'd made this fall sojourn, he still marvelled at how quickly his life of stress evaporated into the gentle landscape of the West Indies.

This time would be different, no companions. His children had grown and had young children of their own, and his wife, Mallory, had passed two and a half years earlier. Towards the end, the two of them had gone down alone while Mallory was still strong enough to handle the trip.

When the plane began its approach into San Juan, Puerto Rico, intimate memories of Mallory rushed over him. Out the window, Jonathan looked down into the hidden courtyards of Old San Juan. El Moro gleamed like a great cake with white icing silhouetted against the deep chocolate, turbulent ocean that crashed against its rock-cliff footings.

A rock on a rock, a white granite tribute to the grandeur that once was Spain. It had stood since the 18th century when Spanish conquistadors pillaged the New World, storing their riches in the underground chambers of Old San Juan, impenetrable to assault, be it human, hurricane or the giant ocean rollers that crashed against its footing. Now, Johnathon mused, it's being assaulted by legions of tourists and Park Rangers, crowding the gunneries for a personal glimpse into a time long passed and beyond reliving. Behind El Moro and the buildings of the National Art Institute, he recognised the structure from a new angle. El Convento.

He remembered their final visit just before Mallory died. El Convento had become their private retreat. After the children left, they'd started taking their time going to St. Augustine, laying over a few days in Old San Juan just to be in love. Neither spoke of what they each knew would be their last interlude, choosing to lose themselves in the romance that hung over the narrow streets and ancient buildings like mist off the bay. ... and, the drooping cords of flowers cascading from the balcony boxes, the smells of exotic chillis and garlic dishes, and music distinct to Puerto Rico half Spanish and half Harlem, half Brazilian with a Jamaican Reggae twist. Their greatest aspects, is sensual and tropical. Conspiring to carry memories into a world beyond time. El Convento, the Convent, was both a modern hotel and a quiet fortress for the ghosts of Carmelite nuns, their shadowy forms slipping with the dawn through the corridors.

They had their own special room overlooking the tile rooftops of the old city and the bay beyond. Giant cruise ships, like great floating cities at Christmas time, slipped beneath their window, silhouettes against the setting sun, time capsules against the rising moon.

They had a routine of walking along the seawall, kissing like teenagers in the gun-turrets that had become the iconic symbol of Old San Juan. Silent sunsets when the language between them was devoid of words and rich in meaning. Supper was always at "Patio del Sam" where Antonio, the owner, fluttered around his old friends, directing the waiters to their needs before Jonathan and Mallory realised they even had needs. He remembered how Antonio hugged Mallory. Somehow Jonathan's old friend sensed that Mallory was dying.

Jonathan had to change planes in San Juan, and he considered taking a day out to rewalk their old haunts, exorcise his demons once and for all. But he knew it was not something that could be erased. In truth, he wanted to experience something other than the numbness, even if it was pain. But also, he wanted to get to St. Augustine. He wanted to get the listing deal over, but this too would be hard because Mallory so loved the place and had wished so often that he could learn to see St. Augustine as she did.

Amazing, just six hours after locking his home in Connecticut, he was getting onto the evening ferry to St. Augustine. Jonathan knew from past experience not to press onto the boat until the gentle jostle of the market ladies, loading their unsold produce onto the deck, had ended. Beside him stood new businessmen in lightweight suits and ties, bureaucrats in short-sleeved Panama shirts, with briefcases held closely to their chests in the commotion.

Already on board was a Christian youth choir going over for a weekend revival. They were performing an impromptu gospel concert for their fellow passengers, who soon sang along. It would be a good trip. The deck chairs were plastic lawn furniture. There was only one deck besides the wheelhouse. Two choices, sit under a covered area beneath the wheelhouse or sit out with the cargo. A pickup was driven on board. Lifts of construction blocks were loaded with a forklift on either side of the Toyota to balance the load. Finally, a horse was led up to the ferry for loading.

He was a hot-blooded, chestnut colored thoroughbred who reared and lunged about on the ice slick surface of the polished concrete dock, terrorised by the sound of the heaving ferry gangplank grinding and clanging against the dock. His iron shoes had been removed. Half a dozen men were pulling on the horse's lines, yelling, until finally, with a single lunge, the horse jumped onto the boat's deck.

Frantically, the ship's crew cranked up the rear ramp before the horse could change his mind and turn back for the dock. With two lead-ropes, the blood's head was pulled down low enough for the jock to put on the blinders. Unable to see, the horse immediately became calm. And though there was a cheer for the handlers, everyone was a little sad that the adventure was over.

Jonathan stood against the port railing watching St. Augustine looming into the horizon. Out of tradition more than actual fear, he joined in a hearty collective "Whoa!" groan with the other passengers as the ferry cleared Nag's Head and the boat keeled to the starboard in the channel's currents. Though surrounded by water, few people on the island of St. Augustine could swim. The fishermen and lobster divers could, of course. Jonathan knew this from his gardener, Mango, who was Jonathan's only tie to the people of St. Augustine. As he looked at the faces of the people around him, Jonathan suspected that some were his neighbours from Poppy Dawn village, but only because they greeted him by name. He had been coming to the Island for seventeen years, yet, he realised, he knew fewer than a dozen locals by either their given or nicknames, and most of those he did know were either bartenders, waiters or hotel staff at the Hotel Lemon.

No, that wasn't quite right. He did know two of his neighbours, Calvin and Alphonso. Each year it was a ritual for the three of them to meet at their common boundary at Jonathan's gates and walk the perimeter of their lands, checking the fence line and visiting about the year that had passed. Jonathan looked forward to the event, for though he understood nothing of what they were saying, he recognised that it was beautiful music.

Midway across the channel, the captain blew the ferry's horn three short bursts followed a moment of silence as they neared the place where the *Christina* sank. Mango knew well the story of the sinking of the ferry *Christina,* on Easter weekend... his mother had drowned in the accident. She and three hundred and fifty-nine others from St. Augustine. The few survivors told of clearing Nag's Head just as a squall came down the Channel.

In those days, there was no inside shelter and everyone rushed across the deck to the other side to escape the torrent… just as the hull keeled from the current. An International investigation followed and concluded that crowding was a key factor, but they also noted that the engines were still running when the ferry went down. The theory was that once the bow went under, the engines drove the ship straight down.

The whole island was affected, particularly in Poppy Dawn where Jonathan lived. Many of the "market ladies" lived and farmed there on the south side of the Island, where the soil was dark and rich, and swept by rain clouds from the windward side as they first caressed landfall.

There was always water for the gardens even when the rest of the island had none. Because of the accident, entire villages just disappeared as family after family dissolved, children being raised by aunties or grandmothers. Jonathan's house was built on the end of a ridge sticking out from the main peak of the volcano. Along the sides of the ridge there was once a thriving community of ten wooden chattel houses and small bountiful gardens. Now there was only scrabbled sheep pasture.

To the laughing relief of the passengers, the ferry came on level keel into the lee of St. Augustine. "Once again we've thwarted death," Jonathan said to the boy standing next to him on the rail.

"Wha's zat, sur?" the boy frowned.

As the ferry approached the dock, Jonathan watched the line-up of flatbed trucks ready to receive the cargo from the lighters that followed the ferry across the channel from St. Sebastian. They looked like the Egyptian boats that still sail along the Nile. Their beams were exceptionally wide for hauling cargo, the cut of the sails was short, with long booms that reached far to the side when running downwind. Once everything brought in from the outside, from soda pop to automobiles, arrived by lighter. But the ferry was starting to haul cargo, and though the lighters were more dependable since they were not plagued with engine problems or gas prices, there was talk of building a deep-water port for container ships, and soon the lighters, like the land relics from the sugar-cane era, would become tourist attractions and finally rotting hulls along Gallows Bay.

No sooner had the heavy rear ramp hit the dock than the horse scrubbed off his blinders and bolted for shore, dragging three handlers behind. On the firm footing of the dock's wooden deck, its hooves, even without metal shoes, found purchase on the planking. By the time he'd galloped to the end of the dock, the horse had lost all of his handlers and was running wild and free up the cobblestone streets of Portstown. Jonathan made a mental note to bet on the chestnut at the horse races the following weekend, though he knew he wouldn't be there.

A line of taxi drivers met the departing passengers. Tropical Rentals, as was their custom with Jonathan, had left a rental car in the parking lot at the end of the dock and at least a half-dozen people told Jonathan not only where the car was parked, but where the keys were hidden. Never happen in New York, he smiled to himself. At least five people welcomed him home, each offering a hand to shake, or a wrist, if their hands were dirty.

"Drive on the Left," said a decal on the right side of the rental-car dash… the steering wheel was on the left. On an island with equal numbers of left- and right-hand- drive cars, the one consistency for Jonathan was that the road's yellow median line was always in the middle… more or less. "Keep the yellow line on the right," became his mantra because, no matter where the steering wheel was located or which way his he was heading, if he kept the line on the right, everything was alright. Consequently, he always requested a left-hand-drive, preferring to concentrate on the edge of the road and pray that it would all sort out in the middle.

Remembering the rules of the road was always the hardest part of the whole trip. There was the written law that he preferred by vocational dispensation, and then there was the common law, or rather the "common-sense law", which often was the law of the moment. It was easy to forget what was exactly the right combination. And even the left-hand rule was on a sliding scale. For example, it was acceptable to leave your lane to avoid a pothole, or a pile of rocks dumped in the road to fix the pothole... or, more commonly, to avoid a parked car since the roads came right to people's fences without benefit of a parking lane. Also,the big trucks rule depended on a number of factors, rum being one, bravado, another.

If you have to choose between a "roadish" — an island expression for a pothole — and a Mack dump truck full of wet beach sand, always take the head-on with the dump, a taxi man once cautioned Jonathan. "Das ways you no gonna be pitching down into Hades right away and you'll still get you's Day of Judgment."

Jonathan stood at last on the veranda of the house he'd had built so many years ago. House to house six hours. But his enthusiasm for the trip was gone. He opened up the French doors and checked the fridge, knowing that Shirley would have it stocked and at least one meal ready to be heated up in the stove. Breaded flying fish with breadfruit salad, cold gin and vermouth, and the added touch, a chilled glass in the freezing compartment. He made a martini, turned off the lights and, pulling a chair out onto the veranda overlooking the Caribbean, closed his eyes and listened to the chorus of the night.

After Mallory died, he'd sit in the dark and absorb the sounds of the villagers doing what humanity had done on island for hundreds of years, eat, visit, play dominoes, sing lullabies and, sometimes, make unself-conscious love. He could follow the monkeys' evening meanderings by listening to the dogs, each sounding the alarm when a monkey appeared on his turf. Great sport for the monkeys, torture for the dogs... and everyone within earshot of them. The main chorus, though, was tree frogs and crickets.

Sometimes after a rain, they were so loud that he couldn't hear on the telephone. For his business colleagues in New York, a phone call from him was a gift from the Island, a blast of St. Augustinian soul.

He wondered sometimes about the lives of the villagers below. Only a few of the houses had radios, and only a few more had electricity. Mind you, he smiled to himself, even those who had electricity didn't have electricity because it was off more than it was on. They had to carry water from the government cistern and cooked their meals on clay coal-pots. Jonathan, on the other hand, had a generator, its tank always full and a spare five-gallon jug of fuel on hand, as well as two 100-pound propane tanks for the stove and thirty-five gallons of water in the cisterns. All for one man? It made no sense. He had to sell the place, if for no other reason than that it didn't justify its footprint.

For more than a year after Mallory died, Jonathan had stopped coming down to the island until finally he decided to sell his house. He hadn't had much of a social life either in that time, resigning himself to his work and his children. Then, the last time he'd been down, just before returning to the States, he reluctantly accepted an invitation to a formal sit-down dinner at the Longstone Restaurant, consenting only because of the hostess, a middle-aged Trinidadian lady who always left him laughing.

He remembered that Danielle arrived late, just before the meal was to be served. He had asked Heidi, the hostess, about the empty chair beside him and she'd given him a thumbnail sketch. She was a local girl, the daughter of Doctor Bordeaux and his wife Maria. They were saints on St. Augustine because they'd brought modern medicine to the tiny Island. Besides being their first doctor, he'd specialized in tropical medicine and had become well known internationally as the Caribbean's Albert Schweitzer. Danielle Bordeaux was her name. She'd gone to New York and got into modeling, then fashion design. And now she was back for a visit. Her father and mother had both died just over a year ago. Huge funeral, letters from important people all over the world. Heidi held the wake at the Longstone. Lasted well into the following morning.

When Danielle entered the Longstone that night, Jonathan remembered, the conversation stopped. She was a tall, fair-skinned native woman, maybe twenty-five years, with high, refined features. She moved with a stride of quiet confidence. She wore no makeup nor jewellery, yet she was elegant in a light, fine cotton dress tailored to her body and a Valache silk shawl.

She smiled at everyone and no one in particular, yet everyone smiled back feeling her smile was just for them. Heidi made introductions to the room, though everyone seemed to know who she was, and then directed the woman to a chair between Jonathan and a man from the northwestern United States.

Throughout the meal, Jonathan cast sidelong glances at Danielle. By her profile alone, she could be Arabic, Egyptian, Creole and combinations thereof. She and Jonathan never had a chance to acknowledge each other, let alone talk, as both were involuntarily engaged by the guests on either side of them. Jonathan was being pumped for investment advice by a wealthy widow woman from Texas, who, by the way, was looking for a new investment adviser she said repeatedly. Danielle listened as the man from Chicago ranted and railed pretentiously that Pablo Picasso was highly overrated as was, in the Chicago man's eyes, the Island of St. Augustine. Only when the coffee was served did Jonathan and Danielle speak to each other.

"Hello, my name is Jonathan Douglas," he offered, extending his hand to her.

She smiled. "You look like a Jonathan Douglas," she said in a quiet voice. Jonathan wasn't sure if he should be offended, but her smile was so genuine that he was quite delighted to settle for curious. If nothing else, she would be infinitely more interesting than the widow from Texas.

"And what kind of person is a Jonathan Douglas?" She leaned forward. Intrigue he asked what that might be.

79

"Strong, solid, the kind of man you'd invest money with. I imagine you standing behind a cannon on guard to defend my money." Her smile set the tone for the rest of the evening as far as Jonathan was concerned.

"Your money... and your honour, should you ask," he replied with theatrical presence.

"And I too will defend yours." They shook hands laughing.

"Tell me, Mister Jonathan Douglas," again her voice was soft, the coo of a mourning dove he thought, a wisp of wind with a trace of a West Indian accent, "what do you do?" Her walnut eyes sparkled with genuine interest.

"Estate planning," he responded quickly, trying not to sound boastful.

"Oh," she said, raising her eyebrows. "I'm sorry," and her smiled turned to a grin.

Jonathan's involuntary snort of laughter had to get out, even though he had taken a sip of coffee at just that moment, and grabbed his napkin just in time to avoid making a bigger fool of himself. That made her erupt in laughter, which made him laugh even more. The others in the dinner party turned to look at them. Jonathan wasn't the least embarrassed and made no attempt to explain. They shared something private and he liked that.

"Well then, Mister Douglas, tell me, what do you <u>want</u> to do?"

For a second Jonathan bristled. He didn't like being interrogated, that was his specialty. "If you must know, I want to be just what I am, an estate lawyer!"

She looked at him for some time. "Oh?" One eyebrow cocked. "Okay... then let me put it another way. What are you <u>supposed</u> to do?"

Sensing a "new age" trap like Mallory used to spring on him when she'd returned from self-discovery workshops, he sought to sidestep it, but he was defenceless against the walnut eyes. "What am I <u>supposed</u> to do? Write, I guess." He said it without hesitation

80

or contemplation, and it surprised even him for he hadn't thought about writing beyond legal briefs for decades. For some reason, this flower beside him made him comfortable to revisit that distant dream, at least for the moment. Maybe it was because she seemed honestly interested, or maybe she reminded him of a time set on hold when he too was in the bloom of possibilities.

"And who are you, Miss Bordeaux?" He adopted an overstated interrogatory voice, the one he used to impress jurors and intimidate witnesses.

The woman was neither impressed nor intimidated. "My given name is Danielle Bordeaux."

"Like the wine?"

"Like the region in the south of France," she corrected and then she leaned forward and whispered, "The locals call me 'Bana, which is short for 'Banana-Champ', which is short for a very long story.

"And...?" He was intently interested. "I've got lots of time."

"Okay." She blushed. "The short of the long is that I like bananas. I love bananas. They are the one fruit I never grow tired of. When I was very young, five maybe, they say I got into a scrap with a monkey over a bunch of bananas." She looked slightly embarrassed, then shrugged nonchalantly. "And, I won."

"You mean fists to paws?!"

"More like a metal dog dish across his head."

For a long time Jonathan sat looking at her, digesting her story and waiting for more. Any name, no matter how delicate, poetic or symbolic, would not do the woman justice. "Which do you prefer? 'Bana-champ the Monkey Fighter' or Danielle?" Jonathan asked.

"For now you can call me Danielle."

"And, Miss Danielle, what do you do?"

She thought for a moment, then puffed herself up with importance. "I... am an estate tailor," she said with playful pretentiousness.

Jonathan laughed. He knew her exaggeration was in fact an understatement. "Let me phrase it another way then. What are you supposed to do?"

"Be an Augustinian and design clothes out of fabrics of juicy jungle colours.

"And...why aren't you?" Jonathan asked.

She laughed and gave his hand a quick squeeze. "You're getting too close to the mark, Mister Jonathan Douglas. But when I have an answer to that question, you'll be the first to know."

When the party ended, they accepted a bottle of Bordeaux from Heidi, who was pleased that her guests had hit it off, and they walked and talked on the beach until dawn. They found they shared something beside working in New York, they both had suffered great losses. She talked extensively about her parents, he about his wife, until finally they'd talked it out and could walk in silence and watch the birth of the new day. He had to race back to his house to get his bags before catching his plane. She rode out to the airport with him to return the car. They exchanged their New York telephone numbers with sincere intentions to have supper together in the city.

In fact, he did call her in New York, but they could never dovetail their schedules. Then, after five weeks in Europe settling an estate that involved a fabric factory, he tried without success to reach her and left a message on her private answering machine. She returned his call to his office, leaving a message with his secretary that she was leaving the city for a new position. It was what she was "supposed to do," his secretary told him.

Jonathan wasn't sure how long he'd sat on the ocean side of the house. He'd had reservations about going up to the garden, but they disappeared as soon as he stepped out of the house into the moonlight and followed the path.

Shirley had left one garden light on, tucked down at the base of an ancient mango tree, illuminating its Buddha trunk and the stone wall behind. Looking back, the house was silhouetted against the silver sea, the clouds were moon-swollen like tottering towers over the gentle carpet of lantern lights in the villages below.

But it was the smell that held him the most. Jasmine, gardenias, trumpet flowers, orchids, ylang ylang. Trees of flowers whose names he didn't even know. It was Mallory's Garden. She'd planted for the smell, landscaping so the breezes fluted across the fragrances. A garden for the nose, a garden for the blind. Scents as though they were colours, a painting of smells for those who could not see. Colours of the Caribbean. She adored the Caribbean. She knew their neighbors' names, their family histories. She remembered little details, like birthdays, and always said hello to everyone.

Jonathan sat down on a bench in the garden and, against all his reserve, he started to cry. He missed her so much. She should have planted vegetables and fruit trees, but she thought of the blind man down the hill and had designed it for him.

Finally, taking his hands from his face, he clapped them on his thighs and rose. He returned to the house, turned the lights on in the kitchen and lit the gas stove. He was starving.

There was a message on the answering machine. Strange, since no one knew he was on-island except Shirley and Mango. It was Danielle. He recognised her voice and the number. The message was short: "Call me when the time is right."

Chapter 6

Mystery Woman

As the bus driver Josiah turned "Isaiah: 43" up "Tired-donkey Hill," his thoughts focused upon the sad state of affairs that cricket officiating had slid into, using a match recently played in San Sebastian as a case in point.

Garth again relaxed, tuned-out and returned to his thoughts of his pending two years on St. Augustine. He thought about the mystery woman. There were times when he wondered if she ever existed, but then he'd remember their first meeting so vividly that he knew, she was certainly real. He recalled the day well, it was a comfortable morning, not too hot with a gentle breeze from the south. He and Caraja had finished early that day, so Garth decided to take the long way through to Poppy Dawn School.

The tap-tap "Bosom of Abraham" had picked Garth up at the agricultural farm and dropped him off at the Gumtree Shoppe. He'd walked the up road into the cloud forest, and turned to the right on a foot path of boulders and roots, for hoof or foot only, that ran horizontally around the side of the island, in and out of ghauts, ending at Poppy Primary where he taught an English class in the afternoon. He never tired of the side of his job.

"Kites" Caraja called them. "Little kites dancing in the wind of their whims." The Rasta would say. And their smiles... man it was great to be on the receiving end of one of them. Poppy-kites in their bright orange and yellow plaid uniforms little poppies flying around the sports field. Running after the balls, each other, themselves, but always running. Bright bundles of energy, released from the confines of their unusually hot classrooms. He thought of their gentle, innocent faces as he walked, their eyes so expressive. His brother had eyes like that when he was their age.

The trail descended into a dry riverbed on polished rocks the size of soccer balls, carried there by flash floods. Through the trees and mist, he could see the sea and the blue outlines of Antigua and Monserrat. The sun was a joyful one, bright and still not hot, it mirrored itself off blades of palm limbs damp with the lifting dew. Even the moss on the stone seemed to radiate the sun yet hold his feet secure.

"So here you are." Came a soft voice from nowhere, speaking with the familiarity of one greeting someone they'd been looking for. Garth startled in half stride, looking up from the trail to a woman who seemed to come from nowhere, who suddenly appeared from the rising mist. "Are you lost?" She asked.

Possibly it was the moment, maybe the light, the breeze, the coo of mourning doves, but she was the most beautiful woman he'd ever seen. She was easily balanced, barefoot on two green rocks in the path, a long, linear, ebony egret lady. Tall, sedate and very pregnant. Her skin was neither bronze nor black, but a changing canvas as shadows and sun brushed its surface.

Her eyes were clear and innocent, the pupils dark like volcanic ash, the whites, a light beach sand. Everything about her seemed sculpted, then polished with a gentle cloth. Her face in particular captured him, smooth high cheekbones, a linear nose, thin precise lips. Her hair peeked out in curls from the lavender turban she wore about her head, like children's faces in a school window, anxious for the time they can run free. Taken individually, her features were striking, together they made her mysterious.

Speechless, Garth studied her eyes. It was a habit he taken up since he'd come to St. Augustine. Seldom understanding the language, he always looked first into people's eyes. Were they asking or answering... serious or joking, confused or informed? Then the mouth, smiling or frowning, lots of teeth or no teeth. With this woman, his survey revealed little except that her eyes were serene yet unsettling for they seemed to hold some knowledge of an ancient truth.

"Are you lost?" She asked again. Only then did he notice that the cotton dress the colour of the sun and shadows was contoured to her body, pulling taught around her swollen stomach,that Garth realised she was <u>really</u> pregnant. Her breasts were fully in the possession of motherhood. And the ancient truth in her eyes was the wonderment of life itself.

He had to say something before she thought him a fool. "My name is Longrass. And I'm <u>not</u> from here!"

"No!" She gasped aghast. "Really mon?!" Her voice was a little too incredulous. "For true?" But, though her face remained placid, the eyes and a grin could not be contained. "No, mon," she laughed, " I's just legging you?"

"Legging?" Garth glanced at her legs, and in that instant lost track of the conversation. Her dress was a pasture dress, light and functional with two slits up each side to mid-thigh for mobility. Her legs were long and strong, yet finely tapered pedestals of raw sensuality. And suddenly Garth wanted to study them, caress them, worship them, explore their recesses to the hidden headwaters. She shifted her weight, twisting her hips to accommodate the unborn baby. Garth felt very embarrassed for his lust, which certainly she must have seen.

"Makes a pregnant woman feel good for a man, look dat way at her."

She smiled, and Garth thought he might just be in love. "Legging' means to tease." She added coquettishly.

"I think pregnant woman are the most beautiful creatures on God's sweet Earth." Garth blurted out

"For true?! Well study at me good, cus I won't be this way for much longer." She rubbed her stomach lovingly as she laughed, sharing her humour with the baby.

"How long?"

The woman looked at her watch. "Any moment now!" She said calmly.

"Oh my God!" And he physically stepped back. But then he caught himself. "You're 'legging' me, aren't you?" When she again broke out in laughter, he gave a deep sign.

"So," she shifted again, "You lost?"

"I hope not. I'm taking the high road across to Liburd path, then dropping down to the Poppy School."

"You're the teacher at Poppy school?"

"Not really, I'm a Peace Corp volunteer working with a man named Caraja, but they've got me teaching English and sports in the schools as well." He said, trying to hide his disappointment of the appointment, the kids were the job's only redemption.

"Where are you from?"

"Western United States." Garth replied, having learned his lesson about mentioning Wyoming.

"As in cowboys and Indians 'Western.'"

"Exactly. I'm like a Blackfoot Indian."

"Well..." she said with both amazement and then pride, "*I'm* an *all* black West Indian." Again her eyes twinkled, glancing at his Levi's. "But you look more like a cowboy." Her grin was expansive and inviting, trying to hide the fact that she didn't really know what a cowboy was, having only seen two movies, neither Western, and one television program for a half hour of WWF television. But that didn't stop her. "Imagine, a real old-west Indian teaching here in the West Indies!"

"And you?" Asked Garth anxious to change the subject.

"Me, I'm but a lamb o' d'Lord." She smiled again making Garth's heart race. But her face grimaced for a moment. Slowly she arched forward shifting her load. "I must be moving now." And she stepped lightly but cautiously towards him. Then just as they were about to pass, a mere hand separating them, they both stopped, looking closely into the other's face. Each trying to figure out what it was about the other, that made their hearts race and yet blood run cold. Complete strangers from opposite sides of the Universe, and yet he felt he knew her better than any woman he'd ever met. There

87

was a familiarity he felt about her -- a play as yet unwritten. Maybe even shared destinies in the spirit world unlikely the past, more likely the future and though he knew not which but felt she felt the same.

Garth was still mesmerized as she turned and proceeded again down the path. She moved like an egret, with smooth, graceful steps, her head held high and back with the stately arch of pregnancy and royalty. But unlike an egret that places one foot in front of the other, the woman stepped from side to side as pregnant women do. Twice she turned back to look at him and smiled. Finally, she shook her head as if to say, "I don't know what's happening either." He shrugged too and waved.

He never spoke to her again, in the two years he was on Island. There were glimpses such as times he and Caraja were working the cow chutes down at the government farm, and he thought he saw her on the path watching them. He couldn't tell if she had had the child because of the waist high rubble-stone wall. The only other time was in the library.

As he began to take interest in the history of the island, he wanted to encourage his students to do the same, so one afternoon he stopped into the Gingerland Library to check out their books on St. Augustine. Garth remembered the chill that follows sweating in the hot Caribbean sun then walking into the old stone buildings, still tomb-cold from the previous night. His eyes saw only dark forms after the outside brilliance.

He stood there in the entry way waiting for his sight to return and when it did, it fell upon the silhouette of a woman sitting in an archway window casement as thick as it was wide, at the far end of the great room. Framed by the arch and beyond the tops of palms and sea receding to the setting sun, a young woman lounged with cat-like leisure, her back arched against one side of the thick casement one foot up against the other. That leg folded back drawing her knee near her chest and supported a book. Her other leg draped languidly down the side of the sill, swinging gently, long and beautiful, as the tail of contented cat. While one hand balanced the book, the other stroked a baby nestled in her lap. It was, Garth saw, the essence of the Christian's Madonna. But an image that transcends religions -- it was the personification of the universal motherhood.

He thought he caught notes of a lullaby but they so closely mirrored the gentle breeze that swept into the ancient portals that he wasn't sure. Then it grew in volume and became a bridge between the dark moody shadows of a past heavy with spirits and the outside vibrance of the Caribbean. What held him in place, however, was not just the serenity of the scene, but the realisation that the woman in the window was the woman he'd met on the trail those first days he'd taught at Poppy Primary. Finally coming to the conclusion that she was not from the Island, for certainly their paths would have crossed before this. Even now however he felt the radar of a wariness a wild untamed animal has for its surroundings even when its attention is diverted.

The woman was absorbed and only when the child stirred did she look up and, feeling him looking at her, their eyes met. Now he was sure of it, he thought there had been times in crowded places when he held them, but each time before he could approach her, she was gone. The eyes looked back at him just as they had the first time, familiar, curious yet knowing.

Was she avoiding him? Was he such a savage that he scared her away – as though somehow she'd seen generations of scalp-takers in his face," he amused himself bringing a smile to his eyes. But her eyes were unblinking. Nor did she move, and Garth sensed she was evaluating the situation like a wild animal, a desert cougar he'd watched as a young man: motionless, yet his muscles under tension requiring little more than releasing a coiled spring when the cougar pounced on the elk calf, and it was that moment when he'd also seen cougars spring up and spin away.

" Are you familiar with our library, sir?" Garth startled to a voice from behind him. It was a cool voice of one who'd been sitting in a cold place most of the day. Relaxed, unfettered and more than a little bored. Reluctantly he turned to meet the face and lose eye contact with the mystery woman. He turned to meet a mid-aged woman with a gentle smile, in a light dress buttoned to the top, long hem, uncomfortable for the outside, the proper attire for the burden of having either air-conditioning or "natural air-conditioning" as they called the combination of wind great stone thermal vaults and shade. The old buildings were natural heat sumps absorbing the cool of the evening air trading it slowly for the heat of the day.

"No thank you" he smiled, "my eyes were just adjusting."

He looked quickly back to the window but as he feared, she was gone. For a second he wondered if he had seen her at all, maybe it was just heat prostration. He excused himself from the Librarian and tried to walk casually across the library to the window where she had sat. As he approached, he saw the book laying where she had been, closed with the tip of a leaf sticking out marking her where she stopped.

"Keenington's Diaries of "Travels in The Spice Isles."

"Excuse me", he returned to the Librarian's desk with the book. "Can you tell me who is the woman who was reading this book in the window just now?"

The Librarian looked to the window. The book and then her eyes sized up Garth. Deciding he must be all right, though in her organised stereotypic ledger, he matched neither good nor bad. Also, she knew who he was and where he was from just by Island rumours. She was definitely intrigued, she'd never met an Indian . "Course I can." She said with conviction in her decision. "Her name is Myah Watkins."

"Does she live near her?"

"Up the mountain high above Poppy Village." She reached out for the book. "Praise be for her," the Librarian laid the book on a shelf behind her, "with television so new to the island, nobody except Myah comes here anymore. Nobody reads the historical books." She reached beside him and handed him a bound book that

90

was one of a large collection that took up one entire bookshelf case. Garth looked closely at it. The pages had been bound blank and the text had been handwritten. "There everything captain's logs of crossings and cargoes, to plantation owners' tallies, slave record, and a lot of them slave diaries."

"You know Myah is very smart. Fact, you know she led the Federation on her graduation exams, received the highest mark for both islands. First time St Augustine has taken the honour in fourteen years. To this day people can't figure her out. Living way up there on the mountain and getting the best marks in the whole Federation. But I say more strength to her and now with a son.

My God, thought Garth, that's right, pregnant women don't stay that way for two years. "Is she married?" He tried to sound casual.

The Librarian chuckled. "Mister teacher, you didn't learn anything during your stay. When people get married here it is usually after the litter is raised. And maybe you consider that's weird to your thinking, but we hardly ever get a divorce." She laughed. Garth too started chuckled, still he knew no more than before.

"Now, if you ask who is the farther, that's a different question." She paused for Garth to encourage her on, but he remained silent, which she interpreted that as interest. "Tell you the truth, even that is a curiosity because as long as I've known her I've never known her to go with a man. She had friends but I don't ever remember gossip of her doing anything more than flying kites with them. Course living way up there, you wouldn't have lots of opportunity to hang out. Which is odd because she is so beautiful. If you hadn't noticed." Her smile was knowing.

"Can't say that I did," Garth said soberly.

"Um-hugh," She teased. "There are three of them, they're all beauties in their own way."

"Her sisters?"

"Well you could say that, but not by blood, all three girls are the best of friends. Danielle Bordeaux, Doctor Bordeaux's daughter and the Ward girl, oh what's her first name?" She paused for a moment, but couldn't remember.

"You know, her father was the head of the Port Authority for years. I haven't seen him in a long time, must'a moved off-Island. She sighed and shrugged to herself. "Doesn't matter. Those three girls are sister-close yet they came from three different sides of the Island and from three totally different backgrounds."

"Don't rightly know how they met, but as soon as they were old enough to ride the Tap-taps, you didn't see one that the others weren't right behind. And let me tell you, they broke every boy's heart on Island, all three so cute, but like I said, none of them paid much attention. In fact, that's what lead them to New York."

"New York?" Garth asked astounded.

"N-ew Yo-rk," she said it slowly that he might hear all the syllables. "It's a city in the United States."

"I've heard of it," Garth smiled, wondering if she wasn't "legging" him.

The Librarian looked out the window where Myah had sat. "Books, for Myah were like ideas suspended in time, ripe mangoes hanging on the tree, waiting to be plucked. Perspectives from the past, about the past. 'Messages,' Myah once said, "sent to me from afar, poems for my soul from my ancestors.' Books were the keys for her imagination that started when her mother would come here to read to her. Seems to me she was reading way before the rest of her friends.

At first, the books she read were about other places and people, but as she grew older she started reading historical fiction and then non-fiction, all about the Caribbean and especially anything written about St. Augustine or San Sebastian." The woman smiled and picked up a book similar to the one Myah left on the window casement.

"Now here's a story for you." She leaned forward as if sharing a secret. "One time about eight years ago the government hosted a conference on island for the Eastern Caribbean Historical Society.

Folks come from all over the Caribbean." She extended her arms to emphasis the expanse and importance of the event.

"Well, don't you know, part of the program was a field walk up to Weller's point. It's that bare knoll high up the volcano way above Poppy Primary. The youth go there to fly their kites. Up there you can see almost two-hundred and seventy degrees, all the way to Antigua out into the Atlantic there, and round to Saba in the Caribbean. Don't you know it was Miss Flarety who was organizing it, and she asked if I knew someone knowledgeable about all the plantations you can see from up there. I told her I knew of such a person but didn't say who it was. Only that the person would meet the folks there on the knoll when they come up." A sinister smile crossed the Librarian's lips and her eyes sparkled.

"Now you've got to picture this. These folks make a religion out of digging around in history, and they take very high stock of themselves. So, imagine that moment when this nineteen year old local girl not only can identify all of the old plantations, including the ruins that most local people don't even know about, but she puts them in historical context with what was happening around the Caribbean. Well, don't you know she held their attention until the sun got so low, that the tap-tap drivers had to walk up and get them down the trail by flashlight."

The Librarian smiled with obvious pride drawing her shoulders back and crossing her arms. Garth sensed that Myah was her justification. Her reason for sitting in a dark cool, building for thirty-four years watching the mildew grow and listening to the bookworms eating away at human histories, devouring great ideas before they could take root in the future. Words forever gone with the decay of the messenger.

"Books are merely the couriers. If they are never read or their ideas don't make a difference to someone's own thoughts, then writing is but folly." She laughed cynically. "I mean, if it weren't for readers like Myah, I wonder how much of the lineage of human experience would be reduced to dust. 'He who reads carries the

93

torch from the corpse of the past to light the way for the creativity of the future.'"

"Wow," Garth was impressed, "Is that a quote by you?"

"Fenton Bartholomew -- First Minister of Education for the Federation."

"So who does Myah share her wealth of knowledge with, besides visiting history professionals. If she were a teacher in the school system, I'd know her."

The Librarian shrugged. "I guess she shares her knowledge with herself and," she smiled, " the jumbies."

"Jumbies?

"Spirits." The librarian continued to smile.

The following week, Garth began teaching St. Augustine Island history from the collection of ancient diaries at the library and gave assignments to his secondary students that required them to go to the library and do research in the archives. When they discovered the journals by slaves who could read and write, his students needed no more encouragement.

Chapter 7

Myah's Perspective.

Myah sat down heavily on the porch swing, thinking about the message her cousin had just brought up the mountain from her brother Caraja. He and a friend would be coming by her cottage in the afternoon on their way to her brother's "High Garden" for a few days. The friend was soon leaving St. Augustine and Caraja wanted Myah to meet him. "It's important." Caraja had told the cousin to stress the point.

Myah felt sick for she had a strong intuition that she knew who the "friend" was, and for almost two years she'd avoided him. She thought of avoiding him again, but that would no longer serve. No, she had to face him; Caraja had made it a special request. Besides, Garth was leaving the island and any attraction she might feel could not develop in such a short time, and when he was gone, the dream visitations would stop. Still, she admitted to having mixed feelings, torn between the desire she still held for him and the fear of the doors it might open. Doors she'd worked hard to keep closed.

While Bantu knelt on the porch with a book in his lap, telling his kitten the story of three mice that couldn't see, Myah leaned back in the swing staring out across the glass-calm Caribbean. How would she act when he came? Normal, usual, like she did before. She thought back to that special day almost two years ago.

Myah remembered waking that morning when they first met, as was her custom, just before the sun. She'd lain in bed, bathing in the warmth of her dream, its feeling lingering though she had forgotten its contents. She ran her hands absently over her swollen abdomen. Most of the time she loved being pregnant, but then she felt only awkward and bloated. Water woman, each step determined by the way the water, and therefore baby, was moving. As she glanced out the shutters at the red dawn on the underbelly of the

95

clouds, she sensed that there would be something different that day. Something exciting, something special was going to happen, but she didn't know what. It was still early for the baby to be born — besides, she hadn't felt any of the signs that Sueky had told her to expect. Still, she thought with a sigh of resignation, she would have to leave her mountain home soon and go down to stay with her second cousin Arabella until her delivery.

It might as well be today. She'd rather remain in her little cottage high on the mountain and have the baby there, but it was her first, and her house was accessible only by a steep, rough jungle trail which, under the best of conditions, was a half-hour trip by foot to the nearest road-head and then if she had luck on her side she would have to catch some sort of transportation either truck or taxi down the mountain. And while it might be acceptable in New York to have your baby in a taxi, it certainly wasn't on St. Augustine. No, she was just too remote for her first delivery, she'd have to stay at Arabelle's.

Moreover, Caraja absolutely refused to assist unless she moved closer to the hospital in case things went awry. She decided that after her garden chores were done, she would pack some clothes and toiletries, and go down the mountain.

Still excited and curious about her feelings that the day might hold something special, she rolled out of bed and, with award movements, walked naked out onto the porch and spread her feet wide and raised her arms to welcome the sun.

"Good morning, Morning!" she sang out to the horizon and then turned to the green velvet mountain behind her cottage as the first rays of sunrise descended its face.

"Good morning Mother Mountain. What new wonders do you hold for me this day?" Her eye caught something moving in the fruit trees below the house. "And good morning to you Mistah Monk, I sees you there sneaking around my orchard. But don't be getting no foolish ideas cause I got's my catapult right here handy," she nodded to her slingshot on the railing, "just waiting to shoot you's furry fannies."

Myah was a tall woman in her mid-twenties. Her skin was black as a rule — when it wasn't purple, or royal blue, or, as it was in the early morning, burnt umber. Regardless of the light off her skin, her flesh was smooth and radiant, particularly now with the pregnancy. She admired how full her breasts were, little beads of milk already appearing on the nipples if she pinched them. Still, though she was crowding nine months pregnant back then when she met Garth, and calling herself "water woman", she carried herself with the same graceful self-assurance that had possessed her since adolescence, moving even in her pregnancy with the grace of an African antelope.

Her eyes danced with excitement at all she beheld. She was endlessly inspired by simple things such as the azure colours of the morning-sea running to the horizon. Or the shafts of sunlight spiking through the clouds on their collision course with the volcano where, condensing and filtering through the jungle canopy, they would supply her with water for her lush garden and orchards beyond, and the purest of drinking water. Her brother Caraja was seldom home and though she lived essentially alone, she was never lonely in her cloud-forest paradise.

Myah had never had serious boyfriends. As her hapless admirers and potential lovers discovered, deep in the recesses of her dark eyes there was a certain absence, the detached look of one who dwells on the edges of the unearthly. And try as they might to catch her attention, the boys were kept at a distance by her lack of interest in their rituals of courtship. Her would-be suitors reassured each other in private that the problem was with Myah, not them. "She has a hole a in her soul," they'd whisper when neither Myah nor Caraja was around.

"You's an old soul," Sueky, her grandmother, used to comfort Myah. "You's wise cus Youse soul be ancient. Nutt'n wrong width dat."

Myah grew up on her parents' farm-plot on the fertile hill just above Remember Me, a small community across the ghaut from Poppy Dawn Village. Back then, her grandmother Sueky lived in the high mountain house Myah now occupied. But tragedy had changed all that when the inter-island ferry *Christina* sank, drowning Myah's parents and much of the rest of her family. Suddenly, with the accident, Myah and her brother were orphaned and with no one left to take care of them, she and Caraja moved in with their grandmother Sueky. When Sueky moved down to be closer to the church and the graveyard, Myah remained on the mountain.

Her nickname as a child was "Sparky", derived from her gift for free and open laughter that resembled the sun dancing upon water. Because her laughter lacked self-consciousness, it generated an equal measure of merriment from all who heard it -- like the time when the circus came on-island from Barbados. Clowns with dogs, acrobats who made a great pyramid — until, she remembered, a large dog escaped from a clown and ran through the first tier of pyramiders, causing the structure to slowly collapse, one elbow, one knee at a time.

As it toppled, everyone gasped... except Myah, who laughed so hard, with her best, sparkling laugh, that soon everyone was laughing.

But the nickname lasted only until her mid-teens — not that her laugh changed, only her hormones.

"My name is Myah," she announced to the last unlucky boy to call her Sparky. "Myah is short for my given name, which is 'Myahlanda', which is African for 'Visitor'.

"In the future I expect you to call me Myah." The authority of the request was based upon the fact that her body had grown much closer to womanhood than childhood, and within a week of her declaration, everyone referred to her only as Myah.

While Myah laughed a lot, she spoke little. She was a happy person but preferred the quiet of books and the song of the jungle. She was used to listening to the inner music of the volcano, much to the astonishment of her two closest friends, Ruthie and Danielle (nicknamed Bana), neither of whom took any interest in tree frogs and crickets, or even the chatter of the monkeys, as she did. On the other hand, when her friends discovered that in her innocence Myah had missed <u>the</u> most important event of the twentieth century, at least in the eyes of two teenage girls isolated on a small island in the Caribbean, Myah had never heard of the "Rolling Stones", or simply the "Stones" or that they had recorded their newest album, *"The Voodoo Café"*, in a Montserrat sound studio just forty miles away by ocean. Her friends took the event as license for them to turn Myah into modern girl. Tragedy provided the opportunity.

After their parents died on the Christina, and Caraja and Myah had moved up the mountain to Sueky's home, they could still walk to school at Poppy Dawn Primary, though it was almost an hour each way. When the time came to attend Senior Secondary, however, Sueky's house was too far away, even if they caught a trans once they reached the Main Ring Road.

The solution, concocted by Danielle and Ruthie, was for Myah to stay with Danielle's family during the week and go home to Sueky's on the weekends. Doctor Bordeaux's wife was delighted with the proposition and Myah, without other alternatives, cautiously agreed. For the next four years, she spent her weekends in her beloved jungle and the rest of the week exposed to 'rock 'n' roll', fashion magazines, thongs, Madonna-bras and a strange *patois* of words like "trashed", "chilled", "git-down" meaning "good" and "down" meaning "bummer", while "bummer" could mean either "hard times" or tight-hipped pants. That is, according to Ruthie who was "super cool" and could out jive-talk any of the "git-down-hoes" of Harlem — at least according to Ruthie who had a cousin in Queens.

But amongst her other peers, Myah was as mute as the dead and some wondered if she weren't a little stupid, or maybe stoned all the time. When she earned the highest school marks in all of the Confederation on the government graduation exams, her quiet presence just added more fuel to the shroud of enigma around her. But the reason for her solitude wasn't much of a mystery: Myah had little patience for "stupidness" or "loose lips", as the old women called idle talk and gossip.

Instead, she was a voracious reader. And, in spite of her grades, her tutoring in the finer points of hip-talk and groove-moves, and her exposure to classical culture through the influence of the Bordeauxs, after graduation she returned to her beloved jungled volcano, hung her thong (a present from Ruthie) over her diploma on her cottage wall, and turned her time to building a profitable market garden.

As she grew into womanhood delivering fresh tomatoes, lettuce, celery and fruits to the Saturday market, the vendor ladies became Myah's main point of human contact. Usually they treated her with respect, but then, on hot afternoons when nothing was moving in the market but the flies, when gossip grew outlandish and became "the gospel truth" because everyone was too tired to dispute its falseness, the conversation would turn to Myah.

"Liv'n on de mountain bound to twitch de brain, make de soul turn to de darkside," someone would remark, and in a single sitting, the hum of the market would drift from "speculation" to "assumed fact" through a questionable course of scientific deduction based solely upon suspicion, having no validity or truth. But mainly it was the rain forest which induced the market ladies to muddy Myah's public image. To most Islanders it was a distant world of darkness and shadows, a sanctuary for jumbies who wailed with hideous screams — "ghosts of slaves skinned alive!" children were told should they hear the cry of a wood-slave or an angry monkey.

"Course you knows she be a grand of Sueky!" Someone would say, followed by a murmur of acknowledgement of the implications hidden in the first premise. "And don't you know dey say Sueky do de Obeah!" was the second premise in the syllogism. Therefore, Myah was Obeah by association.

"Obeah?" one of the uninformed women might ask.

100

"Priestess of de voodoo! Someone what talks with jumbies — and makes all kinds o' mischief."

"Once me hears tell," whispered one of the market vendors in the back of the market, one lazy afternoon, "dat de Swanson woman was losing she garden to thieves and she goes to Sueky and asks she fo' a spell ta vex-up de thieves."

So Sueky, dey say, comes to she garden with a bag full of potions and she take one pumpkin what's close to ripe and she rub de skin with she ointments and say de 'evil words and curses' over it. Den wen de moon be waning, she do de fitful dance, and she leaves de garden fo' de Devil to do He work."

"Weren't but a day later, das somebody done up an' thieve she prize pumpkin. Mad as a hen in de rain, de lady what owns de prize she flies to Sueky, making all kinda fuss 'bout false representation. But Sueky hold up she hand and say 'de game no over yet.'

"And whas you know, dat Saturday w'en de market lady Sally," the narrator turned to her audience, "well, she got's a pumpkin from Banjo whas looks suspicious, and when Sally does open she up to sell in pieces, de pumpkin start to make de noise and talk, saying de thief's name over and over again,' Banjo! Banjo!' Den d'pumpkin-she turn foul and putrid and stink up de ol' market something bad. De police take up Banjo and he gets five weeks! Plus, gotta pay top value fo' de pumpkin. He defends he-self, cus no lawyer wants to deal width he, since most of de market hears what de pumpkin say!"

"Das not true for chure!" exclaimed Lavender, a breeze fanning her enough to muster a challenge. "Sueky, no does de Voodoo. She does go to church every Sunday for all she-life, and choir on Fridays when she can catch trans."

"Girlo, you's blind? Dat's just to cast off suspicions! 'Sides, it's not just Sueky. Myah be de great-great-grandchild to Emma, and she be de only daughter o' dat Eden woman's slave what caused all da trouble… dat 'dusty maid' called <u>Naomi</u> — das de one what commits suicide when da white lady died."

Again, both premises were half true. Myah was the direct descendant of five generations of strong, spiritual women going far back into slavery. And some of them *may* have practiced "de bidding of de afterworld".

Therefore, Myah was not only of the Obeah faith, she was likely a voodoo priestess by genetic inheritance, and thus tied to the legends that were too intolerable to discuss, even in the market. As a consequence of that conversational taboo, most of the market ladies "hung onto the juice" without requiring any substantiating "pulp", meaning truth.

Of course, no one said anything to Myah directly, but it was always their loose grasp of syllogistic logic that was served up when anyone wondered out loud if it wasn't voodoo that had caused some strange event, like the Fergusons' two-headed calf.

Of course, no one had seen with their own eyes any rites or rituals being practiced upon the parent beast, which was itself suspicious enough, for it meant simply that the forces of voodoo moved in unseen ways!.

In her defence, Myah hardly ever spoke at all in public, and never in tongues as she was accused, though there certainly were plenty of others on-island, both in and out of the "Temple of the Most Sacred Nazarene" church, who talked loudly in tongues on Holy Sunday and spoke with other souls in different languages, if "languages" they were at all.

Myah was aware of the rumours about her, but she held no animosity towards any of those who spoke poorly of her.

"When you make someone your enemy, you hold them close, like family," counselled Sueky. "To hate dem is to give dem space in you's heart. Best to pay dem no never-mind a'tall a'tall."

In truth, it was not Myah's lineage, nor her attraction to the jungle, that spawned their consternation. Her only real crime was that she was beautiful and unobtainable to any of the market ladies' sons. Their hostility grew worse when she was invited to go to New York with Bana and Ruthie.

Bana had been invited to go to New York by a friend of her father's who was an executive of a modelling agency. The idea was purportedly to be for a fashion shoot, but everyone knew it was a setup by Dr. Bordeaux and his friend Andres Courseau, the modelling agent, to get Bana off-island and give her exposure to the outside world. Bana, with no serious thought of becoming a model, agreed to the shoot, but said she couldn't possibly go without Ruthie and Myah, which delighted Andres. The phrase "Black is Beautiful" was in vogue at the time in the fashion industry, and three beautiful blacks couldn't hurt his agency, so he graciously extended his offer to each.

For Bana, the City's shoe fit and, much to her amazement, she did become eventually an internationally recognised model. The shoe fit Ruthie as well, but on the other foot. She pursued a different style and became, as one suitor complimented, "a black diamond" in the crown of Manhattan's party scene. Ruthie took a position with one of the city's most expensive and exclusive escort agencies... even a New York State attorney general was a client.

But Myah preferred bare feet to the high heels of the runway and slippers of the boudoir. And while she loved the excitement of the city, especially the Village and its unkempt energy of free-flowing ideas, literature, art, dance and music; it was the "hipster intellectuals", as they were called by their unhip peers on Madison Avenue, who appealed to her the most. She had come to New York for a specific reason ...it was her intention to return to the island with a baby.

It was in the Village that she met Stewart Randall at a rally to save the Indians of the Amazon jungle. He was two years her senior, with blond curly hair, blue-green eyes and a graduate teaching appointment at Columbia University's Department of Philosophy. There was certainly an intellectual attraction, but the magnetism was pure desire. Desire for him, desire to explore her passions, but mainly, though she admitted it to no one — her desire for Stewart Randall was simply to provide her the ultimate souvenir. And as soon as she missed two menstrual periods in a row, she returned to Sueky's little farm high above Remember Me.

Resigned to going down the mountain to Arabelle's, the village midwife, she walked back inside the cottage and looked at her wardrobe. She was down to one dress: a pale green cotton pasture-dress that contoured to her body like paint. Another week or another two inches of girth and its seams would certainly give way. If her pregnancy continued much longer, God forbid, she giggled to herself, she would have to go naked to market. Now wouldn't that give the vendor-ladies something tangible to "tangle their tongues around". Again, she giggled with the idea of going into the market naked with a honey-melon on her head and one in her belly.

As was her plan, after morning chores in the garden and collecting the ripe fruit in the orchard, she shuttered up her house and started down the trail. She sang to herself as she descended, but suddenly stopped before entering the ravine. There between the gaps in the trees below her, but on the other side of the ghaut, was a man moving along the trail entering the ravine from the opposite direction. They'd likely meet in the bottom where the trail turned up the flood-polished boulders in the then-dry riverbed for a short distance. The man's head was down watching his feet as he leapt from rock to rock. He'd taken off his t-shirt and made it into a turban that he'd wrapped around his head for shelter from the sun. Moving with confidence and grace, occasionally he'd stop to study a plant, or insect, or the jungle at large, at which point she'd lean back and disappear into the shadows.

He was beautiful. He wore khaki shorts and hiking boots, with a faded blue backpack over one shoulder. His legs were strong and powerful and as she drew closer she felt a pulse of excitement at how muscular his upper body was, not the physique of one who lifted weights at a gym but of one accustomed to hard labor. His skin was neither white like that of Stewart Randall's from New York, nor black like her own. Rather, it was the bronze colour of oiled leather. She knew he was an Indian like the Arawak and the Carib Indians who once inhabited the Caribbean. She'd heard from Caraja that his name was Garth and that he was an Indian from the western States, which one she wasn't sure. He was good with animals and knowledgeable about their diseases, and she learned from her brother that he was Caraja's friend, which was special since Caraja had few, if any, male friends. But there was much that Caraja hadn't mentioned about Garth that <u>she</u> noticed and those unknown qualities were what excited Myah even from a distance. But there was also something that vaguely unsettled her, like a debt owed or an important promise forgotten.

Maybe it was because Caraja spoke so well of him that she felt she knew him. "So here you are!" she'd blurted out when he finally came fully into her view; he was looking down at where he stepped and hadn't seen her. His head jerked up, startled, and he stared at her for the longest time. His eyes were soft, honest and, most of all, curious. And while he probably wasn't the type of man used to being confused, his eyes betrayed the fact that he was definitely confused by her presence.

"Lost?" she'd asked. He smiled, after the shock of meeting her on the trail wore off. She liked the way his eyes studied her face and her body, and the way he tried to find words but was speechless. When he did speak, he told her how he felt pregnant women were the most beautiful of God's creatures. She loved his words but wondered what he'd think after she'd delivered the baby.

Remembering back to that day, she was a little embarrassed by her behaviour, but she couldn't stop herself. As they approached each other, she slowed her pace, then actually stopped with just a foot separating them, even closer if one included her swollen belly. "I know you," she'd thought, looking into his deep brown eyes. Again, she was struck by a sense of familiarity, as if he were an old friend with whom she'd shared a rich, though very distant past. She felt she knew him intimately, but how could she? In his face she saw that he wondered the same about her. In fact, she laughed to herself, if it hadn't been for Bantu getting restless to greet the world, they might still be there looking into each other's eyes.

After Bantu was born, which happened just hours after her encounter with Garth, she'd take the baby for strolls down to the sea in the morning, past the government farm where Garth and Caraja were usually at the corrals, separating the cows.

She'd stop on the path some distance away so as not to be detected and watch them working on the plank-way above the chutes, their shirts off, muscles glistening with sun and sweat. Garth's movements were slow and methodical, moving at the cows' pace as he shuttled them effortlessly along through the sorting chutes and out into the different corrals. And as Caraja had said, he had a special way with the animals and they seemed to pay attention to him.

But then the promise between them all changed. At first, she lulled herself to sleep with sensual thoughts about him. Soon, however, the dreams turned from being light and softly passionate to dark, confusing and sometimes terrifying nightmares — powerful dreams that followed her into the new day. And while the dreams involved Garth, he was not at their centre. Still, so fearful were the nightmares that she finally began avoiding him completely, which filled her with a deep sad regret. But she held her resolution and the dreams stopped. For two years she was successful except for one brief encounter at the library.

Myah recalled sitting in the open window casement of the old Gingerland library. It was her favourite place not including her beloved rainforest. Quiet, peaceful, it exuded three hundred years of security that wrapped around her. Where others saw the old library as a tomb, for her it was a stone womb. She found for herself a world beyond the present, past and future — a private space inhabited only by the imagination.

Myah also loved the smell of the library. The breeze was seasoned by the seasons. When the mango bloomed, the breeze was scented with its richness. Clusters of palm flowers were the perfumes of Spring. Gardenias and jasmine scents filled the great catacombs in the winter. And through all the seasons, tucked behind the floral scents, was the odour of ancient books, and even that acrid smell reminded her of the dark rich earth that she loved full of decomposition.

The other attraction of the library, for Myah, were the books themselves. She wanted to read them all and she felt she was in a race with time as the tendrils of mould and minute mouths of worms conspired to devour the humans' thoughts written two hundred years ago with the hope that their ideas and histories would be read.

That particular day she'd sailed on an English frigate, reading a handwritten diary from two centuries before, while Bantu, almost two years old, lay out on the casement, his head on her lap. Suddenly, like a short circuit in an electrical connection, she lost her train of thought, of time and place. She felt Garth's presence. When their eyes met, it was as though a sentence half started could now be finished. And part of her wanted to go to him, to welcome him. But she froze like a jaguar caught in a corner. Thankfully, Mrs. Fuller, the Librarian, said something that caused him to look away, and Myah fled.

She'd gone straight to Sueky's and, as was her grandmother's custom in the late afternoon, Sueky was in her garden talking to her plants and trees.

"Girlo, you looks flushed. Is Bantu sick?" asked Sueky, seeing Myah's state.

"No," Myah said, turning her face away from her grand.

"Is you dats fever'n?" Sueky asked.

Myah knew that Sueky would soon discover what troubled her, so she turned and look straight at her grandmother. "I... I saw him today!" she blurted.

"Saw <u>Who</u>? De Lord Jesus?!!" Sueky exclaimed with exaggerated enthusiasm. "You saw de Lord Jesus today?!!" Sueky smiled, teasing her granddaughter lightly, but Myah was not to be distracted. She looked down at her bare feet and the little boy playing contentedly with Sueky's perpetual brood of yellow chicks.

"No," she shook her head. "I didn't see de Lord."

"De Devil den?!"

"No… well, maybe, maybe both." Myah frowned. "I don't know which." She took both of Sueky's hands. "Oh Gran, I don't know what's happening. I have never been so fearful and yet he continually occupies my thoughts ...in pleasant ways, and if I turn my mind ever so slightly to him, he stirs such excitement."

"Wait!" Sueky raised a brittle hand holding some carrots she'd just pulled from her garden. "Child, who 'He' das both God an' Devil be?" Myah had shared nothing about Garth with her Grand until now. Of course, Sueky didn't understand, she didn't even know there was a man in her granddaughter's life.

Myah smiled, a little embarrassed. "His name is Garth, and he came here with the Peace Corps to work with Caraja at the government farm, but they've also have him teaching afternoons at Poppy Dawn Primary and kicking soccer balls with the Secondary boys."

"Disgust'n how de goberment goes on makin' slaves outta de people what's volunteered to be here." Sueky would have ranted on about the St. Augustine government had Myah not placed her hand over the old woman's.

"He's so beautiful and I think he's gentle, the kind of man you'd like. The youths at Poppy school where he teaches adore him. But there is something that scares me and I'm not sure if it is him, .. or something that involves him. It's like," she whispered, trying to hold back the tears, "in these dreams, I associate him with something crazy and awful, but I don't know what!" She buried her face against Sueky's shoulder and began to cry.

"Oh, child, das backtime talk, das you's imagination working after hours. What do your senses tell you? I t'ink you's in love. Nobody can be dat good and dat bad in one soul."

Myah laughed and nodded and they sat for a long time looking at their hands and Bantu.

Finally, Sueky spoke again. "Maybe what you's fearing is love itself. Maybe you's in love an' you's afraid to be in love, and de mon get caught in de middle. Simple as dat." She paused, "Black mon or white?"

"Neither," Myah said forlornly, "and both." She reflected again. "He is an Indian."

"Trinidad come-so?"

"No, from the United States. He's a real Indian." She put two fingers behind her head to represent eagle feathers and patted her open mouth with her palm of the other hand as in a Hollywood "warpath" film. But her antics were lost on Sueky, who had never seen a cinema and only of late a television, and that was as she walked past Sambo's shop perpetually tuned to "WWF Wrestling."

The old woman sighed. "What does Caraja say about him?"

"Caraja thinks well of him. Couple of times he wanted to invite Garth home for dinner, but I always found an excuse to stop him."

"Well, girlo, seems dat you's de one width de confusion. If it ain't nothing he does, den you's gots to ask what it is dat stir brings you's pot to boiling."

Myah thought for some time. It was time to tell Sueky her true feelings. "Since I was little, you've always said I was special. Well, I wanted to think that's what all grands say because I didn't want to be special. And I still don't."

She glanced at Sueky, but her grand remained placid. "But at the same time, I know that I am the first grandchild of Sueky, who is the granddaughter of Emma, and she the great-granddaughter of Naomi, and she the daughter of the African woman Kuwanay. And I know that it is a privilege to be chosen, but I also know that the lineage is for me a curse." She stopped choosing her words. "The power" then she paused for a moment," carries responsibility. "And that's what hangs heavy with me. I don't know what will be expected from me."

"Nothing more will be asked than you can handle, and no more than you will wish," said Sueky patiently.

"I'm not even sure if I want their... their presence in my life. Is there no one else in the family who can take the knowledge, perform the rites and do their bidding?"

"Stop!" Sueky said with unexpected abruptness. "It's not a subject of choice, besides a curse is jus' a blessing dat's not fully formed. And, if you's man be you's destiny, ain't no force you can muster dat's gonna change what's already been set in motion."

Her eyes were as emphatic as her words. "So, child," she smiled kindly upon Myah, "might as well surrender and, love it girlo. Surrender to what you can't change." She held Myah's face with both hands, smiling into the young woman's eyes. "Besides, you's ancestors will never force you to do what you can't do."

"But what about the man?" Myah had asked. "I'm afraid he will turn from me if he knows the whole story!"

"Child, if he is in you's destiny, you'd be foolish to try to change it and chase he away."

Myah gave a deep sigh and her thoughts left the past and Sueky, returning to the porch swing, her son teaching his cat about blind mice and, most of all, the fact that Garth would be passing through on his way up the mountain with Caraja to the high garden.

"What will be, will be," Myah said aloud, rocking forward in the porch swing. Again aloud, she added, "He's coming with Caraja this afternoon and I can't do anything to change it." She said it with resignation.

Bantu, abandoning his book and kitten, tried to climb onto the swing beside his mother. "Swing?" he asked, and Myah reached down and lifted him up beside her, and gently started to swing

110

forward and back. "Three blind mice," she sang. "See how they run...

Chapter 8

Caraja and the Indian Cowboy

Caraja was a big man whose smile was the result of enlightened poverty. On an Island where dentistry was either expensive or reduced to pulling teeth in the back office of the pharmacy, even for simple cavities, few people had their full complement of teeth. Because his parents were farmers and not accustomed to easily accessible cash, Caraja and his sister were not allowed candy or even chewing sugarcane. As a result of this imposed diet, they had excellent teeth. Pearly and straight, Caraja's smile gave off more energy than those of rich people with well-pampered mouths.

His smile was large, welcoming and free. When he smiled, the sun shone; when he laughed, everyone laughed. His glee would issue from his laugh like smoke puffing out of the stack on the St. Augustine's cane train. Short puffs gaining momentum with the fuel of a joke until it hit full-throttle laughter that was both infectious and sincere. His dreadlocks hung around his face like curtains around a stage. And what was playing was always the same show, "Caraja". For twenty-three years, day and night, storm and fair weather, Caraja had never been anyone else. Never even wondered who he was, for he always knew. An old soul, the elders said of him even as a baby. Maybe because he'd never wrestled with his identity, his focus fell exclusively upon the world around him. In fact, Caraja always felt like an observer of his own destiny, willingly participating but always feeling he was following a pre-written script. He sensed himself caught in a reality-play where he was both player and played — both witness and event.

Caraja was the antithesis of consumerism, and everything he needed was provided to him by either the jungle, the sea or the mountain. It was only of late, with his government job managing the Island's herd of white Charolais, that he had a cash income. Shelter, tools, food, love, beauty, passion and Peace ... he wanted for nothing more. He considered himself a man of wealth already though he had neither a bank account nor, title to most of his many dwellings. The first one he did have a deed for, which he and his sister shared, had been inherited from his parents. It was a true dwelling, a strong chattel house made from hand-hewn mahogany planks with thick *cedar* shakes. It sat high up the mountain on a flat, fertile bench shouldering off a ridge doglegged from the volcano.

His and his sister's garden was small but abundant and surrounded by a diverse orchard of natural and introduced fruit trees. Breadfruit, avocados, passionfruit, oranges, juice and pulp varieties of mangoes, grapefruit and even pineapples sprang from the soil, which was rich with volcanic nutrients and attention.

His parents had drowned on the Christina ferry, and he and his sister had been raised by their grandmother Sueky. His sister took to books, but Caraja was drawn to them only when they improved his farming. Maybe that is why he'd agreed to accept the help of the Peace Corps worker on the government farm, believing anyone who had been to agricultural college was a vast source of new knowledge. Or maybe it was just the novelty of working with an American Indian.

He was a practicing Rastafarian, and in the tradition of his faith found fulfillment working the land and animals. When the government put up "free-to-farm" land, Caraja became the role model for all the young Rastas. He had laid in drip irrigation, hand-picked his soil with the attention that monkeys give to fleas, and most of all had negotiated a peace treaty with the monkeys. As a consequence, his crops were often one-again thicker and taller than his neighbours'.

Along the fence protecting his free-to-farm plot from goats, a skull was set on the end of each fencepost. Often they were only dolls' heads he'd found along the shore, but these were interspersed with monkey craniums. The dolls' heads came by chance... the monkeys' by transgression. It took a lot of pestering to bring Caraja to react to the monkeys. "Me and the monks does generally gets on. I tells dem dat I needs de food and asks dem to stay away from it. In return, I'll do dem no harm and leave a little fo' dey. And most de time dey does and I does... until some rogue thinks he can whist he will.

"Den I does give he some licks de likes dat makes de others think hard dat me's a man of me word."

Caraja needed little, and what he did need either arrived on the shoreline just when he needed it or bloomed in the jungle. And what the sea or the volcano couldn't provide, he supplemented from his "special" garden high above his and his sister's garden.

For example, at the annual time to register his well-weathered, heavily patched, topless Mini-Moke beater-car named "J'Loppy.", He'd harvest ganja for a cash income to become legal. For fuel for J'Loppy he'd trade some of his crop with the local filling station owner, who used it for his arthritis.

And Caraja made it even simpler, he quit paying for the license altogether, reasoning that as a government employee, it was a work vehicle and thus the government's responsibility.

The police knew the Moke was illegal and frankly, when they saw it on the road, they marvelled that it lived. "Make she legal, Caraja," Constable Statton would call out to him when he saw J'Loppy in town. "Or it's de cuffs fo' you!"

"You cannot imprison a man whose soul be free of troubles.," Caraja would declare with a grin.

"Ya? Well, make she legal o' we'll see about that!" the Constable would laugh.

"I'm on my way this very minute. Just one stop, den I'm off to the Magistrate. New title of chure" He'd grin.

He'd wave and drive off, pursued by a trail of blue smoke, a Congo drum percussion of loose parts, and an unmuffled muffler. Should the constable stop him again, Caraja would just explain that

114

he was on the same mission — but he first he had to visit a welder's to get his door re-anchored, or when the muffler got so loud that dogs howled when he passed. The magistrate would be next, but he somehow never got there.

In truth, Caraja could walk to the government farm and he didn't have to keep J'Loppy running and legal. There were always buses on the Ring Road. But buses required some money which he earned ten times over one-evening-a-week playing the steel pans at the Hotel Lemon, "Snow" and the Soul Survivors".

When Snow stopped singing to have a baby, the name shrunk to "The Soul Survivors.' They played a unique mix of reggae and rock-a-gospel, with a touch of blues for colour. Caraja's cousin Barker played bass guitar and sometimes trumpet, and Caraja added pan-calypso in part for the tourists, but also it varied the tune when one of the other instruments was on a jazz run. Snow had been part of the original "Strum and Thump Band" or as it was commonly called on Island, the "Bug Band".

Some people thought the name was a knock-off of the Beatles, but in truth it was because most of their instruments were made from parts off a cadaver of a wrecked 1963 Volkswagen van. Caraja played the brake drums and was on set the night that the Bug Band played its final gig, and the owner of the Island wrecking yard, who'd bought the car from the hippie owners, wanted the parts back.

Caraja lived within walking distance of the Government farm, though separated by a deep ghaut that trickled continually, and raged in storms enough to be deadly dangerous. His home was a private piece of land far from the old plantation building-complexes that drew the tourists. Moreover, his home suited Caraja perfectly -- and no one else on the planet!

Actually, it was the land that attracted Caraja to his domain. He had a view of the ocean's many moods and the majestic mountain in the other direction. For Caraja, home is where you can eat, sleep, stay dry, and in his case, be inspired! The fact that there was no central lighting except a kerosene lamp that hung in the

115

middle of the compound was of little consequence. Correspondingly he gave minimum attention to household furniture. In fact, other than flattened stumps scattered around the fire-pit, and a collection of vintage plastic milk cartons, he had none.

His bedroom, if one called two pieces of galvanised roofing, one shingled over-lapping the upper-edge of the other one the ground, and a green plastic tarp covering both and extending to the ground for an entrance, -- a bedroom. To accommodate his bed, he slept in one position mimicking a corpse, even hands folded across his chest. And were his needs more expansive, a coffin and a tarp would serve him fine.

Finally, Caraja had no burglar alarm system, for not only did he not have anything worth stealing, the entrance too was guarded by a spiny cusha tree with limbs sweeping down so low that you had to bend over to avoid their deadly thorns.

Caraja lay in the dark, listening on his transistor radio to the BBC World News out of Antigua. Satisfied that while the world was still going to hell in a donkey cart, global events still had no effect upon him, nor even his side of the island, and he'd switch the radio off. In the predawn haze between night and sunrise, he crawled out and performed his morning ritual of giving thanks for the day and night before, remembering its highlights... ignoring the lows. He asked no more of the day dawning than "understanding" and he gave thanks.

That morning the blossom of passion fruit and lime from the adjacent trees saturated the clearing. 'Paddiwack', Caraja's main dog, began barking and slapped his tail against Caraja's leg to remind him that it was time for breakfast.

"Good morn'n Mista Dog," Caraja bent down, unhooking the dog's leash. Paddiwack raced around the yard while Caraja roared with laughter. "Go dog go!" he cheered until the dog collapsed at his feet. It would be a busy day, he thought as he made a small fire and boiled his thick "bush-tea".

When it was boiling heartily, he poured a cup for tea, then spooned in two hen eggs to make them hard. "Bosom of Abraham" taxi's van would be picking up the yams and papaya he'd collected the day before and would take them to the Portstown market. "Mongoose" would sell them for him, two-one split. Normally he'd carry them himself to market, but he was meeting the Peace Corps volunteer who was coming from someplace in the States called Wyoming.

He didn't know much about the guy except that he was an Indian, real Indian. He had grown up on a horse/cattle ranch and had gone to agricultural school. Caraja was secretly hoping he'd be wearing a feathered headdress or at least a cowboy hat.

Bosom of Abraham arrived on schedule and, after loading the van, while the driver kept the engine running because the battery was dead, Caraja hurriedly ate the boiled eggs and drank the strong tea.

"Okay, Paddiwack, you's de one. You no let in no monkeys no matter how loud they howl come in. You's de one!" The dog wagged his tail and raced off to the property line to start his patrol of the perimeter of skulls.

The ghaut, separating Caraja's oasis from the rest of the world, was formidable, deep and lined with steep walls ending on boulders the size of cows -- all worn round by nozzle-blasting cascades of water when storms saturated the jungle faster than it could absorb. Sometimes he could not cross and Caraja was accustomed to being trapped either away from home, or at home, which ever suited him the best. On the civilisation side of the ghaut, he had friends, and just as they were welcome on his side, Caraja never wanted for a place to stay when the rains closed access to his home.

And though he shared a house and garden with his sister Myah high up the volcano, it was a third residence where his heart resided in with his girlfriend Felicity. But there was a problem at the government farm that had brought him down.

117

More and more farmers were bringing in emaciated animals thick with ticks. And now he was starting to find ticks in the government's animals. The old way to get rid of ticks was to bathe the animals in the ocean and scrub off the ticks, but Caraja saw that it never worked for long and suspected that now something else was going on. He was anxious to talk with the Peace Corps worker about the problem and see if he had any ideas.

At the corrals, Caraja met with his four-man crew and sent two to check fences along the north boundary, while he and the other two went to a far pasture to move the main herd to an adjacent field that had not recently been grazed. Normally by managing the rotation closely, the animals remained fat throughout the season, even in the dry period. Even the ticks could normally be controlled by driving them through a dip-tank. But now it didn't seem to make any difference.

As he walked behind the herds of white Charolais, he never failed to appreciate their primeval beauty. The great horns on the bulls were reminiscent of an ancestral wild beast that might have roamed the plains of Africa. Unlike wild beasts, however, the Charolais had become habituated to their symbiotic relationship with humans, we feed them, they feed us. But of late their moods changed. And Caraja noticed that morning that the herd was unusually restless, the young steers pushing each other, bullying the younger calves. The cows were grumpy with each other, and collectively ornery towards the bull. Possibly they knew that it was time to wean the calves.

"Watch 'em close," Caraja called out to a man named Benji. "I's a feeling de moon is making dem ill-tempered. Dey could cause us all sorts of mischief if we's lax, so look sharp, think spry."

One cow in particular was continually trying to break away and get around them with her calf. At the road separating the two pastures, the gate opened out onto the road, cutting off the animals from running down it to the sea. Benji stood on the other side so the cows had no choice but to cross the road. Suddenly the

118

cantankerous one bolted at Benji, knocking him down and charging up the road towards Poppy Dawn Village, turning what should have been a simple transition into a morning of full-throttle drama, with cows racing back and forth and the crew running twice as hard trying to cut them off.

Finally, by midday, they got the herd situated in the new pasture and had cut out the dozen cows and calves for weaning back at the corrals, just as the Department of Agriculture car pulled into the yard. Caraja quickly stepped behind the fence where his pack lay. He put on his clean shirt, brushed his locks from his face and started across the corral to greet the two men, turning his head and attention away from the cow who'd started the morning's problems.

She suddenly charged him from behind. Caraja hadn't even seen her coming when Garth, without thinking, jumped the fence into the corral, grabbing an empty gunnysack hanging there.

"Hey! — Hey!" Yelling and waving a gunnysack he started running at the animal, which was circling around for another shot at the Rasta. Waving the bag to catch her attention, Garth pulled her away from her objective by making himself a preferable target. The cow spun at him and lunged, but the Indian was ready and shook the gunnysack in her face, stepping to the side as she heaved past.

"Fuck they're as stupid here as they are at home." he flashed. Again, she turned and came for him, and again he controlled her with the bag like a bullfighter fanning his cape.

Caraja had fallen so he scrambled to his feet and limped to the fence, watching the Indian over his shoulder with disbelief. His initial fear for the Peace Corps worker turned into astonishment as he realised that the Indian had complete command of the cow.

With each pass, Caraja became more animated until, between huffing hard with laughter and cheering Garth, he gasped for the Indian to stop. Garth decided to seize the moment and make a good impression.

Holding the cow's attention on the burlap sack, he started spinning her around and around in a tight circle until she was disoriented and dizzy. When he finally dropped the bag on the ground, the cow stood still, head down, looking at it, swaying slightly from side to side. Garth moved cautiously away and eased behind her.

Then, he spun around to face her and ran full speed at the dazed animal, he put both hands on her hindquarters and frog-jumped onto her back with the ease of a gymnast. Her head jerked up and she lurched forward, but, before she could buck, he swung off.

Taking up the burlap bag, he bowed to his audience.

"You see that?!" Cried the government agent. He slapped Caraja on the back with an intimacy unusual for St. Augustinians. "Bravo, Bravo!" Caraja was wiping his eyes, red with tears from laughing so hard. He suddenly saw a whole new lesson to working his cattle, at least the wild ones. Keep them confused.

"Me's never! Never in me sweet-loving life!" stammered Benji when Garth dropped to the ground on their side of the corral. "Me no gone do dat.... Ever!" He said.

"Mon, I owes you my first-born child for dat! Dat crazy bitch has been looking all morning for a chance to trample me." Caraja looked through the fence-boards at the cow, who was still wobbling, head down.

"The Lord didn't allot cows too many brains, so they're easily confused," said Garth.

Caraja wiped his hands on his once clean shirt, and stuck out his right hand.

Garth, not knowing what to do, wiped his hands on his shirt before shaking.

"I'm Caraja. Or, as my mother had me christened, 'Archibald Brauwn'."

"Which do you prefer?" He laughed.

That got Caraja to laughing again. "Which you t'ink mon?"

"Well then," Garth grinned, "Mister Archibald, I'm Garth Longrass."

"Those were pretty cool moves you made on her. Where you learn dat?"

"I wrote you that I lived on a ranch. No limit to what kind mischief kids can get into when they're bored enough." Then Garth chuckled and confessed, "Naw, in college I did a little rodeo-clowning." He could see by Caraja's face that clowning meant something different, circus clowning, but the words "rodeo-clown" had him thrown.

"Well, I hope you won't be bored on St. Augustine, no telling what trouble you might get into ... well, that's not true."

The tour of the farm began with the government man pointing out the new corral system, the pump system for the watering tanks and the concrete pads for the squeeze chutes. But it wasn't long before Caraja was directing Garth to the animals.

"I'm <u>very</u> glad you're here. I think we got *'una problema grande"!* Caraja said it exclusively to Garth; the agent from the Ministry of Agriculture didn't like to hear the word "problem". "When you're ready," added Caraja. "When you're ready."

Garth looked at a couple of the cows. "I think I know what's happening already."

Then he smiled." Anyway, we'll sort it out, you got me for two years, might as well make the best of it. Think of the Peace Corps as kinda reverse slavery."

The government agent bristled at the remark, but he also realised that Garth might actually do something helpful for the island which few Peace Corps volunteers actually did, so he didn't respond.

"When do you want to start? Caraja asked.

"I thought we had?! What time should I be here?"

"Seven a.m. and look sharp, don't want no slackers on my crew." And again, the Caraja's private train started puffing merrily along, still fueled by memories of Garth and the cow.

Chapter 9

Rainbow's and the Blackwater Picnic

As Jonathan approached the cluster of thatched roofs and the sounds of reggae music reverberating through palm-frond walls and across the white-sand beach, mixing with the late-afternoon sounds of children laughing and playing out in the ocean, he thought how much all beach bars looked identical all around the Equator. He remembered one called "Slouchoes", along the coast of the Baja of Mexico. It was the only structure from horizon to horizon on the desolate beach, and yet, inside, out of the scorching sun, it was elbow-to-elbow humanity fortifying themselves against dehydration.

Rainbow's beach bar was strategically situated between the Sheraton Hotel and the rest of St. Augustine. It was an intersection of classes, classless but classy, the kind of place where people of all shapes and colors, fortunes and fame, drank Rainbow's 'Killer Bees" and mixed with egalitarian confidence that what happened in the bar stayed in the bar.

Before his eyes had adjusted to the shade and he could look for Danielle, he was greeted by a large man behind the bar, dressed in a multi-coloured caftan, with his hair plaited into cornrows, a massive smile and round eyes full of merriment.

"Welcome to Rainbow's where it makes no difference, mon." Rainbow spoke with Shakespearean eloquence, delivering a well-practiced soliloquy: "whether you's snowbird-white, blood-pudding black, expensive saddle-leather bronze, down-and-out, broken-hearted blue or simply too-much-sun lobster red' Rainbow's is for all colours. They all come to Rainbow's because a Rainbow is <u>all</u> colours!" His hand swept the reaches of his establishment, "You knows what I mean, mon?"

And so it was. Rainbow's was a watering hole where the privileged and pampered could go native, and the natives could indulge their nativeness in the non-stop carnival that Rainbow kept running and on course. Behind him, stapled to the bamboo wall, was a rogues' gallery of famous patrons who'd taken refuge and solace at Rainbow's. There was a photo with Rainbow's arm around Madonna's waist, another shoulder to shoulder with Oprah, one fist to fist with Rod Stewart, and many more with people Jonathan didn't recognise but whom he assumed were rock musicians from their hair and the rings in their faces. He immediately saw that a poster of Danielle was one of the most prominent. It was the center of the display, a two-by-three-foot fashion runway photo of her at Dior's in a powder-blue satin gown. He knew it was Dior by the "Dior, Paris" inscription across the bottom of the poster.

"I sees you around de island for some time now, mon." Rainbow wiped his hand on a bar towel and stuck it out to Jonathan. "How is it you takes so long to come to Rainbow's?" he asked.

"Circumstances," Jonathan grinned, immediately taking a liking to Rainbow, yet still lawyerly cautious.

Rainbow, the club owner introduced himself.

"Douglas, Jonathan Douglas."

"Welcome to Rainbow's rainbow where de carnival never stops... nor even slows down for school zones." Instead of a straightforward suit-and-tie handshake, Rainbow guided Jonathan through a complicated choreography of hand moves, ending with a knuckle-to-knuckle meeting of their fists, at which point Rainbow leaned so close to him that Jonathan could smell his cologne and marijuana. "Respect," he murmured. Then he handed his guest a glass full of amber liquid with grated nutmeg floating on the surface. "Killer Bee! Don't spill it on anything important."

"And for de lady?" Rainbow said, looking over Jonathan's shoulder.

Jonathan turned to see who Rainbow was talking to. It was Danielle. She was as enchanting then he remembered, her smile even more disarming. Her hair had been plaited into long, tight braids, then turbaned around her head, the tips of the braids hanging like tassels, framing her Cleopatra countenance. She wore a jungle-patterned dress that tied at the waist and around her neck. "Would the madame have a tall Ting with ice to the rim as usual?" Rainbow asked.

She nodded to the proprietor but looked at Jonathan. "Hello," she said to him, reaching out with both hands. More complex hand jive, Jonathan feared. But she leaned close and gave him a kiss on each cheek. "You look great! A little pale, but some Augustine sun will turn you black in no time."

"And older and wiser," he smiled. "You look wonderful too."

"Older and a lot wiser!" Danielle smiled back.

"And for Bana I make de ice width de purest bottled water," Rainbow broke in.

She tasted the drink, her eyes settling upon the wall of pictures behind the bar. "And what did you do for Madonna to get that picture?" Danielle smirked, pointing to a newly added photo of the pop singer with Rainbow.

"Well," he said with an air that foreshadowed a great story. "She does come here one evening from de Sheraton with her entourage, samples de 'Bee' and asks for de recipe." He shrugged. "We haggle some, an' I asks what she can offer in return, cus I'm not willing to settle for a few autographed pictures and some CDs. So finally she offers a night width she, 'she'n and me'n', fo' de formula." Danielle laughed, but Jonathan wasn't sure what "she'n and me'n" meant.

"Hard choice cus I's sworn to de death upon me long-passed mother's grave to protect de family recipe. But den I figure, a night width Madonna gonna kill me anyway, so I comes up width a solution. I does take she up on she's offer, and oh Lawdy what a night dat be. De Sheraton want to send me a bill for de broken bed and de complaints for all de noise." He looked at Danielle very seriously. "But when it's all over and time for me to settle me end of de bargain, I's so exhausted dat I gets confused on de formula." He roared with laughter. "And she go away width recipe for Shagboy's rum-punch that's got the sting of a butterfly!"

"Oh, Rainbow, you are so full of it," Danielle laughed happily.

"How you guess so soon?" Rainbow conceded.

"What do you do, Jon?" he asked, pronouncing it "Yon".

Jonathan liked that — at least at Rainbow's, he was Yon. "Well…" He looked at Danielle, then back at Rainbow.

"He's a writer!" she spoke up before he could say estate lawyer.

"Yah? Anyt'ing I know?"

"*Barbarians at the Gates*," Danielle stated matter-of-factly.

"Wow! Das you, mon?! I knows dat book, I wolfed it down." Jonathan and Danielle groaned, acknowledging that they caught his joke. More patrons came to the bar and Danielle led Jonathan to a cabana on the beach with a table between two chaise lounges facing the setting sun.

Only then did Jonathan look closely at the dress she wore. The material was obviously quite expensive, the kind he saw on the beaches of the French Riviera with Rousseau jungle print animals with big eyes peeking out of the folds.

"One of your designs?" he asked.

"The design is mine, but the material was one of the perks that came with the job," she said. "Perks like unlimited access to the best fabrics in the world are hard to give up."

"Came with the job? In the past tense?"

"Oh my God." She clapped her hands together with excitement. "I didn't tell you! I'm through, no more runways, no more design sessions, no more photo shoots… 'I's done-be gone'. I live here now!"

"Really?" He was astonished. What could a woman of her sophistication and exposure find interesting here in the backwaters of the Caribbean?

"Das so, mon," she laughed. "Other than a trip to Europe and maybe one to Asia to sell my designs once or twice a year, I'm rock-bound." She raised her Ting, "A toast to new adventures in familiar places." They toasted, her eyes revealing that she was happy with her decision.

"And you?" she asked. "I tried to call you in New York, but your secretary said you were away in France. Lounging on the Riviera?"

"Hardly," he scoffed. "Business. In fact, it seems anymore that it's always business. But it keeps me occupied and my mind off Mallory."

"And is it business that's brought you to 'St. Aug'?"

Jonathan took a drink of his Killer Bee and looked at the kids playing in the water's edge. One young boy was busy making sandcastles only to have them demolished by rogue waves. He wondered if his children had done that when Mallory brought them down to the island alone -- which was most of the time. Business, always business. He turned back to Danielle. "Well, not really business, I'm putting my house here on the market."

"I thought that was why you were here last time."

"I was uncertain then, but now I'm not. My lawyer here on-island said I should come down to sign the listing papers. I think he just wanted to see me one last time, but I don't mind, it gets me out of the office."

Danielle turned to look at the mountain behind them and nodded to the giant thunderheads looming over the peak of the volcano, raking the dark burgundy jungle with shrouds of rain. No sooner did the rain land on the still-hot jungle canopy than it turned to steam. In turn, the sun caught the vapours, turning the volcano gold in the sunset. "Granito de Oro" she said, "that's what the Spanish called the mountain. 'Golden Rock.' This really is the most beautiful place on the planet."

Strange, Jonathan thought. In, all the years he and his family had come to St. Augustine, he'd never really thought about the Island's beauty, though Mallory would continually draw his attention to it. It was enough, he somehow thought, that at least one member of the family saw the Island's treasures.

"My secretary said you called, but when I tried to call you back, your number had been disconnected."

"I wanted to tell you something," she said, turning her attention back to him and leaning forward, "but didn't want to say it to your secretary." Jonathan arched one eyebrow. "Please take this in the right way... I'm not coming on to you," she smiled. But the thought had never occurred to him that she could possibly find him interesting.

"I just wanted you to know how special it was for me the night we walked on this beach and talked. I kind of bared my grief to you that night, about losing my parents and all, but I knew you were hearing me and were likely feeling same the emptiness because of the death of your wife." She spoke with sincerity but Jonathan, embarrassed, just waved it off.

"Likewise," he confessed, then thought for a moment. "It was out of character for me to open up, but you know, it did me a lot of good. It is I who am indebted to you!"

"Listen to me, Jonathan Douglas, you are a fine human being. You are a kind and gentle man, and I haven't met many of them in a long time. In fact," she paused for a moment, weighing whether or not to continue, but then decided to say it. "In fact, if you hadn't noticed, I too came early," she blushed.

"Excuse me." Rainbow came to the table with a tray holding a covered dish, two place settings and two glasses. "I wondered if you might sample a new recipe — compliments of the Chef."

"Oh, Rainbow," Danielle cooed, lifting the metal cover. "Lobster thermidor, my absolute favorite!"

"Naw, ain't dat a'tall. It's just some fresh lobster some divers dropped off dat I slathered with some spicy cream sauce and a little cheese for colour and broiled in de oven for three minutes."

Danielle was delighted. "Oh, Rainbow you're the best! 'Slathered?!'" she grinned. "You're still so full of it, no wonder Madonna adores you."

127

"No wonder." Rainbow grinned to Jonathan, handing him another Killer Bee though he was only halfway finished with the first.

The lobster thermidor was the first of many diverse "samples" that Rainbow brought to their table, including Jamaican barbecued ribs, jerked Haitian chicken in a Creole sauce, and one dish of scallops glazed with walnuts and served flambé. Each dish, as Jonathan marvelled, was more exotic than the last, far better than any he'd had in the Sheraton's four-star restaurant — or at least that was his conclusion after his third Killer Bee.

Danielle talked about how easily things fell into place once she'd made the decision to leave the fashion industry and start her own line of clothes. "I decided it was what I am 'supposed to do'. So, with some friends' encouragement and help, we started "Bana Designs". As you guessed, this is one of my creations."

"I'll be your first customer when you start producing them," Jonathon smiled.

"For yourself? Or for your girlfriends?"

"Funny on both counts. For my daughter and daughter-in-law. Couldn't you see me on Madison Avenue in a frock designed by Bana?" He laughed freely, fueled by the Bees.

"No one would even notice in New York. And if they did, they'd think it was a new fashion statement and rush out to get one for themselves." She smiled at him. "I can't imagine you any other way, except behind a cannon guarding my money."

"And your honor," he added.

They both fell silent, as the sun set on the Golden Rock and soon became haloed by the moon behind. Both felt luxurious with the moment and comfortable in each other's company.

"I don't suppose" Danielle started to say, but paused and looked away. "I don't suppose you would like to go on a picnic tomorrow — to a special place?" she asked, still avoiding his eyes, not wanting to face the rejection. "There is someone I'd like you to meet."

Unfortunately, he had booked the entire day. He was meeting with his lawyer in the morning, and with the real estate appraiser and a surveyor in the afternoon. That was Thursday. Friday he would pre-sign the government tax agreements and the property release papers in case a buyer was found immediately, then he was having supper with the Premier. Saturday he'd catch the early-morning ferry to St. Kitts, then the 9:00 a.m. American Eagle flight to Puerto Rico. He had a four-hour layover in Puerto Rico, and had decided to take a taxi into Old San Juan and have lunch at Patio del Sam with Sam. Afternoon flight to New York, an hour's drive to Oak Mills and he'd be home in time for the nightly news. He'd go into the office on Saturday to finish the Tennyson probate documents and prepare for the board meeting on Monday.

"I'd love to," he said. The Killer Bees had stung, dissolving the compulsive cells in his brain. "What can I bring?"

"Sure?" Her smiled radiated. "I'm not pulling you away from something important, some estate planning or something?"

"Only my own, and it can wait... maybe it's <u>supposed</u> to wait!" He shrugged as the Bees buzzed merrily in his head.

Chapter 10

The Domino College

Stripped to its purest form, the "Pelican Perch Shop, Lounge and Domino College" — abbreviated on the Carib Beer sign out front to "The Pelican Perch" even though there never had been any perching pelicans since the shop was far from the sea, and, high up on the volcano! It was merely concrete slab on which rested a village of wooden rooms with roofs running in varying directions, at various angles and pitches; all bound by at least by one common wall. The Perch was a composite of add-ons and subtractions that mirrored the village's history of interests and needs in the course of its evolution.

The founding parent structure was a wood chattel house that belonged to a goat farmer named Pap. When the delicate fragrance of rum became more intoxicating than the earthy bouquet of goats, Pap stopped farming and opened a shop that sold a variety of dry goods, including "wet" ones.

But... what is a shop without a lounge where patrons can relax out of the sun with friends and a Carib bear or a "Hammon" the local moonshine rum; so, a second building was added, then a third ... lodging for Pap so he could keep the lounge open longer. More walls were added to accommodate patrons' main entertainment dominoes.

When Pap thought someone had "teeved-up" three bottles of Bacardi, a "secure" storage shed was nestled into the complex to separate "de teevable from de teeves". But when it was found that Pap had drank the "thieved" merchandise, the room became the television room, along with another addition to the complex that was demanded, mainly by the boys between the ages of six and sixteen that another chattel house was added to the slab to accommodate a television. An ancient set from the dump that shifted red, green and blue bands slightly ajar from each other, requiring the viewer to

130

assemble them into a single focused image in his mind's eye. However, since the television had only one channel available, and it played "World Wrestling Federation' matches exclusively and... nonstop; a focused image television was not essential!

The actual legitimate "Shop" wing of the Perch was stocked on the worn shelves with rows of Campbell's vegetable soup and Breeze laundry detergent (sold by the box, the bag or the cup). Vienna wieners for lunches were a mainstay to be eaten with small baguettes, called *"loafers"*, and pickled sardines. There were matches that lit only in dry weather, dry jars of penny candy costing up to three cents for the hard Tootsie Roll Pops, and most of all fishing line for flying kites.

Also, at the shop you could buy kerosene if you brought your own empty rum bottle and cap. Fortunately, the lounge sold bottles with rum in them that tasted like kerosene. As well, you could buy soda pop, real sarsaparilla and root beer made from the roots in the garden behind, plus beers of all fashions from Heineken to local ginger beer.

Jamaican rum, mango rum and vanilla rum and, for the well-accustomed connoisseur of cane, in search of the novel, and deadly potent there was the very local "H*ammon*"... the indigenous white lightning brewed upon demand, served by the jigger straight. And sometimes Pap made a special batch called "*knock-you-flat" that he kept for special occasions!*

It made no difference when one patron who drank heavily "flat-back" died and the coroner, in front of the deceased family, took the man's liver and hit it on the surgical table, causing a dent in the metal tray!

The Perch was the only commercial venture in the village. Thus, it was where deliveries were made, directions dispensed to the lost, packages and letters left by the Postman. It was where the soda and beer truck delivered full cases and picked up empties. And it was where political rallies droned on well into the night, second only to religious revivals of varying Christian faiths, performed by fledgling pastors who, without benefit of an ecclesiastical nest of their own and a paying congregation, tested (with God's help, they claimed) and a bullhorn for promoting both their ministerial talents and vocal-cord strength.

On a bulletin board on the Leeward side of the building, there were handwritten notes about choir practices, pan-band practices, notices of church services, posters for cricket matches and, of utmost importance, the TV schedule with the days and times of wrestling matches and pages out of "*Grapple Magazine*".

"Masked Marvel Annihilates Body Snatcher" or "Electrifier versus The Crusher in a Fight to the Death.

Beyond supplies, entertainment, rum and rest, the most essential role of the shop was that of Town Hall. Be it a thatched roof in the Amazon jungle, a mosque in Morocco or the Hotel de Ville in Paris, the human spirit needs a gathering place. A place where the community congregates and discusses matters that affect them all. Poppy Dawn had no mayor, nor wanted one, though in truth it had many — Nine to be exact. Called "The Smart Ones!", Bueno was a member of that august fraternity. They governed by respect and wisdom. And before there were Island Courts, the Perch was enough to dispense justice.

It was the "Smart Ones" opinion that was always sought first in all matters from bad children to boundary disputes.

Garth said goodbye to Bueno and Raymond, at the junction before the Perch, and continued up the right fork. "Remember," Bueno called out to him, "turn up-so at the Perch and don't dally or you'll will never reach Caraja's." He waved to the left, "And every time you comes to a branch in de trail, take de lesser path."

Garth laughed. Caraja had told him to follow the path "best hidden". But there was little chance of getting lost. As he passed the Perch rumours had proceeded him and Pap waved to him and pointed to the road leading straight up towards the volcano's peak. Along the way he passed two young boys walking a pig down the mountain, five piglets squealing behind. Again, before he could get the name Caraja out, they pointed up towards the peak.

"Garth-something. Works with Caraja down at the Government Farm and does some teaching at Poppy Second. Dey say he's a fine fellow. Real Indian too."

"Trinidad?"

"Texas, I t'ink I hear somebody say."

"Snap!" came a loud crack from the adjacent room. For all of the functions of Pap's building, the real reason for the structure was the "Domino College"! Scattered around the College there were a half-dozen tables, all polished shiny with fingers well-greased by fried chicken and barbecue sauce from the ribs Pap cooked on Friday nights.

Each table was surrounded by a rough collection of salvaged chairs, some with missing legs, though none missing more than two. But the "butt-bench" of seats of preference was a wooden Carib or Coke case turned on end.

"Snap!!" Pause… then an explosion of exclamations and laughter, bantering and boasting.

As the evening advanced, more and more villagers gravitated to the Perch. Bueno's crew sat across the road, along the top of a stone wall like tired disciples at the last supper. Bueno was in the college, studying and honing his skills with the ivory cubes and sipping a Carib.

Villagers gathered in small groups around the intersection. Large wooden cable spools, the cable long since strung on poles, had been rolled out and turned-on end to serve as tables. On one, the undertaker cooked fried chicken and ribs, while around another, boys hunkered over the spool playing gin rummy. On polished rocks sat small groups of men and women and couples talking quietly beyond the hubbub of the Perch.

Younger children sat in the trees like opossums, watching, and giggling at a drunk winding his way down Uptee Doon Road.

To the side of the perch was a garden plot, in the middle of which sat the cannibalized carcass of a Volkswagen. The frame, cab, fenders and hood were all that remained for the rust to eat. The hood latch was sprung, affording enough room for a green tongue of vines to protrude from the metallic mouth. Eventually, the tongue would consum the whole face, threading back through the empty windshield sockets. But its life <u>after</u> death was illustrious — if not inspirational.

The Van had died a quick and merciful death, a heart attack caused by lack of oil. It was slated for a "round-to-it" transplant, but when a donor engine didn't materialise, the body became a donor for other patients until finally, thoroughly gutted, it became inhabited by the jungle. Then one day in a game of street cricket, a batter drove a tennis ball far into the garden and when Macaroni went to fetch it from under the truck, he discovered that, in fact, not every organ had been removed from the engine.

With the muffler, he made a toot, with a special downsized mouthpiece, and a "scratch". The scratch was made by repeatedly creasing the outer wall of the muffler with a hammer and the edge of a file. A dry hardwood stick could be scratched across the ribbing, creating a percussion accompaniment similar to the cow-fart toot.

Brandice pulled the wheel hubs and welded them onto a stand, and into a xylophone-type instrument that in Caraja's hands sang sweeter than real steel pans... though it took three men to carry it to the venue.

But the most ingenious instrument was an old carburetor, found behind the seat, it sounded like a piccolo when blown through the intake port, with the jets for fingering into the notes. Close enough for music, it too became part of the band.

The members of the "Soul Survivors" were gifted musicians foremost, and at first the van ensemble was a light deviation from their real instruments and their "real" music, ranging from Haiti and Harlem.

Macaroni would set up a theme on his keyboard, then Brandice would do a jazz variation on the hubs. It worked, and soon they were getting around-island performances — until they did an off-island gig on the island of Dominica... where the actual owner of the van lived. Having heard the story from a sister of his in St. Augustine, and noting the popularity of the Survivors, greed got the upper hand and he demanded payment for his parts. There were words, and pushes, and the judge awarded custody of the instruments to the original owner of the vehicle!

Still, the Soul Survivors survived and went on with non-petroleum-based instruments to become famous in Latin America, and the van was dismembered, its parts scattered between the St Augustine and a backyard "git-around-to-it" dream of a metal band in Dominica.

Across the corner from the Perch and recessed on the back of the land, was the chattel house of Sammy Speaks. His property was surrounded by hedges on which hung plywood, hand-painted sayings that Sammy spoke. On Friday afternoons, he would stand on a wooden pulpit of his own making and speak to the people of Poppy Dawn.

There Sammy Speaks spoke to the attending, but not attentive audience gathering on the corner, including the Smart Ones when important decisions had to be made.

"Anywhere on dis planet you's gonna find de word of God! Wherever you go ... even go to Jamaica Youse gonna find de word of God... sometimes. God is <u>everywhere</u>," He'd stressed the word, cuing his audience that he was coming to his point, "everywhere there's de word of God is where you're gonna find it!"

No sooner had Sammy Speaks spoken, and his message was forgotten, than there came the clank of tin cans on the road, and Delbert-He-ain't-crazy-you-know-mon appeared. His feet clopped with a metallic clack from the beer cans he wore bent around each foot.

On his head he wore a hat made out of flattened beer cans laced together along the edges with heavy red yarn to form a mix between a helmet fashion-statement that made him who he was. In his hands he held two empty Carib cans, which by clapping their

135

ends together in cadence with his vocal rant was only intelligible as he drew near. Today's rant was, "De end-she nigh, de Earth-she mad, de end-she nigh, we's soon gonna die."

Heralding "The End" was common fare for him, but environmentalism and global warming had given it new direction, the beer-can costume adding special importance to his message.

The world was of two opinions about Delbert. "He ain't right in de 'ed", was one belief. And "He ain't crazy... ya know." was the other. Still, some thought that even if he wasn't crazy and was just putting on an act, he <u>was</u> crazy to consciously create such delusions.

Of course, others of the "sane camp" argued that he was the master of guerrilla street theatre. And there were many vocations attributed to Delbert-he-ain't-crazy-mon: For example, he was the Portstown Gardener hired by the Ministry of Agriculture, Town Clown hired by the Department of Tourism, and either a Master Thespian of Shakespearean dimensions... or a Master Nutcase!

The latter position was a debate that gripped the Island when there was nothing better to talk about. Did wearing tin cans bent around his feet, sounding like a flamenco dancer's castanets on the cobblestone and concrete streets, bringing a grin to everyone he passed, mean he was crazy? Or did the time he was Jesus, beating himself with switches and wailing for the plight of humanity — buff-naked on Main Street at midday, settle the issue! It was decided, he was "crazy you know mon!"

"Lock um all up, throw away de key! De revolution she be neigh!" That was the time he jumped in the back of a sound truck in which there rode a political candidate ... with a speaker system, stumping his merits and promises. And, once in the back of the truck, Delbert began waving a bleached banner for Breeze detergent, proud as if it were a tattered flag of Che Guevara.

"Clean up government, throw de bums out! Dey's all a bunch of crooks. Throw de bums out!" Immediately Delbert and the truck disappeared, heading north. But long after they were out of sight, a mixed refrain could still be heard: "Delbert get out of here!" And

"Throw de bums out!"

"Dat Delbert, he chure be something else!"

"He ain't crazy, you know mon."

"Why is it always the end? Why not the beginning?" Gitlicks yelled from the shop and everyone laughed.

"The end is the beginning!" Delbert yelled back. Then he thought about what he'd just said and took up a new chant. "The end is the beginning!" he chanted and turning towards his home at the top of the hill, he waved and clattered away like a monotone evangelist of an ever-changing God.

"He ain't crazy, you know."

"Play or pass," grumbled Gas to Gitlicks. "You either gots the right domino or you's don't."

"Maybe me does and maybe me doesn't. But maybe I got choices — like dis," and Gitlicks slammed down a double six, sealing off both ends of the chain. He grinned, looking from one man to the next. No one could play and grudgingly they pushed soiled blue five-dollar bills and maroon tens at him.

"He does trap you, boys," laughed an old man who was watching the action.

While the Perch was the commercial center of the village, the "heart of Poppy Dawn" was a great boulder terraced with flat ledges scattered randomly across its ponderous face. Seats carved by slaves was the rumor. Back in those days, Poppy Dawn and Remember Me, across the ghaut, were no-man's land, where slaves could slip away from the surrounding plantations and talk long into the night about Africa and freedom. Though the topics had changed and the Island's occupants were no longer held against their will, the "Rock" was still the place where people sat in the cool of the evening, listening to tree frogs and the murmur of soft voices in gentle conversation about the latest outrages committed by the government; such as not repairing the sanitation truck in a timely fashion, or giving the road contract to the Minister of the Interior's second cousin. Neither topic much affected anyone in the gathering except to give them a topic upon which to agree and take the moral high ground.

Worrystone was another rock-perch, but it was reserved. Located just up the road from the main boulder, close to the action but professionally detached; Worrystone was the office of the Worrymon. He had not a worry of his own, so he took on others... for a small fee! For a Heineken beer in the evening after work, he'd take on somebody's problems and worry them to death. Sometimes a problem had so many issues that it would take two Heinekens to worry them through. Some said he was a Saint sent to ease people's burdens, some said he did it because of his work at the abattoir — when you're in close contact with death daily, the mundane concerns of life are easy. Others scoffed that he just liked free Heineken beer. Still, everybody used him. Worrymon physically fit the title and was everything one could want to confide confidences to. He had a curly white beard trimmed close to his face, which, coupled with mischievous round eyes and a full set of his own teeth, distinguished him with the wise aspect of a black Christ look-alike. On the other hand, dressed in a different set of clothes and circumstances, he could have passed for the U.N. Ambassador from an African country.

Worrymon had also mastered the yoga discipline of contouring his body to the recesses and ridges of a rock. It was unclear if he was exhausted from his work or others' worries. But the way he moulded into the basalt as though it were a feather bed, his eyes closed, it was little wonder many thought of him as something of a Holy man.

He never offered solutions as he took on the things people couldn't change, but he was good at getting the people of Poppy Dawn and Remember Me to consider alternatives for the things they could change. Worrymon specialised in the worries which people couldn't do anything about and was rigorous about the size of his client list, taking only two clients a day, which was also the number of Heineken that it took to round him off before going home, and, it

138

was the limit of burdens he could carry per day. Someone, probably Sammy Speaks, printed a sign on the pear tree by Worrystone: "Why Worry, Be Happy!"

"Worrymon." Bueno approached the man labouring over the first concern, and beer, of the evening. He opened his eyes and look at Bueno's empty hands. "It's not a professional visit," Bueno laughed.

"In dat case, hither you rest." Worrymon tapped an adjacent stone as if it were softer then the others. "The day's too heavy for standing."

"Das de point me wants to discuss. I does see Sueky for de afternoon, and she say dere be something in de wind. She don't say just what, but she does say 'be prepared'." Bueno watched to see if Worrymon understood the weight of Sueky's opinion, and for the first time in Bueno's memory, a moment of personal worry clouded the man's face.

"I does speak with Fluteman about it", Bueno continued, and he hear de radio say a hurricane dey's calling 'Hugo' supposed to punch Guadeloupe dis evening," Bueno continued. "Montserrat tomorrow and maybe St. Augustine the following day. I figures best not to say too much, but dere should be a meeting of de Council tonight before de masquerade competition. Den if dere's something to be done we can discuss it with the whole village." He looked away from Worrymon. "Das all I has to say." He reached out and touched the man's wrist. "Until."

"Until" said Worrymon, nodding but not looking up from the lip of the beer bottle-- there was a worried expression on his face. Hurricanes come and go. Every season there were at least one or two alerts, and most of the time the hurricanes turned away. Occasionally there were brushes, but never in his fifty years, a direct hit. Normally he wouldn't worry. But Sueky didn't waste others' time with false prophecies. Then Worrymon felt another flush of unaccustomed anxiety... how do you prepare for a hurricane?

A large woman, whose breasts rode comfortably on her

stomach, came up to Worrymon with a beer in her hand. A troop of children with dirty faces and oversized clothes wove around Sophia's legs as she swung them forward, their eyes darted between hers and his as she explained that her brother had eaten poisoned fish and been taken to the hospital, she couldn't go for having to watch all the little ones and she was worried.

"Kids and poison fish, that's a lot of worrying, gonna take me the better part of the weekend. I'll trade for charcoal. For now, leave de kids here and we all's gonna watch dem."

Sophia nodded.

Black, the mortician, had set up a chicken-and-ribs barbecue on the corner near Poorman's, but he wasn't getting much business.

"I jus don't likes the idea of eating chicken what's prepared by de same hands what prepares a corpse." A girl holding a baby confessed.

"And besides," laughed Petro, Ester's oldest, "You's never truly chure dat it's chicken."

"Petro!" Julie barked, startling her nursing baby. She picked up a bottle cap and threw it at him. "Das so sick."

"Takes sick ta see sick."

"Say dat for true," replied one of Petro's friends.

"Now that's the dumbest thing I ever does hear," Julie retorted. "It don't take sick to see sick. What about doctors, dey don't have to be sick to see sick."

"'Sides, it wouldn't be that different from eating monkey."

"Mon, you never gonna see me eat no monkey," exclaimed Julie.

"You never know what you's gonna eat till you does it," teased Petro.

"You disgust me."

"SILENCE!" Pap cried. "SILENCIO!" he repeated for the two Spanish-speaking day-laborers on Bueno's crew. Then he turned up the television's volume.

"We interrupt our regular programming for an urgent public

140

announcement. Tropical storm 'Hugo' has just been upgraded to a class four hurricane. It is presently situated just south of the Guadeloupe Banks, advancing north by northeast at a speed of 23 knots with internal speeds exceeding one hundred and twenty knots per hour, and building.

"The Miami Hurricane Center warns that the storm is growing and a Caribbean-wide alert is in effect. This applies particularly to the people living in the Leeward chain: Montserrat, Antigua, St. Christopher and St. Augustine. The Red Cross advises people to be prepared to move to storm shelters at a moment's notice. All coastal residents are asked to look for shelters on higher ground. Stay tuned for hourly updates on the storm.

The last word of the broadcast had hardly settled before the domino game began again.

"Wait," Pap spoke up. "Dere's pictures from Guadeloupe." Images of waves crashing over the sea wall palms were bent almost to the ground appeared on the screen. An amateur handicam caught the galvanised roof of a house ripping off sheet by sheet and flying up into a funnel. Everyone in and around the Perch gasped.

"Doddy, Doddy, Guadeloupe does take some mighty licks." Two kids who'd been watching the TV ran into the domino college. "Is Mr. Hugo coming for us?" one cried, frightened to tears.

"Let not de heart be troubled," Gas assured his son, pulling him close. "St, Augustine ain't been hit in sixty years, de Lord ain't gonna change He stride now."

"Hmm? Me no so chure," Gitlicks said, cautiously laying down a four/two domino to freeze one leg of the chain. Satisfied with his move, he leaned back. "I wish it <u>does</u> come here! I'd like to see what Mr. Hurricane does really do."

"I agree," said someone in the back.

"Me too!" came another opinion.

"Mon, don't talk such nonsense and stupidity," an ancient voice rose from the corner where the shop met a large stone.

"Me sees one hurricane sixty years ago on dis very Island and to dis day I pray me never sees another." Stephen Liburg said from his piece of the stone throne. He was Aunt Josey's older brother but he didn't know by how much. Still in case it was his responsibility, he made it a point to attend every funeral on that side of the Island assuming others would follow his lead and go to his.

"What was it like?" Loverboy asked.

"Mon, he be legging you," Fredrick laughed.

"But I does tell you somet'ing dat ain't foolishness," said Stephen. "After dat hurricane, me mudder could stand right dere in she yard and see all de way to de high goat pasture cuz dere weren't a leaf left on any tree... what few trees remained! Dat mountain was as bald as dat baby's butt." He pointed to Caddy's baby crawling around on the pad.

"Another beer, Charlie?" offered Bueno.

"Best not." The old man raised his hand. "Me donkey, Miss Asuwink dere," he pointed to a donkey tied to a ground tether, "she don't walk so straight no more. One more beer," he winked at the domino players as he rose, "and she be weaving all over the place, maybe fall down in the ghaut and kill-up both us." He laughed. "Best not. 'Sides, I gots a lot of worry on me mind dis night."

"As usual." Bueno laughed.

"No, dis be different. I keeps feeling something strange in de air."

Fluteman came hurrying up the road. Catching Bueno's eye, he motioned for him to come outside. Bueno turned his domino hand over to Hilo, who was standing behind him, and left the table.

"You sees Guadalope's being mash-up by de hurricane? I think now's de time to call a meet'n and make our plans," said Fluteman.

Bueno nodded. "Paca," he called to his son, who was standing near Big Rock with a small group of boys looking through a wrestling magazine.

"Paca, take some youths and call out to da Councils' homes. Say dey must come quick-sharp, we must hold a meeting."

Obediently, the boy ran back to his group and conveyed the importance of the message, and immediately they all took off in different directions.

Quadros, the furniture maker, who lived near the corner, was the first to arrive. He was seventy-eight years old and though much of his day was spent over a large work bench, his back was as straight as the planks he planed by hand, giving his bearing a sense of dignity. His craft was well respected around the Island and he had a waiting list for beds and armoires and great tables two years in advance. Jonathan and Mallory bought his first four-poster pineapple bed. They had four children because of it, Quadras believed, because pineapples carved on beds assured fertility, and Mallory's was a veritable garden, from a plant in full bloom on the headboard to ripe fruit capping each post. In fact, it was Mallory who first saw Quadras' talent, and they loaned him the money to buy good-quality mahogany from Guyana for the bed. The hotelier Gage saw the bed Mallory bought and commissioned a complete bedroom set for the Hotel Lemon, then four more, and then four more ... each completely different from the rest and only the honeymoon suite using carved pineapples.

As she hobbled towards the corner along the corrugated path, depending heavily upon her long, knobby walking staff for balance and companionship, Aunt Josey hummed a Christmas carol though Christmas was still three months away. Unlike her brother, who fixed his gaze on the horizon, her eyes were set on the trail just ahead of each footfall. One of the children dropped from the Baobab tree and scampered up beside Aunt Josey, taking her free hand. An older girl brought the old woman a chair, and no sooner had she sat down than the younger child crawled into her lap.

Fluteman saw that all of the councillors were present, and he began. "Most of you know dere be a big storm loose in d'Leeward dat might jus' come here so." There was an audible grunt of affirmation from Josey at Fluteman's words.

"Some figures we's safe, but to my thinking, we's foolish not

143

to make plans." The committee nodded. "Some of us have endured hurricanes before and know what must be done. So we need to discuss these thoughts." Again, there was murmured assent.

"First, each must find suitable shelter of dey's own liking," said Ginger, Fluteman's oldest cousin and postmistress in Poppy Dawn. Her mind followed an orderly line, as though directing mail into its proper slot. "And provisions must be laid in accordingly."

"Food and water dey's de most important," added Josey. "All food what can be gathered even if it's not full mature cuz there may not be any more once Mistah Hurricane is done width us — and, if memory serves me, de land won't spring back for some time."

Bueno's thoughts raced. "And save can-goods for last cuz dey no gonna rot over time. Also, we may not have electricity for a goodly long time." Poppy Dawn had only been electrically wired a couple of years before, and while refrigeration was a luxury, the people of Poppy had not had time to become too habituated to it. "Coal pots and plenty charcoal," Bueno added.

"And tools," said Quadros. "We'll need tools to rebuild if de storm does give us licks."

"And if Mister Hugo don't come so?"

"It serves us no good not to make plans. If'n de storm smack us, we's sitting pretty like de King of England. If'n it don't, nobody gonna be no more de lesser, and de Anglican's Church gonna be full o' believers for once!" Worryman smirked.

The meeting finished. Fluteman was chosen to speak to all the villagers after the try-outs and immediately the masqueraders began.

Boom, boom, the base-drum thumped through the hamlet as Gobo, standing on the shop slab, tuned his instrument. Soon Conga arrived and began limbering his fingers on the conga drum slung from his shoulder by a strap. From far down the Eaton Estate road came the faint cords of ukulele. By twos and threes, the musicians and people of Poppy Dawn gravitated into a ring in front of the shop.

The dancers and the boys trying out for the two recently

144

vacated positions had gathered behind the shop, putting on their costumes. Clown suits, tight at the wrists and cuffs, ballooning out everywhere else with long, flowing strips of brightly coloured cloth remnants. Their head-dresses were constructed of real feathers of many colours that waved in dance like a peacock's plumage. They all wore tennis shoes.

When the leader, a tall man named Domino, heard the music, he called out to the dancers. And when they all were ready, he picked up a whip from the ground and swinging it high over his head, he gave it a sharp back-snap and it cracked with the bark of a bullet. Again and again the whip cracked, twining into the rhythm of the drums. Letting the music take possession, Domino arched backwards, then leapt into the air landing onto the slab. The whip whirling above him, he spun and landed a complete rotation. "SHEAWWEE!", he yelled and the other dancers took their places.

One, two, three, Fluteman counted, nodding his head on the downbeat, and the head-dresses folded into the circle, then swept backwards and the dance began. There were no single auditions; everyone danced and the troupe leaders watched the competitors to select who would fill the vacancies. It was too short for the audience's liking, but it was sweet and when it was over, since there were only two serious contenders and two positions, Paca found his place in the troupe.

Unaware there was more to come, the crowd began to disperse towards their homes.

"People." Fluteman stepped up onto Sammy's pulpit, and when the towns people returned, he laid out the situation and what they could do.

"Fools!" cried Stederoy, staggering towards the center of the group. "Ain't no hurricane gonna do us no harm. You's scar'n de chillens what width all dis talk, Fluteman. De Anglican say God no-gonna let He's chosen get mash-up by some ol' windstorm. We's be de special ones."

"Well, de Anglican might be assured of his place in de Glory-

Ever-After, but me's still looking for my mine, so maybe I's gonna prepare just de same," said Agust, one of Priscilla's sons.

"Ye of little faith!" Stederoy exhorted, "You's faith is what set Youse free."

"Mon, dat's donkey talk if me ever hears so," said Bueno.

"You call'n d'Anglican a donkey?!" Stederoy adopted a fighting stance, weaving slightly from rum rather than pugnacious posturing. "Blasphemous!"

"Idiot!" laughed Bueno. "Just how secure is Youse place in Heaven to take de risk of getting killed?" Stederoy hadn't thought about that and after a long minute of evaluating his own moral history and balancing the tally sheet of bad against his good deeds, he grumbled and slunk back to the Perch, pursued by laughter and catcalls.

"Better prudent than landing in San Juan Harbour, Puerto Rico!" teased old Stephen.

Chapter 11

"Stomp" the Stamp Lady

"No practice fo' de afternoon?" Josiah asked as Garth got into the front seat of the tap-tap bus. There were only the two of them, which suited Garth just fine. He was in no mood for being social.

"Too wet," said Garth without any encouragement for further discourse."

"I's on de way ta Portstown and beyond if'n dere weren't so much water cutting thru Baines Ghaut." Josiah shrugged. Where are you headed?"

"To hell!" grumbled Garth.

"We's all headed dat way if we no change our sinning ways. What's de problem, brother?"

"You know a woman named Stomp?"

"De stamp-lady?" Josiah asked in astonishment. Then, after a pause, he started to laugh. "She vexes Youse up, mon?"

Garth nodded.

"Mon, I's tell Youse how she be. Dat woman is all about she-own-self, dere's only she in she mind, but I figure dat's because she's 'fraid dat she be nothing. You follow? Me thinks Stomp starts being who she be even when she but a baby."

Garth settled into the van seat, content to learn everything about his nemesis without having to make a contribution.

"You see, she's de youngest and de princess in de fadder's and de mudder's eyes. Get what-all she want, and when she no get it she'd stomp around and make all sorts of noise until she does. Pretty soon she becomes a bully, and lazy, and bigger. Soon everybody grow more and more 'fraid of her till she is where she is today."

Garth didn't know where Josiah got his psychology, but he probably wasn't too far off the mark.

"If she's got everything she wants, why's she so angry?"

147

"Cuz me thinks she knows she gits dere fraudulently. Even she's job she got just to satisfy she sister who's married to the Premier." Josiah glanced at Garth to see if the man understood.

"He'd rather face the wrath of the people rather than she ... De thing she hasn't got is love or even passion. Which brings us back to your problem. Because she makes she-self so disgust'n, she gots no love-life 'cept who she can intimidate into rubbing up with she. I think she's horny and it sounds like she's on the rut."

Today would be Garth's fourth trip to Stomp's office in less than a week. In fact, a week ago he'd never heard of Stomp. Only while getting Garth's departure papers together did he discover he needed a special 'Exit Stamp' on his passport. A rubber imprint stamp which he could only get from the office of a Miss Packard, nicknamed "Stomp" in the back of the treasury building.

He figured, by the way people rolled their eyes, that Stomp's power was in her position and her proportions, which were great in influence and dimension, respectively. She was the final turnstile between freedom and being stuck on the rock in a bureaucratic limbo while the paperwork filtered down from Washington. As far as he could tell, Stomp's sole job was to control the departure of non-nationals who had worked on St Augustine in a volunteer capacity, which translated to all Peace Corps and VSO workers, of which there were at least four a year.

Her second anchor on power was her substantial size. As Garth discovered in detail, she got her position in the government because of her position in her family, who were terrified of her. Her second-oldest sister was married to the Island Premier and he would rather face an angry mob of constituents than the wrath of his wife and Stomp, so she was given a rubber stamp, a title and an office, and by the authority of an Order in Council, the "Stamp-lady" suddenly loomed in the path of all outward-bound expatriate volunteers.

He well remembered how it was the first time he went there last Monday. He was happy that day, he was on the down slope,

148

termination of his contract with the government, and he'd done it with the distinction that he'd actually done something to help the Island. He was booked on a flight out the following Monday: St. Augustine to Saint Kitts, Miami, St Louis, Denver and then Pinedale, where his Dad or brother would pick him up for the hour-and-a-half pickup ride out to their ranch.

Jude, Garth's dog, would be so happy he'd be jumping and spinning around in the back of the truck. Garth would be just as overjoyed and, once Jude calmed down, he'd be allowed up front in the cab between Garth and Dad, or his brother. Sage... the dog would be smelling of fall sagebrush. They'd have elk steaks for supper and wild rice and garden potatoes with rich brown gravy.

But the first thing he would do was walk. Down the haying roads and into the fields and from there he could see the mountains. Granite claws in the sky. He craved space, horizons that extended the imagination. Horizons that you could walk or take a horse to and not swim to as he had for the last two plus years.

. His mother was pure, undiluted Shoshone. When she and his father decided to nest, she walked and walked the land. She sat and slept upon it until finally she found a slight knoll facing the prairie to the west and the mountains to the east, and that was the hub around which their lives and the ranch were built.

At times, Garth hated the jungle. It had no horizon, just a tangle of green, a mask of a thousand faces seeing and seen, but not recognised. Back home, he knew all the plant and mammal species; here he felt crowded and exposed. Compared to Pinedale, there was no privacy: the island was not only crowded, it was crowded with gossips. And that, rather than fear of embarrassing the Peace Corps, seemed to be the one factor that held him back from jumping into the Augustine culture and experience.

As he looked back at his time on the island, he marvelled at how differently it had turned out from what he'd expected. At first it was dreams of making a difference, and he felt good about how he'd helped. But he had envisioned working in the low end of the third world, teaching agriculture to a starving country, bringing water to a drought-ridden land.

But St. Augustine wasn't starving, nor a Third World country. It was a different world altogether. Caught in the backwater of time, it was neither new world, nor old, yet part of both, and in their technological nonchalance, the Islanders met the technology on its way back. For example, Garth learned that since Augustinian farmers knew nothing of the newest cutting-edge agricultural science, all they had going was experience. Yet they had achieved surplus production with rudimentary technology, and without commercial pesticides or herbicides. The island had only two tractors, both owned by the government. Short-wheelbase, powerful tractors that could manoeuvre even in tiny plots around basalt boulders.

Caraja was the first farmer Garth met on-island, and the most successful small plot farmer. The thing that St. Augustine had going for it was self-sufficiency, but it did export fruits and vegetables throughout the Leeward chain.

Still, Garth was ready to leave. While everybody, except for a couple of enemies he had cultivated, was civil and sociable, sometimes he was a bit of a curiosity. White folks from the States and Europe were common, but Indians were not. In fact, he was a curiosity to the white tourist. Also, it was only of late that he'd most of the time understand their language. Even though he spoke English and Shoshone and some Mexican Spanish, he was never sure he was understanding the Island jokes. He was never sure the expressions his students taught him weren't slurs, slanders or provocation to have his throat cut… though that was highly unlikely since his students never out of personal choices missed one of his classes. And situations with bureaucracy, regardless of their nationality, tied his stomach in knots.

"Well, dere she be," said Joshua and he parked "Ezekiel 2:15:6" in front of the Federal Government building. Garth sighed and handed the driver two E.C. dollars.

150

"On me, man. Was going dis way anyhow... 'sides, de condemned deserves a break in dey's last hours." Joshua roared with laughter.

Garth slowly climbed the ancient grey stone stairs of the Treasury Building, a two-story colonial cut-stone structure, fortress-pragmatic, austere and devoid of pillars or statues. Its only adornment was the wide flight of stairs leading to the upstairs. The treads had deep troughs worn into them by commerce and three centuries of the financial affairs of state. Authorisation, taxation, registration, even auctions of estates when debt or neglect dictated. Once, humans were sold into slavery on the Treasury steps. In another time, the Declaration of Emancipation was read there on those steps a hundred year before. In fact, so was the Title of Self-government to free them from the Crown.

Other than the timid shafts of light that peeked in from the open door behind him, the only source of light was one long, dim fluorescent ceiling bulb that hung low on chains from the cantilevered ceiling. Its vague illumination reminded Garth of Jake's Pool Hall back home in Wyoming. At a table beneath the lone light, hunkered down over a book, her face hidden in the shadows, her fat fingers covering its cover, was a woman of such massive size that her buttocks hung like jowls over the sides of her chair.

Between her and Garth was a long counter with a heavily worn lignum vitae top. When he first came to the office, Garth wondered what incredible transactions must have transpired when this room was filled with gold from the plantations, and plunder from passing pirates — finally currency of the crown. The financial intrigue presently that kept historical superiority alive was money laundering.

"Hello." Garth tried to sound upbeat and courteous like the first time he had been there five days before ... though now he felt neither; especially when it became obvious that Miss Packard (as stated on the plastic imitation-brass name plate) was not going to acknowledge him.

In the disheartening gloom, he remembered vividly the first day he came to her office. "I'm here for an Exit Stamp." Silence. "Garth Longrass, Peace Corps Volunteer, Agricultural Ministry?"

Still no response. "Mr. Malcolm has signed the releases and all I need is the "Exit" stamp," he said, wondering if she was deaf, asleep, or maybe dead..., which he doubted, since he saw her thick digits turn the book's pages.

"And I'll be on my way." ... silence ... "out of here... trouble you no more... moccasin tracks over the horizon... gone." His rant strained his ears with its hollow echo. He stared hard at the form, trying to communicate that he was not to be intimidated.

Slowly, with the sigh of one intimately familiar with long suffering, Miss Packard took a pen from the desktop and underlined the sentence where she'd stopped reading the paperback novel. With great effort she lay it down on the desk, front cover up. Garth saw it had the telltale illustration — an impassioned, intertwined couple: swarthy, black-moustached man resembling Rhett Butler holding a limp but eager woman with long auburn hair — a Harlequin Romance.

Placing her palms flat on the table, Stomp began to push herself up from the desk. And as she rose into the light, Garth realised that her command of power was not limited to the stamp: she also possessed the formidable air of a mean sumo wrestler or a Samurai warrior.

The trip from her desk towards the counter was laboured, as her hips swung with ponderous gravity corresponding to the advance of each thick leg, creating an inescapable parallel to a giant movie-monster made by an inept scientist who never figured out that walking is a scissor action, left foot, right hand, rather than a swinging from side to side of such significance that the camera would shake with the tread-fall of each step.

Still, Garth realised that there was not a weak or unsteady movement in her assault. Her advance became even more ominous as she moved from behind the desk and crossed the floor towards

152

him, her backlit shadow growing, falling first on the counter, then up across his papers, his hands and finally him.

Garth spread out his packet of papers and dared to look into her face. He marvelled at the fat: her eyes hidden down tunnels of fat, her mouth sunken behind rolls that once were cheeks. She licked her mouth with a tongue that emerged like a slug, back and forth across her lips, leaving a wet streak. Her nose was but two more tunnels.

One by one she singled out his documents, staring at each without uttering a sound. Suddenly Garth wished he had more, maybe a letter from the Prime Minister of the Federation, or maybe from the President of the United States, written personally to Miss Packard, though somehow, he sensed even a letter from God would not satisfy Stomp.

"She needs for a stamp," the woman growled, and shoved one of the pages back at him.

"That's what I came to get from you."

"Not that kinda stamp!" She stared at him with a mixture of disgust and disbelief at his stupidity. "Mon, she wants for an 'Assumption Stamp'."

"I don't understand. Where do I get an 'Assumption Stamp'?" He tried not to mock her allusion to a consumption stamp.

"Where? ...The Pilli-Burro."

"You mean the Philatelic Bureau?" Then Garth realised what she was talking about. "Oh, you mean that kind of stamp... the kind you lick and paste on. What does it look like? They've a lot of stamps at the Philatelic Bureau."

" D'usual." She slurred, with a note of entrapment such as an executioner might emit while placing the noose around the victim's neck. "Git de one with 'St. Augustine' written under a big bird. I guess de bird represents flight and freedom." Then she began to laugh. "Das a good one for me to put me stamp over." She shook like jelly. "Das good. De one with de free bird on it."

153

"You mean I have to buy my own stamp before you can stamp my papers?"

"Chure," she smirked. "Dey does it all over de World."

"Babylon coming!" Caraja used to say when he saw trouble ahead. Three more times Garth returned to Stomp's office over the following four days, getting every form of verification that he could, from the signature of the Premier himself to statement from all three offshore banks that he had no debt or offshore accounts with amounts more than $100,000 USD.

Now, as he watched her study the papers of his labours, he thought there were other alternatives: strangle the woman; ink up her stamp and place it on the bird of freedom himself; walk out and simply get on the plane without her stamp and spend the rest of his life on the run from the Augustinian Interpol. Since his plan was to spend his last weekend with Caraja up in the mountains at "Rasta's Roast", as Caraja called his encampment high up the volcano beyond all civilisation, maybe he would go there and hide out for the rest of his life.

Maybe it was as Joshua had said in the van: maybe she had plans beyond the decorum of her position. Garth decided to stop the cat-and-mouse game with Stomp. He was her amusement. Her revenge for all the hurts harboured from years of Harlequin Romances. He saw the situation for what it was, the practiced sadistic joy of keeping him on a tether.

He even smiled when she claimed, "Das not de Minister signature. I know'd he hand, and das not it."

"Babylon coming," he said to himself.

"Of course it is, I witnessed it myself," Garth said defiantly. Then, for reasons that he could only describe as sadistic, he extended his index finger and ever so lightly stroked the back of her hand, grinning and probing the recesses of her tubular eyes for her reaction.

There was a strange gutteral groan from far down in her throat, but her eyes neither exploded in rage nor smouldered with lust. Again, he stroked her hand, keeping his eyes fixed on hers.

They glazed; she took a deep sigh. "Come back to de desk." It was a command, but one tempered by foreplay. "We discuss dis problem."

Garth leaned his lips close to her ears. "Al'sho-tsoyo!" he whispered seductively.

"What does that mean?" she almost purred.

Garth collected his papers and passport, turned and walked to the door.

"Al'sho-tsoyo? It means, in Shoshone, 'Not in this lifetime'," he said, though in reality it was an expression more closely conveying, "I'd cut off my dick first!"

He wished he had a burlap bag like the one he'd used on the cow that tried to trample Caraja when Garth first arrived on-island. He'd wave it in her face, coax her to charge. But his anger cooled enough by the time he opened the door and felt fresh air, that he experienced a charitable feeling of pity, as one might have for a three-legged dog. He turned and rubbed his hand over his crotch, "Umm." He smiled, rolling his eyes, then stepped quickly outside.

Unfortunately, no sooner had he slammed door behind him than the daylight of reality evaporated his sense of humanitarian compassion and freedom, and again his frustration turned to anger. "FUCK!" he yelled with one Portstown-piercing scream.

Suddenly from inside, her voice screamed. "Me still controls you's ass, and On-island you be till your pecker rots off!"

He heard her yell, even through the thick solid mahogany door.

Chapter 12

Garth Meets Caraja's Sister

"How'd it go with Stomp?" asked Josiah when Garth got into the taxi bus.

Garth smiled. "Well, she's still got her stamp and my passport still needs it, but Lord, her price was too high. To answer you, that woman no longer has a hold over me and I'm considering options."

"You's an' illegal alien', dat's what Youse be. Naw, me thinks she be the kind of woman who'd rub up with you then kills you cus she hates she-self so much, and she hates you even more for push-push'n she pussy."

"*Psychology Today?*"

"*TRUE* Magazine," Josiah grinned. He'd bought an issue over at the Saint Augustine newsstand and took the title of the magazine at face value.

"You take me to the airport Monday for the Antigua flight? Maybe you could speak to your cousin in Immigration?"

"Chure. No problem mon. Anyt'ing for an 'illegal alien'."

Josiah took Garth all the way up to Poppy Dawn Village's shop where, as Garth has learned, most of the community gathered regularly to relax, or "lime-out" on a Friday afternoon. This time, many of the youths were there awaiting the tryouts for dancing roles in the Christmas Masquerade group. Garth got out and started to pay Josiah, but the driver would not take his money., saying he'd catch him on Monday.

Bueno intercepted Garth.

"You a freemon?" Bueno asked.

Garth suspected that by now everyone knew he had gone to see Stomp, and likely her technique for granting exit visas. "You mean, did I fuck her?" Garth asked with an edge of indignation.

156

Bueno looked at his feet, embarrassed that Garth understood that was the core of his question. "Naw, she'd probably kill me afterwards."

Bueno laughed. "Maybe. We never does see no more dem 'Volunteers' after dey goes width she. We just t'ink dey so ashamed dey leave island quick as dey gets de stamp from Stomp. Maybe she's got bodies with her dere in the Treasury."

"That's disgusting!" laughed Garth. "But tell me this, do the women volunteers have to get an exit stamp the same way?"

"Probably, cuz she's desperate for rub-up."

Garth let the topic drop. "Where's Caraja's cottage?" he asked.

"Same as it's always been, up de road and at every junction take de right tread up-so. Maybe you should leave your wallet width me, dem Rastamons be slippery bunch. Maybe I expand you's fortune width de dominos, split de winnings equally." Bueno smirked.

"Right. And the losings? I think my money will sleep in my pocket and take its chances with those slippery Rastamen."

"Suit you's-self, but I offer Youse de chance to be a rich mon, mon." Bueno laughed and pointed to the road leading past Big Rock and climbing up into the jungle. Soon the road degenerated to a one-lane donkey path lined by rubble-stone walls, dividing fields and pastures. "Afternoon," he'd call out to those in the fields, knowing that even if he didn't see anyone, someone would be there tending them.

"Afternoon!" came greetings of unseen origins.

"He be dataway!" said a man Garth met on the trail who was carrying a large bundle of vines called simply "pig food" on his head.

"Who he?" Garth smiled, knowing full well that the jungle telephone had relayed that he was coming and where he was going.

"Caraja-he. You's de cowboy what work de cattle width Caraja."

"Indian, not cowboy."

"Come-so Trinidad."

"Come-so Wyoming."

The man shrugged. "Pass de day in peace, brother," and he resumed his portage down the path.

After two more forks in the trail, each cutting in half the upkeep and maintenance, he found himself on a trail from his youth, the invisible trail, a game trail walked by hooved animals where there were certain places to step, and once you saw the stride, the path appeared like magic. It was a case of looking for the signs and not the underbrush. On a face of a hill shouldering off the volcano, he came upon an orchard, a mixed and widely varied plantation of fruit trees ranging from mangoes to passion fruit, exotics like star fruit and kumquats, and a couple that Garth didn't recognise at all.

The ground was clean; all the brush and sheddings had been cleared and composted or burned, and the jungle trimmed back. Many trees had their own "git-some poles" -- a long stick with a strong natural fork at the end, or a long stick with either a sawblade or a very sharp knife lashed into the end. Each pole, Garth knew, was for that particular type of fruit. Oranges were best picked with the forked end. This was done by hooking under the fruit with the fork and giving the pole a hard jag upward, snapping the stem. The trick then is tracking the orange's descent as it bumped and jumped through the limbs like a baseball player tracking a fly-ball, and then catching it with two hands. Coconuts required a saw and breadfruit needed a knife.

At the top of the hill was a large flat area. Garth stopped on the lip of it and, looking back, he was awestruck by the vista. He could see 270 degrees, all the way to Montserrat in the south and St. Maarten to the northeast. The Caribbean, blue and green in the afternoon sun, was so clear that every whitecap on the ocean was distinct, though thirty to forty miles away. In an hour or two the sun would be setting in the west, not into the ocean but behind the western shoulder of the volcano. The jungle would turn gold then.

The trail rose again, through an orchard of wild and planted fruit trees, and then flattened out on a large bench that butted against a high, monolithic cliff covered with foliage. Snuggled between two large juice mango trees was a cottage, light green with lavender gingerbread and tropical-blue shutters. The yard was clean, there was a clothesline along one side of the house, and an open hearth with pots hanging from a cross-pole. On the far side of the fire, half hidden by the smoke, was a woman squatting down tending the fire. It was the universal "at rest" position for people of the land: squatting to shuck peas, to take a pee, to have a baby, to repair nets, to participate in endless conversations, to throw the "bones" (dice) and gamble for pennies. Or as was the case with this woman, squatting to wash off potatoes before dropping them into a pot hanging on an iron rod over the fire. The smoke curled around her like loving hands.

At the base of a mango tree to the west, a child of a year and a half maybe two sat happily shredding a banana leaf and talking to a kitten, which was further shredding with equal enthusiasm what the baby discarded, sometimes rolling on its back and scratching the husk to shreds with its hind claws.

While the view of the wide Caribbean had taken his breath away, this scene was the ultimate intake... a gasp at how much he felt it. It was everything he'd wanted St. Augustine to be when he was first assigned here.

The sound of the woman's singing added yet another dimension. It was an African song full of lyrical stories, and throaty grunts set the rhythm, which she sometimes timed with her hands when they were free to clap. A working song, a marriage of the soul with what one is doing, the cadence set to the beat of the labor. Maybe a slave song. For a moment, the smoke between them blew away and he saw her face clearly.

It was her! It was the young, beautiful woman he'd met when he first arrived on the high road to Poppy Dawn primary. For two

159

years he had looked for her. Only once seeing her in the library, but she had bolted before they could speak.

The baby must be the child she had carried in her belly on the path and later, at the library. Here she was and he wondered if his attraction would be as strong as he had imagined. The scene, the woman, the child, the fire — all were mesmerising. It suddenly occurred to him, she must be Caraja's sister!

Of course, it was the house that Caraja shared with his sister. But an ugly second thought occurred to Garth. What if she was not Caraja's sister, but his woman? Wouldn't it be a cruel irony if the woman of his fantasies was the girlfriend of his only close friend, Felicity? Caraja talked about her so much. For a split second, Garth considered turning back in disappointment, but immediately the desire to go further up the mountain with Caraja convinced him that he had no choice.

He stepped back down the trail a few meters. "Inside!" he called out, as is the custom for alerting someone at home, so they don't feel spied upon, which he had been doing. He waited. But only the baby responded, with an echo attempt at "Inside".

With curious eyes, the baby studied him until Garth drew close enough for the child to decide that Garths were friendly creatures, and it welcomed him with a face full of smiles and arms flailing. The woman seemed to pay no attention to him, but he noticed that her hands had stopped and the song was silent. Only when the baby shrieked in silly delight and laughter did she look to see the cause.

Garth was balanced on one leg, his arms sweeping in slow Shiva-dance while making foolish faces, crossing his eyes, protruding his tongue. It was too much, even for her, and as much as she'd coached herself to behave while he was there, she could not hide her joy completely. A smirk burst into a smile, and when she saw the hilarity of the baby's laughter, she too broke into carefree laughing.

160

"My name is Myah." Her eyes held a hint of embarrassment that she hadn't acknowledged him.

"We've met."

"I know."

He had to ask, "Do you live here?"

"Yes," she smiled, "I'm Caraja's sister."

It was the best news he'd had since he came on-island, except maybe the slamming of Stomp's door behind him.

Myah knew Garth was coming because Caraja had told her, but she had sensed it before. And she'd given a lot of thought to the moment they would meet. She decided to do the obvious and continue her work as usual. She wouldn't overly encourage him. If he felt as strongly as she, he would make the first step. She thought about when they first met, she remembered clearly what was said, but what she remembered foremost was what was not said.

She remembered how muscular he was. Like men who work with their bodies, like Caraja. When they had passed, they had both stopped, their bodies very close. They had just stood, each studying the other. Then, not knowing why, on an impulse she had brushed his cheek with the back of her hand. "So here you are." She would have followed him anywhere, he had but to ask. But of course, he didn't, and she knew that pregnant woman are not the most attractive to most men though he'd said she was beautiful. And when they'd looked into the other's core. she wondered how she knew nothing about him, yet felt that she knew everything.

God, he is so beautiful. She had smiled to herself, her head bent down, looking at her feet, for fear he'd catch a glimpse of her real thoughts.

What had happened that changed her so much? It wasn't long after their meeting that Garth began invading her dreams, sometimes even passionately. But only cautiously would she let him in, and then for only minor roles. But the visitations, the "frequentings" as Gran Sueky called them, began taking over her dreams, growing sometimes into stark nightmares full of almost uncontrollable

161

terror… and loss, and sorrow and Garth. Since the incident at the library, he had begun playing feature roles in her dreams, but she was never sure if he was an anchor against all of the chaos, of the visitations… or the cause of it.

She spied on him constantly when he and Caraja were working the animals in the corrals in the morning. She'd find excuses to take the goats and Bantu down to Windward beach. They'd spoken only that once, but she'd heard nothing but good things about the man. So why was she so afraid?

"Afraid to feel," was Sueky's diagnosis and her cure was equally direct. "If dis writt'n, den dat gonna be and ain't nothing Youse kin do to stop it. So, you might as well surrender." Surrender to whom, to him, to the nightmares, to the heavens, to the Lord Jesus? In the end, she decided to keep her distance, and now, when he's leaving, he comes into her yard.

Garth, still standing on one leg for Bantu's amusement, lost his balance at the news that Myah was Caraja's sister.

Her instinct was to reach out to shake hands, but fear held her back. Still she offered her wrist, as is the custom when one's hands are dirty. Garth took her hand instead, with both of his, much as a politician would, and gave it an awkward shake. Realising that he was holding her with two hands, he quickly jerked both back to his side.

"I always thought the wrist thing was too much like enslavement." Enslavement! He screamed at himself — why did he choose that word, knowing that some St. Augustinians were still raw about it?

"What was that song you sang? It sounded African."

"It was. It was a Masai song about village life, teaching the children the lessons of the land. I don't know much."

"How did you learn it?"

"I don't know. I think I learned it from a Masai, so I must have been very young."

"Have you been to Africa?"

162

She shook her head no. "New York once and that was about as much of the human jungle as I ever want to know." She smiled, a twinkle coming to her dark brown eyes. "You wouldn't believe the wild animals they have there in that preserve they call Manhattan." She chuckled. "Have you been there?"

Garth noticed that her English was impeccable.

For some time they stood there in silence, neither feeling compelled to speak, comfortable without words. Mostly they watched Bantu, though sometimes sneaking glimpses of each other. Each knew the other so well and not at all.

"Geronimo!" boomed Caraja, his shout echoing off the great wall behind him. The Rastafarian came out from the foliage curtain of hanging vines that draped from the rock wall behind. He'd changed his red turban for a weathered grey-blue one, his pants were short cut-offs, and instead of the work boots with steel toes that they wore at the farm, his feet were bare. In his hand he carried two cutlasses, and under the arm a tied load of burlap bags and a backpack.

"Hey, mon, good ta see ya," he greeted Garth.

"I see you meets Bantu and he mother?" Caraja scooped his nephew away from the kitten attacking the child's legs.

"Ja," Myah's tone was serious. "Wha's you plans? Me-sees Felicity dis after and she getting dat look. Of any time now You hear-so about the hurricane? Maybe you wants to postpone your trip to de herb garden until after the baby?" Myah pleaded but knew her brother too well to think she could dissuade him.

"Can't do dat cuz Geronimo here is headed back to de reservation dis Monday come. But just in case, I lays in provisions in de cave and Sueky wants ta stay-put at de Anglican Church. And another thing you can count on, we's gonna be de first what sees what dat storm gonna do. We'll be out of there and down here lickety-split. He stopped talking and directed Garth with his hand to the pack he'd leaned on the porch. "Can you give me you's strong back and weak brain?"

163

"Besides," he turned back to Myah, "St. Augustine ain't gonna take no licks. Jah gonna look after us. If anything goes sideways, we's back in a flash. Send Bantu up to get us if you hear different." The baby smiled as if pleased with the thought.

"Right, he gonna crawl all de way up to de roost?" Myah turned away from Caraja but gave Garth a smile. "Maybe you'll be the voice of reason?" She asked him.

****

The trail leading up along the side of the cliff face was steep and treacherous. Garth had seen nothing like it. Even the rocks were green with algae and moss, so different from the arroyos back home. The trail ran beside, sometime in, a gentle stream that wove through a labyrinth of boulders and roots. A great curtain of vines hung hundreds of feet from above, curtaining from the very treetops of the jungle canopy. The trees stood like giants, stealing the light for themselves before it could reach the forest floor. Even in the waning afternoon, the jungle was thick and humid, wet clouds sweeping across their tops like a shroud of gauzy vapour veils masking the top of the mountain, molding to the contours of the volcano's ghauts.

Caraja was barefoot. He carried a canvas pack slung over one shoulder. In his other hand he swung a cutlass with tireless effort, cutting back the ferns and elephant ears that had choked the trail in just the week since he'd last passed. A tall man, he walked with long strides, leaping easily from rock to rock, from root to root. At one point in their ascent, Garth realised that they'd stopped walking on the ground, and were moving instead upon a root webbing a meter above soil. The route was visible only by the worn roots, their skins peeled and polished, shiny in the mountain mist. They were slick like "loon shit as his farther used to say.

"Take off your shoes before you hurt yourself," Caraja advised.

Suddenly, the trail they had been following veered up the ridge of the ghaut into an almost vertical pitch. From there on, it

164

was hand-over-hand climbing on a ladder of roots, with vines for handholds.

To Garth's amazement, the trail landed on a wide, flat bench, sheltered at one end by a giant baobab tree, its long arms intertwining with the limbs of an ancient mahogany tree to form a canopy. A rope hung from the interlocking limbs.

Like the roots on the trail, the earth beneath the cathedral was worn and polished by activity. A green tarp covered a bundle wedged into the elbow of a baobab root. Caraja lay his pack against the tree and began untying the tarp.

Spreading it across the clearing, Caraja caught the rope and hitched the hook to a ring stitcher with heavy fishing twine fastened to the center of the tarp. As Caraja drew on the other end of the rope, which Garth realised was the down-end of the center rope, the tarp began rising high over the clearing and into a tent.

Caraja tied off the center line and the four ropes attached to the corners of the tarp. He handed two to Garth. "Take these over to that side." He pointed at the baobab tree and then, with the other two lines in his teeth, he climbed the mahogany and tied one to a limb on the far right, the other to the far left. The limbs in the center had been cut back. Garth turned to the baobab and, after some inspection, found the marks on the tree where the ropes had been tied, and tied his off accordingly.

"You learn quick." Caraja climbed down from the mahogany tree. "Use a slip knot so we can drop she from the ground. With that, the Rasta pulled on the center rope and the tent rose fanning out like a butterfly. Garth, who had pitched many tents in many configurations, was impressed. All the shelter you needed in the tropics, a pulley, a tarp and ropes, thought Garth.

He looked around. The clearing stood above two steep ghauts. Looking down on the tops of trees, he saw that each edge dropped hundreds of meters into pools of vegetation. In one ghaut he could hear the sound of rushing water.

"What do you think of me babies?" Caraja said, pointing and grinning.

Garth looked to find, nestled into the roots of the baobab, a couple dozen plants in tin cans. They had been pruned into little bushes spilling out of the cans. "They wants to be grounded soon, so maybe we does dat wa' you're here. Youse being an agriculture expert and all..."

Garth pick one up and studied it: "Cannabis Sativa". Known to cause fits of insanity and an obsession for junk food he laughed to himself. "Yes, it is a plant I know from textbooks, but I have as yet to try it."

"Fo chure?" Caraja looked incredulously at Garth and let out an elephant laugh that startled the doves from the surrounding canopy. "I'll make a Rastaman out of Youse yet."

"You be my assistant," he said, then laughed again. "Now dere's some irony, me teaching a Shoshone Indian come St. Augustine de ways of Haile Selassie." He handed Garth a black plastic garbage bag, then picked up his cutlass and a bucket made from a dried calabash about the size of a soccer ball. There was a hole the size of a fist cut in one end, with a leather strap tied to each side for carrying the gourd like a pail.

They climbed the spine of the ridge for a few hundred yards, then turned abruptly onto the steep side face and into the ghaut. Again, they were no longer touching the earth but walking on living lattice of roots. Even Caraja used one hand for balance. The sound of the rushing water soon muted even the noise of the jungle. Egrets sailed out over the ghaut, like white messengers above an emerald sea.

Caraja stopped and stood looking at the hillside above the trail. "Well, doc, how are my darlings doing?" Between the roots and pockets of topsoil he'd carried on his back up the mountain, Caraja had created a garden ...no, a forest of ganja. Thick, bushy and six feet tall, each plant was cradled and anchored in the curl of a root. Garth ran his fingers into the soil. He took a pinch and studied it, black loam with sand. He smelt it. Cow shit.

"You get many cows up here?" Garth laughed.

"None 'less you carries dem. Every inch of dat mold and dirt, gits here on me back. She's my cash crop!"

"Now to work. Pay attention." He held his cutlass in the middle of the blade and cut the bud by pulling the stem across the blade rather than sawing, and carefully cutting the limbs free. Each branch of buds was the size of an ear of corn.

"We'll take one from each bush and study dem tonight." He dropped the cuttings into a black bag tied to his waist. "We water dey well tonight, and on de morrow, when de day's good and hot, we'll liquidate our assets with withdrawals and invest in other securities. Dat's my business plan, for chure!" His laugh echoed, even above the roar of the falling water.

"Now, take-up you's pail and follow me cus you's me assistant." Caraja followed the path around the wall of roots towards the cascade. Then suddenly they were looking at a waterfall dropping two hundred feet below them from a polished rock ledge another five stories above them. As Garth inched forwards, he watched the shaft of water plummeting into the thick green pit, striking ledges, spraying a fine mist of rainbows across the canopy-tops of the giant trees lining the ghaut. In the absence of soil, the jungle was nourished by the eternal mist from the falls.

"Watch me close cus I only does dis once for Youse," Caraja smiled, reaching up and with his left hand grasped a rope coil of thick vines and wrapped it around his wrist. Anchoring his feet on the thick root, he leaned far out over the abyss, swinging the pail into the falling water, holding it as long as his arm could take the weight, then letting the gourd swing out of the torrent as he twisted and pulled hard on the vine, carrying the gourd into a controlled landing at Garth's feet. "Youse catch all dat?" His grin was full of teeth and mischief.

167

"You's turn to de wicket. Watch de deck, she slick with slime and all. Now take she vine and loop she around you's waist, den loop she round you's hanging arm. Which arm you hang by?"

Gath shrugged, he wasn't used to hanging by either arm .

"You survive dis and a Rastaman you be.." The Rasta grinned at the Indian. "Know for true dat we's half monkey when we needs be."

"Come on, man, what's next?" Garth said impatiently.

"Think she through. Den clear you's mind and just does she so!" Then he added, "And don't drop de' water gourd, I does have she for some time now and it'll come out of you's pay."

Garth hadn't expected the force of the water, and he was jerked off balance by the violence of even a small stream at terminal velocity. He grabbed the vine with the bucket hand and the gourd hit him in the face. For a second he was blind with adrenaline, and then he was back on solid root. Caraja had expected the scenario and pulled Garth back with the vine end the second he lost balance.

"Youse didn't clear you's head of fall'n to you's death!" Caraja laughed. Garth started laughing, until they were howling like monkeys.

"Give she another try, shorten your grip on de vine, and take she's water from de side. The beat's not so strong."

"When you's head's clear, Youse can do most anything." Caraja walked back out on the root platform, pulled together a rope of vines from far, far up the ghaut face, wrapped his leg around the vine, kicked the end into the ravine... and was gone!

A bird in flight, a black egret gliding down into the mist, far out into the gorge, far beyond the waterfall face. His arch carried him to the far wall, and with a hard kick, he descended again into the mist, parting the rainbows, growing bigger, until he was once again standing on the thick root platform with Garth..

Caraja folded over at the waist and shook the water from his thick braids, catching his breath as he stood erect. Garth was silent. He'd never seen anything so beautiful, so graceful. The human body

168

in flight, with nothing more than gravity and a vine rope. It was what he imagined as a kid from his grandmother's description of trapeze act she saw in a Salt Lake circus. A dance where a human seldom touched the ground, at least according to his Grandma Ellise.

"Wow, I could never..." Garth said in awe. "Never in ten lifetimes. There is no inducement that could make me do that."

"When de mind is clear, it's effortless as flights for a bird. You's carrying too many rocks in your pockets." His look was more of a question than a statement. "Come along, assistant, let's water dose sweet plantlets, and den we's do something bout light'n you's load."

They took turns filling up the gourds, and once Garth shortened his grip on the vine and anticipated the force of the falls, he began enjoying catching the water, even insisted on doing the last two gourds.

"Come assistant. I have the medicine to lighten your heavy load so you can fly."

They sat down on a large rock protruding off the ridge and Caraja produced what appeared to be a hand-rolled cigarette. From his pocket he took out a small disposable lighter and lit the cigarette, puffing until it glowed and then inhaling deeply. "You's turn, Rastaman," he said, still holding his breath, and handed the 'joint' to Garth. "Take a shallow puff at first till you's used to it. Hold de smoke in you's lungs."

Garth took what he thought was a light drag, but he suddenly started coughing and his eyes began to with tears.

"Try again," encouraged Caraja. This time the smoke felt smooth, and Garth held it until he had no more oxygen in his lungs and had to exhale.

"I's surprised you's never smoke de herb. I'm told dat ganja and tobacco come from de Indians."

"Tobacco for sure but don't know about marijuana. We've got lots of mind-altering drugs without it. Peyote is the one my people use for sacred rituals and vision quests. I have been on a couple without jumping off a cliff."

"Mind altering? Mon, das de stuff what makes you's mine right." Caraja laughed and his laughter was infectious, until soon Garth was laughing for no other reason than that it felt good. He took another puff and stared at the vista stretching below them. Over the trees, Garth could see the roof of the Domino College and Big Stone on the corner across from it.

Beyond, nestled into the green canopy of orchards and gardens, he could see the Anglican spire and the graveyard. Roofs of villages defined the Uptee Doon Road as it led down to the coast and the white lines of beach and waves rolling from the deep blue waters of the Atlantic and Caribbean. Floating on the water, Garth could see the islands of Redonda, Montserrat , Antigua, Barbuda, and a dark spot, barely visible, that Garth assumed was Guadaloupe.

He saw different great bulbous clouds that rose thousands of meters into the sky above the islands, their shadows floating like galleons on a pirate sea, an armada all set on the same course. The evening sun turned their boiling, bulbous sails ruby red and silver grey, and gold poured from their bellies making rainbow pillars on which the galleons floated. Garth and Caraja sat as observers upon the world as it stretched out below them. Looking up at the setting sun, Caraja unfolded his legs and stood up on the boulder. "I sees you's load is light now, dis time."

"Nothing much to it," coached Caraja. "You want as momentum as possible!" He smiled, So, again two points to remember. Don't let go! And don't stop in the middle

Take a hard run, then <u>throw</u> yourself off de cliff with the courage of a Sioux warrior!" He patted Garth on the back. "When you comes to de far wall, face it so you can drive yourself back with as much force as you came over with." Did I can mention that you no want to let go, nor stop in the middle?"

"Swing until you're as closes as you's gonna go to the opposite wall, fold up so you can push off the face width de legs."

170

" I'll say it again because adrenaline sometimes muttles things..., no matter what happens, don't let go, you will come out on the other side." He stood, raised his arms like a Pope giving to a crowd of thousands his blessing. "May the Force be with you." He grinned.

Garth wrapped the vine rope around his left arm and grabbed a handhold above it with his right. His heart was pounding in his ears as he looked over the edge and the polished granite holders hundreds of feet below.

He turned and walked back from the edge a few strides with the vine. When he could feel the vine-rope tighten, he tugged on it a few times, returned to the edge wrapped it around his waist, with a final loop around his right arm. He adjusted the tension so when he lay back he could feel the tension on it, and without further thought, eased to the edge of the rock protrusion.

"Run and jump!" commanded Caraja. "Clear de mind, t'ink you's a bird."

The sense of euphoria that followed the smoke also gave Garth courage, or at least dulled his fear of certain death, and rocking back, he lunged over the lip of the root platform into the cauldron of boiling mist. His heart stopped as he felt the vines sag under his weight, and he felt he was going down more than he was going out.

But soon the vine began to draw taut, swinging him out of the tempest, lifting him up towards the opposing wall, which seemed to be moving towards him at an alarming speed. He turned facing it, and when he thought he'd certainly collide, he drew up his legs and pushed himself hard off the green moss-covered face. His arms ached and for a split second, something deep and primordial inside of him entertained the idea of stopping the pain by releasing his grip, but he held on, sweeping past the center point. Then he could feel the trees holding the vine flexing back, and suddenly he was up, but above the platform from taking slack at the far wall. swinging above the platform.

"Drop!" yelled Caraja. "Le-go de rope!"

Garth was already swinging back outwards the ravine when he released his grip. Caraja grabbed him at the last second, pulling him firmly back onto the platform. "Man, you's going for a second spin?"

Garth was soaking and gasping for breath, which he had held for the duration of the flight.

His arms ached, his legs were weak, but his head was full of flight.

"Wash me-so," said Caraja. Stepping back and reaching as high as he could, he grabbed the vine and went running at the cliff, swinging his feet up and lying back. He dropped from sight, then went sailing out across the gorge, into the mist close to the face of the waterfall, out of the mist, against the opposing wall, and with a mighty thrust of his legs, propelled himself out over the ghaut, arriving finally back on the platform.

"I think I've got it," said Garth, taking up the rope of vines. And back and forth the two took turns swinging into the setting sun. It was only when a few of the rope's vines snapped and went slack from above, that they decided to stop for the night.

Chapter 13

Home at Last

The old Jeep bounced and jostled up the jungle road over boulders polished black with years of tyre rubber spinning and gripping at their surface. On the straight stretch, Danielle saw a troupe of monkeys scrambling and gambolling on the roadway ahead. She remembered so clearly when she was young, before she had her driver's license ... but still drove on the back road and any monkey on the straight stretch was fair game to chase. She'd accelerate, pedal to the floor, horn honking, sending the monkeys scurrying into the thicket screaming with a mixture of terror and raw anger.

Then one day, a monkey leapt the wrong way, onto the windshield. Blinded for a moment, Danielle swerved off the track and went far enough into the jungle that her father had to winch the jeep out. She knew he was really angry because he didn't say a word.

"What were you going to do if you hit one?" he said finally with a voice level and measured. "Were you going to bring him to the hospital and give me more work, when I can't even handle my human patients? Foolishness."

That was not her first encounter with the monkeys. One year the monkeys had become particularly brazen; maybe the yard dog had died, or maybe, as Lottie would say, "He learned to swing in the trees by he tail," which meant the dog became friends with the monkeys. Danielle was around three and was sitting on the back veranda picking through a stalk of bananas that had been left there by a neighbour. She loved bananas, still did.

Spying the stalk guarded only by a toddler, some monkeys started teasing her, hoping to get her to chase them around the corner so another monkey could slip in and steal the stalk. Danielle was having no part of it. Taking up a metal pot used for feeding the dog, she started yelling "Bana" so loudly and angrily that Lottie could hear her in the kitchen. The "snatcher" monkey finally made his move and she hit him square with the dog dish, and from that moment on "Danielle" was known as "Bana".

What Lottie saw was Danielle swinging around 180 degrees with her weapon and the monkey sticking his head right in front of the incoming pot. The way the story swept the island was that Bana and the monkey had engaged in a fierce battle and she had won — and almost knocked the monkey's head off. Many years later when Bana was a supermodel, the tabloids ran a headline, "Jungle Model Fights Monkey for Bananas." "Danielle" or "Bana" which name depended upon the circumstances, and now she had chosen to change her circumstances.

It felt wonderful to come home after New York. In some ways she wished she hadn't, but part of that was wishing that she didn't have to grow up. She'd observed racism in a country where all were supposedly "equal", ghettos next to skyscrapers, places in Africa where the dogs ate better than the people -- unless the people could catch the dogs! That was the hard part, seeing the raw edge of the World's human condition while working in an industry based upon indulgence. She had become the rage of the industry. But after years of modelling, and then designing, she'd come to realise that fashion was founded upon promotion and exploitation, and once "Bana of the Jungle" understood this, the magic was gone!

On the other hand, she was coming home with a Hermes wardrobe and two Gucci duffels full of beautiful clothes and fabrics, plus her own copyrighted design patterns and dozens of important business cards. Though burned out, she still cherished the memories of all the exciting things that had come to her -- life in New York, then London, Paris, and finally New York again. No, the problem was that her childhood was too good! She wasn't running "from" something as much she was running "to" something by coming home. If anyone was going to exploit Bana, it was going to be her.

Finally, her jeep came to an opening where the bush road stopped. The grass was short, recently grazed.

"I'm home!" she yelled to the monkeys. "Spread the word, BANA's home, so best keeps you's fury-fannies far away from me. Hear!" She reached in the back and took out her bags. At the edge of the opening was the beginning of a path and a gate on a sagging post. She lifted it and walked it open, then, setting her luggage inside, she walked it closed. Every gate on-island sagged for a purpose, she was told as a child by Lottie. "If mister gate swings free as the breeze, the animals gonna go as they please."

She walked but a few meters further before coming to the edge of a large clearing where the sunlight streamed through the open canopy. She dropped the suitcase and duffels and just stood there in awe.

It was even more beautiful than the day she last visited a year ago. The Aztec gold sunlight came through the clouds in shafts, igniting the boulder gardens, highlighting the bird-of-paradise plants and the delicate jungle orchids. Trees of trumpet flowers hung heavy with blushing pink blooms. The limbs of the great mahogany tree were cocooned with monkey-tail vines and long antebellum tassels of Moss's moss, and of course there was her "vulcanised" Goodrich rubber-tire swing.

It was there she had worked out the complexities of her youth, crying broken-heartedly over her first love lost. Now she couldn't remember anything about the boy. A large calabash grew at the far end of the clearing like a fertile woman laden with big hefty babies — round pods the size and shape of soccer balls hanging from her mammary limbs. That tree had been the source of many hours of amusement. When the tree babies were dry, she'd roll them like bowling balls at equally dried zucchini nine-pins. When the pods were green, she'd carve their outer shells with mysterious Arawak designs, then cut them in half for the sacred bowls and holy basins required for her secret Arawak rituals. In them she'd pour vile potions of jelly-water, blood-red sorrel seeds and black water from

175

the swimming cistern; mix it up with a few choice words and feed it to her dolls. Once she tried feeding it to the cat, but it scratched her.

The tyre swing swayed casually in the late afternoon breeze, beckoning to her like an old friend, medicine for the soul. Birds talked to each other from around the clearing, the pauses in their conversation filled with a chorus of donkeys, dogs, chickens, laughing children, radios, singing, preaching, praising, ranting and then the donkey again. The odd motor joined in on the chorus. It was a jungle paradise made more magnificent with age and jaded to the amenities of the outside world.

Along the southern side of the yard was a long escarpment facing out towards the ocean. From a distance, the main house, which sat on the ridge, was indistinguishable from its jungle surroundings. But upon approaching, suddenly, there was a large two-story structure surrounded by wide verandas from an era gone by. The structure was grounded by a large plantation staircase that fanned from the upper floor of the house out into the yard. The bottom story was made of hand-cut stone blocks, probably by the hands of slaves since the keystone read "B.R. 1783".

The second story was all bamboo: bamboo walls, bamboo pillars carrying bamboo beams. There was not a nail in the structure except for the flooring. The bamboo was lashed together with vine-ties that dried like leather in both strength and colour. Bamboo trusses carried bamboo strapping for the thatched roof. Danielle's New York agent made much in the media of her being raised in a thatched-roof house. She was a little embarrassed at her good fortune and secretly felt sorry for those who lived in steel and concrete.

As she rocked in the tree swing, feeling the lift and dip of the bough, the tree groaning and sighing as it always had, she thought she also heard humming coming from the garden. "Lottie, das Youse sing'n so fine?"

176

There was a long silence, then suddenly an old woman flew out of the garden, skirt and apron flapping around her, her hands waving excitedly in front of her.

"Bana!" she yelped. "Praise de 'oly mudder a'God! Bana, 'tis you, 'tis you!"

"I's be de one. Danielle Bana Bordeaux. And Youse must be de one Miss Lovely Lottie me hears so much about?" The two women flew into each other's arms, hugging and laughing.

Danielle grabbed the old woman's face, kissing it with little pecks to the cheeks, forehead, the eyelids. "Oh, I missed you something awful."

"Oh girl-so, me does too! Me does say a prayer fo' you every day and wonder how you be git'n on."

"Lottie," Danielle finally turned to look around the yard, "the place looks fantastic. Who's helping you?"

"Just me… and me, as usual."

"As usual." Danielle smiled.

"Come, girl, sit with me a spell, de heat gonna melt me down."

"Into a beautiful puddle of chocolate. And I'm going to get a spoon and eat you all up."

"Well, dat'll be alroight, but make chure you does wash de spoon and put she away." They looked at each other, laughing, their hands interlaced. Together they climbed the staircase to the house.

The windows and doors were open to air the house out as was Lottie's custom when she came to look after the garden. The furniture from the deck had been taken inside and covered, with the other furniture, by sheets.

"Take dis." The old woman pointed to a sheet draped over two sedan chairs. "Might as well act like you owns de place and sit in de best seats." They carried the chairs one by one onto the veranda and found the end table that normally sat between them. Danielle sat down while Lottie went to the kitchen to make a pitcher of "whacbac", a local drink of ginger-crush, lime and papaya juice (and local rum if necessary).

Danielle hadn't had 'whacbac' in a long time, and never with local rum called "Hammon", which her father said could make one temporarily crazy and permanently blind, or was it permanently crazy but only temporarily blind? She suspected neither, but she hated the taste anyway. Danielle closed her eyes, listening to the sounds of dusk's intermission between movements in a symphony. Soon the peace that comes from deep happiness carried her into a dreamless, unguarded sleep.

Danielle awoke gently to the clinking of crystal Tibetan bells from a mountaintop. She opened her eyes to see a tall, stately apparition coming towards her from the shadows of the house. Tall and stately, proud and regal, a Masai woman warrior carrying a pitcher of whacbac and two empty glasses on a wooden tray.

Danielle leapt to her feet. "I'm sorry, let me help you." She took the service from Lottie and set it on the table.

"Dere's no ice, de fridge she be sleep'n since you's last here," she said apologetically. "Why you no tell a body dat you's coming-so?" She said, a little perturbed. "I always thought I raised you better. I'd have dis place looking smart... not shabby like you sees it. Maybe now, you'll t'ink Lottie a little shabby she-self!"

"I was afraid you..." Danielle paused. "I was afraid you wouldn't be here."

"Girlo, where else me gonna be? I ain't gonna be nowhere else but here... or heaven."

"Hmmm... that's what I was afraid of," Danielle confessed. "That you might be in 'de Glory-be-gone'."

"Well, when dat day does pass, jus' rejoice dat I's width you's mother and father."

Danielle looked away quickly, tears coming to her eyes no matter how hard she tried to stop them.

"Oh little bird, I's so sorry. Lottie never means to grieve you."

It was Lottie who had delivered her because Danielle's father was away on the other side of the island, doctoring a fisherman who'd been attacked by a shark. Maria, Danielle's mother, said she waited until Francois was out of the house to have the baby. Danielle was born in the very bed where she would sleep that night.

As the two women sat on the porch sipping 'whacbac', Lottie secretly looked over at the young woman whom she'd known as one of her own. True, Danielle hadn't passed through her belly, but everything else a mother could do, she did. And some things that Francois would normally do, since both Danielle's mother and father were dedicated to bringing modern medicine to St. Augustine. Lottie had no children, so she was the parent who took Danielle and her friends on walks in the jungle, or to the top of the mountain. Sometimes they took a "tap-tap" down the Uptee Doon Road to the beach where the fishermen stowed their boats. Then they'd walk up over Camel Back Hill to the next lagoon so the girls could play unobserved in the surf... naked. The Anglican Priest would be horrified at this, especially since one of the girls was <u>his</u> daughter. Lottie would sit back in the shade of the baobab tree and marvel at how free they were, without a care, dolphins splashing sunbows at each other.

Raising Danielle was a symbiotic procedure. Lottie taught the girl to tie her shoes, the difference between left and right, right and wrong, proper and foolish behaviour. In turn, Danielle taught Lottie how to read. And that is why Lottie could speak impeccable English... if she were around impeccable English.

Even as a child, Danielle's skin was a deep rich tan, not from the sun but from inheritance. Her father called her a "mutt of many races from many places". Her features were neither white nor coloured, but the best of both, according to Lottie. East Indian, African and mainly French from both sides of her family. As a result, she had long black hair, a fine thin nose, big, round, honest eyes, high cheekbones and a mouth that smiled easily, or could slip into a seductive pout with the slightest turn of her lower lip and downward cast of the eyes.

She was the hue of fine saddle leather, soft and smooth like the best saddles the jockeys saved for the special races. The saddles they groomed with as much care as they groomed their horses. The jocks were the prime prizes for making babies, and the ladies at market used to laugh that it was because of the jock's gift for grooming... "gentle hands and a knowing touch."

Most of Danielle's first friends came from Poppy Dawn Village, though soon her net spread all over the Island. Boys came and went, and occasionally Lottie held her hand through loves lost. She suspected the girl also broke many hearts, likely without intention, or even knowingly. Never a malicious child, but always strong willed.

Both of her parents and even Lottie herself wanted Danielle to go off-island to school, which she did after senior secondary, but until then she was firm, she wasn't leaving St. Augustine. Still, she didn't miss out, her folks brought culture to her. The house was filled with books and classical music, even played outside through speakers in the garden to keep the monkeys at bay. In reality, it probably attracted them, Lottie guessed, for when Danielle discovered rock 'n' roll, it was Elvis, the Beatles and Hendrix that stripped the surrounding trees clean of monkeys. Inadvertently, Lottie developed a taste for classical music and preferred working the garden to Chopin even more than to the birds, especially the peacocks.

The Bordeaux home was also a gathering place for interesting people from exotic places. "Monkey Tails", the name Danielle's father had bestowed on the bamboo palace of his creation, guests would be friends for life, for the Bordeaux lived the dream many sought but could not live themselves. And soon the Hospital Fund was receiving substantial donations from foundations controlled by the secretly envious visitors from outside. How fast time had passed since those elegant evenings.

Now the Island had three resident doctors, and the hospital had an X-ray machine of its own and a modern, air-conditioned operating-theatre. Still, there were only two wards, one for women and one for men, and both were overcrowded. There was talk of adding a new wing, but the government was financially strained. A few years before, St. Augustine had decided to secede from the protectorate of England and become a sovereign nation, and their newly discovered nationalistic pride put the financial burden of social services solely upon the residents shoulders.

When Danielle left, she attended Bryn Mawr College for two years before being offered a job with the Ford Modeling Agency by Jason Carmichael, who knew her family from the Island. She became a star model, as Lottie knew she would, and once when she was doing a show for Valache in Miami, her family, including Lottie flew up. Tony Valache treated them like royalty and the press ate it up. Dubbed Albert Schweitzer and Audrey Hepburn of the West Indies.

Francois died just over two years ago. It was the largest funeral ever held on-Island. Then Maria passed within a month of him, and again the Island people turned out en masse to pay their respects and gratitude to the Bordeaux family. Everyone said Maria died of a broken heart because she and "Doc Borda" were so much in love. But Lottie knew that the woman's health was never good, and that she never attended to herself because of her determination to share her dream with her husband.

Danielle had quit modeling a year before her parents passed and was working in design in Paris for Dior when she heard of her father's death. She rushed home for the service, and within the month, her mother died in her arms with Lottie holding her hands. Devastated and confused, Danielle moved back to New York, and only once since then had she been back to St. Augustine. But here she was now. "Hold love while you have it," Lottie used to say.

As Lottie studied the young woman, she wondered if Danielle had changed. Living off-island does that, she knew. She blew a

181

strand of hair from her view, a habit she had when her hands were busy or full, or when she was worried about something.

Convinced the young woman wasn't going to volunteer any information about how she'd been and what she'd been doing, Lottie decided to take the lead. "So, you come to see if me's been work'n?" Lottie turned and look squarely at Danielle, expecting an answer.

"As usual," Danielle said absently, staring straight ahead, still absorbing the view of the ocean and the top of the jungle canopy — a green carpet woven around multi-colored roofs, a full spectrum from calypso blue to canary yellow.

Where some islands had ordinances dictating single coloured roofs, usually red, the people of St. Augustine were individualists. A ship loaded to the gunwales with loose cannons, Danielle smiled to herself. If her Islanders were sheep, not one herder could keep them as they'd be going off in their own directions immediately. Still, Danielle also understood that there was a current of social responsibility ingrained in the community, probably running as far back as slavery and emancipation. It was still a "We" society, while the rest of the West Indies had become "Me" islands.

Suddenly, the phone rang. Both women jumped. "I thought I'd had that disgusting thing turned off last year," growled Danielle.

"Can't say, das de first peep me hears from she since you last passed."

"Hello?"

"Danielle?"

There was a long silence. "Jonathan?"

"Yes. I just arrived on-island and found your message on the machine," he said.

Suddenly she broke into laughter. "Oh my God," she gasped. "I left that message last year. The morning you left. I knew you were gone, but I still wanted to leave it." She fell silent for a moment. "I too just arrived. Came in on LIAT from Antigua."

"But my secretary said you had left the City to take a different position."

"I did. I've moved here permanently to start 'Bana Designs'."

There was a long silence.

"Could I see you?" he blurted out, astonished at himself.

Lottie rose and went around the veranda to get Danielle's bags. She set them in the bedroom. From the closet, she took out a set of sheets and smelled them for mildew. They smelled fine, but had she known of Danielle's arrival she'd have washed them. Lottie removed the duvet from the four-poster bamboo bed, and spread the sheets, smoothing them hospital flat. How long would the young woman stay, she wondered as she lit a candle and put the hurricane glass over it. The house had electricity, but Danielle preferred the "Arawak way", whatever that meant. Finally, Lottie returned to the veranda, carrying another lit lamp.

"So," she smiled. "You've a man already on-island?" she teased, then she extended her hand to Danielle's hair. "Girl, you's hair's a fright. Let Lottie give she some love."

"I'd like that." Danielle got up and retrieved a brush and a comb from her bag.

Realising Danielle was still not going to offer any information, Lottie was again direct. "Dis man, what sorta man he be?"

"The man…" Danielle thought for a long time. "He's someone I met here a year ago when I was last down. What can I say? A really nice man. He hadn't a clue who I was, or anything about the fashion world… two big assets, in my book.

'He's a respected lawyer in New York, but I have this feeling he's looking for something else. Lost his wife a couple of years ago about the same time as Papa and Mama died."

"Dem's de facts," Lottie said, wielding the brush with long strokes. "But what kinda man he be?"

"It's all very strange, we have little in common. And yet I feel… well…felt," she corrected herself, "good when I was with him.

183

You know how, with some people you might have everything in common, but there is nothing special. With Jonathan I felt a certain correctness, even though he's almost the age of my father."

Lottie smirked at this.

"No, not as a mate," Danielle was quick to correct, "more like a friend that you can trust." She thought about all he'd said on their walk on the beach that night.

She considered for a moment. "I guess the attraction was that he was like this closed door that I wanted to open."

"Why fo', girl?" Lottie asked in amazement.

"Because I believe there's someone really special on the other side." Lottie rolled her eyes and gave Danielle's hair a pull.

"Ow!" exclaimed Danielle. "I think there's this young man, full of curiosity and adventure, trapped in the prison of someone else's choices." Then she laughed. "Mind you, New York itself is a minimum-security prison."

Silence followed except for the crickets: the second movement of the symphony called "nightfall" had begun. Lightning bugs flashed across the veranda while the moon, three-quarters to full, inched up out of the Atlantic.

Now that she was firmly home, she allowed herself to be philosophical, and she saw the New York fashion experience with detached amazement. "Lottie, do you believe some folks are in our lives because of destiny?"

"Like who, de Devil?" Lottie twinkled.

"Like Jason Carmichael from the Ford Agency. The man who invited Ruthie, Myah and me to New York."

"Chure I does." The old woman looked at Danielle with a playful smile. "Why else does de Lord bring you's parents to St. Augustine?"

"To be the Island's doctors?"

"No, silly girl, because St. Augustine is where Lottie lives!" She stopped brushing and gave Danielle a light peck on the cheek. "How else me gonna raise you, if dey don't come-so."

"Oh Lottie, I love you!" Danielle's hand reached up to touch Lottie's. "But sometimes I still can't believe they've both gone. I always thought that Papa would be around forever like that great mahogany tree in the yard. You must miss them a lot too."

"Me does, and me doesn't. We had more den our share of happiness together. But happiness isn't forever, it's a present dat de Lord bless us with to keep us going while we's here. We can either take de present and use it or leave it wrapped." She thought a moment. "Now I takes me happiness in me garden. Den every once in a while, me gets another unexpected present, like you's coming to visit."

"No, Lottie." Danielle realised that Lottie didn't understand. "I'm *not* here to visit..." Lottie looked puzzled and disappointed. "...I'm here to _stay_!"

The old woman's eyes opened wide in disbelief. "For true?"

Danielle nodded.

"Well... das good," the old woman said quietly, though her heart sang. "Me'll slow down me brushing, cus now we gots time."

"Time," Danielle nodded. "That's what it is about, isn't it?" she said reflectively. "Here we have time. In the cities I had no time, and what time there was was poorly spent. Hurrying here and there in a chicken coop where none of the chickens even talk to each other, let alone know each other, or look at each other. You don't even see the stars, except for camera flashes."

"Why'd you go dere in de first place, child?" Lottie asked, starting the first braid.

"Opportunity. Freedom. Flattery. Time for change. I guess I was a novelty in a business always looking for something new. 'Jungle girl', daughter of the West Indian Albert Schweitzer." She stopped talking, overwhelmed by the abundance of the stars, the fireflies, and her love for the old woman braiding her hair with fluid fingers.

"Just between you, me and the tree frogs, I came home because I was starting to believe my own press clippings."

185

Danielle talked, while Lottie listened and braided, far into the night.

Chapter 14

Gage: The Hotelier

Though Gage had been up late playing poker with his guests, he was the first person into the Hotel's kitchen that morning. A cup of fresh-ground Colombian coffee in one hand, a pack of Benson and Hedges cigarettes in the other hand and he took his usual chair just outside the kitchen doors, on the verandah facing the pending sunrise. Like Orpheus with a hangover, he felt the day might not come were he not there to welcome it. On those rare occasions when he wasn't present and yet the sun did come up, he wrote it off against what God owed him, credit that he'd accumulated with the Almighty.

Why he had credit wasn't clear even to Gage since he'd lived the kind of life that the Pastor at the Evangelical church just down the hill spent entire sermons railing against. Cautioning adventurous souls who might be tempted to follow Gage's ways that it was a fast and slippery slope to "Eternal Damnation". Still, for all the pastor's best efforts to tarnish Gage's reputation, or maybe because of it, there was a waiting list of applicants for positions at the Hotel, positions which were vacated only by retirement or death. And over the years his staff had become as integral an attraction to the Hotel as the hand-cut stones in the old plantation buildings.

The original plantation was a complex of a dozen heavy stone structures with walls a meter thick, faced both outside and inside with hand-hewn stone blocks while the center was filled with a mixture of clay, called "tara", lime from charred coals, and cane fiber. Because of the walls, the resulting buildings could withstand hurricane-force winds, yet they were sufficiently malleable to flex in an earthquake.

187

The Roosevelt Plantation was built in 1764 around the sugar mill, a great conical tower, flat on the top to carry the turret supporting the blades of great windmills, which caught the wind and turned the giant rollers that crushed the cane stocks for the juice to make sugar, molasses and most of all, rum. Gage had turned the top floor of the mill into the honeymoon suite. Stables, a coopery, cisterns, warehouse, foundry, baking ovens, slave quarters, and of course the main mansion, called the Great House — collectively it was a self-sufficient village, all converted by Gage into Le Hotel Lemon.

Gage fit well into the Caribbean. But he fit well wherever he landed, his ranch in Wyoming, the polo team at Cornell University, the 21 Club in Manhattan, and especially, on Island at Dick's Bar. Especially Dick's Bar on a full-moon night when the tree frogs and brass trumpets caught a reggae beat that turned the human form fluid in dance.

"Like writhing well-oiled eels in de bottom of a coal mine," Gage would tell his guests, enticing them, after Saturday night supper at the Hotel, to come with him to Dick's. Most did. Returning with stories of dancing until they thought their hearts would stop or explode, then dancing some more.

Gage got on well with everyone but one, the pastor down the hill from the Hotel. Gage was a sometimes theist who had little use for organised religion, particularly as it was practiced at the "Church of the Holy Jump-up Jesus", as he called the Pentecostal Evangelical Church of the Second Coming down the hill.

Gage preferred to gamble with God rather than begging or negotiating. From the pastor's perspective, Gage was a constant source of material for fresh sermons.

"Writhing Like Well Oiled Eels!" became one of his most popular sermons. In it, the pastor likened Dick's Bar Saturday night to Dante's Hell... except that the oil on the "writhing eels" was boiling -- for Eternity!

Gage was of average height, solidly built and grounded with long arms and large hands, and even though in his mid-sixties, he was handsome, with the rugged countenance and stature that were the material ad agencies used to sell cigarettes. His features were the product both of living with his face to the elements, and by inheritance from strong German stock. Being both a realistic pragmatist and an incurable romantic accounted for his success in gambling. With Gage you never knew what he was holding. In crisis, of which came only occasionally, he was the cause. Gage was unfaltering, possessing that easy-going confidence of one who has seen humanity's worst horrors and vowed not to contribute, instead filling life was his horizon. No matter how hard his situation, there was solace in knowing he'd experienced the worse.

But it was his eyes that set the man apart and left an indelible impression. Engaging and open to getting to know you, they were, one sensed, holding secrets. Calm eyes, kind eyes, grey-blue from sitting downwind of too many campfires, he claimed, and endeared Gage particularly to his enemies. Accepting, non-judgmental, at peace with whatever they beheld. Humour that saw the best first and didn't dwell with what he couldn't change, that attracted friends, both men and women. He never meant to attract, and maybe that was his attraction. Gage never boasted, bragged nor shared confidences. Moreover, he was excruciatingly honourable, discreet and ... unrepentant.

He was a man's man, but by choice of his own. It was the very beginning of the war and the allies were looking for young pilots. He trained and went to Canada to go into combat since the US hadn't committed

.   He'd been a teenage pilot, surviving sortie after sortie over Europe in World War II, until death caused by a single act, made thousands of feet above the landscape, meant fear had no hold upon him except curiosity. When Gage was 25, Ernest Hemingway befriended him in Colorado and they fly-fished for rainbows in the

189

ripples just off the fast water with the art of concentration, timing and delicate finesse.

Later, when Gage took the boat El Lemon south from Miami, destined for Venezuela, they fished in Cuba for marlin, and drank Pimm's gin and tonics till the dawn, and then fished again.

"Each man," Hemingway wrote of those times, "was addicted to the suspense of anticipation... adrenaline addicts waiting for that electrifying moment when the fury of the sea exploded, and the scream of the reel grudgingly gave line against the drag of a raw superior force. It is sex with the sea. A mortal struggle with a savage lover that you can neither subdue nor change, only capture and kill."

The attraction of Gage for the ladies was that he was attentive! Never a seducer, he was easily seduced. His greatest sexual delight was in giving his partner pleasure; learning her body, the contours and the way it was wired was an ultimate aphrodisiac for both lover and loved.

The Caribbean helped fuel Gage's attractiveness. The smell of jasmine, the sounds, the colours predisposed women to seek romance, or create it when it wasn't there. With Gage, it always was there, just on the other side of his smoky blue eyes. If he had a technique, it was the same as trout fishing... the art of concentration, timing and delicate finesse. Occasionally a lady, bewildered by the abundance she felt for Gage, would try to take possession. But it always ended tenderly sad, and reluctantly they returned to their husbands.

It was his boat *El Lemon* and a hurricane named Maria that brought Gage to Cuba and finally to St. Augustine. He had won the boat in an upstairs salon on the second floor of the 21 Club. By others' measure, the stakes were high, but in the wee hours of the morning, mere money is no longer interesting to the men with too much, against a wager of man's possessions or, better, his destiny was the only intrigue remaining. On one of those nights, Gage had put his ranch (which he'd recently inherited from his mother) up

190

against an investment banker's teak-and-brass sport-fishing boat. In truth, Gage wasn't risking that much, for he knew that the State of Wyoming would never recognise a title secured in a card game held in a foreign land like New York.

And so it was that when hurricane Maria drove *El Lemon* with her small crew of women, neither of them his wife, onto the rocks off St. Augustine, Gage accepted his fate with characteristic savoir-faire, and with the insurance settlement for the over-insured *"Lemon"* he bought the ruins of the Roosevelt Plantation.

And, with the same enthusiasm as one on a mission for the Lord, he converted the ruined estate into a quiet hotel catering to rich romantics, some of whom he had known since childhood. Born to old money and an only son with four sisters, Gage knew nothing of poverty nor abandonment. When his father died, and his sisters slipped into Madison Avenue mansions, Gage went West, trading his Princeton letter sweater for a deerskin jacket. It was there that he'd inherited a long-neglected cattle ranch at the base of the eagle-claw mountains in the Rockies. And pooling his charm and uncommonly good common sense, he parlayed his assets into a successful summer guest ranch.

But his winters were boringly quiet, and when fate dealt him three queens against a banker's two pair, and the hurricane Maria converted his once floating winnings into the Hotel, Gage invited his summer guest-list from the ranch to join him in a <u>new</u> "Wild West" ... the West Indies. He was offering his long time guests two retreats; the working dude ranch in Wyoming, and in the winter the joys and climate were resorts for all seasons, offering both summer and winter amusement and adventure for those who had neither.

As the first shafts of morning sun struck the volcano behind Gage he flipped his cigarette ashes over the railing into the hibiscus. There was an ashtray on the verandah table, but according to Gage, cigarette ashes, like the ashes of the cremated, are best set free to the wind. The same applied to the burning cigarette butts, much to the anguish of Santavos, the gardener.

"Mon, someday you's gonna burn she doon and den where we be?"

"Let her burn," Gage would say with a nonchalant wave of his hand. "Put us all out of our misery!"

"Maybe you's, but <u>not</u> mine, Mis-ah Gage."

Soon Felix joined him on the kitchen veranda. He was a tall black man who moved with a controlled grace and the energy-saving stride of a basketball star walking back to the bench after six straight points. Felix was the bartender, assistant manager, and as much a part of the hotel as the great windmill which ran the plantation. He was born just down the road and had been behind the bar since before he was old enough to drink, (which he didn't do), let alone serve, and there was no drinking age on St. Augustine.

At the plantation, he had evolved from a cricket-crazy, gangly youth who knocked mahogany nuts across the ghaut in a pretended test match between the "Remember Me" village and the rest of the world; into a long-of-leg, handsome man — the descendant of a line of Zulu kings, according to one of the guests with self-proclaimed psychic powers.

"Morning, bossman," Felix now grinned at Gage, his gold star tooth catching the rich morning light. "What's on for the day?"

Gage was slowly sifting back through the past evening's events, trying to remember who said they wanted to do what. "Cantrells want to go over to Henchcliff reef fishing this afternoon, so best have the boat fueled and ready. Other than that, it's pests and pestilence as usual!"

Felix went into the kitchen, poured himself a cup of coffee and flipped on the cook's radio before returning outside to sit down beside Gage. Both men sat quietly staring out at the Caribbean Sea as it transformed from Tabasco-chili-red to Tasco silver, and finally to the Caribbean pastel-blue that paint companies tried to mimic ... but never successfully. Unaccustomed to being part of the World News, the two men listened intently that day to the BBC's local relay out of Trinidad about the building hurricane. "You think that storm off Guadeloupe gonna give us licks?" Felix asked.

"It would be about time. The island hasn't had a good cleaning since Maria." Gage said it without enthusiasm. "But I hope not."

Mildred, the cook, bustled through the door, flustered as usual that the two men were there *before* her. Early each morning was the only time Gage came into her kitchen and she worried that maybe she'd missed a pot in the sink, or one of the girls had failed to sweep the floor. Mildred was a living endorsement of her own cooking: though each morning she had to climb the long hill to Hotel Lemon, she only grew sideways rather than up. But on an island where wide women are sought after, she abounded in suitors and joy. Each of her seven children had a different father, yet all shared their mother's physique and propensity for happiness.

"Disgust'n." She slapped a dishtowel on the kitchen counter near the verandah doors, chasing off invisible ashes that might flutter in from Gage's cigarette. "It's a filthy habit you got's. Why you never partake of the ashtray?"

"Don't want to cause you any more work having to wash it." Gage smiled.

"Da truth be known, Youse more work den all me chillens lumped together."

"That's my point. You have too much work already."

"Disgust'n." She flapped again and mumbled to the stove as she turned on the gas. "Felix, we gonna need a new tank dis day."

"Consider she done, my love."

"And don't you be 'my loving' me. I got's enough chillen what wants my time without one of yourn."

"Mildred," Gage winked at Felix, "why'd you never come to me to make babies?"

'Cus you's the most stubborn mon what God fetched to dis earth. Stubborn with disgust'n habits! Now, out of my kitchen and do you's skullduggery elsewhere while I make the breakfast for civilised folks."

193

The men leisurely finished their coffees on the verandah and soon the kitchen filled with the rest of the staff, and like prayer flags on a Tibetan prayer-wheel, orders for banana pancakes, papaya fritters and crepes d'Lemon and soon began to flutter over the stove. After having breakfast with the early-rising guests who had gone to bed at a reasonable hour, Gage walked across the central courtyard where once slaves were sold and families and lives destroyed.

Lucy was standing in front of the big reservation board talking on the telephone, " I'm sorry, we have nothing available between January and mid-May". She listened and frowned. "That is next year. If you wanted to book for the year after that, we can accommodate you.

Alright, thank you for thinking of us, Mr. Brookes. I'll pencil you in. Is there an address we can reach you at as the date comes due?" Dutifully she wrote it on the board.

"Which Brookes?" Gage asked his reservation manager. Lucy was an attractive native woman who treated everyone with an extra measure of attention. But the real skill that made Lucy invaluable was efficiency at doing many tasks at the same time. She was the nerve center of the hotel, booking rooms, monitoring the finances, coordinating the staff. And she was very pretty and loved to dress in stylish clothes, making her own outfits from pictures in *Vogue* of "Modern Maidens". The guests enjoyed being around her class and youthful energy.

"Doesn't matter which 'Brookes', Gage, we're still booked for two years in advance." She'd worked for Gage for sixteen years, since she was sixteen.

"Who's coming into Bungalow #10?"

"Richard Sutter and his wife. Remember him, the man with the International Red Cross? Are you here for supper?" Lucy asked. "Jonathan is bringing Bana for dinner."

"Jonathan Douglas and Bana Bordeaux? Now that's an interesting combination."

"Don't you be devil-mouthing Bana, boss." She feigned a warning look. Bana was the role model for a large number of Caribbean women who studied the fashion magazines to see what Bana was wearing or designing. Now the word was out that she'd come home to stay.

"Lucy, I've known Bana since she was born, I knew her father as my brother, but she is such a breath of fresh magnolia blossom, and Jonathan is, well…" He sifted through the list of characteristics of a New York banker and Harvard graduate lawyer, settling for "a connoisseur of fine wines". But then that, Gage realised, sounded like he was "devil-mouthing" Jonathan.

"No, I mean, Great! Of course I'll be here for supper, I like them both very much. Have Cannon bring up a bottle of Chateau Cordinny 1958 from the cellar and ask him to remove the label. We'll see if we can finally stump Mister Douglas." He reached to the back of his desk and turned on the radio. "Why was the radio off?"

"I got so tired of the storm warnings for Guadeloupe and the Lesser Antilles that I shut it off."

"Lucy?! <u>We</u> are in the Lesser Antilles! Did they say anything about St. Augustine or Saint Kitts?"

"I don't know, I turned it off, remember? Come on, boss, pick up the pace," she teased. "Now what about the Sutters?"

"Of course, put them at my table, we can catch up on the latest world disasters and calamities."

The phone rang, but Lucy stood there looking at him without answering it. She was waiting for something, but Gage didn't know what.

"And?" Lucy looked down and rubbed her eyebrow with the long silver nail of her forefinger but didn't say anything more.

"Ok, Ok," Gage smirked. "I understand. Bana is coming tonight." He let the statement stand, then added. "Will you be my dinner partner tonight?"

195

"If you insist! she smiled and returned to her desk to answer the phone.

The local radio was on but only on background. Gage was interested in the weather report and his plans for fishing.

"... and now for weather for the Caribbean... Sun with some high and overcast for the near future. The National Association for Ocean and Atmospheric Administration reports a tropical depression forming north by northwest in the Atlantic ...

Gage turned the radio down. "This time of year, when isn't there a tropical depression forming" Gage muttered to himself.

"Lucy, have you seen Felix I haven't seen him since before breakfast?"

"He passed a few minutes ago in the Land Rover, going to the garage."

"Ok, there's been a change of plans. I think we could get hit by this hurricane and I want Felix to prepare a few things just in case."

"What about the Cantrells?

"I'll take the Cantrells fishing." He started to leave, and turned, "and Lucy I need you to listen to the radio on the hour and get the coordinates of the storm, and the speed and direction. Then put it on the map in the phone book.

"Don't be late coming home. We have a date."

"If I am, maybe you could be the hostess and chat-up Bana?"

"You can count on that!"

Gage caught up with Felix loading the fishing gear and explained the change in plans. "I think we need to be ready just in case this hurricane turns left instead of right."

Felix was relieved; he'd been through a hurricane on Barbados as a kid and knew that you <u>had</u> to be prepared.

"So, what I think we have to do is get the gas company to bring up five or six bottles of propane instead of two. And then take some bleach and pour it into those two upper cisterns so they'll be purified if we need them. Also, would you have Sampson put the pool furniture in the shed and just leave a few things out for the guests?

196

Oh, and get an extra drum of petrol for the generator. If we do take licks, we'll have to run the refrigeration and pumps off it.

"What else?" He thought for a moment. "Oh, and the most important thing, bring up a few cases of booze from the well house so if we get hit, we can have one hell of a party."

"And if we don't?"

"Well, we can have one hell of a party to celebrate that we didn't!"

******

Captain Palli had *Le Petit*, a smaller version of the *Le Lemon*, that had sunk bringing Gage to the Island was at the dock when the hotel van arrived. Palli was a short man with arms the size of his thighs, each sporting a shoulder tattoo that was reduced to smudged blobs and no longer intelligible, both done in Miami's Dade County jail. He wore a sleeveless t- shirt, ragged cutoffs and a baseball cap that read, "Le Petit Lemon" and below that "Gone fishing".

"Palli," Gage hailed him. "You remember the Cantrells from last year?" The Captain frowned. "Oh, sure you do, you and their daughter, Chantelle are old fishing buddies." The girl was seventeen, tan and athletic. She stuck out her hand, obviously happy to be going fishing again with Palli the pirate. She too wore a "Le Petit" cap, though hers was not as faded as Palli's.

The Cantrells had been coming to the Hotel for years and Chantelle had grown up deep-sea fishing, landing the smaller ones her father hooked, graduating to marlin and blue fin. If she had her way, they'd fish every day of their vacation. Equipped with rods, bait, ice cooler and a large food basket that Mildred had prepared, they cast off.

Gage took over the wheel while Palli went downstairs to the galley, returning with two "soft" (virgin) rum punches for the ladies and hard scotch on the rocks for the men. He also carried a platter of hors d'oeuvres. Gage turned on the tape deck.

"Mario Lonza ok? Might as well settle in, it's about a half-hour run out to the banks." Chantelle and her mother went below to

197

change into their bathing suits. Palli climbed the stairs to the wheel deck and handed Gage his drink. The two men stood silent on the top deck for some time, scanning the horizon. "You got a valid passport?" Gage asked in a low voice that only Palli could hear.

"Si claro!, por que?"

"If this storm comes north, I may want you to take the boat up to the US. Virgins tomorrow. We'll watch it but just in case, when we get back, fuel up both tanks and I'll bring some food down and the ship-to-shore radio on board tomorrow. There may be guests who want to get out if the planes haven't already flown out of the airport. *Comprende?*"

"U.S. Virgin Islese... no es possibla... Hay una problema con los Federales."

"Ok, how about one of the British Islands?" Gage asked. "How about Antigua? Are you wanted there... Antigua?"

"Esta muy bueno... puedo tambien Juanita?"

"Juanita?! Mon, this is not a paid holiday for the staff. Business as usual."

"As usual," Palli smirked. "Ok, if I'm to die, a man should not be alone," he said in English to make sure Gage got the message.

"If the boat isn't full of guests, she can go. Esta bien?"

"Esta bien."

"I thought you got that 'thing' with U.S. Customs straightened out."

"We did." Palli looked at Gage and smirked. "They takes me boat and I got me freedom. Nothing to bother about."

"I *don't* bother, because my name is 'Gage' and I can go wherever I please."

Palli shrugged. *"Manana."*

Palli had just appeared one night at the marina in Cuba, in fact, the night before Gage and his female crew were setting off for Venezuela to go bone fishing. Said he'd heard from Hemingway that Gage might need a skipper who knew the Caribbean, and he was anxious to get off-island.

198

Since the trip from Miami to Cuba had been easy, Gage said no thanks. Later he'd realise that had he hired Palli, the El *Lemon* would still be afloat. But then he wouldn't be in St. Augustine. Then, a few years later, Gage bought another fishing boat, much smaller than the *El Lemon*. Shortly thereafter, Gage recognised Palli at Dick's Bar, asked him if he was still looking for work, and hired him on the spot. Gage had a policy that he trusted everyone until they proved that he shouldn't. Palli had been captaining *Le Petit* ever since.

****

"So how did you do?" asked Felix when Gage and the Cantrells got back to the hotel

"Chantelle landed two nice tunas, a forty-pounder and one that was close to sixty-five. Chantelle is happy, the cook will be happy, what more can a man want from the sea?" Gage laughed. "How did it go with you?"

"We did everything on the list, but I wonder if we shouldn't disconnect all of the down-spouting from the roofs to the cisterns. Who knows the shit the storm might leave on the roofs. Also, I think we should pull the radio antenna out of the mahogany tree and run it under the eaves of one of the buildings.

"Both good ideas. But let's wait on both until we know for sure the hurricane's coming. Neither job will take too long. What about you and your family? Where will you go if "huff" comes to "puff"? You know that you're welcome here. This place has seen three hundred years of hurricanes, it should withstand another.

"I'll think about it and bring it up with Eulanda,"

"Lionel called from Zetland." Said Felix "They want to know if we want four freezers of frozen meat. Their generator has been waiting for parts and if the Island-power is turned off, the meat will just spoil, so best someone get some use out of it.

199

"Four freezers? Where can we put them where there are already outlets? I assume they are 220 volts?"

"To my way of thinking, we could set them up along the wall of the cooperage next to the kitchen doors. Maybe cover them with tarps and tablecloths and use them for sideboards. No telling how many mouths we's gonna feed before this is over."

Gage picked up the phone on the corner of the bar. "Lionel, Felix told me about your offer for the freezers. Our generators are working fine, but we'll take the freezers only if you and Ronda and your two children move down here. Do you have any guests?" He listened.

"Are they anxious to get off-island? Because Palli is taking *Le Petit* to Antigua and they could go with him. Tell them that I want to make our move tomorrow at first light before the seas start building, so they'll have to either come here or meet Palli at the dock."

Gage listened as Lionel explained the situation to his guests and then came back on the phone. "Great. They'll come down in the morning and ride out with Palli."

"Since you won't have any guests, why don't you and Ronda and the kids move down here with us? You can stay in the Sugar Mill."

There was another pause, then Lionel returned. "That's a generous offer. When do you want to get the freezers?"

After the two trips it took to haul the freezers and their contents over, place them in the Cooperage, fill them again and cover them with tablecloths and floral arrangements, Gage barely had time to change before it was time to sit down for supper -- but his presence was unnecessary.

Lucy was the hostesses with charm and gaiety, taking drink orders, introducing the new guests. And, of course, making sure Bana's "Ting" was full... and by association that Jonathan's scotch had ice.

Though the dining room was originally a large, cavernous space, Gage had divided it into little islands of privacy, with lights at the

200

bases of stone walls and exotic ornamental plants casting leafy shadows on the vaulted ceiling, creating an atmosphere of elegance and grandeur reminiscent of a romantic period inhabited by antebellum Ladies and Lords of the manors. The furniture was expensive bent bamboo from Borneo covered with light pastel, tropical material.

The overall effect was peaceful indulgence in the shadow of history. Lucy had obviously given some thought to the seating. Jonathan and Bana had both requested, independently, to sit next to each other, so she put Mrs. Sutter on the other side of Jonathan and, as Gage expected, she placed herself next to Bana, leaving Gage to sit between the Sutters... normally a bad position because while one half of the couple was trying to tell a story in one ear, the other half would be correcting it in the other. But the Sutters were very interesting people. She worked with Doctors Without Borders, while he was Northern Hemisphere Director of Emergency Response for the International Red Cross.

A chronic student of human nature, Gage was intrigued watching the dynamics between Jonathan and Bana. They were certainly in deep "interest" with each other, and neither was apparently concerned over the difference in age or background. Gage was non-judgmental. What he found most interesting was seeing a completely different side of Jonathan.

God, he was such a stuffed-shirt when he first came on-island twenty-five years ago. He'd designed his own house, financed it and watched as it was built, but it was his wife Mallory who made it happen, building a bridge of mutual respect with the workmen, ultimately forming bonds between her family and local community, insisting that the Douglas children go to the local public school in Poppy Dawn rather than to the private school.

Then Mallory died and Jonathan had become a rogue elephant, wandering the night trumpeting his pain. Gage sought out at least one interesting thing in each person he met, and in Jonathan it was his gift for recognising wine. He was a connoisseur par excellence, figuring out the type of grape and narrowing its origin down to one of three vineyards, but he was humble, adding tentative phrases such as "I believe it could be…" and "I may be wrong," though both he and Gage knew he was right. Gage was in awe, challenging him to expand his taste for many wines he'd never considered.

The main course was fresh tuna, compliments of Chantelle, cooked in a light dill sauce on a bed of curried rice, with fried plantains dusted with coconut gratings. After supper, Gage rose to make a toast.

"I have a few introductions I'd like to make, but first I'd like to offer a toast to Madam 'Sea Huntress'." He raised his glass, "to Chantelle Cantrell, who provided the fabulous yellow tuna for our supper… and many more suppers to come."

The guests lifted their glasses. Chantelle rose, embarrassed, wearing the lovely dress of a young woman but with the arms of a young man and the Pirate Palli's faded cap on her head.

"Also, I want to thank Mildred Rutherford for preparing this magnificent feast." The cheers and calls of the diners demanding her presence and finally Mildred came out of the kitchen. She beamed, as did four of her seven children. Numbers five and six were home looking after number seven, she explained, and everyone, especially her four proud children, laughed.

"Disgusting!" she growled under her breath at Gage as she passed on her way to the kitchen.

"So, for those of you not from the Caribbean, or for that matter the world, I'd like to introduce" — Bana caught his eye and shook her head pleadingly — "to introduce Bana Bordeaux straight from the Tanner Estate very near here." Which was technically true, with side trips to New York, Paris and Rome in between. "And her distinguished escort and Island toy-boy', the eminent barrister Jonathan Douglas, wine connoisseur extraordinaire." Gage enjoyed teasing Jonathan.

"Here, here," toasted the gathering, having made the transition from saluting the person to saluting for the sake of the salute and the drink that followed.

"And finally, I'd like to introduce Richard and Linda Sutter, who have been coming here for twelve years now. Linda is with 'Doctors Without Borders' and Richard is 'honcho grande' with the Red Cross." Glasses were raised again, and Lucy made sure they were refilled promptly.

"So. With that out of the way, there's something else I'd like to mention," he said while the tables were being cleared. "As you likely know, there is a hurricane south of Guadeloupe, which is roughly 150 kilometers that way from here." He pointed beyond Montserrat. "Right now they do not know which way it will go; by tomorrow morning the weather bureau will have a better picture… and it's unlikely that we will be in its path. Last prediction was that it was headed back out into the Atlantic, but hurricanes are like women, they can change their minds in a minute." There was polite laughter, restrained by concern. "Otherwise, if they were predictable, they'd be called 'him'a'canes." This time the laugh was louder, but it was nervous energy escaping through vents.

"For you who might want to get off-island, *Le Petit* is going over to Antigua tomorrow, if necessary, and you can go on from there. And you who decide to stay put, may I point out that old Roosevelt Plantation has seen many hurricanes, including the one that brought me to St. Augustine in the first place. However, I take no responsibility for your safety, only your entertainment. And understand, if you decide to escape our company, do not feel you are showing the white feather. If I didn't have to be here, I'd probably not stay." Again, there was polite laughter, and no one took the comment seriously. "So, think it over, have a good night's sleep and we'll talk about it in the morning."

"To hurricanes!" came a toast of bravado and rum punch.

"Oh God," Sutter of the Red Cross groaned.

"To *Le Hotel Lemon*, long may she stand!"

"I see it now, an epic film," said the movie director from southern California who saw every situation as a movie script. "Mariah! That's what we'll call it. A multi-million-dollar movie about humans fighting against the ultimate forces of nature, an ultimate action film, monster cars fleeing the wind, men with tawny muscles grappling with the hurricane, women with ..."

"Oh God," groaned Sutter again. He'd seen too many disasters to think of them as anything but the tragedies they were. Hopefully the producer would leave on *Le Petit*.

Chapter 15

Rasta Roost: Evening

"Twenty-three," Caraja said through his inhaled breath. "Dat's how many mill towers I counts from where we sits. Das a lotta land and cane to feed all de machinery, and a lot of souls." He passed the rollie to Garth. "De whole of de cane industry was fueled on souls." He exhaled.

"That vex you up?" Garth asked, stealing language from his students.

"Naw, das den, and now's so." The farmer shrugged after a long silence. "Look towards Guadeloupe. Look-at de horizon. See how de clouds being pushed."

The tops of high, roly-poly clouds were being knocked down flat by high winds from the North. "Das not a good sign, but whatever the weather gives us, we must give thanks."

Garth watched Caraja, mesmerised by the ease with which he sat on his haunches on the edge of the fire-pit, crouched like a monkey, eyes quick to detail like a mongoose. That was a good way to describe Caraja, half mongoose, half monkey, with a brain superior to most homo sapiens.

For the longest time they sat in silence, staring into the fire. "This place is paradise, way up here in the clouds." A thick moving curtain of clouds had settled above the mountain, revealing glimpses of the full moon through tears in the cloud fabric. Since he first saw Caraja's and Myah's cottage, nestled into the jungle, he had a feeling that in the two years he'd occupied The Rock, he'd missed the most important part, the rhythm of the local life of which he was slowly becoming.

"Naw mon, de air's too thin up here. All you get is headaches and nosebleeds. Leave you dizzy and you's headset full of foolishness."

"I thought dat be de smoke." Garth unthinkingly slipped into St. Augustinian slang.

"Naw," Caraja said incredulously, "De 'herb' be what keep you's head clear," and he laughed. But soon, silence settled over their camp.

"I see de fat lady come to de fire," Caraja said into the flames.

"Which fat lady das-be?"

"You's fat lady. 'Stomp'... de Stamp Lady what wants to hold you here on-island till you's an old wrinkled-man."

Garth laughed. He <u>had</u> been thinking about her at that moment and wondering how he would get the exit stamps by Monday, or if he even needed them. Maybe he should just say to hell with it, catch Brother's fast cigarette-boat that the smugglers used to run to St. Maarten — go over to St. Kitts and fly out from there. Immigration would not care over there. Let the St. Augustine Interpol track him down in Wyoming.

The idea made him laugh. But maybe he should stop in at Stomp's office on the way to the airport and see if her attitude had changed. Maybe she'd had a man over the weekend."

"She no gonna change, ya know." Caraja looked at Garth. "You see, de t'ing dat hold dat woman back from ever grow'n-up is she-own-said-self. When you look at she, you see right off how big she be. She carry six stones of *waste* and she don't want to part with it for nothing. She'd rather dream someone what loves she 'waste' gonna come along and snatch she up like in ' her novels — rather than loose an ounce."

"Josiah Taxi said de same," Garth said with a grunt. "Whatever ails she, to my way of thinking she's the most disgusting woman in the Caribbean!" He shook his head and reached for the joint.

"Mon! Das a bad attitude. She's no more disgusting den a spoilt child what got to have she-own way all de time. And when she don'ts get she, she play de bully and fuss and make all sorts of noise 'til she does. But de truth, she's afraid of change. And she's gonna do everything possible to make chure it don't come to she. She'd see you and me dead 'fore she give up she habits, so' she fat."

Caraja took back the spliff, took a long pull and rocked his head back, his eyes closed. "Dis gonna be a fine crop, I t'inks dis gonna be de best year ever! Tomorrow we harvest de rest of she, and water what not ready to spring."

He exhaled, his mind returning to the last thread before the tangent. Caraja maintained that the loss of short-term memory was just a momentary problem, like a train going down one track, then exiting the station on another track. Sometimes the train gets sidetracked to a far-distant village of the imagination, but if you are patient, he believes, it will finally return to the starting station — or so he believed, and because he did that was how it was.

"And another reason das a bad attitude…" Caraja blurted, on track again. "When you make someone you's enemy, some part of you holds dem close cus of anger, hatred, revenge and de like… sometimes closer den you hold dose you loves. 'Me no-know de mon's name.' Das how we deals width it when someone really vex us up."

"Meaning?"

"Meaning, from then on you are always strangers with that person. You no longer know he name, who he be."

Stomp didn't warrant that, Garth thought, she was but a momentary problem. But he did manage to make at least one serious enemy while he was on-island, and his name was Settee. Settee began testing him from day one on the Island, making loud and public remarks about the Peace Corps and Indians. "Wagon burner," he once said of Garth, loud and in the market. No one noticed except to question, why would one burn his wagons… what a waste when wagon/carts were so expensive.

"Well, dere is one I'd keep close just to keep an eye on him." Garth's brows folded into a scowl. "De mon dey call Settee."

"And what he do to you?"

"He's a racist. If you's not black, you's someone to ridicule. I watched him on the streets with de tourists. Telling dem dey should stay home, dey's not wanted."

"You're a racist," said Caraja casually. "Not a Klan racist 'bout black folks, but a soft racist against whites. Dey's not you kind but you still have a lot in common, and you don't like to notice she cus you want to be separate from dem."

Garth was taken back. "Ja! I sees you width de tourists and dey's looking for help and you just walk by like you's deaf." Caraja didn't lift his eyes from the fire.

"'Bout Stomp, most people now days got more choices den dey know what to do with. Stomp don't have any, in she own self's view. Maybe she sees how unhappy some people be with so many choices, so she turn de udder way." He took a toke. "I see in de people what comes here... dey can't just be someplace and enjoy where dey is. Dey's always weighing de choices, mov'n round for a better perch. And den dey feel bad when dey can't decide which perch be de best. Dat make dem frustrated and unsatisfied."

Garth thought about Caraja's analysis. "Das fo chure, mon!" he agreed, trying desperately to follow the Rasta's train.

"Instead, dey should let Jah have He grace and rejoice what He lay before dem. De old ones say, you learn to eat what's before you and wants for no more. If mangoes in season, we eats mangoes. Mango soup, all kinda mango drinks, mangoes on you's cereal in de morning, mango stew at de end of de day. And when she be potato season, we does eat potatoes, maybe trade for dis or dat what's also in season, but eat mainly what's before us.

"Today —" he started to laugh, his huffing-train getting traction. "Today you go back to Wyoming and go to de supermarket and you can have mangoes with you's potatoes anytime Youse want!"

The train was building steam. "Maybe... even a french fry and mango sandwich, mango and monkey-water, mango and communion water. Too many choices," he said with a sigh, handing what was left of the home-rolled back to Garth.

"But Stomp is a special. She gonna take up what Jah give she, and what Jah give you. She got no choice."

"No choices and too many, das de problem! Oh, I's width-chew, mon." Garth was starting to slur, marveling at how brilliantly Caraja had distilled his thoughts upon an attuned audience and a sympathetic audience. Not one to usually imitate, he was proud of his language and his heritage, and was surprised at how much the local dialect had seeped into his speech. He knew that the dope had freed his tongue to swim with speech, but, of late, he'd noticed he was starting to dream in St. Augustinian, words full and round, sliding one into the other without collision, syllables divorced from one word and married to the next. And not just the speech of the characters in the dreams, but his own responses were brilliant. He wondered whether he might have a West Indian accent when he got home. No, it was the dope. When he got home he'd be right in the tongue. The desert sun would dry up the mildew growing between his brain cells. Anyway, with Caraja, there was just one language.

"How you come so wise, Caraja?" Garth teased him, studying the Rasta's face in the flames. Caraja's smile danced in the glow for a long time until, just as Garth was going to ask again, he spoke up.

"Licks!" he said firmly. "When we is youths, we's taught respect. Respect for all sorts o' things. Things what most people don't give a second thought to. Respect for work, for example. Everybody had dey chores, gett'n de goats, pack'n water. And when you slack back and say naw, me no go fo' de goats, maybe de horseraces suit me better. right?" he asked rhetorically. "When dat happen you disrespect Youse duties. And if I does partake of de races, chure enough me mudder was gonna hear-so an' give me licks. And bad ones too! With de palm broom she use to sweep the yard." There was no resentment in Caraja's face or speech.

"Respect for all sorts of t'ings. For de land, Youse-self, Youse neighbors, even Youse enemy. Most folks say, like I said,

'Me no-know de mon's face' when someone speaks of his enemy. The enemy do no longer exist in dey's mind. We's taught you greet all adults when dey pass, even if dey be me worst and give dem da greeting. And if she spies us going by dat person without wishing dem de "goods"... good morning, good health, so on, boy-Lordy we'd get de scolding so bad we'd wish for licks instead. Give respect. Respect's is the glue what holds us all together on dis rock."

"Which rock, St. Augustine or Earth?" Garth lay on his back against the mahogany trunk, watching embers from the fire rise to the heavens, wishes, hopes, prayers, messages becoming stars.

"Both! Dey be de self-same!" Caraja huffed, but the train was too tired to build much steam even though he thoroughly enjoyed the analogy and made it a note to study it more closely at another time. Garth decided it was the most profound thing he'd ever heard, and particularly on a night of such dazzling ideas like the "choices" diatribe.

Garth dozed off. When he slid just as easily back to consciousness, the fire was but a few hard-knot coals. Caraja still sat by the fire. Slowly Garth pulled his body out of the contour of the tree. His eyes, accustomed to the dark of sleep, found the trail to the edge of the ghaut. Holding the swing vine with one hand, he peed out over the abyss. As a kid, he loved doing that off mesas in

Wyoming. Buffalo jumps, ridges with long, gradual slopes leading out of the prairie, terminating in vertical cliffs hundreds of feet high. His people herded the buffalo over the cliffs.

"For de t'ings of de night, dis fire be like dey's Fourth of July." Caraja raised his voice above the noise of the night when Garth returned

There is no silence in the jungle, Garth realised as he returned to ancient mahogany tree. Especially at night when all the cold-blooded or light-sensitive, or merely timid, creatures come out to feed and court. Tree frogs as loud as the tabernacle choir back in Salt Lake City. Crickets, geckos and woodslips; and they're just the "callers"; beyond them there is another layer of sounds. If he listened closely, he could pick out the shrill, aerodynamic whistle of a fruit bat, diving for insects that had become mesmerised by the fire and were flirting with suicide. Fighter planes, they dropped from the night "Shee...uph!" and climbed back into the dark in a perfect hyperbolic arch. One less moth to die in the flames.

His thoughts seemed to have a mind of their own as they flowed over him without effort, he a passenger on a train when moments before he was the stationmaster. Again, he attributed it to Caraja's ganja. Garth had done peyote, but that was always in a spiritual ceremony. The herb was not nearly as hard on his body as the cactus buttons.

"Sheee-uph!" came another dive-bomber bat, scooping in flight a cocoa moth hovering above the fire. He remembered then a song, "Fruit Bat Love".

It was by a group from St. Augustine that had gone off-island and made it big. In fact, Garth heard them in Washington, D.C., when he was there training for the Peace Corps.

"Ever hear of a group from here called the "Sole Survivors?" Garth asked.

Caraja looked up from the fire to see if Garth was teasing him. "You legging me? Mon, dey's me cousins!" He looked back to the fire. "I was dere when Trump and Thump first tried dey's turn at music."

"Who's Trump and Thump?"

"Deys de two main men in the Sole Survivors."

"You mean the trumpet player and the drummer?"

"De very ones, mon, de very ones. Jacob Webbe and Alvin Liburg, known on-island as Trump and Thump... and to de rest of the world as de 'Sole Survivors'."

"Wow. How did that come to be?" Garth leaned forward to hear better.

"Hmm." Caraja thought for a while. "What really does happen to set de ball moving was dis hippie van dat got mash-up cus

211

de Rastas driving was laughing too hard and paying no attention where dey's going. And bam!" Caraja clapped his hands. "Off de road and into de bush where dey finds a big mango tree to hit."

"And?" Garth asked.

"And dat's dat's. Das where she sleeps for de rest of she life."

"I'm missing something. How did Thump and Trump enter into the picture?

Caraja pulled a stick from the fire and, using the ember, he lit a roach between his lips. He took a deep pull and handed the spliff to Garth.

Garth waved him off. "Too short."

"Wheww!' Caraja finally blew out. He was ready to tell the story.

"What really does happen to de Trump and Thump Jump-up Band goes so. Trump was born just down de lane to his neighbour and does know some how to play de trumpet he acquired from he Uncle. Alvin, who dey come to call "Thump" cus he's a natural drummer, can make sentences into drum rolls, and de drums into love poems what make de women wet, de women say.

"So, de hippie van gets mashed-up in the bush b'side Cannon's mango tree... which is across de road from Trump's house. Rastas don't have insurance, so dey just leave she corpse where she dies. Now in dem days, folks figured dat after a sufficient amount of time, whatever de Lord leave in front of you is you's to use if nobody else has a need. Or legal claim, Captain Tat said she's like a ship abandoned at sea, 'cept dis be a boat abandoned on land and de village had salvage rights. Besides, my cousin Zackerie wins ownership in a domino game from somebody who say is dere's. But he don't mind none if someone gots a need for she parts, he's off to St. Thomas to join the U.S. Army.

First de seat covers and tires goes, den some t'ings from she engine, like de carburetor. After that, she was leaned-up on she side and held dere with white cedar poles like a ship keeled over in a wave, her underbelly exposed for the pick'ns off she. Finally, after

212

all de village needs be met, she corpse became open to dose dat just has "wants". Which means de kids and dey's imagination. Thump for one sees possibilities in de brake drums and goes around she, wrenching each one off in turn. Trump, he's fixed on the exhaust system, figuring she make a good scratch, and chure enough, he gets she off in one piece, manifold to tail pipe.

"For a good spell we doesn't hear so much from dem, 'cept you see a few more parts disappearing from de van. But it's a real race cus de Lub-vine is coming in thick and fast, and the chocks what's hold'n she up is getting weak with rot and ants."

Caraja threw the roach into the fire.

"Boyyo!" Caraja blew out. "When I t'ink about it, none of us knew it at de time, but in looking back later, it was a significant event for dis island.

"De first time dem boys does parade out dey's band of auto parts, dey's a dozen strong. Girls and boys, maybe eight to twelve years. Not everyone had an instrument from de van. Some of de girls sang and some de youths has real instruments like tambourines.

"One of de girls played the guitar, which she mother make she learn to back up a jump-up church choir. Everyone saw right off she talent and everyone say dat with practice, she'd be milking de notes out of dat guitar under de big revival tent!"

"'Cept fo' she, de trumpet and de tambourine, de rest is pure Volkswagen. Thump gets he brudder's cousin to weld de brake drums onto a hanging stand and…"

"Wait a minute," Garth interrupted. "Isn't his brother's cousin also his cousin?"

"Same mudder, different fadder. Come on mon, you gots ta pick up de pace… I can't be slowing down the train cus somebody's fallen off. De drums is on a stand four in a line, each like mushroom cap. De music she made was so sweet, like a steel pan with a Detroit Motown ring. And de air filter cover, lordy she sounded like a bass. And Thump strike dem like a piston.

"One kid played a toot from de length of exhaust pipe, and another kid made a scratch out of the muffler." In anticipation of what was coming, the cane train began to huff. "Another kid is playing a set of chimes made out of valves hanging from throttle cable.

"Mon does they look good to all of us, but when dey first actually play, it's torture. Jenanne, de main girl singer, knows only religious songs, so dey attack "De Rock of Ages", but dey finally run de neighbors and de saints off when dey slaughter "When De Saints Comes Marching In". The cane train was once again running full throttle.

"But don't you know dey stay with it, and eventually, dey comes along till one day dey try it again on us. Dere's a third less de number of kids, but a million times dey's improvement. And dey does all kinds of music, but mainly 'rock 'n' roll', and love ballads for the girls. Thump is laying in a pad of percussion, and just to keep de girl width de tambourine occupied, dey also does a good lick of gospel and she's a pretty fair wailer.

"Das when dey decide to shake things up a bit by doing gospel songs to a jazzed beat, and then rock 'n' roll songs in de old-time Bible-thumping way. Oowee, things does get lively. Mon, dey do a Fats Domino song called "Blueberry Hill" width all sorts of wailing and 'amening' dat make you t'ink you's clap'n and rock'n up Calvary Hill.

"Bout den, don't you know, Walter-he-ain't-crazy-you-know does step to the wicket as dey's manager, and right off he books dem into the Carnivarama Competition. Course, it's open to everyone, so dere's no problem getting a spot. Drawing a crowd is a different matter. Walter comes up with dey's title 'De Original Thump and Trump Band and Associates.' Or, 'De Bug Band.' Word circulated that most of their instruments were made by Volkswagen and, besides, they were a 'Walter-he-ain't-crazy Production' production and dat alone gonna draw a crowd.

"Dey's booked dem last act on de Thursday eve. But what a job dey does. For dem, it's de first time dey hear demselves on de feedback monitors, and in front of microphones and amplifiers instead of just feedback off de palm trees. Boy, dey took to she like a mongoose to chickens, and when each does a solo, you jus feels dem pushing beyond what dey's ever done before. And mon, when dey pull she all together for 'de Saints'... dere ain't no one sitting. Took more energy <u>not</u> to dance than it does to do she. They didn't win de competition cus it usually goes to a solo singer for coronation as King or Queen of Carnival, but dey won de hearts of de islanders.

"So after dat, Walter is getting dem into Dick's Bar over in Brick Kiln on Saturday nights and playing at a different church every Sunday. 'Let dem sow dey's wild oats on Saturday and pray for a crop failure on Sunday,' Walter-he-ain't-crazy said in a radio interview." Caraja grinned as he stoked the fire, then leaned back onto his haunches.

"Roight," Caraja said, picking up his story again. "Well, Walter's remark about the wild oats causes such a stir with churchgoers and parents of those daughters what goes to Dick's dat dey have to stop playing both Dick's and de holy houses. But no one in de band complained dat much because it took two pickup loads just to move de instruments of the Bug Band, not mentioning the drunk musicians who had to be sober for church service. Well, Walter figured accordingly that they had to be more selective anyway, so he booked them into the Hotel Lemon on a regular basis. Gage, the owner, had them every Sunday evening during the season for their Calypso Cuisine Barbecue. And everything's sliding smooth for dem and pretty soon de folks is coming from other islands to hear the band what plays a Volkswagen. But den, disaster hit."

Caraja stopped his story and turned his attention to rolling a new spliff. "Wanta try you's hand at rolling?"

"You understand, I have a distinct advantage." Garth gave Caraja a cunning smile and took the papers and bag of dry leaves.

215

On a banana leaf, he shook out a small mound of the leaves and spread them with the edge of the rolling-paper wrapper, then picked out a few short stems, leaving only leaves. Satisfied, Garth scooped the pure leaves into a line, drew out a cigarette paper, creased it, and again using the edge of the wrapper, laid the herb into the trough. Rolling it between his thumbs and forefingers, he brought the paper into a tight cylinder. Ceremoniously he took a match, tapped in the ends, and handed the joint to Caraja.

"I thought you say you never smoke the ganja."

"I've never smoked marijuana, but that doesn't mean I've never smoked rollie-cigarettes. Bet you never knew that most people buy cigarette papers to make cigarettes."

"For chure?" The train began to puff. Caraja lit the spliff from a fire stick and held it admiringly to the firelight. "For chure!"

"So what happened to the Strum and Hump Band?

"Das a good 'un, de Trump and Thump Band... De 'Bug Band' is what we starts calling dem. 'Strum and Hump', humph... sounds like a pornography film.

"Well she come down like dis, cus I was dere. De man what plays de valve chimes takes ill and dey calls me to sit in. Well, everyone in de band is feeling good. Walter-he-ain't-crazy went a little crazy width dey's success and he takes he share and flies to St. Maarten, and comes back width a cape, and a high hat width a feather, and his new name 'He-ain't-crazy' embroidered on it.

"It was 'bout then that Ollie's Bar offers them a gig on New Year's Eve. New Year's Eve at Ollie's, mon, is like nowhere else in de Caribbean. Normally Ollie's doesn't open he door until midnight except on New Year's, and then it is 6:00 in de afternoon. Even then she fill up fast, and a lotta people spend de changing of de year out in de alley waiting to get in, talking to de pigs in de next yard, or walking de beach.

"From de stage, de bodies look like greased eels packed in a plastic carton. And when we does find our groove, oh Lordy how dem eels does slip and slither and snake about.

216

"We does close our first set around 2:30 a.m., and no one has left the floor. De next set starts round 3:00, and she seems like just a continuation of de rest of de night's antics. Everything's cool till Cousin Webbe comes in, dressed in he army combat fatigues — he was a cook in Vietnam. Seems he's got it in he brain dat he also wants to start a van-band, and he comes up to de stage right off, demanding his parts back. Well, when he leaves for St. Thomas, Thump and Trump just be kids, but dey grow'd some and dey's not likely to give she up without a scrap. Course, as soon as the fracas begin and de music stop in mid-note, de fans sizes up de situation and throws dey's lot in with Trump and Thump.

"Boyyo! Dat was some commotion." Caraja was rocking and clapping his hands. "Cousin Webbe, for all he training, ain't no match against everyone else, and de few friends he's gots with him looks over the situation and goes AWOL real fast. Finally, big Kong, who's still dancing though the music's been silent for some time, opens he eyes and grasps de nonsense going on, and he grab de Cousin and give he a toss. Unfortunately, he land on Thump's brake drum set and it falls onto de engine block and mash-up both. Well, dats dat, and de boys and girls in de band sees right off dat dat's de end.

"After de police come and send everyone pack'n, dere's no one left 'cept de band and what's left of dey's instruments. 'Well, well,' laughs Trump, cus he just gotta smile at all the commotion. 'Looks like we's de sole survivors of dis night.' And from dat day on, dat's what dey's called, 'Soul Survivors'. Mind you, de boys does finally take up real instruments and Thump buys a drum set from Puerto Rico, and Trump learns to play he Uncle's trumpet real sweet. Dey figure dat the world's gonna turn a deaf ear when dey abandon de Volkswagen sound, but dey's talent carries dem true and de rest be history."

Garth was laughing so hard he started coughing.

"No, mon." Caraja held up his hand. "Dat's de gospel truth how dem things does transpire."

217

Chapter 16

Rasta Roost: Dawn

Like steam rolling out and over the edge of a cauldron, a thick grey mist settled down the sides of the volcano's jungle as the atmospheric pressure tendrilled into the deep ghauts, and through the jungle canopy along the ridges. In the pre-morning haze, the mix of mountain and mist formed a delicate veil through which limbs and leaves appeared and disappeared behind phantom shrouds blurring further the edge between fact and fantasy.

At times in the night rain drove hard against the tarp just inches above Garth's hammock. He lay through the night dry, lulling in the highest of human primitive pleasures of being dry.

Likely the ganja, Garth decided. Hopefully the brilliant ideas from the night before were more permanently burned into his memory than was his actual memory of the night before. As the light of dawn seeped through the grey mist of clouds which by now drifted through his shelter. When he could see, his eyes settled upon a Darwin finch perched on the hammock rope near his feet.

"Not a bad place to weather the storm, Mister Finch." The finch cocked its head to the side starring curiously at Garth. "Look around for yourself, we have green papaya, ripe red mangoes, coconut milk for your cereal and the herb for your head." Then he coughed, from the thick smoke of Caraja's morning fire that had collected in the top of the trap-canopy. The bird flickered to the ground and fresh air. "Lordy Lord!" Garth coughed aloud, "even paradise is polluted."

"De Rasta mon riseth!" Boomed Caraja from the edge of the firepit.

"Roight," Garth rolled out of the hammock onto his feet, then he ducked below the smoke line, "You may know the jungle, but Indians know build a fire without smoke, your wood's too green."

"Mon das donkey-talk, you no noticed? All wood here is green, even the dry stuff. What do you eat for breakfast in Wyoming?"

"Bacon, eggs, oatmeal, juice and pancakes with maple syrup on them.

What do you eat on Augustine??"

"Bout the same, fried breadfruit salad, boiled eggs, tapioca Johnny-cakes with mango jelly, goat feta, when I can get it," smiled Caraja.

"Great because I'm starved, all that swinging like monkeys worked up my appetite."

"Well, you's appetite is in for a disappointment. We's eating bush food dis morn'n. Salt fish and root-tea."

"Do I have time to go to the falls and wash?"

"No set time. In the bush we eat when we's hungry."

Caraja had been thinking about the Indian since he'd got up. Garth should stay on Island. It would be best for him. He fit in. In fact, Caraja suspected that Garth was just beginning to see the real Island... as an Islander, a passenger on a boat of humanity surrounded by water.

Too bad. Garth wasn't like most of the Peace Corps volunteers who'd been assigned there. Garth had made a difference, especially down at the Government Farm. He was a real hand working the animals, taught Caraja's men a lot about working cattle. In fact, Garth was the one who saw that it was a virus from the ticks causing in the animals a fever that sucking down their health. The concrete dip pits were also his idea. And when the cows, the goats, sheep, even the horses started putting on weight, the farmers saw Garth in a different way from his predecessors and they gave him respect.

Garth would stay, Caraja figured, if he had a 'squeeze' -- a lady in his life. But he wouldn't settle for someone ordinary. She'd have to be very special and quick of thought and pretty so their babies would be beautiful, and content within their skin.

"Uncle Cara! Uncle Cara!" The call came from down the ridge. It sounded like a youth, a younger one at that. Someone from the family for only they knew the secret trail.

"Bouyo!" He called back, "I's bove you. Up here width de Lord." Soon the boy, maybe eight years burst out into the clearing.

"Myah say you must come-so <u>NOW</u>!" The little boy threw himself on the ground, panting. "She say der's gonna be a hurricane and you must come-so and stop it."

"Dose she exact words?"

The boy nodded.

By the time, Garth returned from the falls, Caraja had the camp packed into the tent fly and lashed in a bundle in the top of the mahogany tree.

"I've got to stop a hurricane!" Caraja said to Garth, then he turned to his nephew. "Bouyo! How big dat hurricane be?"

The little boy extended his arms as wide as he could reach. "Den some," he added, his eyes equally as wide.

"Well," Caraja shouldered his pack, "sounds like that's a might bigger than I can handle alone. Maybe I best take my partner here along, he wrestles hurricanes on an island called Wyoming." The little boy looked at his Uncle disbelievingly.

"For true?"

Again Caraja swore so, but the boy wasn't buying it completely.

The boy led, Garth, then Caraja. At the crest of the shoulder on which the camp sat, Caraja turned to look back at his private oasis. Maybe, depending on what he found when he got down, he and Garth could return in the afternoon to harvest his crop. Judging by what they'd smoked the night before, it would be his best crop ever.

Chapter 17

A Lamb Is Born

"Soon, I hope!" Felicity gasped. "I can't take much more! The spasms have been coming hard but not close together." She looked at Caraja for some assurance as she stood and walked with short pigeon steps towards the door. Then suddenly she gasped and cried out with pain. Caraja caught her and carried her into the house, laying her on the bed. She curled up drawing her knees close to her chest and moaned. Caraja stripped off his pack and retrieved a plastic bottle of medical disinfectant, and an envelope of surgical gloves.

"Camora," he said to Felicity's niece , "brew up a big pot of tea of ginger root, cinnamon and honey. Do you have that?" Camora shook her head that they did. "Good, chop up the ginger small and put a palm of cinnamon powder in a cloth pouch and brew it. When its color turns golden, ladle in the honey."

Gently he rolled Felicity on her back and pulled up her dress and visually examined her vagina, then pressed his hands on her thighs and belly.

Suddenly, involuntarily she dug her nails deep into his arm and the pain of a contraction forced her to cry out. She'd already emptied the forest of birds with her screams.

When the contractions had eased, Caraja kissed her lightly on the forehead and slipped out of the bedroom to the kitchen. Camora was there prodding absently at the pot with the honey ladle trying to retrieve the ball of cheesecloth that held the cinnamon and ginger.

"She gonna die?" She started to cry. She turned and handed the tea pot of Caraja, her eyes were already swollen from crying. "She gonna die?"

"What?! Das foolishness, girl. Babies come healthy and strong every minute of every day, someplace on d'planet, dis one gonna be no different."

"'Cept dis one's coming with a hurricane!" She started to sob.

"Hush girl, you want to terrify poor Felicity? Now take de bush-tea to Youse sister, and stop crying?" Caraja scolded, moving to the sink. But as he passed the girl, he put his hand on her shoulder. "Just fine... she gonna be just fine. And so are you, you'se my assistant."

At the sink, he washed his hands with a lime and a bar of aloe soap, then a herbal disinfectant, drying them on a clean towel from his bag. He took out his pocket knife, and held it by the blade while pouring scalding tea water on it and then across the blade. He looked out of the kitchen window at the clouds ripping through the jungle's canopy.

"Jah" he said to himself, "be with me on dis day of dread." He mumbled putting on the surgical gloves he'd picked up at the drugstore and returned to the bedroom.

The contractions continued through the afternoon. More honey was added to the tea to give Felicity strength, and sweet ginger for the muscle spasms and to fortify her will. Then, about two hours after the Island's power was shut-off and the first tornados had circled the edge, the storm hit the Island hard...and her water broke!

However, after half an hour passed, Caraja began to worry. He couldn't understand it. It seemed that she was as dilated far as her vaginal muscles would allow without tearing, and her pelvis was certainly wide enough for the baby to pass. The baby was definitely ready, but each time the top of the baby's head appeared, it stopped ... and then receded!

223

His mind raced. There was nothing obvious on the outside -- then suddenly he swore! There's something inside holding the baby back. The reality that this was his child, scrambled his thinking. If Felicity were in a hospital they'd do a Caesarean and for a second he thought about going for an ambulance, but that was even more insane., the storm would certainly have closed the roads by then. Confused he rose, walked bewildered into the kitchen and slumped against the counter, staring without seeing, as the backdoor bulged with the force of the wind, preparing to explode in any minute. What would he do if it <u>weren't</u> his baby?

"Fuck!" He exclaimed suddenly. He'd failed to do the most important step in problem solving -- find the cause!

Camora poured a few drops of pure coconut oil into Caraja's palms, which he rubbed over his glove hands.

"My love," her looked into Felicity's anxious eyes. "I think dere's a problem." He spoke in a confident and comforting tone and she seemed to relax.

"Not a big one, but I believe the umbilical cord is wrapped around the baby... and the only way I can tell is to push the baby back a little so I can feel what's happening."

" Can you elevate your hips?" He said between contractions. Felicity said nothing but arched her back and lifted her hips on command.

"Camora," He turned to the girl, "Quick! Fetch some pillows, or a rolled-up blanket." The girl disappeared into the other bedroom.

"Now, just lay back and try relax your hips." Caraja said, and she complied.

"I'm going to rub some 'balm' on your muscles that will sooth your whole body with the feeling of mist off falling water when Youse really hot." He spoke without attention to his words. "And listen to the sound of my voice. I'm going to

224

sing to our baby a welcome song... a back-time song." He spoke quietly as he slid pillows under her hips.

"Wah-hlie-yo, wah-hiee -ah!" He whispered repeated the phrase again and again while rubbing the sides of Felicity's vagina with coconut oil, messaging gently the muscles along her thighs, relaxing them between contractions.

Once Felicity's hips were elevated as much as possible, Caraja placed the palm of his gloved left hand on the top infant's head and began applying pressure, pushing it away from the pelvis bone. The pressure from the hurricane seemed to help and slowly the fetus moved back a few inches.

Quickly he slid two fingers down the back of the baby's head just in behind the ears and then around the shoulders. Following the same procedure on the other side, he suddenly felt the problem!

As he feared, the umbilical cord had indeed looped around the child's shoulder and neck, and each time the baby advanced it was yo-yoed back.

Caraja drew his two fingers back a little and slid them under the cord.

Now the question was, which direction was it wrapped. Cautiously he turned with his other hand the fetus slightly counterclockwise and immediately realised that it made matters worse, causing Felicity to cry out.

"Jah, don't leave me!" He prayed, and taking a deep breath, he again pushed the baby back and rotated it slightly in the opposite direction.

Felicity gasped with the pain, but the move was enough to loosen the umbilical cord a little and Caraja, arching his fingers backwards under it, gained enough slack to draw the cord over the baby's head. Immediately, just as the hurricane gave a mighty punch that slammed a tree limb into the house... the baby came into the world!

"Praise given to Jah!" Caraja began to cry. "In the face of such violence," He whispered to his wife, "our lamb is born!"

He cut the umbilical cord and tied it off, turned the baby head down for his lungs to clear, almost immediately as he turned it upright, the baby gasped for air and started to scream and gasp for air.

"Where'd he learn that?" Caraja marvelled.

"He?!" Felicity asked

"Yes, we have a son… a Him-a-cane!"

Immediately as soon as it was laid on it's mother's breast, the tiny lips began to suckle.

Then, after some time holding the baby as it nursed, Felicity whispered, "I guess we have no choice but name him 'Hugo'!"

"Not very African." Caraja grinned, "but it will do until another hurricane comes along!"

Exhausted they fell asleep, with the baby between them ... full of the freshness of a new life... unaware of the forces of hell-unleashed and raging just feet away. "In the face of such violence, a <u>lamb</u> is born," Caraja whispered again to Felicity.

Chapter 18

"A Friendship of Intimacies."

The week had passed without notice as Danielle and Jonathan added layers of history and intimacy to their friendship. Each day was spent walking side by side along the beaches.

"See this," she'd say, picking up something inconsequential and giving it her own meaning. "It's an Arawak cell phone," she'd say, carrying a conch shell and holding it to his ear. They'd laugh and Danielle would drop the treasure into her fishnet bag, to be added to the collection of beach memories she'd gathered in twenty years of active beachcombing.

In the evenings they'd dine at one of the hotels, sometimes dancing to a steelpan band. Usually, they just walked the shoreline by moonlight and talked. And while they had never so much as kissed, both were afraid to give their relationship definition -- nor look at the absurdity of it, but the first person each thought about with the sunrises was the other.

For the first time since Mallory was diagnosed, Jonathan was joyful to receive the day. He had spent too many mornings lying in bed, dreading the loneliness which had come to fill the hole once occupied with happiness. He'd occupy himself with work that he took no satisfaction in doing, staying at the top of his profession because of his diligence. On weekends he'd see his children for a few hours to play with his grandchildren, only to return to an empty house.

Though they never spoke of Jonathan's dilemma of selling his practice and moving to the Caribbean or putting his St. Augustine home on the market and returning to his life in New York, in the last week, it weighed heavily upon him. He had to decide soon: he was booked for a Saturday morning flight to New York and a board meeting Monday morning. He'd be back in a few days, he'd said to Danielle, but it was a placeholder comment until his final decision.

Late Friday afternoon, as he walked along the white sand beach turned copper by the setting sun, Danielle galloping ahead like a child exploring the surf for new treasures, Jonathan realised that he had in fact made his decision. As much as he wanted to believe that the week had been the liberation of a youth never exploited, he knew at his core it was not him.

He realised that he had purposefully not thought about what a relationship with Danielle might be, because he knew it couldn't be. And it was not that she was almost half his age. Rather when everything was considered, he would have to change so radically, his very philosophical underpinnings would be in jeopardy — and he was too old to experience that. He had spent his whole life counselling others on how to maintain their financial and social status and demonstrated its merits by his own example.

Eliminate the financial risk from people's lives, that was his job: protect them so they didn't have to change. What he offered them was well-thought-out, pragmatic insurance against change so they could maintain their routines right through to death, and, if he'd counselled correctly, they'd leave enough for their children to do the same. Every detail: "Make sure there is something for the mortician," he'd joke with his clients. He was an estate planner, not an adventurer.

No, he would list his St. Augustine property with the local realtor and return to the familiar — the firm, his family — and follow to the grave beside Mallory the path he had mapped out back when he first articled in law. It was what he was accustomed to, all he'd ever known from boarding schools to board rooms. He was too old to take a new direction.

Besides, he thought that Danielle wouldn't be attracted to him beyond the short term. She was so young and vibrant; she could have any man on Island. Considering all possibilities, he wondered if Danielle could live in Connecticut and share his life there, but he saw immediately that the pull of New York no longer held her. No, the Island was her place, her chosen destiny, and just as the Island was the fabric for her designs, she was an intricate thread in its tapestry, a wide-eyed tiger peeking out of a Rousseau jungle. He would tell her that night.

"What's the matter, big boy?" she said as she loped up beside him. "Barracuda got your tongue?" In her cupped hands she clutched broken pieces of Delft pottery that had once been used for ballast on the trading ships from England, only to be jettisoned into the Caribbean as their holds filled with kegs of Caribbean rum, spices and raw sugar for the Continent.

"A barracuda in a bikini," he laughed, trying to mask his deep sadness.

Since it was his last night, Danielle insisted on making Jonathan a local meal at his house. She could take his vehicle home afterward and return it to the rental company the following day, and he'd take a taxi to the airport. Inez Morton waved them over on their way through town. She had been a close friend of both Danielle's mother and Mallory and had helped Jonathan's wife collect the exotic plant perfumes she needed for the garden of heavenly smells.

"Dannie, dawling," Inez called out, "you heard 'bout d' hurricane?" Since the rental didn't have a radio, they hadn't.

"No? Hugo, dey calls he. He's at Guadeloupe, sleep over tonight and expected to visit Montserrat midday tomorrow." She waited until the information had settled upon Danielle and Mr. Douglas, then added, "And they's saying we's next!"

Immersed in a universe of their own making, for all its lack of clarity, they'd heard nothing in their cocoon, and the news was hard to comprehend.

"You must take precautions for dey's calling he de 'Hurricane o' de Century!" Inez exclaimed.

"What do you think?" Jonathan asked Bana. "Maybe we should skip supper and you should be preparing your place for the storm."

"No. Who knows when you'll be back? Tonight, I'm going to cook real West Indian food for you and we'll watch the moonrise from your veranda. Tomorrow I'll prepare."

"Spoken like a true island-girl," Jonathan laughed. Still, he wondered if she suspected his decision that he wouldn't be coming back after the meeting in New York was finished.

They stopped at the Bordeaux's home for Danielle to pick up a change of clothes as well as some spices and other ingredients she'd need for the supper. "Bana!" voices called from out of the dark as they drove along the winding roads leading to Jonathan's hilltop fortress.

"Roight!" she called back and waved.

"Everyone on-island knows Bana except me. I gather there's a long story to go with the short one. Why do they still call you Bana?"

"Hmmm," she said, "it's a name that's followed me since I was very young, maybe six, when a monkey got in the way of my fixation for bananas, as in 'bana' for breakfast, lunch and supper. In the market, they would set aside hands of them for my mother so she wouldn't go wanting."

"Of course" ... she smiled at Jonathan, "when I left New York to move back at the end of this last fashion season, my friends there called me 'bananas' for my decision." She laughed. "Depends on who you talk to, I guess."

"Stop here!" she commanded, waving her hand in front of Jon's view to make sure he knew she didn't mean "around" here. He braked immediately in front of an open gate in a hedge of stonewall, draped in grapevines. It was Paulette's house. The market lady sat on her front porch surrounded by baskets of produce, separating them for Saturday's market. Danielle leaned over Jon and yelled out, "Does you have ripe breadfruit and onions for de evening?"

"Come-so," Paulette called back "You won't be disappointed,". Danielle got out, and when she returned, she carried a large bushel basket, heavy with vegetables and fruit. Crowning the cache were two great hands of bananas. "I hope you're hungry!" she exclaimed, setting the basket in the backseat of the Suzuki.

"Do you have a coal-pot?" Danielle asked as Jon set the basket on the counter.

"*I'll* make supper," he announced in a my-kitchen-my-meal tone. "Is spaghetti alright?"

"Mon, you's legging me on, you no-know how ta cook bayou-boccon and papaya and mango-posito?"

Jonathan grinned, "There's no such thing as Bayou-boccon and papaya au mango pasta. You's legging <u>me</u>."

"You are plenty smart, Mistah Douglas, but not so smart to keep me from cooking the meal of your life. I have all of the ingredients and," she slipped back into slang," Me does plan she all de day through! And you thought I was just having fun."

Jonathan laughed, shrugging. "No coal-pot, only a barbecue. But I do have a bag of local coal… in fact, many bags." Each time he came on-island, Mango would set in stores for his stay, including a fresh bag of local charcoal. Mango's sister was a coal lady. Making charcoal was a long and labor-intensive process that suited large families. It began with gathering the wood, meaning days of standing over a blown-down mahogany, hacking at the limbs, turning them into chunks small enough that two or three children could pack out of the jungle. Then it was stacked on top of drier wood in a large pit covered with banana leaves topped with dirt. When the weather was right, not too dry, not too wet, the coal lady would light the wood and artfully smoulder it. If it got too hot it turned to ash, and the weeks of labor were lost.

For days, the mound smoked beneath its mantle of fresh soil. If the burn went well, it was dug into and the contents raked across the open area beside the pit. Like everything on-island, it was a family affair: the children scurried around picking out pieces of charcoal from the dirt and placing each in a burlap bag, which, when full, was tied at the top and added to a stacked row.

Jon paid the equivalent of four dollars U.S. per bag and felt embarrassed that it was so cheap. But Mango would say, "Naw, mon, dat's de going measure." A small bag of charcoal briquettes in Manhattan would cost twice as much for a tenth the quality. Jonathan learned from Mango that when the local charcoal was mixed with a few pieces of dried coconut husk, the food tasted so much better.

As Jonathan lit the charcoal in the barbecue, using only paper and matches — no fire-starter — as Danielle had told him, he could hear her chirping away in the shower. The embers swelled, carrying heat to those adjacent lumps until Jonathan had a good base of glowing coals.

"That's perfect," she said, standing beside him, her wet hair wrapped in a towel. She wore tan linen pants that flared loosely from her hips. Her feet were bare and she wore a man's sweater. "Go take a shower while I prepare supper. You've done enough for the day."

"I've done nothing for the day." Jonathan smiled.

"Bet you couldn't say that two weeks ago." She teased him. "See how much you've learned."

Jon caught a glimpse of himself in the bathroom mirror. It was still a younger man's body, he noticed. A life of tennis and workouts at the gym. He did it not to stay in shape as much as to free himself of his daily tensions, and thus he kept fit despite the pull of gravity regardless of the pressures of his position. Suddenly a wave of self-consciousness and sadness gripped him as he stepped from the shower. He was resolute to tell her of his decision.

Jonathan couldn't imagine that the feast came from just the produce basket. Every course balanced and complimented the others before. Pumpkin soup spicy from a variety of onions and peppers; breadfruit salad, tart and reminiscent of potato salad with an added taste of walnuts. Breaded plantains fried in coconut oil, and, of course, bananas sautéed with sugar and set aflame in vanilla rum. Only when Jonathan had cleared the table was the rich silence

232

between them interrupted as Danielle put on a tape of Gregorian monks performing the passions of Hildegard von Bingen. She flipped the switch to play the tape in an endless loop and returned to the table.

"I won't be coming back," he said, unable to look at her. She looked at him with a hurt that made his heart sink, then her eyes fell to the table and the table flowers that seemed to be wilting. "But you must understand, it is not because of you." His eyes darted across her face. It was just what he didn't want to happen. "You're wonderful — in fact, at the risk of sounding like a soap opera character, everything is... well, too wonderful."

Danielle reached across the table and placed her hand on top of his. "I've known that for longer than you, and I too see the reasons." She drew her hand back, picked up her wine glass and gestured for a toast. "I would like to propose a toast, to a nice man with whom I've had a lot of fun this week." He frowned, embarrassed.

"Island life is not your life my friend. You're a man of order and the Caribbean island-life is chaotic at the best of times, more so than even the Island of Manhattan. Island life here thrives on the relaxed acceptance of the unexpected. I would like to drink a toast for the week that was, and to the night that will be." He started to say something, but she cut him off. "Enough talk. Tonight is a night for the mute of tongue, "a symphony for the deaf."

They moved to the veranda, and in the double-wide hammock, the two of them lay back, side by side and watched the moon rise out of the Atlantic. Danielle looked out to the sea. It was a moon full that rose out of a pirate sea, doubloon-round and golden. Clouds, backlit by the vibrant moon cast dark, ominous shadows upon a silver ocean. And like Spanish galleons the shadowy forms of cloud-ships sailed towards the Island, dispatching thousands of longboat-waves, conquistadors racing out of the ship's shadow, assaulting the tiny Island shore from three sides. "There is no hope," sighed Danielle. "We are about to be conquered and Spanish will

233

surely become the language of the morn." But she underestimated the strength of a mountain and the waves of conquistadors died without valour in a white-foam, back-surge surf.

It was a night without edges and Jonathan allowed his mind to wander aimlessly between imaginary war ships and Wall Street from the seventy-third floor of his office building. From jungle village lights to the lights of "villages on top of villages" like towering torches from a million sparks. On those nights he stayed in Manhattan and worked late to avoid going out to Connecticut and the empty house, he often found himself standing in front of the floor-to-ceiling window, mesmerised by the beauty. If man is the instrument of God, skyscraper cities have to be His greatest achievement. In those almost sacred moments, he'd see the city not as a place to make money but as a shrine to God.

He never felt as alone even in the wilds of Canada, where he'd take the kids canoeing, as he did standing there in the heart of Manhattan. He felt close to Mallory in those moments, but she'd passed on when the people behind the wall of lights were again flesh and blood. It was not necessarily a bad time, for he found his time full of wonderment. Who are these people? What are their lives like?

Slowly, his sleep-hooded sight fell upon the Poppy Dawn village lights twinkling at him through the jungle below. Who are these people? he wondered. Mallory would know. He listened intently. There was a mariachi band on someone's radio, and a soft crooner who made the heart embrace the moment. "You no gonna go Banky's," warned a mother 'less Youse takes you's sistah along ." There's a long quiet spell, filled with crickets and tree frogs., "Ah, Ma?!" But the wind swept away his protest.

"Hear the monkeys?" Danielle whispered, her head resting in the crook of his shoulder and arm, Jonathan listened, but all he heard were dogs across the ghaut in Remember Me. He shook his head no.

"Exactly. The dogs are saying, 'We sees you dere mister Monk skulking about in dem bushes.' And then, 'Hey, Bassarios,

234

dey's com'n you's way!' ... until everyone is on the alert. Okay, now listen. Hear that screeching? That's the jack monkey telling his mates to come on down, the stage is set."

"Now the dogs will really go crazy," and they did until finally a man's voice rang out, "Monks git outa dat sop tree!" followed by someone else beating on a pot. And no sooner did the metal pot percussion stop in one garden or orchard than it began again in another plot. "Boyo! Git Youse catapult. Dey's sit'n big as can be, right dere under de yard light."

"Phumph!," came the sound of a slingshot firing a rock, followed by the yelp of a monkey and then the courageous yap of a dog in pursuit. Yard by yard the tumult went on until the troupe passed further down the ghaut from the village.

"Lullaby of Broadway ala St. Augustine," Jon laughed as the evening fell quiet, and finally enveloped the villages below.

As the night progressed into deep and deeper layers of solitude, the distant surge of the sea, grinding longboats to foam, souls to sand, could be heard all the way up the mountain. They drifted in and out sleep, interrupted only by Danielle shifting beside him in the hammock, but eventually even her restless movements failed to wake him from his dream travels. And in the morning, well after the sun split the line of the sea from the horizon of thin flat clouds lulling across the Caribbean, Jonathan realised that he was alone. Danielle was no longer beside him.

"Bana," he called out, but she wouldn't answer to the name. "Danielle?" Still no response. On the mirror she had left a message.

"Took car to check on Lottie. Be back in time for your plane. Thank you, thank you. D." The phone rang, and for a moment he wondered at the sound as dreams from a distant time rushed to escape capture by his consciousness.

"Seems like you join de dead." It was Mango. "I come-so, and call you's name, but it seems you does desert to a different place."

"Not a different place," said Jon, "just a different perspective of the same place."

"Well, whatever. I tells you true, you's best polish up you's senses cus we gots company. Dere's a hurricane's com'n, mon!"

"Oh Lord," Jonathan remembered Inez' warning. "What needs to be done? I've got to catch a plane in a few hours, so we'll have to hurry. I'm going back to New York for a board meeting."

"Well, Youse best be on de phone to dem cus dat Board's gonna haf'ta stop Mistah Hugo fast... or you's gonna haf'ta learn ta fly. Dey's pulled all de planes in de night and de ferry's gone out to deep water."

Jonathan stood stunned. Surely there was some way to get off the Island. Maybe he could hire a charter helicopter to come over from Antigua. What was the name of the company?

"Leeward Air, but deys airport's closed. 'Sides, all Antigua's planes done gone to Barbados. You's stuck width the rest of us!"

Jonathan had never been stuck. There was always a contingency plan, a different envelope in the portfolio of his life. He always had options, ways to capitalise on the situation. Never stuck.

Danielle arrived at the gate in his jeep a few minutes later. "Well, what's the word?" she asked as she got out. "You've heard about the planes and the ferry?" Jonathan nodded. "The Lemon took a load of guests to Antigua this morning, early enough to catch the Eagle to Puerto Rico."

"Are they coming back?" A faint hope sparked for Jonathan.

"Eventually, after the storm, but for now they're headed for Trinidad." said Danielle.

"Jonathan, I've something to ask." She looked at him directly. "Lottie and I have emptied the upstairs of the house down into the lower, stone level because she has a feeling in her bones that "Monkey Manor" may not fare so well in the "Storm of the Century". Lottie is going down to be with her children at the Saddleback Shelter." She looked at him, hoping he would pick up the thread. When he didn't she said, "May I come for a sleep-over?"

"Of course you may." He hadn't even thought where <u>he</u> would weather the weather. "But I don't know even if this place will survive, sticking out like it does."

"You might lose your roof, but this concrete and steel fortress is not going to be flattened, that's for sure."

"Das fo' chure!" mimicked Mango, appearing in the doorway.

While Danielle unloaded the jeep laden with an abundance of produce from Lottie's garden, Jon and Mango carried up sheets of three-quarter-inch plywood from the generator room, standing them beside the windows and doors.

"Before they cut the power, you must set each in place and turn deys hurricane bolts here on the sides," Mango said while he showed Jonathan how to turn the handles of each door, thus pulling the plywood tight against the opening. Many of the windows especially on the garden side of the building had shutters, which they closed and dead-bolted.

"When de hurricane-he comes so, open de shutters on de lee side, but don't forget to close dem when he change he direction. And make chure not'n's left outside what de wind can lift."

Mango smiled at Danielle. "Seems like you puts in provisions for de 'whole island," he said, looking at Paulette's basket still full of vegetables coupled with what Danielle brought, and then the shelves of canned goods. "I had de cooling gas tanks topped 'fore you come, so you should have lots. But de youths' gonna come soon width some more tings you'll likely need. Maybe a stand of bananas?"

Danielle laughed, "But what about you? Do you have enough for you and your kin? Here take some of this."

"We's plenty. No belly gonna go empty, least fo a while." He turned to Jonathan, "Let's seal de cisterns with tape and take off the down-spouting. No tell'n what dis Mistah Hugo does carry in he winds… nothing any <u>good</u>, das for chure!"

When they'd done all they could, and Mango had walked the property, assuring himself that all was in order, he gathered up a

237

cutlass and some packing straps stored in the pump room. "It's time ta make me move." he said. And then as an after-thought, "Best does you's phoning now ta dat Board you's meeting with cus only de Lord gonna know when you get Youse next chance."

Jonathan called his daughter Nancy. "Oh, Daddy! Where are you? We heard about the hurricane, it's on all the television stations. They're calling it the 'Hurricane of the Century'. Guadeloupe has had a number of deaths, and reports claim that the capital of Montserrat has been destroyed. Where are you, in Miami?" Then she spoke away from the receiver. "It's Daddy," she called to her husband, "get on the other phone."

"Jonathan, are you alright?" Dwight, his son-in-law, came on. "Where are you?"

"I'm at the house here in St. Augustine. Beautiful day... a little windy," he laughed, trying not to raise their concerns.

"Oh, Daddy, get off the Island immediately," his daughter pleaded.

"Can't, they've taken all the planes south to Trinidad, and the ferry, according to Mango, has been moved out to the deep seas.

"But listen, there are things you must do. Call Brenda and JJ, I believe they've taken their families up to the cottage for the weekend. Tell them we're fine. You know this is a strong house, and nothing is going to happen to it. Mango's made sure we have everything we need."

His daughter started to interject.

"Also, tell JJ that he must go to the board meeting on Monday. I'll fax him my proxy as soon as I hang up. Tell him to vote his conscience. You get that?"

"Yes, sir," said Dwight.

"Who's 'we'?" demanded Nancy.

"Give the children a hug from me and tell them Grandpa is fine and loves them very much."

"Who's 'we'?"

Jonathan put his finger on the disconnect button. "Your turn," he said.

"I have no one to call. Everyone I love is on this Island." Jonathan sent the fax, disconnected the phone knowing that Nancy would be calling right back. He didn't want to be explaining his relationship with Danielle at least while Danielle was in the room, particularly since he didn't understand it himself.

Later that day, Mango's two youngest boys arrived, carrying a huge stalk of bananas. Jonathan offered to take their load. "No, Mistah Douglas. Papa say dey's for de misses and no other."

Soon Mango's wife appeared with a plastic grocery bag. It was full of handmade candles from the "Honeybee" honey factory.

"Mango said to use candles and save de generator, it may be a long time coming fo dere Island current is on again."

Chapter 19

Back to the Dark Ages

Sparky drove the company's pickup into the yard of the Electrical Department's generator station and turned it facing the side of the building where glass blocks let the headlights stream into the control room. Even the crunch of the tyres on the crushed seashells seemed ominous.

Fight as he might, his spirit was low and the task before him weighed heavy for all its uncertainty. Reluctantly, though resigned, Sparky reached across the cab seat and took up his ear protectors, flashlight and hardhat hanging on their hooks beneath the dash. There'd be no foreman nor safety inspectors at the site that evening— even the night watchman had left his station to help his family prepare — but rules were rules and as the head of the Generator Station, Sparky put on his helmet. That was why he'd been picked for the job, attention to details.

From outside, the roar of the giant diesel generators overpowered the sounds of the night, muting even the ocean waves driven crashing against the rock cliffs on which the building sat.

Sparky walked to the corner of the building and peered around, but the blast of salt air made him recoil. He knew then that he had to do it. If he waited much longer, the wind might trouble his pickup when he crossed the open ridge at Browne Pasture.

The door handle to the great concrete building felt clammy and gritty like the thick air, stale and stagnant in the lee of the structure.

Inside the concrete and glass-block building, the roar of the generators was deafening, even penetrating his ear protectors. It was maddening as the sheer power of the beast quickened the heart to pump adrenaline to even the most minor muscles. He likened being there to standing out in a violent storm, every sensation alert.

He could recall with vividness his first day of work thirty years before, how he had trembled at its force. The Government had sent him off-island to train in Barbados. Back then, the Islanders knew him as Santos. But soon, after the generator electrified what little bit of island grid there was wired, he was nicknamed "Sparky, Carrier of the Current". And the more the Island became dependent upon electricity, the more esteem was bestowed upon him. He was not an ambitious man; but he did accept the moniker.

Sparky was pleased with the hum of the machines. As he walked through the generator room, feeling the concrete floor pulsing beneath his feet and the raw energy vibrating off the walls. He recalled that day when, following two years of construction and assembly, the beast was first awakened, how terrifying it was when they started the great turbines. The building quaked, the floor trembled with fright and didn't stop except when they turned on the auxiliary system and stopped the main for maintenance.

The Island had never had electricity and hadn't had a machine of such size since the cane era, and those were driven by wind or steam... never with fuel delivered in a truck from a ship that got it from someplace far away like Venezuela. With nothing to compare it to, he recalled, his first thoughts were of a mythical dragon imprisoned in a concrete cave.

"Dere's a dragon in dere," he teased his children when he returned home after his first day of work. "And he be so mad chained up and what dat he blows electricity out he nostrils. For true! And I's de only one he no turn to cinders cus we's friends."

Using the headlights to see his keys, he unlocked the control room and walked over to the large control panel and, beside it, the grey box housing the island's main throw-switch. For a long time, he stood there looking at the handle, thinking about the consequences of pulling it down. In the few years since the island was electrified, its people had become, both dependent, and accustomed to it. He held the power of Zeus at his fingertips.

"Back to the Dark Ages", which were not that far back since people were still accustomed to oil lanterns, meals cooked on coal-pots, and blocks of ice on lighters from sister islands. He marvelled at how attached they'd become to the conveniences and luxuries electricity brought, but they were yet not necessities. Still, maybe he should just leave the power on until they knew for sure which way the storm would go. Maybe the hurricane wouldn't hit the island at all. He'd heard stories of last-minute reprieves. Maybe… no, no, he knew what was about to happen, and it would take an act of God to change the Island's destiny. In fact, maybe the storm was an Act of God with purposes unknown. He could wait no longer. Already reports were coming in from the coastline. What if someone was electrocuted or there was a fire from a fallen live wire?

He wondered how long it would be before power could be restored. Maybe only a few hours. Maybe if the storm skirted the Island, by morning he'd be starting the big diesel generators and laughing at his melodrama. Twenty-four hours at most, he hoped, but by the feeling in his stomach, and judging by the wind's intensity, it would in fact be a long, long time.

He placed his hands on the handle. The breaker bars were corroded, and he had to use both hands, but suddenly the friction broke, the giant switch snapped off, and the Island was plunged into the dark ages.

Chapter 20

The Cave

With Caraja delivering his baby, Myah, Garth and Bantu made their final move into the cave at dusk. They put the bounty from the garden and orchard far in the back of the cave with the bundles of hanging ganja plants with the supplies Caraja had left, plus the household items Myah had brought from the cottage. Garth marvelled at their abundance, particularly since it wasn't certain in his mind that the hurricane would even hit them.

. Soon Myah had a fire going in the fire pit contained by a ring of rocks in the center of the main chamber of the cave. And while she busied herself with pots and frying pans, a cutting board and various vegetables and fruits, Garth amused Bantu with more magic. Even the kitten had taken a liking to the show and tried to expose the magician's magic by retrieving missing marbles and breaking invisible strings.

The meal they ate that night in the cave, sitting cross-legged on bamboo mats before the open fire, was far from just "breadfruit in the fire" as Myah had warned.

It was a feast that began with fresh avocados in a lime brine, with thin wedges of pickled plantains. The next course was a spicy chilli pepper and peanut soup cooked in coconut water. The main course was breadfruit fried also in coconut oil plus a dish of dried christophene smothered in a tomato, onion and garlic red curry. For Bantu, she'd made a porridge of grated cassava root, mashed bananas and a pinch of brown sugar. After feeding him, she sang him to sleep.

Following supper Myah took over the cave, laying out sleeping mats that Garth noted were side by side. She consolidated the wood near the open hearth and stoked the coals around a cast-iron pot full of boiling water, while Garth took the dishes to be washed.

Clean water wouldn't be a problem since the rain along the front edge of the advancing hurricane was just hitting the peak above them, condensing into rivulets that channeled and braided together into torrents of deep rents in the peak's vegetation.

Cascading off the cliff hundreds of feet above the cave, a waterfall had appeared across the entrance. As he watched it grow, Garth realised they would soon be sealed inside until the storm was over. He wondered if that was good or bad, but whichever-- there they were. He liked the idea of being trapped with Myah and Bantu. He liked being in their presence.

"Who is this man?" Myah wondered, watching him as he washed the cooking pots. She had been mesmerised by his beauty when they'd first met on the trail leading to Poppy Dawn school two years before. Now his black hair was long and pulled back into a ponytail, but back then it was Peace Corps short. His eyes were clear and dark, his skin the colour of oiled leather. He walked like a God, erect, head high, the features of his face strong and smooth like a mahogany carving sold to the tourists. She could tell by his hands, and the square of his shoulders, that he was accustomed to hard work. In fact, everything about him was hard, everything but his manner... and his eyes. They were rabbit-skin soft, gentle, understanding.

"So here you are." She repeated to herself the first words she'd said to him when they first met.

About a year after he arrived, Myah had heard that, much to the astonishment of the Agriculture Department, that Garth had diagnosed the problem that was knocking back the island's animals. And with Caraja, they had started a tick-dipping program that, after another year of hard work, they had all but eradicated tick-fever on the Island.

Myah's thoughts wondered back to those times when she used to take Bantu down to the sea past the government farm and watch him working with Caraja. Stripped to the waist, working the animals in the corrals, his skin was kindling to her imagination as the sun and his sweat defined his muscles. Strong and focused, he prodded and diverted the cows through the maze of new corrals and the dip tank, sandwiched the chutes. It was hard work and by mid-morning his Levi's would be soaked with perspiration. She could tell by the way the men treated him that he had their respect.

How strange that she should now be with him sealed in together behind a waterfall with a violent storm just beyond.

Why him? She asked herself, and suddenly she could hold herself in no more. She began silently crying as though years of tears could no longer be contained, for she had a glimpse of the source of her sorrow and depression. She knew the answer, she, like her grandmother Sueky were different... but so was he.

She wiped her tears and busied herself in the cave, avoiding eye contact.

"I'm Myah," she blurted, as though they had never met, when he returned with the dishes in the growing dusk of the cave. "I'm Caraja's sister." It was her way of clearing the slate, starting afresh, for now she accepted her destiny.

Garth smiled playfully, feasting on her beauty in the firelight, trying to keep his face from betraying how much turmoil he felt inside. Then he grinned, his teeth sparkling with merriment. "I'm Garth Longgrass, Caraja's friend."

"You're the cowboy from Wyoming."

"Indian," he corrected her.

"Indian," she repeated, fully intending to make the mistake again.

"And you're the beautiful <u>West</u> Indian woman I was warned about in the village."

"Warned?" Myah's smile turned into a slight frown.

"I was told you are the kind of woman that men make fools of themselves around."

"You mean men aren't fools all the time?! Everyone I've met acts-so." Her smile assured him there was no malice in the comment, and more — that she found Garth anything but a fool!

"We appear that way to you," Garth observed, "because we act that way around you and that's why you pass judgment upon our foolishness."

Counter to the sounds of the growing waterfall and the swelling storm, the dusk in the cave was deathly silent. Even the tree frogs in the back of the cave were quiet as if not wanting to divulge their presence to some predator that lurked at the mouth of the cave: a predator hiding in the winds that slapped the vines across the front of the cave, back and forth with the clack of crab pincers. The crickets, donkeys, dogs and monkeys, all of the island's familiar sounds of evening, were on the other side of the waterfall. For a moment Myah felt dizzy, as though suspended in midair, and she grasped Garth's forearm for balance, anchorage. He did not withdraw, and after a moment she released her grip. They sat close together until exhaustion slowly drew over and while Bantu slept in her lap, she slipped into sleep with her head on Garth's shoulder.

"Where's Caraja?" she demanded with a start, sitting suddenly bolt upright from her sleep.

"He's gone down to deliver a hurricane," came a voice from the dark.

"Oh," she said with slow acceptance, finally remembering where she was, and the events of the day. Bantu now lay on his mat asleep, Garth's hand absently brushing the boy's hair. Why was the man here, she asked herself again. The answer came again with simple clarity: because he's supposed to be.

Both dozed and then awoke briefly as the wind started lashing the long vines harder against the cliff's face. Now the lines slapped against the bare rock with a whip-crack bark of unrestrained violence.

"I've always thought that I would die young," Myah said so quietly that Garth was unsure he understood her words. "Maybe now's the time."

Garth put his arm around her. "You won't die this time, no room for a body <u>and</u> Caraja's crop!" He assured her. She welcomed his strength and allowed herself to surrender a little to his comfort.

"When death came last," she whispered after a long time filled only with the storm and the crackling fire, "I was an old woman, and it came without violence — restful and peaceful as an old one's passing should be." She lapsed again into thought, the storm's howl swelling back to fill the void. "But not this time. I will die young, and it will be violent and insane... and senseless!"

"We're not dead yet. Not even close. Besides, you can't die, I'd have to raise Bantu and his kitten." Garth nodded to the young boy with the kitten curled in his arms, then he gave her a comforting squeeze and immediately she felt foolish for her fears.

Garth lay awake beside the woman curled in his arms as she came and went in and out of sleep. The hurricane, he thought with a smile, bellows with the fury and volume of the bull Charlie back on his folks' ranch when they finally castrated him. Savage violence slamming against the stock pens with such explosive force that posts set in concrete flexed and snapped off at the ground, shattering side boards, until eventually there was little left of the working corral — with their work half done. A single knife slice through the scrotum, and before his Dad could pull out the testicles and cut them off, Charlie exploded. No one dared to run, they had to stay with him and get control. If he escaped into the bush, the bull would eventually die from infection.

Ropes were put on him, but he snapped them like thin baling-twine. One of the hired cowboys tried to get a blindfold on the bull, but it was more courageous than effective. Garth wasn't really sure how they completed the operation, for suddenly the bellowing and yelling had stopped, his eyes filled with white light, and a silence that bore no memories, engulfed him.

Knocked out by a hard blow to his head from Charlie's considerably harder skull, the next thing he knew, he was in his bed, his grandmother Ollia pressing his forehead with a moss and sage compress and chanting a Shoshone prayer of safe passage for the dying.

Boom! It was as if a clap of thunder had struck <u>inside</u> of the cave. A giant limb from one of the grandfather trees high up the volcano snapped and caught in the plunging water, free-fell until it slammed against a ledge on the cliff face, then catapulted out into the ghaut below, crashing against the sides of the walls of the ravine with more volleys.

"It's okay," he was saying into Myah's ear. "It's okay," he repeated without conviction, "it's okay." Like the corral planks under Charlie's force, he felt he too would explode, his lungs collapsing from the outside pressure, then ballooning in the vacuums.

"Talk to me," Myah gasped, gripping his arm against the storm's force. "Tell me about where you come from, about your family, about being a cowboy."

"Indian," he laughed. "I'm an Indian. Totally different worlds."

What could he say that would make sense to her? He sought some common ground they might share. He thought about what he'd written to his friend Cowboy Bob soon after he got on Island, "Somehow St. Augustine is just like home on the reservation, except nothing's the same."

"Well," he began, "I live on a ranch on the edge of a great desert, along the base of giant mountains that rise thousands of feet above the desert floor. Some of the peaks have year-round snow, others are raw rock so steep that even a snowflake in winter can't catch hold." He glanced at her to see if any of this interested her. She looked back at him with rapt attention.

248

"The ranch is a cattle and horse ranch, which is rather ironic since Indians are, according to the movies, supposed to steal them both, not raise them." He laughed, as did Myah, for she suspected his family was far from horse and cow thieves.

"Both my mother and father are full Shoshone Indians. Our ancestors were nomadic, following the herds of buffalo and elk across the great plains of North America for tens of thousands of years before contact with the Europeans."

"Mine too, and we are also black of foot... from Africa," she smiled.

Garth reflected on her words. "Divine Ordination! That's one thing we have in common, we have been the victims of a class of misguided humans driven by its own conviction of self-importance. Orphans of Divine Destiny. These people killed off the buffalo and most of the wild game we lived upon. Killed most of the Shoshoni too, and those of us who were left were stuck on reservations... until recently, when there was a war and the whites needed us to go fight."

"I guess St. Augustine is a black man's reservation," Myah mused to herself. Their histories had a lot in common because of the European colonialists. Exchange the word "Indian" with "West Indian", "massacre" with "slavery", "reservation" with "plantation" and "racism" with "racism", and they actually shared a very similar past, on opposite sides of the planet.

Myah marvelled at how openly Garth admitted to venturing into the spiritual realm, describing how in his culture Spirits take animal and with some special people, human forms. On-island, SpiritTalkers never talked to others about their gift.

"Sueky is a Spirit Talker... I guess I am too!" Admitted Myah "but... I resist it!" She looked away from him into the fire " "Do you have brothers and sisters?" she shifted the subject.

"One younger brother, Daniel, and of course dozens of cousins and grands."

249

"Grands? That's also what we say," she smiled. "Another thing we have in common."

"Only three blood grands alive. My mother's father was killed in a drunken knife fight. But" he shrugged, "in our culture, the family extends across most of the tribe, meaning I have hundreds of relatives." He smiled, "Which is both a blessing and a curse." Myah frowned, not understanding. "The blessing is there's always someone looking after you…"

"The curse?"

"There is always someone looking after you. Nothing goes unseen… including things that never happened." He chuckled. "A bit like here. You see, another thing we have in common."

"Ain't das so!'" Myah laughed.

They sat in silence for a while. "Oh, and I'll tell you another thing about here that's like home." Garth mused " Children are recognised as people from birth, and they're shown respect and taught respect by example. In my culture, we believe that every child is an ancestor returning. And every child has special knowledge and a gift to be nurtured."

Myah lifted herself up onto her elbow and looked at Garth. "How do you mean? You believe your ancestors live through you?" There was a resonance of intensity in her voice that told him the questions were not casual to her.

Feeling her sincerity, Garth tried to select the right words, but his ideas suddenly jammed like logs in a narrow gorge. He feared he would scare her, so he settled on the coward's way out.

"Well, let's say our ancestors are never very far away." In fact, he had conversations with his ancestors frequently, though usually they were one-sided. Normally it was him telling them of the day's events. Also, Garth made a point of not asking for more than "understanding" from his ancestors. Asking spirits for a favour, he believed, could be a double-edged blade. If you want something from them, there may come a time when they'll want something from you.

For a while they lay beside each other in silence, listening to the endless roar of the storm and the falls. "Do you believe," she broke the silence, then hesitated "...do you believe that Spirits can... occupy people's minds and bodies?"

He thought for some time. "Mind yes, but body I'd have to think about it. In my culture we believe that spirits exist in everything from the buffalo to the gecko. We communicate with the animal spirits, and often they bring us messages. So, I guess to answer your question, for us there is no separation between here and there; the physical realm and the spiritual realm are one and the same." He smiled, looking up through the fire, "Opposite walls of the same cave."

"But" he added, "we also believe there is a single entity called 'Spirit' that is the totality of *all* Existence."

"Pantheism," Myah said, to Garth's astonishment. "That's what it's called."

"Pantheism," Garth repeated, pondering whether the word captured his people's belief. "Exactly," he said, "and ---then some. You see, I believe," he wanted to choose the exact words, "that man has a purpose and that is to bring consciousness to God's creation. Not just to marvel and give thanks, but to actually experience it. My grand- mother had a saying which roughly translates as, 'Do for God what God cannot do for Herself." He paused self-consciously. "Am I ranting?"

"You're yelling, but just to be heard over the storm." She laughed but continued her query. "Is it your belief that through our consciousness, your God experiences Its creation?"

Garth grinned. "You sure you're not a Shoshone Indian?"

"West Indian," she smiled back and turned her back to him, holding her knees to her chest as she stared at the fire's reflections against the cave wall. Her thoughts were on his words. He was very strange. Strange that he spoke openly about communicating with the Spirits. She too talked with her ancestors, and she too found the hand of God in every aspect of

Its creation. And she too believed we are God's eyes and hands. But he'd missed her question about the visitations, about being taken over by a Spirit.

With her back still to him, she asked cautiously, "Do you believe people can go into the realm of the Spirits of the Dead and return?"

Garth pondered long about her question. "I have been there. Yes." He offered no further explanation for some time, then spoke. "A shaman named Albert was the first to show me the path as many believed I have the gift. And for a long time he was my guide. Even now, though he is long since dead, I communicate with him. Only once have I gone alone without him into the desert for guidance and spoke with the dead. Maybe it was just to confirm that it was possible without him."

Myah could feel the blood rush to her face. Faltering, she had to ask more. "Do you believe our dead ancestors can take over someone's... someone's living body?" she blurted out.

Garth sat weighing her words. "You mean Spirits taking human form?

"No, more like taking over a living person, pushing them aside."

"Maybe." Then, realising that the question deserved more, "I know that during some of our traditional dances, especially the three days of the Sun Dance, I have seen others possessed, their bodies inhabited... and yes maybe even me." Again, he held back for as long as he could, but again he felt the interminable violence of the hurricane driving him towards a deep honesty. "Yes, I have passed from the land of the living, and yes, I have shared my existence, my body, in the Sun Dance," he said with both resolve ... and finality.

"So, now's your turn," he said. "Tell me about you. Were you born on-island?"

"Born very near here on a farm down the mountain, near "Remember Me" village. And like you, I am pretty well related

252

to everyone back there. My father and his three brothers and two sisters proved up title on an abandoned plantation land around there, so between the five farms, every school class down at Poppy Dawn Primary was half relatives."

"Five farms? I thought you said there were six children."

"One brother got the calling to "Save Sheep" rather than herd them and became a television evangelist in Texas."

In the firelight, her eyes grew soft with happy distant memories. "We had the best of times as a kids, Caraja and me. Always making kites and flying them up to Heaven, playing on huge vine swings. In fact, Caraja still has one that'll carry you clear across Hanley ghaut from wall to wall."

"I know, I did it."

"Me too," she smiled. "Thought I was going to die that first time."

"Me too."

"Someone was always trying to make a go-cart out of scraps of wood and pipes, and of course cast-off baby-buggy wheels. And if somebody had a set of four matching lawnmower wheels, he had a 'swack' of friends for the whole summer.

Water fights, trying to catch monkeys, even chores like collecting the pasture animals in the evening, were fun back then. See this scar," she turned back around and showed her leg in the firelight, exposing a six-inch-by-three-inch scar along her calf, the kind that comes from a bad friction burn.

"One-time Caraja and I and a cousin named Sully made a go-buggy that was so cool. It was a platform on four wheels that you could sit on, two in the back and two in the front, with a turning axle that swivelled in the middle for steering. And had tyres nailed into the axle ends. But... that was the problem that gave us fits, we could never get a real axle shaft for the wheels to turn on.

"The summer would be over before we could find something, so we decided in the meantime that if we held the wheels on with washers and nails driven into the ends of the two-by-four steering stick we might be able to navigate it"

"We knew we were riding the edge, but oh Jah was it exciting!"

" It was great for a few runs and I'm telling you I bet Coney Island has nothing that's comparable!"

She started to laugh as memories came forward with vivid content. Her laughter was that of an unrestrained child's. "But mon, when that nail snapped-she off or pull-she out, we'd crash 'Mama' hard."

Garth noticed she'd slipped into dialect, but then she caught herself. "You'd think a bad accident would stop us, but the rides were so wild and fantastic, it was worth the risk. And we figured when our number came up, we'd just put in another nail, a little deeper, and go until we crashed again.

"Most of the time they weren't bad crashes. Like if it was a rear tyre to fall off, you'd just skid on your butt, but sometimes on those steep hills above Remember Me, you'd lose a front steering wheel and then it was 'landing-in-de-spiny cusha-tree' rough. Caraja has a scar like mine, but bigger, on his shoulder.

"Oh Jah." She started laughing and "Oh Jah-ing' so hard, remembering their recklessness, that she feared she'd pee on the floor if she didn't stop. It had been some time since she'd laughed so freely with a man that she wasn't related to. But then, just as abruptly, she saw the dark cloud and fell silent.

"None of us thought we'd ever be unhappy, but then the *Christina* sank and now I sometimes wonder if I will ever be that happy again."

"Excuse me," Garth interrupted her, "I don't understand. The *Christina* was the ferry that went down back in the '60s… between St. Augustine and St. Kitts?" He looked at her. "Did you have family on it?"

"Are you ready for this? It's heavy," she sighed. "My mother, father, two younger sisters and a younger brother, three aunts from my mother's side, two of my father's brothers and eleven cousins drowned!"

"Holey! Holey!" Gath exclaimed.

"Three hundred and sixty people died that day and twenty-two came from my family." She fell silent, then grew anxious as the storm raged again into the vacuum.

"Oh God, will this storm ever stop?" She had to keep talking, engaging.

"Where was I?" She thought for a moment, then, "Oh yes, Portstown Academy. That came next. I always did well in school, so when I was ready to leave primary, the headmistress recommended that I go to the Academy in town for the rest of my education. It was a blessing and a curse, as you say. I decided as soon as I got there that, after so much death, I was going to become a student my family would be proud of, even from beyond. And much to the Principal's delight, the Academy and the Bordeaux family opened my eyes to a huge world of possibilities. I guess I kind of absorbed everything I could."

"And the curse?"

"The curse was that I missed so much of village life, blood-family life, little things like sitting around in the evening sharing gossip, talking about the day's adventures, the hide-and-seek games in the through the orchards. But... that's not completely correct to say I had no blood-family life. On weekends, I had Sueky, my grandmother on my father's side, whom Caraja and I initially went to live with after the *Christina*. Maybe someday you'll meet her." She thought about it and smiled, "In fact, I would like that very much.

"I think that, because of Sueky's stories, I know as much about my ancestors as I do about my parents. One in particular, a back-time slave named Naomi." She caught herself and chose a new direction. "If truth be known," she stared into the flames, "those days of village life ended for everyone after the *Christina* sank. Also, after I moved into town, Caraja went to live with an

Uncle on the other side of the island to learn farming and we didn't see each other very often." She fell silent for a moment. Oh, I missed him so much."

"During the school part of the week, I stayed with the Bordeaux family, and it was because of them that I was introduced to the world that books had only hinted at. The visitors to the Bordeaux home were remarkable people from all around the planet, interesting people who achieved great things. Doctor Bordeaux was himself a famous man in tropical medicine, something of an Albert Schweitzer of the Antilles. One of my two closest friends — in fact, to this day we call each other sister — was his daughter Danielle.

"And your other friend?"

"She was another girl I'd met at the Academy. You may know her — Arabelle Johnston? Her father was the harbourmaster for thirty years." Garth shook his head No. "Everyone calls her Ruth, or Ruthie."

"Auntie Ruthie!" Garth's mind raced, but he held his tongue. The irony hit him that the woman who kept one of the classiest sporting-houses in the Caribbean was best friends with a woman as in tune with the natural harmony as Myah. He smiled to himself. Auntie Ruthie was also one of his best friends. Not long into his Peace Corps tour, loneliness and lack of female companionship had guided him to "Ruthie's Snackette" as it was called back then. She was young, beautiful, charming and seductive. But when she learned he was with the Peace Corps she made it quite clear that sex was not on the menu of the Snackette.

"The United States government doesn't hassle me. And I don't wage wars or collect taxes, and they stay out of the Snackette business… meaning I don't entertain their employees."

"But" Myah continued, "my absolutely best friend, is Danielle. After graduation, she moved to New York… we all did, for a little while, but that's another story. Danielle is beautiful, and she became a well-known model with the Ford Agency.

We'd nicknamed her 'Bana' as a kid and that became her *fashion 'nom celeb'*".

"Bana? I know of her," Garth said, surprised that he actually did, at one time her face and form were common on every magazine from *Vogue* to *Rolling Stone*. And it wasn't the kind of face one forgot.

Like Myah's, in fact, like Ruthie's. There were certainly differences: Ruthie's eyes were soft, easy-going and brimming with mischief; Bana's were innocent and almost shy, while Myah's were wise, confident and always a little sad. They all had long, sleek bodies and that was the original bond, for they were all athletes, distance runners all through high school.

"In truth, other than living in New York for a few months," Myah reflected, "I haven't been even as far as the Gulf of Mexico. And what travel I did around the Caribbean was just for debate competitions and sports."

"I'd heard from the librarian at Poppy Dawn," Garth interjected, "that you were rebellious, yet you had won highest marks in the Federation on the graduation tests."

"That was years ago, and it was probably because the Bordeauxs didn't have a television set back then and I was too ugly for boyfriends."

"No... there was another factor. I was very angry and disruptive as a student, and finally the Head Mistress threw me out of school! But just to piss her off, I'd sit outside the classroom and learn that way."

And yet you got the highest marks in the Confederation?" Ask Garth.

"Go figure!' She laughed. "I guess I was so ugly I had no choice but learn!'

"Roight. I'm sure that's it." Garth laughed.

"What is your gift, Garth Longgrass?" Myah studied him.

"Don't know yet. That's why I came to the West Indies, I guess, to figure out what steps in Gods' dance I'm supposed to do. But let me turn the question back to you, what's your gift?"

"I don't know either," she reflected, "but I've sensed for a long time that something important will be asked of me."

Garth held up his hand, cutting her off. Except for the sound of falling water and its thundering echo off the ghaut walls, there was silence!

"It's the eye," Myah realised.

****

Leaving Bantu asleep on his mat, Myah and Garth crawled to the entrance of the cave. The force and volume of the water now caused it to cascade well beyond the entrance trail, far out into the ghaut below, leaving the footpath accessible, but grease-slick with mist on the moss.

At first Myah thought everything was miraculously fine in the light of a brilliant full moon peering through a cylinder thousands of feet high in the clouds — a giant eye looking in to examine the damage.

But, as she drew closer to the yard, the moon revealed that nothing was right. Petrified by the storm, the only movement was the earth shivering and spasmodically recoiling from the beating it had just received. The silence resonated through every nerve ending in her body, and she realised her eardrums still vibrated violently, as though they'd explode from built-up pressure. The hurricane still resonated in her head, hollow and empty but terrifying just the same, making her pulse continue to race, after being overloaded, over-sensitised. But it was not just her hearing, all of her senses were traumatised and she trusted none of them.

The air, though stagnant, was still full of electricity, standing hairs on end, causing her body to itch, to sweat and then shiver involuntarily, like the earth itself. The air tasted of salt, decay and the metallic bite of death. But her senses did not

258

betray her completely, and what she had experienced was indelibly written upon her. And what she saw of her farm, particularly the tree orchard, her livelihood, was a shambles.

The mahogany tree between the cabin and the cave had split in two, one half snapping over into the garden, the other towards her house. The chicken coop was crushed, the chickens gone. Somehow, in the moonlight, Myah found one egg.

Garth suddenly clasped her arm and cupped his hand to his ear, listening, gesturing for her to do the same. They could hear the wall of wind coming across the Caribbean again!

Immediately they ran towards the cave, but an advance gust drove them to the ground. Garth struck his head on something hard, and for a moment of severe pain, he thought he would vomit. Myah grabbed him and tugged him onward. But then, just as they started for the entrance, they saw in the fading moonlight that the opening was blocked once again by the waterfall.

"Bantu!" Myah screamed.

Then another blast of wind struck and in disbelief they saw the wind lift the waterfall into the air and propel it far out into the night, away from the cliff. They rushed through the entrance and instantly the wind subsided and the waterfall returned, sealing them inside.

They were soaked by the time they got to the back of the cave. Bantu was crying in the dark, holding his kitten close.

"Oh, baby, is okay." Myah rushed to the child. "Is okay," she said again and again, and held him close. Holding his head in the curve of her neck, she stroked his locks, rocking him, talking to him in as calm a voice as she could muster. Soon Bantu stopped crying but continued to fuss. She sat down on a mat and pulling the bodice of her dress from one breast, she began to nurse the child, though he hadn't breast-fed in months. He soon fell asleep.

The fire had gone out, leaving a small cache of coals that Garth coaxed into flames before laying in fresh dry wood. Taking the ladle from the pot, he poured hot water into a calabash bowl and added some tea and two tablespoons of brown sugar. When it had steeped, he filtered it through a cheesecloth into a second calabash bowl, which he gave to Myah, still sitting on a mat with Bantu in her lap. She was shaking with cold, her hair and dress drenched.

In his pack he found a t-shirt, a pair of shorts and a pair of boxer underpants. There was also a pile of towels that Myah had brought from the house before the storm. He took two fresh towels and the clothing to Myah. She smiled up at him with tired eyes, and he motioned to the towel and then her hair. She nodded. "Take off your clothes," he said, and again she nodded, drawing her dress over her head. She wore neither bra nor panties.

When her hair was dry and wild, she put on the shirt and underpants. The shirt was tight and the pants were loose, but both were dry. Myah drank the hot tea. Garth sat behind her, his legs on either side of her, pressing his chest against her back for warmth, his arms around her, while she wrapped hers around Bantu, forming a cocoon against the storm's awful force until finally she stopped shivering. Garth lay back on the bamboo and Myah curled beside him, placing Bantu between them, her arm reaching across the baby and resting on Garth's shoulder.

For all his fatigue, Garth couldn't remain asleep for long and lay there for some time thinking about Myah. From the first moment she spoke to him, he had felt out of balance. She was like no one he'd ever known. From the moment they met on the trail, he was in love. Love like he had never felt, as if he had never known love at all. There was a rightness to it. But this line of thinking was silly, he realised.

He was leaving soon. As soon as the storm ebbed— he was gone. Why had this singular fact eluded him? Why did he allow himself to become even more infatuated with her in the light of his imminent departure? So often over the past two years he'd relived their first meeting, and now here she was in his arms, and he was thinking of leaving. Still, both the irony and the tragedy of his circumstance seemed somehow irrelevant in the face of the hurricane.

He recalled how she walked that first day, tall and graceful, like a beautiful ebony egret that held its head steady and correct as the rest of her being, moved beneath it with natural assurance and choreography over the rough terrain. She was pregnant at the time, her swollen abdomen drawing her dress tight around her, revealing her long legs, the lift of her buttocks, the form of her breasts above her drooping belly. Her face had the presence of royalty, long, rich cheekbones and a jawline of determination. Her presence was also punctuated by the strength of her eyes, confident and without fear, without compromise. Yet there was also something unsettling in their recesses.

Something unresolved as though wisdom and emotion were at a crossroads and she couldn't decide which to choose. Thick black coils poked out from her turban like eager schoolchildren from the windows of Poppy Dawn primary. Cleopatra, he decided, an African queen emerging from her emerald palace. He could not speak until spoken to.

When she spoke, her mysterious catacomb eyes were flooded with a genuine warmth and familiarity that he hadn't known since he'd left his family and friends in Wyoming. Her first words emerged before she could catch them. "Oh, here you are," she'd said, as though finding something or someone she'd been looking for. She spoke it with the innocence of a child. He was speechless, thoughtless, or maybe overwhelmed by the thousands of potential responses that crowded his mind — all equally stupid.

He understood why they'd said at the shop, "Myah-she makes grown'd men be-fool demselves." Garth saw something

261

more, for he believed pregnant women are the most beautiful creatures on the planet. They wear an aura of life, the fragrance of new birth, and carry about them a field of radiance that moves loud men to quietness,

Chapter 21

"He Ain't Crazy, Ya Know"

Delbert-he-ain't-crazy-mon was a large man with thick hands, feet and brow. His face was predisposed to looking crazy by the fact that one eye turned more skyward than level, while the other studied everything from eye-level down. It was the right eye, the one turned upward, that people figured was Delbert's problem because he often had conversations with various Deities on high. On the other hand, the leveller eye was often more on the level than any other perspective on-island.

The difficulty was knowing which eye had control at any given moment. Also, the face itself was hard to get a focus upon, as it passed through various contours, from innocence, love, humour and even, occasionally, lucidity. Each contortion matching what possessed his imagination at the moment. Never dangerous, and always genuine.

"He Ain't Crazy You Know Mon" wore his cap facing sideways, adding an aura. to his manic mystique. When asked why he wore his hat so, he would turn it proper, bill facing forward, the correct way, and say "ON!"

Then he brought 90 degrees, a quarter turn: "Lock!"

The air through the day had been a thick, suffocating soup that sat almost motionless until dusk, when the wind picked up enough to push out the haze. By evening the wind was growing and Delbert was anxious to make his move up to his tiny jungle shack on the edge of Portstown Ghaut, facing Montserrat where the storm was coming from.

Delbert believed his bamboo and thatch house would likely come apart if the storm came to St. Augustine, but at least he would be home. "Going country" was the expression: half an hour by bus up the volcano from town, then another half-hour walk beyond the last stop. He had spent the day since dawn at the helm of the town,

Captain of his ship preparing for the storm. Mainly he directed traffic, unsnarled bottlenecks. Like when Lobster Louise had to make talk with her cousin Gateneau about hurricane Hugo — in the middle of the War Memorial intersection! It was Delbert who guided them smoothly through the snarl and into a parking place down Alley Road without a break or even pause in the ladies' conversation.

When one store ran out of something, he'd direct folks to those that had it. At the end of the day, he was helping the shop owners close their shutters, lay blocks on their galvanise roofs for weight. He was resolved to remain aboard his ship until the last man, or in this case, woman, was on safe moorings.

Miss Williams was alone; her sons were in Canada. Her grocery store sat at the strategic heart of the town. She was the last, staying open until the last possible minute so everyone could get their provisions. Miss Williams never extended credit... except that day. "When money holds less importance than friends helping each other it is time to "git on".

"Delbert," she asked as he passed with his arms full of large wooden crates, "Why you bring in boxes dat's empty?"

"Better Delbert bring dem in den let Mista Hugo throw dem thru somebody windows."

She smiled. He set them against the cereal shelf. "Delbert, people just don't know all what's gonna befall dis place if dat hurricane takes a notion to turn on us. Nothing is going to be the same. Mark my words, Nothing going to be da same."

"Fo'chure, Mam" he nodded in agreement. "Dis is da last of da t'ings dat de wind gonna touch. Les' not tarry any longer," he suggested, growing anxious to get the last porthole of the ship closed tight. In truth, he didn't believe that the hurricane would actually hit. On the other hand, a person in his position of responsibility must always err on the side of caution. He had arranged earlier with Samba Taxi to stay in town to the last. Samba Taxi had been helping Miss Williams too, but now he sat in his car, the engine running, the radio set on the storm report.

"Me t'ink she be time we makes our move!" Delbert said with finality in his voice.

"Yes, it's time to make our move," Miss Williams sighed.

Delbert was stunned by what confronted him when he stepped out of the shop. It was more than a ghost town — there weren't even any ghosts. There had been no time for the ghosts to set in. In the course of two hours, the town center had gone from a teeming beehive of activity — half the population of the Island swarming through the streets — to now a barren roadway void of life. No people, he'd expected... but no dogs, chickens, not even birds?

That was what scared him. The closest thing to life was a line of flags that had pulled free at one end from a palm at one end of the park. Caught by the growing wind, it swung its tail in great serpentine coils, slapping up against the shutters of the Treasury Building, then whipping across the square to give de Longstone Café a few licks. Delbert shook his head to drive out what he now knew — the hurricane was going to hit them straight on!

Miss Williams locked the old brass padlock while Delbert and Samba Taxi wedged in the cross-arms over the shutters. "Good enough," she said with a heavy heart, and she began to weep as she looked one last time at her store before getting into Samba-Taxi's car.

Samba-Taxi raced up the main road. There was no traffic. No concern over hitting a donkey or chicken: everybody and everything had disappeared. Delbert hurried Miss Williams to the door of her house. She pleaded for the men to remain in the shelter of her strong home, not for herself but for their safety. Yet each wanted to be in his own nest. Samba-Taxi dropped Delbert off at the bottom of Shaker's Hill.

When he began, he was sure he'd make it home. But less than halfway up the second pitch, sheets of galvanised came flying across the soccer field at him, and Delbert saw the hurricane was upon him.

He had to find shelter. But just as he turned, a blast of wind caught him and sent him stumbling, slamming him into the side of an ancient fig tree. His ears ached from the pressure, his nose bled from the impact. Desperately he clung to the tree, waiting for the wind to ebb, but it grew only worse.

One careful foothold at a time, he inched around the giant tree, stepping over the great root hips. In the lee, he slid down into the pocket of one of the roots, curling into an exhausted ball. He could not breathe; the air was full of mush. He covered his face with his hands and pushed himself as deep as possible into the dirt.

It was the sound that drove Delbert mad. Relentless, the wail of death unleashed from the grave engulfed him, deformed souls no longer contained by the earth, or even human imagination. It had been a long time since the wail got into his head. Before Hugo, the sound came upon him when the storm was only in his head. He never knew when it would come. His hands flew to his ears. But it was too late; the sound always got in.

Since childhood, he was at the mercy of his affliction and no amount of yelling or screaming would drive back that awful wail. Why did no one else hear it? He'd rush from person to person. "Mon, don't you hear she?" Of course they heard it. They must be playing a trick on him. But... the pain, they couldn't have hidden the pain. Sometimes he could not see because of it. Sometimes just a sliver of light sliced like a welding cutting-torch into his brain. And sometimes it was too much, and Delbert would fall to the ground writhing in revulsion to the thing that possessed him.

Though the physical pain was severe, what terrified him most was the flood of grotesque images that swept through him. Thoughts without order, bougainvillea flowers ... then body parts. Faces in agony, others calm, black people, white. Sometimes they spoke to him, more often they screamed, with open toothless mouths at him.

And then one day, a Sunday at the intersection of the Methodist, Anglican and Wesleyan Holiness churches, as each was unloading its congregation, Delbert was taken by a seizure... and then a vision. He was standing in a freshly picked field of sea-island cotton. Goats wandered around eating the weeds amongst the cotton plants. At the far end of the field was the soft blue Caribbean reaching to the horizon, and great cotton-ball clouds. Everything was clearer than if he'd seen it with his eyes open. And the goats were fat, the sea full of fish. Along one side of the field stood a lone mango tree, an old lady resting in its shade.

"Come sit-fora -spell. " She motioned to him. She looked like Sueky, the obe' down Hanley Road.

"Me does study you for some time, Delbert," she said to him. "And me sees da Lord does give you a heavy burden. And me sees Youse does struggle with it. But da burden be no more den you can carry."

She looked at him hard. "When da load seem too much, remember dis: Delbert, you's one of God's chosen!"

And with her words, the seizures stopped! The change in Delbert made many wonder if he hadn't been taken to San Sebastián and had shock-treatment. Others said he took 'mood' drugs "like dey's liquorice". Delbert had had a job at the dock, which he promptly quit. And for the first few weeks, he just walked about town looking it over, studying the people, their habits. And then one day, the drab, uninteresting town-square, the "War Memorial Square' in the middle of Pottstown was an explosion of flowers, ribbons and artistic forms from the dump. .

The "Square" was actually a triangle, created at the main intersection of Dock Road and the Ring Road and a street no one knew its name since it only fifty-metres long. Its justification was as a pedestrian safety crossing. In the middle of traffic, it was a place to make decisions in the safety of a few benches and the serenity of a scrubby dead palm.

But suddenly, overnight it became an extravaganza of flowers from neighbourhood gardens, *objets d'art* from the sea, and sculpting of empty tin cans.

'He Ain't Crazy! the Islanders agreed, pleased with his work.

Chapter 22

"Insanity of the Storm"

The fury of the storm grew stronger into the night. At first there were just violent waves punctuated by brief windows of relative calm. But around midnight the hurricane's full force hit the Island. And even deep inside the cave. The air became saturated with a thick mist of debris that was once a vital living jungle of leaves, lizards and birds; all pulverised into a thick mist of choking pulp. Even the fire, tucked deep inside the cave fluctuated between near collapse in a breathless vacuum, then there'd come a sudden violent gust that turned even thick chunks of whole logs to crushed splinters.

At first, Bantu, huddled in a protective clutch of his mother and Garth, whimpered, but soon he slipped into the same comatose silence of the adults.

The forces of chaos and violence possessed the land. Garth was beyond exhaustion and still the intensity of the storm's bellow grew louder. And, as fatigued as he was, there was still no relief in sleep as he was enveloped with nightmares unrestrained by the limits of sanity. Then, sometime in the night and the storm, something snapped.

As Myah and Bantu slept, Garth stared into the flames of the fire. At first, he thought the flames made the usual apparitions that he'd seen so often in campfires..., but this time they were different. They coiled and crafted into a figure...a woman, a white woman dressed in a white dress, a wedding dress.

Suddenly he saw her face. The eyes were wild with sorrow... maybe insanity!

Then they widened as they fell upon him, Bantu and finally focused on Myah.

268

"Naomi!" she screamed from the flames, focusing exclusively upon Myah. "So now ye finally come to me to pay fo ye sins!".

Garth pulled Myah and Bantu closer to him.

The apparition growled in the back of her throat, low and guttural like a jungle cat defending its kill, or maybe preparing <u>for</u> a kill! Then, without warning, the pupils snapped into view and Garth gasped in horror at her eyes... intense, animal -wild...<u>demonic</u> eyes that darted around the cave finally falling upon him with such fierceness that he tried to escape, but his body would not move.

"Myah," he shook her, trying to wake the woman beside him, but she didn't respond.

Then suddenly the woman moved with practised grace away from the fire towards them.

"Naomi" it cried out. "The Lord has finally delivered you unto me for ye sins! Finally, d' time is neigh for ye to know the consequences of your deeds. The time of reckoning!" She screamed

"Myah!" Garth yelled as he felt the woman's delirium upon her. The woman moved with focused stately strides in contrast to the mad, grotesque frenzy of the fire. The apparition's back was straight, its head held high! She was ghostly pale, the colour of chalk. More striking, her clothes...a wedding dress from an ancient time, crinoline in layers, internal hoops casting wide shadows across the floor. A fear more powerful than the hurricane overwhelmed him. He felt he had gone insane!

Advancing, the woman now stood quietly on the edge of the fire. She was cultured, with an aristocratic poise that comes from generational breeding. Then she lifted the bridal veil.

He recoiled! Etched by the fire's reflection he saw the details of refined pampered features. Her dress was a wedding dress!! Her blue-grey eyes bore down on them with malicious hate!.

"So, at last ye cum". She yelled, the words hanging in the air, echoing off the cave walls, muting even the hurricane. "Ye come to curse me further ill with what ye doon for selfish spite?"

Each syllable was precisely pronounced in a back-time brogue of the Scottish Highlands from another century.

"Ye come to plead for mercy for what ye've done?" She looked questioningly, as if seeking a response from Myah, to whom she spoke, though Myah lay unconscious on the floor.

"Know ye true, Naomi, 'cept for ye, dis day Ay'd be wed! Er nay for ye Ay'd pass with he, free from this immortal hell of neither death no life!"

"Aye," she repeated, "er nay for ye dis day Ay'd be wed." She fell silent, starring at Myah.

"Desires are empty dreams o' things jus' beyond thine hands of want!"

"Ye cannot satisfy thine-self with only one!" She laughed. "Nay!" She screamed, her head rolled back; her cry was vile and vitriolic, "Ye cannot have but one!" she yelled at Myah. "Ye take ye BOTH!" She screamed above the swelling wind of the hurricane.

"So, art thou too not trapped upon 'ere rock as Ay, when ye were both slave and hand-maiden be?" The eyes rolled inward, then flashed full force upon Myah, then him and the child

"Oh, how true does fate aboon that thou condemn ye-self and me condemned upon 'ere wretched rock. But more cruel for me than thee who knew thine harlot's joy with my men, while Ay should pass, my sex intac..., unto eternity."

Tears rolled down her cheeks and fell upon the cavern floor, hissing like water droplets upon a hot skillet. But then, the swollen eyes suddenly focused on Bantu.

"Nay" she shrieked. "Ye cannot take jus' one, but both, and now ye bring day's child t'mock? A bastard child, who he father be? He? Or he? Or both?!" She screamed.

Confused, Garth recoiled when he saw her insane focus had fallen now upon Bantu. Myah remained unconscious, oblivious to this delirious nightmare.

Then he saw the woman's purpose, and pulling Bantu from Myah's lifeless hold, he leapt to his feet, clutching Bantu in his arms away from the apparition's reach.

"Nay, slay-up de innocent that ye may feel de cutting cold and dark of an empty life's as does I!" The woman screamed at Myah! 'Smash he head, as ye my heart for what ye does to me!" She wailed and lunged once more with burning eyes for the child in Garth's arms.

With Bantu in his left arm, way from the screaming woman, he rocked back, and in the empty light of the dwindling fire he swung with all his strength - his right fist striking her a full blow ... the hit had substance!

She dropped hard onto the earthen floor in front of him. Now full of fight, Garth jumped at her, his fist raised, ready to strike again and again should she make another move.

But then ... she disappeared!

He waited fists clenched holding Bantu while the storm bellowed in his ears, his chest full of war and warrior - full of her madness.

Crazed with adrenaline, he finally looked down.

"Oh my God," he cried with disbelief and shock…. it was Myah he had struck!

Suddenly his senses were confused... unreliable. Suddenly Garth realised something else; the storm had grown more intense like the sound of an airplane taking off! Then suddenly a blast of the hurricane far stronger and savage than what they'd known crashed against the cliff face and the mountain itself shook with an explosion of an impact that drove the waterfall back upon itself ... and into the cave!

Like a cresting ocean wave, it crashed through the entrance, driving Garth, Bantu and Myah further into the cavern. Still clutching Bantu for a fleeting second Garth saw Myah's arms flail above the froth before the water drowned the fire and all went black!

271

Then, just as suddenly the wind collapsed upon itself, and immediately the water inside the cave flushed out of the chamber with a force and fury equal to its entrance - dragging him still clutching Bantu helplessly towards the entrance and the vertical drop into the ghaut far, far below.

Garth clawed fruitlessly for a hold... then, in desperation, with both arms, he threw the screaming child as far as possible into the back of the cave and above the waterline. Then in the back-surge, he grasped wildly for Myah in the foam and turbulence. But trying to find her in the dark hopeless and he was being pulled out of the cave!

Only, at the very entrance did he feel her arm, and grabbed, catching it by her wrist

He no longer had the strength to pull her out of the back-surge but anchored his feet against the entrance wall and fought to hold solidly until the water flushed away!

He knew not how long they lay exhausted, motionless on the sodden floor of the cave.

Desperately fearing that the wind might again turn the waterfall back upon them, he grasped Myah under the arms and drug her to the rear where Bantu flailed screaming from the bales of Caraja's ganja. There far back of the cave was a section still dry, untouched by the wave, and he carefully laid Myah on the floor beside Bantu and collapsed beside both crying with relief and thankfulness that they were alive.

***

Finally, as dawn illuminated the inside of the cave with grey fingers, Myah brought her face close to his. He could feel her breath when her lips moved, but her voice was weak with little force.

"No more," she whispered, looking up expressionlessly, "no more." Her eyes closed and she was gone!

Garth pulled her body close to his and began to cry, then sob without control, from fatigue and loss! It was an emptiness more profound than he had ever known! In the insanity of the storm, he

272

had lost the very person he believed might be his destiny. He dared not move nor awaken Bantu, nor affirm that the woman he held in his arms was dead!

Finally, when he had no more emotions, he felt in the faint wisp of dawn that the storm had passed.

"Bikini!"he cried in Shoshoni "*Bikini!* Give her life." he begged his ancestors. "I ask for nothing more." Again and again, he pleaded!"

Then, as though in response to his prayers, he felt her move within his arms. He saw her chest rise and fall. He kissed her brow. "E-wisa, e-wisa!" he cried in shoshone. "*Thank you thank you*"

Myah and Bantu slept undisturbed as Garth sat wide awake for the rest of the night. He felt bitterly alone and longed for his family and home in Wyoming. In fact, he'd settle for something, anything, familiar, something stable... someplace untouched by the storm!.

"When this is over and I'm off this forsaken Island," he vowed.

Easing away from Myah and Bantu he found the pile of blankets left by Caraja in the far back of the cave. He wrapped Bantu in one of the towels and gently dried Myah's wet body with another.

All there was that wasn't soaking wet was the marijuana, and even the it took a little time to build a fire of dried marijuana, Over a makeshift fire-pit in a cast-iron pot that Caraja had put away in the back for washing the dishes, he boiled water and poured some into a calabash and put in some tea bags he'd also found in Caraja's supplies.

Crawling back to Myah, he dipped the end of a towel into a bowl of warm water delicately wiping the mud and ash her face.

He knew now that he'd been broken by the storm, and he felt sick with shame that he had struck Myah, supposing her some fire-phantom spirit. He'd always thought himself of stronger mettle.

Before the "Storm of the Century", he had been happier than he ever remembered. He realised that when he was around Myah --

before the storm, he'd never felt more heroic, more tender, more confident. But, he caught himself.....and now more unsure... confused ...and... maybe.... Insane!" How odd he thought, to survive the storm and lose confidence in one's own mind.

Chapter 23

"Delbert and the 'Emperors of Saint Augustine"

The hollow of a fig tree where Delbert had found some shelter was now being lashed straight-on by the brutal storm, the sounds and the seizures came back upon him. The "dung demons", he called the cries as a little boy when the sound, the pain and the fear came upon him. Ever since he was ten years old, he had expected to die when the seizures began. He felt that way now, burrowed into the crook of the tree roots as the storm howled above him. The pressure, the fear and pain were so strong, he wished for death that he might escape their hold upon him.

Finally, when he could take it no more, he screamed. "If she-be da Lord's will…" he gasped, resigning himself to the uncontrollable, "…den das wha she-be!" And the great uprooted tree of emotion crashed within him,

"Me surrenders!" And he sobbed and sobbed until he could cry no more. It was finally over. He released his fear. He no longer carried its burden, for death itself no longer had a hold on Delbert.

But then he realised with the passing of the eye that he was not going to die. In fact, he somehow felt strong, for indeed he had rested in the crook of the root. He must leave the fig tree and make his move for home once again.

He ran up the empty road, but just as he passed in front of Browne's house the storm came again, this time even harder! There was no other sanctuary near, and he had to find shelter.

No one came when he beat on the door. He tried the shutters. All but one were secure and that one had only a half-inch of play. His ears started to hurt again from the pressure changes. The wind now had both sound and matter, burning his skin as though it were blasted by beach sand.

Desperately he worked his fingers into the loose shutter and pulled slowly and steadily, but it would not budge. Rocking forward, he threw all of his weight backward, yanking with all of his strength. This time the board holding the shutter on the inside broke and suddenly the shutters flew open, throwing Walter onto his back on the ground. Fighting, he rose and crawled through the open window, and pulled the shutters closed. With the longest piece of the broken board, he jammed it closed and slumped to the floor gasping for breath.

Cautiously he started to move in the darkness, immediately knocking over a chair. Then, from the middle of the room came scurrying sounds like a pack of fruit rats scrambling away into the far corner. Pulling a box of matches from his pocket, he lit one.

"Ayyeeeee!" came a blood-freezing scream so violent and unexpected that he dropped the match in alarm. There was something, or somebody, in the room with him!

"He a jumbie, be?" whimpered a tiny voice.

"Worse..." came a second, older, boy's voice. "...is Delbert!"

The timid voice began to whimper louder and louder, until it was crying full out. Delbert lit another match. Six sets of eyes, round and dollar-size, stared at him in numb fear. He found a candle on the table between them.

As the flame swelled, there was a gasp from the children as Delbert disheveled countenance became clear. The screams were so terrifying that they scared even Delbert. All the children covered their eyes and yelled — all, but one. That one was Emily, the youngest. When she peeked between the tears, he was not the horrible monster she had imagined, but simply a man... in fact, the funny man from the Memorial Park who used to make faces for her amusement.

"Ohh-ee-gurl." He knelt down to her level. "Dere's nothing be afraid of. Es jus' me." He made one of his silly faces, and her face muscles relaxed into the slightest smile. "Come here, dearest.

Es jus' me, Delbert." He extended his arms, and again there was a collective gasp as the children pressed even farther away… all but Emily. She paused but a moment, looking hard at Delbert, then she rushed into his arms and began to sob out her story. Slowly the rest of the children moved forward, adding parts left out by the littlest one.

Their parents had gone during the eye of the storm to see if their grandmother was safe. Her house was down at the bottom of Hickman Road, a long way off. They thought they could get back, but they hadn't returned when the second side of the hurricane hit.

"Well! Now dat's just da best luck ever!" Delbert grinned in the candlelight. "Da best luck dat I does come along when I does!" He turned to Emily. "You believes in Angels, little one?"

She nodded.

"Well, everyt'ing gonna be just fine, cause I's an <u>Angel</u>!"

"Das a lie," barked one of the older boys. "He be da crazy man what hangs in da Square."

"He ain't crazy," Emily snapped back "He's an angel!"

"Hey, Little One," Delbert whispered in her ear. "You like stories?"

She nodded.

"Well, how would you like it if I told you a story?"

"Wat's it about?"

"Is about da mongoose and da monkey, and how dey come to rule da kingdom of Saint Augustine. You know dat story? No?! Well, you know dat we has a monkey and a mongoose for Emperors? Yeh… for chure!" he assured her. "And you know why, cus da very first monkey and mongoose what comes to St Augustine does be sons of da Emperors way in back time in Ah-free-ca. Yep, das so. What's more, dey used to be da best of friends till dey get on da boat."

"Which boat?" Emily asked.

"Eh… da boat what Mistah Noah he-same-self does drive."

"Was it bigger than the Queen's?"

277

"Oh, much more so."

"Bigger than the cruises ships?"

"Jus' dat size. Yep, but dis one only for da animals. And all dose lights be staterooms for every animal on da Earth, even da birds have places for nest up on she top.

"But then comes d'trouble den dere's da trouble. Since dey be da best of friends, da monkey and da mongoose ask Mistah Noah if dey can bunk together.

"He t'inks long time, cus he's not so chure, but dey begs and swears upon dey's paws dat dere be no problem to he-Lordship. Ons and ons de go until finally, Captain Noah got to laugh and say 'Go so'!"

"Now, since dey both be royalty, da monkey and da mongoose is used to having dey's own way. And da way of da monkey is "shenanigans"! But da mongoose, he be da serious type, always watching and sorting things out in he own time. And at night when da mongoose want to lime out and read on he bunk, da monkey wants to swing on da ceiling light.

"'Mistah Monk Mon,' scolds Mistah Mongoose, 'does dey lets you act like dat in Youse palace?'"

"For a long time da monkey stops swinging, thinking bout what d' mongoose has asked. 'No,' he admits, 'we <u>all</u> does it back home at da palace! Everyone from da baby monks to me Auntie Agatha, we all does it. We figures, if Youse can't swing by it, what good a tail be? 'Sides, it takes more effort not to swing den it does to do it."

"Then one day... Boom!" Delbert made a big noise that startled the children into laughter. "You know what does come so?" The children nodded with delight.

"Da light broke!" they said in unison.

"Das exactly right, de ceiling light mesh-up! What's more, da monkey does take a hard knock on he nogg'n and have to go to da ship's doctor.

"'So, I sees by Youse bump,' says da nurse, who is a no-nonsense nanny goat, 'dat you be swing'n on da ship's chandelier. Does dey let you acts like dat at home?'

"'Chure!' Mistah Monk says."

By now, even the older children pressed against Walter, some with their arms around his neck, others sitting beside him on the floor... all trapped in his spell! And while the storm pounded upon the block house. Delbert had turned his hat sideways, to the "lock" position.

"Well, Captain Noah he none too pleased neither and he wants to separate da two right off, which da mongoose t'inks might be just fine. But not da monkey! He sees nothing wrong width what he does, and he wants to stay width he best friend and teach *him* to swing by his tail... da mongoose has a mighty fine tail for swinging.

"Now Noah does figure dat da influence of Mistah Mongoose on da monkey, plus da bump on da head, might change da monkey's ways. But don't you know just da opposite does happen!

"Chure enough, da next t'ing what rubs Noah wrong is deys complaining 'bout da food. Being royalty, dey Mistahs Mongoose and Monk be accustomed to certain luxuries. But da ship serve ordinary fare like tanya fritters, pumpkin soup, corn meal dandies and da likes, -- especially since she be a vegetarian cruise. Now dat doesn't bother de monkey too much, but da mongoose does like he frogs and snakes now and den. And what really ruff-up da mongoose's tail-fur is dat Captain Noah bring aboard plenty of frogs and snakes... den treat dem like any other passenger ... instead of supper!

"But da very last straw is when dey gits into de rum!"

"Oh, oh," everyone squealed in anticipation.

"Da monk begins by pestering da mongoose to start using he tail more, and eventually he wears he friend down to where Mongoose agrees to wrap it around things, then give them a pull, then a tug, until at last he is actually hanging by his tail like a possum."

"What's a possum?" Emily asked.

"It's like a fat mongoose hanging by its tail... but not so furry."

Emily nodded with a clear picture in her mind.

"Well, all is good, and soon da mongoose is learning to swing like a monkey. Den da monkey find da rum."

Again, there is a collective, knowing gasp.

"Don't you know, but dat dey don't finds deys way out of the rum room until dusk! And by den, dey's more den a little wobbly on dey's tails, but Mongoose is also feeling unusually brave and he takes a few swings off the starboard rail, out over da ocean. Mistah Monk-mon is mighty impressed and t'inks deys should show da others.

Now, on Captain Noah's boat, sundown also means supper in da big dining room, and all da animals are there at once with plenty chandeliers for swinging. Monk is t'inking dat maybe once da animals see Mistah Mongoose, deys all gonna be swinging from da roof and having a gay old time demselves. And off dey goes like two rum soaked fools with tails."

The children were now squirming around in excitement, each with a clear idea of what was to come next.

"Da monkey does swing into da room with a grand 'Ta Da!' yell, like a Circus Master. And Mongoose almost does the same, but he misjudges for da rum and his head hits da tray of da penguin waiter, sending everything flying..."

"What's a penguin?"

"It's a black and white mongoose!" scolded one of the children. "Now hesh-up!"

Once again, the storm rushed into the vacuum of the story, swelling the house with its force.

"Hesh up!" Delbert yelled at Hugo.

"Hesh up!" the chorus echoed. And suddenly the roar of the wind dropped into a hollow howl and the room filled again with Delbert's story.

"So, what does happen?" asked Emily.

"Well, don't you know da commotion of da flying food and dishes does bring everyone to alert. Monkey, seeing he's got dey's attention, does a double flip dat lands him hanging from the first chandelier. He figures everybody gonna applaud instead of gasping with horror!

"Mistah Mongoose almost makes it to da chandelier but again he misreads for de rum and dis time lands in a bowl of seasoned slugs for da egrets.

'Grab him!' Captain Noah commands, and drunk or not, Mistah Mongoose is out of dere like a mongoose running for he life.... down da length of da table! Over platters of sea moss for the platypus and buckets of breadfruit for da polar bears. And he would've got away if'n he hadn't tarried to take a chomp out of a frog's foot, and dey catch hold of 'im. Dey never does get Mistah Monk Mon, down from da lights, but he can no git to the floor either.

"Well, Captain Noah walk very straight and stern up to da Monk, pull'n Mistah Mongoose by the scruff. "Gentlemen," he does say, and everybody on da boat gits real quiet." Delbert furrowed his eyebrows as though he was the angry Noah.

"'Even though Youse be royalty, you does vex-me-ups once too often!' he say to dem. 'See dat island.' He points out da porthole at a rather lonely volcano sticking out by she-self in da Caribbean. 'Well, das you's new home, cus dey's no room on dis boat for swingers and toe-biters!'

"And, chure to he word, he does set dem off!"

" Well, don't you know da mongoose and da monkey are not too pleased width being stranded in the middle of the Caribbean, and each blames da other for dey's predicament.

Dey even does goes on for a while like dey no-know de other's given name. And when dey meet, dey eyes look right through de other. Mind you, sometimes Mistah Mongoose does turn and give Mistah Monk-Mon a nip on he tail. And sometimes Mistah

Monk does turn and gives Mistah Mongoose a knock on da nogg'n just to pester he.

"'Enough be enough,' says da mongoose one day! 'Here's what we gonna do. We's gonna divide up da food stuffs. You's a vegetarian?'

"'Cept fo de odd grub worm or beetle I does take to cleanse me breath out," says da monkey.

"'Das okay, I doesn't take no pleasure in dem. I's a carnivore, and nothing suits my palate more den a nice juicy, slimy, squiggly snake..." Dexter acted like he had one in his hand, causing Emily to crinkle her nose in disgust. The children crowed with delight. 'Or a fat, floppy, hoppy toad, all covered in warts.'"

"Yuck!" Groaned Emily.

"'And de land --,' Mistah Mongoose continued. "We gonna divide de land. You goes up da mountain to da rainforest, and me gonna stay down on da lower plane.'

"So, they shook paws on it. And to dis day Mistah Mongoose and Mistah Monk-Mon does share dey's kingdom equally. And das how dey come to be here to St. Augustine. And das why St. Augustine gots two Emperors, instead of just one, like most places."

"But we does have one Prime Minister, not an Emperor," one of the older girls corrected.

"Oh, he just be for show... for da people-kin. It's da monkeys and da mongoose what really runs dis Island."

Everyone laughed. "Das for chure," commented one of the older children.

"Listen!" Delbert raised his hand. "Listen up." He cocked his head.

"I don't hear anything," said Emily.

"Exactly!" Delbert bellowed with a great roaring laugh. "Mistah Hugo does get tired and move on!"

Everyone listened. It was true. The storm was over!

Chapter 24

"Sueky During"

Sueky rose early in spite of only a couple hours sleep having been at the beach most of the night. Curiously she found she still had the energy of one who was rested from hours of sleep and immediately alert to greet the day. She thought of the evening's events, of making the" Salvo d'morte". She looked at the small clay jar and lid, hoping that she had forgotten nothing, for the salve must be potent. She wondered if the manchineel apples were strong enough, they seemed dry and reluctant to release their caustic acid. Then she smiled to herself, seeing the burn in her apron, no, it had power. Besides, Emma would not let her stray from the formula and the ritual sequence for preparing it. So often she thought about Emma, first Sister of the slave Naomi, their birthmother who was consumed by her obligation to the white lady Elizabeth.

Emma never knew her mother well. Emma spoke across time to Sueky though devoted to her sister saw Elizabeth was like an opiate upon her Aunt, demanding all her time, and even in the white woman's insanity, pulling Naomi to her side, away the outside world, child that she was.

Sueky was so thankful the Spirit of Emma was with her that night on the beach to collect the ingredients for the salve. "Use your strength well, for it will not come again." Emma counselled her great, great-grand child. "This is the last that anything will be asked. But it must be done right. The cloak will pass soon to another." Sueky knew who that would be and did not seek affirmation. The knowledge came to her only as required, there was no exception.

"Sueky!" Mrs. Sutton passed and called from the old woman's gate. "Where-ya gonna spend d' hurricane? I's going to Anglican Church. Come-so? De priest say de storm no gonna touch us, but dere's so many people what's frightened, mes not one of them ya-know but he gonna open de doors for deys what wants can take solace in de Holy House. She made of stone so she good and solid, if'n you seek shelter dere.

"Das good cus das de plan all along." Said Sueky as though she'd known that was where she was going, though not for the reasons all others sought its shelter.

"Tell Sambo Taxi den dat he must pick up me too."

"He coming by me, me'll see he stops fo' Youse."

"Thanks you dearie. You's okay?"

"To be alive in these troubled times be a blessing and a curse," sighed Mrs. Sutton, "And only de Lord knows which. But give praise... to be alive is enough." It was a phrase of a generation where speech, even more than writing was the vehicle of expression.

Sueky cleared her thoughts of the night before, and focused on what had to be done, starting with her animals. She threw chicken food on the ground under her house, but closed off the wood n'wire gate to keep the chickens out it until the time came to move them. Midera would be there soon, she could help.

"Grand!" Midera's voice rang out. A pretty girl fourteen years of age stood at the gate. She had big soft eyes and a well-practiced, comfortable smile. Her hair had been plated with attentive love into long corn rolls. Dressed in shorts and a halter-top, she carried a bag with a dress and a few toiletries she'd need for the Church.

"Come so girl," Sueky called out to her extending her hand. "Midera, my love, me t'nks dis gonna be a mean wind we gonna know well, and de pig and de sheeps best sleep at de mill width de goats. Go so and fetch back de donkey he tired in Miss Sutton's pasture, cuz we gonna need he to tow de pig.'

Mistah Pig think he should be snoozing at de Anglican width us, but I tells he true dat chure as dat some o'dem parishioners gonna want he for bacon b'fo dis night pass. Sides Mistah Pig be in good company at de mill."

284

The girl sat her bag by the gate and went over to the Sutton pasture. Immediately the donkey began to bray, happy to be moved to new grazing.

"Enjoy yourself," laughed the girl, "for it maybe a long time before you know joy again."

She was surprised how secure Sueky had tied the animal, usually her knots were loose, and her animals remained tethered out of loyalty to their mistress, but there had been a change in Sueky over the last two days. She seemed younger, stronger, her mind more alert and clear instead of allusively wandering through the fog of age. It had caused Midera such concern of late. She didn't know the source of her grand's vitality, but she said a prayer of thanks.

"Come beast, we need you to do some towing." Without argument, the donkey followed Mirera's lead.

"Good, we take down the sheep first. Mistah Pig could vex us some so we'll save he fo' last." Sueky said, taking the donkey from the girl and tethering it to the mango tree in front of Sueky's bright pink and blue chattel house.

"Good to no go." Sueky said giving the tether line a pull. Open the gate and wait up d'road to turn de sheep down." It took little encouragement to collect the sheep and push them through the gate and down the road.

Midera ran ahead to open the barrier Sueky had pulled across the Mill's single opening the previous day. Again, Midera was surprised, that Sueky alone had moved the heavy bedsprings when it was all she could do to simply tip it aside. The goats tried to over-run the opening, but the girl was too quick and finally out of frustration and fear of her flailing arms and flying, they moved to the back of the old sugar mill.

"Here dey come!' And her sheep dashed into the inner-sanctum of the old cane-crusher mill. They were not happy to be confined with a bunch of goats and immediately they bleated their discontent loudly.

"Bes' git used to it, you's gonna be roommates until dis t'ing does pass." Sueky laughed, casting a loving eye over her flock.

As predicted, Mistah Pig had no intention of leaving his soft wet muddy, messy pen. The donkey, had to pull hard on the pig's tether while Sueky slapped his backside with a stick. The strength of a donkey is unrivalled and Sueky's beast simply leaned harder into the task. and soon they were moving the pig and clumps of rank smelling mud from his pen -- the pig's hoofs leaving deep furrows in the mud. Midera led the donkey while Sueky walked beside the pig coaxing it with gentle words and empty threats of using the stick she carried in her hand on his hamhocks. Still, the procession moved slowly down the Uptee-Doon Road.

"De abattoir in the odder direction." Said old Charlie coming up the road from the beach on the back of his own donkey, Asyouwink.

"Is not for bacon dis pig, dis day... so don't let Youse mouth take to watering."

"Suit Youse-self, but das a fine pig for roast'n." Charlie teased, for he knew how attached Sueky was to her animals.

Squeal as much as the pig might, the donkey with his unfaltering gate drug the reluctant animal past the bedspring gate and into the abandoned sugar-mill.

"What about the donk?" Asked Midera untying the tether between the pig and the donkey.

"He no gonna like it, but we'll leave him be here with de rest. It ain't de Four Seasons but we can afford it and das enough!" Sueky announced to her congregation of animals. "Just be happy you's no's stuck in a boat like Mistah Noah done width he animals. At least, here you's no gonna get seasick!"

They rocked the bedsprings back in place against the inside wall of the door frame. "That should hold 'em," the girl smiled at Sueky.

"Hold maybe the goats, but not Mistah Wind. He wouldn't even be'd slowed down de way dey is now. We mus' anchor she

286

width somet'ng." She looked around the yard, her eyes settling upon a cane crushing roller.

"Me t'inks dat could make a good anchor," she pointed to the rusted cast-iron calendar, three feet in diameter and six feet long, embedded deep in the ground by its great weight and the crush of time.

"Gran, we no gonna move dat!" exclaimed Midera appraising the weight of the rolled to be many, many tons.

"Oh my love," Sueky cooed lovingly, "not even Mistan Hugo gonna move dat, and dat's why we's gonna lash she to the bed springs." Gathering all the tether lines she'd removed from the animals, she and Midera made a rope and tied the bedspring gate to the cane roller.

"No wind gonna move she" And true, the storm would have to drag the giant piece of iron to release the tension holding the bed-springs against the inside wall of the sugar-mill. "We'll just see what Mistah Wind does with dat."

The last thing left were the chickens which was not much of a chore for they had spied the corn in Sueky' threw under the porch. "There you go my lovies, grow fat and lay lots of eggs while Sueky's away and don't be faint of heart over de commotion. You gonna be just fine."

She closed the porch gate and wedged against it a forked pole Sueky used for hooking papaya out of the trees. "Poor souls," she muttered, "deys gonna be so frightened. Me doubts we gonna see an egg from dis brood for a month."

Finally, Sueky climbed the two porch stairs and went into her house, soon appearing with a small bag of clothes, two bamboo mats and most of all, the small medicine pouch on a cord. She glanced inside examining it, assessing its contents of a small clay jar one last time before pulling the drawstring closed and hanging it around her neck-- and then tucking it under the bodice of her dress out of sight. She dropped her Bible in her dress pocket. She was ready. Then with some effort, she and Midera lifted and shifted her front door closed enough to line up the deadbolt and lock into the hasp.

It was an effort purely for Sueky's sake more than an actual deterrent for thieves. In the first place, Sueky had nothing to steal and secondly, none of the windows had latches and a thief need only lift the sash and crawl in. "Ready to go."

Midera noticed that Sueky wasn't wearing her Sunday hat, nor her best dress, nor her leather shoes. In fact, she dressed as though she was going to cut cane.

"Roight on time!" She said to Sambo Taxi as his van stopped in front of her house. Midera offered to help her grandmother climb in the van but the old woman stepped up with agility, sliding tight to the far window to give Midera room on the seat beside her. It was only then that she noticed Mrs. Pemberton in the front passenger seat.

Mrs. Pemberton feared God along with everything else. So great was her fear that she spent much of her time praying for all sorts of improbable things not to happen to her, which further fueled her faith by proving how well the Lord looked after her when she considered how few terrible things had happened to her in the face of infinite possibilities that <u>could</u> have happen. She feared many people, but no one terrified her more than Sueky, for she was said to be an "Obe'" and her powers were beyond the Bible, which was Miss Pemberton's sole solace and anchor.

When not in prayer, she devoted her time to scanning the Bible for transgressions that others might have missed and had inadvertently been practicing and if she thought you were unaware of your "ungodly" behaviour, she felt it her duty to tell you so. And if you were not around, or ignored her piety, she told everyone else. A sin unnoticed was still a sin.

When there was no more room, Sambo's Taxi-bus lumbered up the rough road to the Anglican Church with its cargo of elders, mainly ladies over seventy, plus two orphaned brides -- their husbands off working on another island. Few spoke, each

288

fixed on their thoughts and their fears. All except Mrs. Pemberton, who babbled to the enclosed congregation without pause or mercy, about things she was afraid might happen. Sueky paid her no mind, and counselled Midera to do the same. And focused her thoughts outside the window.

The Anglican said that the hurricane wouldn't hit them but Sueky knew better. She didn't always agree with the Anglican, he was a "young soul", as Grand Edna would say of those who looked but didn't see. He saw through a veil of ecclesiastic verse and hymns, and church politics and Saturday night socials.

Still, she went to his church and praise d' Lord with song with all her heart! It was not for his sermons that every Sunday but for the music, for the companionship of her friends and yes, she had to admit, the smell of the incense. She loved the thick pungent aroma as it followed her home pressed into her clothes, lining her nostrils until it became mixed with her usual Sunday fried flying-fish.

Sueky eyed the graveyard closely fixing in her mind upon the placement of the graves between the four stone boundary posts. There was no sanctified wall between the 'bounds' and that was the problem. If she gave it thought to what she had to do, she'd be paralysed with fear. She couldn't do that, she had to follow the Lord's commandment and blindly accept that she would not be asked to perform any rite she was incapable of doing. Her long stick fingers caressed the clay pot she held in her lap. "What's in the pot," Sambo Taxi had asked as her when she got out of his van.

"Balm for de dead," she started to say but all that came out was "potion." She wanted to get started before fear welded her old joints together, but she knew she must wait until the 'message' for her to move came upon her.

"Sueky, where are you. I does been talking to you a goodly long time and now me sees you don'ts attend to a single word I says." Said Mrs. Sutton sitting behind her. "Does you see something out de window? Maybe de future come so? Wha's gonna happen?"

"We's never be de same again." Sueky said with a sigh. "Das all me knows!"

The Anglican Church was a large stone structure with meter thick walls, and like the other two Anglican churches on Island, it was built in the shape of a cross: the main entrance at the foot of the cross, the alter at the head with two "fire-exits at the end of the arms. The churches were built at the height of the plantation era when cane grew like grass across the West Indies and rum ran like rivers, and the Leeward Islands were awash with wealth.

Somehow in those times it must not have been disrespectful to walk on the dead, for the floor was made up on marble inlaid headstones over graves of wealthy plantation owners, Island Governors and Bishops of the commonwealth. Carved in inch deep letters were the names of those who acquired great wealth and had built churches instead of tombs.

Peale, an albino black man met them at the door. His position had no Ecclesiastical station. He was both bell ringer, custodian, welcoming committee, handing out Sunday service programs, hymnals, and gossip. The first to come in the thin dawn, the last to leave by moonlight, he was respectful yet cautious of Sueky because of Miss Pemberton's warnings, but he did like Sueky's granddaughter, Myah. When she came to services, she made him nervous for she was too unruly. On more than one occasion when the Anglican was flailing away on sin and repentance, she'd stand and walk out of the service. She was too smart for her own good and spoke freely and unconcerned where her words landed. Besides that, he thought her the most beautiful creature he'd ever incurred. What little arousal he allowed himself was stimulated by Myah and he hated her for it, for he thought she dressed so just to tease him, to test his faith.

Peale greeted Annie and Midera and suggested a spot in the rear corner of the church because it was close to the bathrooms. But Sueky purposefully chose seats near the side doors. The atmosphere inside the church was almost festive as the

290

congregation indulged in nervous conversation.   Many people brought food dishes, and there was a group of ladies working around two long tables setting out the dishes. In another corner, lanterns were being filled and tested.   There was mood of congeniality among the congregation -- all secretly happy to have the support of each other in facing the ordeal ahead. Also, it was also an ecumenical gathering, a mixture of age, colour, creed, religion, intimate relations, and a few strangers simply in need of shelter. The only thing that all shared were the meter-thick walls, still that was enough to bridge generational rivalries.

Groups of old people chatted in pockets scattered around the church, including Sueky who sat down with a group mid-church talking amongst themselves.

"Dis hurricane ain't gonna be much," said Miss Pemberton said making her rounds of the groups, "I's been in a hurricane." She boasted. They all had, it was nineteen and twenty-six when Hurricane Audrey struck, leaving the Island completely denuded and seven dead.

"I know'd Audrey was gonna be bad and me tells me mother so but dis Hugo ain't gonna prove to be anything."   Mrs. Pemberton rattled on, "I only came here for the food and company."

"Miss Pemberton, don't you be talk'n such nonsense.   Dis hurricane gonna be bad!" Sueky said clearly without inflection beyond the weight of the words themselves. "He gonna be real bad and ain't no use tell'n folks otherwise."

"Oh! De Obe speaks, does she?" snapped Miss. Pemberton and a hush fell over the gathering.

"You mocks Sueky, but de truth gonna mock you." Sueky smiled and rose taking hold of the back of the next pew for balance. "Oh Lord," she sighed feeling some pain as her knees took weight, "You sure Sueky's gots to do this?" she thought to herself. With the clay pot secured in both hands, she walked down to the isle and up to the front of the church where she sat down alone in the first pew by a door.

"Yea, dough me walks t'ru de valley o' de shadow of death, me fears no evil for Dy rod and Dy staff does comfort me," she muttered again and again.

The Anglican and his family came over from the rectory to bless the meal and give thanks for the fellowship. Malinda, grand daughter of a parishioner Sarah, brought Sueky a plate and sat down beside her. Sueky felt the girl's frightened eyes on her.

"Well?" Sueky asked. "You don'ts need to be shy around Sueky girl, I does be de one what gives you you's name."

"Are you an Obe? Like Miss Pemberton says."

"What you know about Obe, girl?"

"They say that it's worshiping the dark side. Dat de Obe deal with Satan to gets things done."

"Lor--dee!" Sueky cackled. "You t'ink an Obe be sitting here in dis church, eating God's food and praying Holy words if de devil and me is thick together? Das just some foolishness an ol' women prattle on about t'ings she no know anything about. Miss Pemberton don't understand whats she say about me so pays she no-never-mind."

Malinda looked down at her hands, then she reached over and placed one on Sueky's.

"What I can tell's you, girl," said Sueky " it's humans what gots to stand up to da Devil when he knock. And when d' Lord come asking some folks to do for Him what He no-can do He-self, das soul must do He bidding."

"What can't God possibly do for Himself?"

"Confront de Devil. Find out what's de Goat got's planned." Suddenly Sueky's eyes bored hard into Midera, "Das how I knows dis wind she gonna be bad." Then she softened, and taking her hand out of Midera's, she put her arm around the girl and hugged her. "Now girl, don'ts Youse be troubling your heart none. You's gonna be alright through dis, me knows das for true."

"And what about you?" The girl lay her head on Sueky's shoulder.

Sueky sighed. "Sueky does de job de Lord asks... and He gonna keep me safe in de Bosom o Abraham." She smiled and started rocking her grand. "I don't knows why de Lord's not ready to take-up Sueky as yet, maybe me crown ain't got enough jewels in it."

Lanterns were lit when the power was cut at mid-night. A few of the older people went to the mattresses and lay down. Midera lay down beside Sueky for a little while, but the building wind made her restless. She got up and walked to the back of the church. Two girls from her school were there. They sat around on the floor in a small huddle, holding hands and whispering.

"My Auntie says it won't be bad," said one girl, squeezing the other girls' hands. "Auntie say she heard the man on the radio say that the satellite predict the storm will swing west again, out to sea. What we'll get will only be the edge."

"I hear so too." Said Bernice. "You watch, tomorrow morning's gonna come like nothing ever happened, and we'll all have ourselves a good laugh.... Not that I think it is funny to be cautious," she hastily added, not wanting to tempt fate.

"No," Midera said solemnly. "It will come. And it will be hard! And we must prepare ourselves for it, cuz when it comes there won't be time!"

Evan as they talked, Midera noticed the sound of the wind grew louder. To her it sounded like a drum, a steal fifty-gallon drum rolling down the mountain getting louder and louder until it sounded like it would momentarily crash through the Church walls. One of Midera's girlfriends began to cry. Then without warning, there was a vacuum of silence, and the sound of ocean water being pulled out from in front of a breaking wave. Then suddenly into the void, "BOOM!" and the silence was shattered as the barrel slammed headlong against the church's front doors. Lanterns swayed wildly, murals of the twelve steps to the cross

293

heaved from their pegs on the walls and crashed to the floor, a stack of freshly washed dishes cascaded off the table and crashed onto the floor tombs in an explosion unheard by the dead since against the hurricane Sandra.

"Sueky!" Midera screamed and scrambled through the chaos, pushing around people trying to get to the back corner. The old woman's mattress was empty. "Sueky," she called rushing down the aisles.

"Move away from the chandelier," the Anglican grabbed her arm. Looking up she saw it swaying wildly, the roof rafters groaned hard against the walls' anchors.

"Have you seen Sueky?"

"She must be here, the door-bars are latched." The Anglican was now yelling over the swelling next assault.

"I saw Sueky go into de bathroom not so long ago," said Calvin.

Midera rushed to the toilet but it was empty, and the door to the outside was closed, but then Midera noticed the inside brace wasn't against the door jam. She turned the handle, pushed with great effort on the door and quickly looked out not really expecting to see anything.

Sueky must be inside she concluded, but just as she started to close the door, she saw one of Sueky's shoes lying on the top step. "Sueky!" She screamed but the storm was too loud.

****

On her hands and knees, Sueky made herself mongoose thin and weaselled herself through the door. A shoe came off as she pulled her legs through the opening. The wind pounded upon her full gale, deflating her lungs. It swirled demon-shroud clouds about her head slapping her face, blurring her vision. Sueky clawed back at them,

"Yea dough me walks tru' de Valley ..." she cried, and the demons retreated. She gasped for breath, realising it was fear, not the storm that controlled her breathing. Unable to stand against the side of the church, Sueky crawled along the wall. Without candlelight, her night vision grew strong, but there was also a strange faint green glow that lay over the graveyard. She could barely make out the walls of the church and the graveyard, the big tombs, trees and the main corner posts. Her touch and intuition were her only reliable guides.

Mercifully the wind ebbed for a moment and she crawled to shelter in the lea of the first corner of the graveyard post near the building. She reached to her throat and caught the cord holding the bag around her neck and pulled it over her head. Removing the lid she poured some of the contents into the claw pot. Fighting the wind that tore around the sides of the pillar she rose carefully to a kneeling position. Holding the open jar in one hand, she ran her right hand across the flat stone, inside face of the pillar that the souls would be contained within the graveyard. By feel alone, she found the pillar's center. "*Siempre la mort esta mortum.* May the dead be dead.""

She whispered, and her words soon fell into a chant and for a sideways second there was no storm. Then she plunged two fingers into the container. The paste smelled foul, the dry sea-cucumber, crushed and boiled with the bark of black-bay root, the poisonous manchineel apples and the blood of agave cactus. The potion hissed and steamed, and heat snakes rose from the face of the sanctified granite post as she laid the paste in lines that made the sign of a cross that glowed with a phosphorescence yellow/white sheen behind her passing fingers.

The potion was strong enough to etch the stone, and yet, it did nothing to the old woman's skin.

"One step at a time," Sueky thought to herself as she abandoned the shelter of the first gate post. "One step at a time", except she could not walk! And as soon as she exposed herself out of the shelter of the gatepost, or a tombstone, the wind pinned her down. She couldn't even crawl on her hands and knees, instead having to lay flat against the earth she squirmed along like a worm.

"If it be dis way, den dats how she be." Sueky mumbled in her mind, her lips pursed tight against the wind. She began to a recite a prayer as she moved. "Yea dough me go through de Valley of d'shadow o'death, I will fear no evil .... yea dough I go ..." and she began worming towards the second corner post of the church yard. Just when she felt she could move no more she came into the lee of Clemont/Stanton Malinda, "Beloved Father, Husband, Overseer." Cecilia Stanton, wife of John Philip Stanton". One headstone at a time. Sueky was thankful for the rich families, who loved their dearly departed enough to build a large, elevated memorials that Sueky could hide behind. The great Vanderhussen Mausoleum was a God-sent for it was there that she rested for the route to the second corner bound.

She reached the second post and followed again the ritual of making the sign of the cross on the stone pillar with the potion, and again it burned and hissed and glowed in the dark etching the stone. She allowed herself a moment of respite. She was half-way through the graveyard, then she felt something that struck new horror in her heart, the ground beneath the graves began to shift and she knew she must hurry.

At first the shrieks were muffled beneath the sod but like the wind they grew in intensity to high piercing wails of souls in burning and tortured deaths! They became so loud in her ears she had trouble focusing all her being on advancing to the third pillar, and her hands shook violently as she etched the salve into that stone, the lines of her mark wavered but still the symbol was unmistakable.

Quickly she sealed the jar, closed the sack around it and began scrambling to the final and furtherest bound. Miraculously, the wind shifted to her back, driving her head long to the next grave in route towards the final post.

Suddenly she felt a hand grasp her leg, she jerked hard in revulsion, the grip had no strength, and she broke free easily. All around her there were now hands trying to grab her, hold her...

strangle her. Flailing, clawing, screaming with the same intensity as the dead, she brought herself to her feet again and in an act of blind trust that her God would guide her, she stumbled letting the wind drive her towards the next post. Grotesque faces now lunged in front of her, each had sunken eyes and protruding teeth. Their skin was that of lizards, their tongues of snakes.

Finally, the wind slammed her hard against the last bound, and she grasped the gate hinge with one hand fighting against the phantoms trying to reach her medicine sack. Individually there was no substance to their attacks but still Sueky had to hold them off and somehow complete her final rite. In the insanity of the apocalypse of the dead, she dropped the clay jar, the lid fell off, and suddenly the fluid ran out onto the ground!

Horrified Sueky scooped the precious liquid into her hand and hurriedly drug two fingers across her palm and slashed at the stone post. Again and again, she struck until she went blind, then deaf, then totally senseless as though she too were dead --- the demons of the dead swarmed around her body. She was helpless against them. Then... the wind that had propelled her across the graveyard to the final bound, suddenly ripped her from the post and carried her high into the air beyond the bounds of the graveyard, throwing her like a rag down into the ghaut.

Chapter 25

"Symphony for the Deaf"

From birth, Fluteman was impish towards life, just as he believed life was towards him-- much to their mutual amusement. Music was his core, the substance out of which his bones were made, the corpuscles of his blood flowed to their own beat. Music was his purpose, for he was a channeller picking up tunes from the air, giving them substance. When he played, he danced a little in-place two-step that kept him bouncing from side to side sending notes flying in every direction.

Music gave him perspective, clear and uncluttered by baggage or any false sense of self for he was what he claimed, a mere maker of music without more ambition than making people happy. He held no grudges, no lingering sorrows, nor guilt, nor any of psychological pitfalls that keep psychiatrists, clergy and rum shops busy, for just as fast as a trauma befell him, he sent it flying through his flute. He had had many protégés over his fifty-plus years but none so eager and gifted as his youngest grandson Fife.

Fife as well, began his career in music soon after birth, bouncing in his grandmother's arms, then later dancing, well more like prancing, as soon as he could walk. Mrs. Flute attributed this to her dancing so much soon after he was born, simply grand- prenatal mimicry. Being married to Flute, she had to dance whether she wanted to or not... and she wanted to. Fortunately the grand-baby was of a like mind, "Mon, dat's gonna be one dancing baby" Flute observed when the new baby began moving and kicking and leading the dancer. For Fife's fourth birthday Flute made him a little pennywhistle. Then a single note flute when he turned five. To accommodate his one note partner, Flute wrote a duet that was complex and all over the scale, with windows at just the right time for a single note – the one Fife knew!

Fluteman's coaching stimulated Fife's appetite and by the celebration of his sixth birthday, he had mastered three notes on the pan flute and expanded his accompanying skills to the point that Flute promised him by the time the boy could grow a beard that Flute would let him play in the Hornets.

"Why so long?" Fife asked his grandmother.

"Because all what goes on at dem dances ain't suitable fo' young eyes and ears. When Youse of beard age, den you can know such goings-on."

"But Mother does go to da dances and she don'ts have a beard."

"Das my point, where you t'ink you comes from?"

"She found he at a dance?!" Fife's eyes grew round with shock.

"Not at-all, at-all my love. I'll explain all to you when Youse can grow a beard."

Flute thought he saw the shadow of a whisker when Fife was eight and he let his youngest grandson tag along with the band to Sunday afternoon socials.

Fife would stand beside Flute on an over-turned beer case, and in front of Alabaster and his toot (a straight length of three-inch diameter of PVC water pipe that gave a didgeridoo sound that had little range or variety of notes but grounded the beat.

The Hornets were a mixture of profoundly brilliant musicians and village idiots. Their uniforms fit the name, yellow shirts, black pants, black vests with "Hornets" embroidered on the back in yellow letters. All wore rumpled fedoras in various stages of slouch. Fife got his own hat, actually an old one of Flute's with a weekend edition of the National Times stuffed around the inside brim.

Fife was literally born in his grandfather's shadow in that Flute was beside his daughter for the delivery, and the first sound the infant heard was that of the flute, a spontaneous, short happy little tune.

If Flute leaned against a post with his thumbs in his pockets, Fife shadowed him against the adjacent side. And like Flute, Fife had the same gentle, happy inquisitive and disarming smile, and at an early age he too would look intently into people's eyes with a smile that open doors into their thoughts. As with Flute, there was no judgment in his eyes and since he didn't understand what he saw at dances, he had no need to pass it on. In fact, Fife was too preoccupied with music to notice, let alone tell tales from the dances anyway.

On Saturday, the day before Hugo was expected to landfall St. Augustine, Fluteman's family spent it securing their shelter, anchoring shutters, setting in supplies of water and food. The house was tucked down between two ancient mahogany trees, and while it lacked view, the sunlight that filtered through the foliage was a cascade of greens and yellows bathing the house in a mood of harmony and contentment. Their home was a bigger than the usual block house due to their extended family which often included the various members of the band.

And since word had gone out of the pending hurricane the house began to fill. For not only was there the Flutes, Mister and Misses, Fife, two older brothers, two married daughters and four grandchildren; there was Sister Hermando, a self-ordained Baptist "nun", as well Alabaster, the Hornets "scratch" player, and Banjo who played a three string ukulele at times with Carnegie Hall quality, though more often it was plunk with the delicacy of a percussion instrument ... depending on how much rum he'd had. If he had just the right amount of rum he'd give a quality performance, but too intoxicated and the rest of the band had to mask his discord ... too little and he was introverted and played without courage.

While the men in the family attended to the heavy lifting getting their shelter ready for the storm, Mrs. Flute, and her daughters filled the kitchen with vegetables which they grated and chopped into cooked dishes to feed their ranks for a number of days, including a big basin of porridge they could fry-up for breakfasts.

They ate early as was their custom, usually to accommodate a dance gig at one of the hotels -- the adults sat on chairs along the walls of the living room, the children out on the front porch, and a table in the centre of the main room with the prepared food.

"Lord may dis whats we partakes," Sister Hermando prayed over the meal, "nourish us in Youse Glory be on highest dat we's sustained through de trials what's you sets before us... and anoint us in de blood o de lamb and d'glory' de kingdom ... what comes as sure as de Holy Rock what was rolled away from d'crucified Lamb's Sacred Tomb. and der sits He... Alive in You's Glory! .... AMEN ... Hallelujah!"

Everyone 'Amen-ed' in kind... but no one really understood what she said, only that it had all of key phrases, plus some of her own making. At least she wasn't "speaking in tongues" as some of the "Rollers" did... or, in Latin like the Catholic Priest in Portstown did.

"Dis gonna be bad." Moaned Alabaster. "Ah's in Dominica when "David" mash-up she up. Den Ah's in Cuba when Floyd come so. And now I's here and look what gonna happen here at home.

"You sure you's de cause of all de mayhem?"

"Fo' chure Ah is."

"Den tell me why you weren't in Guadeloupe yesterday when it got hit? Can you explain that?

301

Alabaster thought for a moment then his face lit up. "Chure, Cousin Arnie is der now and he looks jus like me!" Everyone laughed, bewildering Alabaster

"I'll tell you one thing true," said Flute philosophically, "I doubts for a fact dat God does chase you round de Caribbean." He smiled. "De Lord just figures de Caribbean needs a little dustin' off from time to time. And it is time for a little house cleaning. We're simply in de way. No, I doubt de Lord holds any more malice or pity for us, as one of us taking a feather duster to cobwebs and the spiders."

"Das maybe so, but Ah's a little fearful." Alabaster said aloud to himself.

One skill Flute had learned playing at the hotels was when to start the music, and when to stop, and when to simply take a break. He'd start playing after the guests' supper and the moment one of the one of them yawned or commented how exhausting it was sitting out in the sun all day; Flute and the Hornets would have them dancing about like a marionettes

Knowing when to stop for intermission was also important. Leave the guests grateful that you've released them from the dance and thirsty for a drink at the bar, yet still thirsty for more music afterwards.

With the pending hurricanes, Flute realised the time to start playing is when the first tendrils of fear and panic grew with each warning punch from the storm.

"You's scared" He said to Alabaster, who embarrassedly nodded.

"Then is time to pick up Youse toot and let's chase de fear away." And immediately he took up his flute. Fife ran to his room and fetched his pan-flute where he kept it from under his mattress. And when all were assembled, Flute began to play his theme song a long wobbling bird note that danced with the happiness of a yellow bird at sunrise. The Band started with the traditional songs that everyone knew,

Belafonte from Barbados, and even some Bob Marley and reggae from Austin Texas.

"Come on Gregory take up the bongos." He'd call out.

"Rose, where Youse Jew's Harp." The table was pulled out of the middle of the room, the chairs pushed tight against the walls and soon there was no audience as everyone had become a musician, even Mrs. Flute who played the spoons and two-stepped in tandem with Flute.

Then when the music had enough momentum to carry itself, Flute and his Missus started dancing, for forty years the same moves, even doing some hip-bumping and bum-rubbing, much to the delight of the younger kids and the horror of the Sister Hermando.

Soon everyone was laughing and having a great time. Because it was now dark in the room, except a few battered candles on the windowsills, and simple collisions on the dance floor, of which there were many, making the laughter grow quickly to hilarity; muting the growing roars of the storm with the human spirit.

An outsider would call it a "party" and not a hurricane watch. Yet, finally, as Flute sensed a total collapse of the musical dance troupe from exhaustion, he began the familiar reframe of his wrap-up ending, a piece that left his audiences yearning for more.

It was intermission at Fluteman's home, and though the storm continued to swell and howl and beat upon their shelter between the two mahogany trees; everyone was still laughing hard and gasping for air.

Missus Flute brought some out some Johnny-cakes they'd made before supper, and two large bottles of mango "knock-your-socks-off" home-brew she'd been saving for New Years. And though limbs shattered in the trees high above them, causing splinters of flying quills; the mood inside Flutemans' home was that of carefree happiness.

"Mon, you dance like Delbert-he-ain't-crazy-ya-know mon." Said Seminole to her older brother Fife.

"Mon, Aye tells you,"He shot back, "when Me gits to dancing Aye's a 'going-concern'! You best be on guard... or be off de dance floor."

"Mama do something 'bout him, he does talk like dat to me in front of my friends! Always showing off and smart-talking thems. You gotta do something!" She pleaded, using the opportunity of the congregation's full attention to call their focus to her long social suffering, and bate her brother to prove her point.

"Whats Youse think dat 'something' gotta be?" Mama Flute asked. "Maybe cut he tongue off?" She suggested.

"Dat's de very least!" Said Seminole. "Fact to my way of thinking when Youse in de cutting mood, you could cut off something else of his. Maybe he'd stay home width de family more, instead of tomcatting around, flirting and fuss'n with me friends."

Flute sensed in their banter the seed of friction, the fatigue of fear and as the storm grew stronger with the passing of each gust, he began to play again.

This time it was an unfamiliar song which no one except the simple instruments like the "toot' and "scratch", could follow. But the storm grew and changed its course. To which Flute changed his direction, and the music shifted from calypso to foot tapping, thigh slapping gospel, collecting a few 'hallelujahs' and a 'hosannas' in toote. But the storm undaunted by the Christian sanctums gained force.

Flute to picked up his pace, though losing his band in route. But, as if the hurricane was being pelted by his notes, it blew even harder ... causing Flute to play still harder.

Soon he lost his accompanists ... each terrified for they had never seen Flute play so.

It was a wild insane music full of primitive patterns, punching the notes as if they were drumbeats, hurling them at the storm. It was music if played slowly would be beautiful even haunting, but when played with the power of a man possessed, caught in mortal combat; it was gripping, compelling, courageous and ... terrifying!

Faster and faster Flute played, harder and harder Hugo blew catching leverage on a piece of tin-roofing at the back of the house, making it groan from the strain.

Sweat poured from his brow, soaking his shirt. Flute was crazy, yet his notes came flying at the hurricane, fighting with it for the piece of roofing.

Mama Flute begged him to stop for fear that the storm would seek revenge and carry him away.

Still Flute stood in the middle, arching his back, sending his notes like fists into Hugo's belly. Then bending far backwards he'd suddenly, like a prize fighter, threw himself forward adding the force of his weight to the strength of his muscles into each blow, going for the knock out punch.

"Grandpa stop!" Fife screamed. Others pleaded but no one went near him. Their pleas were wasted!

Then, suddenly as the speed of the conflict reached beyond even the fortitude of Flute ... he broke!

Ripping the flute from his mouth, he let out a shriek of rage that even the storm couldn't push back, and his cry raced clear across the Caribbean.

Suddenly, it was over, and though the man slumped to the floor -- the fight gone from him; the ferocity of the storm abated!

Seemly the storm stopped, stunned but not mortally wounded. But the wind died down with such abruptness that everyone held their breath, waiting for the next really strong punch -- maybe the one that would level the house.

But the strike didn't come!   And soon the sudden quiet -- their fears turned to relief.

They were in the Eye.

"Anyone else got's something to say to Mistah Hugo?" Banjo cried hurrying to the middle of the room where Flute knelt, his head bowed, panting, dazed.   Banjo put a hand on his shoulder, and suddenly everyone started cheering, surrounding him, hugging him.

"No?!" Banjo bellowed, "Seems that Mistah Hugo got's nothing to say!" He yelled to the others.

"Oh he will," said Mrs. Fluteman, standing over her husband.   She knew there was certainly more of the storm to come.   She put her arms around the man.

"And when Hugo comes again ... " She looked at her family, "he gonna give us a mighty wallop!"   Her voice trailed off in thought, understanding what must be done, and, that she had to do it... Fluteman was spent!

"Gregory," she ordered, "Go out with William and see what can be done 'bout dat loose piece of tin."

Soon they returned, "De edge of de galvanise begins to lift, and me t'inks it gonna go anytime."

She thought for a moment.   "OK... what you got'a do is run a rope line over the roof at dat weak place and tie each end down to de base of de tree roots.   And then jam some cinderblocks up under the rope to give it extra bite."

"<u>And</u> de rest of you comes width me and we'll look for shelters if'n de roof does take flight." She picked up one of the candles and a procession formed behind.   Under beds, cabinets closets – last-ditch protection.   She knew the worst was yet to come and even Flute would <u>not</u> be able to soften the blow.   And soon cabinets, closets, ever cubby hole had someone in it, until the family was hidden from flying objects should the roof tear off. In their room she lay Flute beside the bed and pulled the mattresses over him and crawled in under it, beside him.

"I can do no more but wait." She assured herself.

Chapter 26

A Single Sad Note.

The wind folded in on itself the following morning, but then the rain began. The island was exhausted, the Caribbean was exhausted ... and still the storm continued its rampage north to Puerto Rico, where it beat upon old San Juan with a fury the ancient citadel hadn't experienced in centuries, flipping over airplanes at the airport, filling the old gun-turrets at the Fort of San Sebastian with mulch from both the Leeward and Windward Isles.

The hurricane then turned west, hitting the Dominican Republic, Haiti, Cuba and Jamaica before beating a swath north through the Florida Keys. There would be no unfettered, peaceful sleep in the Caribbean for a long while. And for many, the sleep of innocence without fear would never come again.

"Youths, come out! Hugo's gone!" Flute called through the rooms of his house at sunrise, tapping on cabinets and closets. Door by door, room by room, cautious eyes peered out. Eleven was the count: Fluteman and Tasco, two daughters, two sons, a son-in-law, two grands and two musicians crawled and staggered from their hiding places in varying degrees of bewilderment and shock, the heavy shadow of terror blanketed each.

"Oh My," Cried Tasco. She fell to her knees and began to weep as her fingers touched a pair of porcelain salt and pepper shakers on the floor — both smashed. In her grief, she failed to notice that, overhead, a section of roof was gone!

Flute wandered outside and sat on the edge of his porch, staring. What lay before him was incomprehensible, and try as he might to focus his attention, nothing made sense, nothing was familiar, and both his sight and mind wandered aimlessly over the embattled landscape, absorbing nothing. He felt he'd gone mad. There was not one building, one tree, one color, nor sound, smell, or any other once-familiar perception upon which he could tether his sense of place and time. He thought about how he had played the flute at the height of the hurricane, and wondered if that was when he'd gone mad.

One by one the family silently joined him on the porch, each glancing sideways at him, hoping for some indication of what he was going to do. For a long time, they all sat in silence.

Slowly, an imperceptible seismic shift quaked through Flute and he realised he'd found his anchor. It was right beside him — his family. For them he would commit himself, his strength and his will to do everything possible for them to recover.

"Hugo!" he whispered, "you can mash down de whole damn planet but you ain't never going to break our spirit." And with his words, all at once; he looked afresh at the carnage, and he saw not destruction but a bounty of building material.

Still, what could one man do?

Probably nothing, Flute admitted to himself. But a lot of people working together could do a lot.

He gave a great sigh of resignation. "Good enough!" he shouted aloud. Slapping his hands to his thighs as though signalling that the work-break was over, he got to his feet. Once his course was set, a plan of what must be done appeared before him.

"Slat," he called to his second grandson, "I want you and CJ to light out for Bueno's, Sambo's, Priscilla's... all de Council of Elders, call out for dey to come to Worrystone as soon as possible."

There was a collective sigh of relief and the mood of the family changed: Flute had found his moorings. The boys jumped up, happy to have a task, and scampered off the porch onto the road.

Flute turned to Tasco. She held a piece of the white porcelain in her hands. He knelt beside her, putting his arms around her shoulder. "Give thanks we's all still have life. Dat's what's important, not dis." He reached down and gently took the piece of porcelain from her. "Dis time too shall pass," he whispered and rose. Taking up his flute, he shoved it into his belt, then picked up a cutlass and left for the road to the shop and Worrystone.

It was hard going through the maze of downed powerlines and toppled, splintered trees to Worrystone. When he got there, he was staggered by what he saw. The shop was gone! Nothing but a slab of concrete remained. All signs of the shop's many commercial ventures, the store, the bar, the television room, the Domino College, had been erased from the community. Even the field adjacent to the shop had been swept clean better than a crew from the Department of Roads and Sanitation could do.

With the loss of the shop once called, the heart and head of the village of Poppy Dawn had been surgically severed. Flute wondered, looking at the slab of clean concrete, if the village could survive without a head. Once again, he had to fight off the lethargy that accompanies feelings of futility. Still, on the arrival of Calvin and Sambo, the only two council elders that the boys could find, Fluteman knew what had to be done.

They spoke in hushed voices, though there was no one near to hear. Fluteman explained his idea, and after quietly fine-tuning it, they agreed it was the way to proceed.

Flute rose and, bringing his flute to his lips, he played from the heart a single sad note that reached out over the village, the island, the entire West Indies.

It was a cry of such sadness that the wind wept tears in despair. Finally, the note became so heavy in its grief that it broke apart into more notes, slowly assembling into a pattern, into a song that lifted above the carnage on melancholic wings, touching every ear, every heart. It was a dirge for the dead, for dreams so violently destroyed, desires never to be fulfilled. And all who heard it began to cry from the very core of their last resilience.

One by one they came out of their hiding places, dulled by shock and fear; some shattered, some needing help, some beyond help. They gathered around him as he played, and as he played, he studied the eyes of each, assessing their damage. Each carried the mark of death and dying, and it was up to Fluteman, like Jesus unto Lazarus, to bring them back to life.

When the assembly could take the grief no more — holding each other, hugging, crying in groups for support — Flute stopped his tragic lament and took the flute from his mouth. His eyes swept the gathering of villagers, waiting for the pain to flow from them until it ebbed into deep gasps and soft, pitiful whimpers.

Then suddenly his face broke into a broad, toothy grin and, lifting the flute to his lips again, he began to play the music that had come to him in the night when he fought the storm. Without introduction he played, shocking the assemblage with the fiery, lively piece that defied anyone not to smile and move their toes. It was more than a song of defiance, it was a song of life; of giving thanks, rejoicing for each breath. Faster and faster the song grew until it now danced of its own accord, and even when Fluteman had to stop from exhaustion, the melody played on in their heads.

"People," he said finally, "I'm not gonna linger on de self-seen, We's taken some bad licks from Mistah Hugo and that's a fact, and we can't be afraid to look them in the face.

"In fact, that's de first thing we got to do is to look de Devil in de face and take inventory of who needs what. And we can't be afraid of anything now and can let no task, no matter how hard it looks, to hold us back. If we can survive Hugo, ain't nothing gonna touch us afterward, is there?" No one commented, but the tune continued to play in their heads and with it came the courage to face even the unfaceable.

"Now de way I sees it, we's been dealt a tough hand and now we gots to decide how to play it." He paused. "We can mope around and feel sorry for ourselves — Lord knows we got reason — and wait for de Government to come and help us, and I can play de sad and sorry song until your hearts break. And we can be selfish and scrap with each other over every little thing what de land gives up, so everything we does is dripping with 'me' and 'mine.'" He studied the confusion in the people's faces.

311

"Or — we can go another way." He let his voice build. "One for all," he let it hang like an evangelist recruiting souls, "and ALL for each other." Again, he paused; the silence had force. "All for each — and each for all." His eyes smiled, sweeping the congregation. They were feeling his fire.

"In my opinion," his voice turned from the pulpit and returned to that of reason. "Dat's de kind of people we are! Cus know for chure, de Government right now ain't gonna be coming around with any help. Fact, I bets de whole damn Caribbean done mash-up, and we's low on everyone's priority list. Besides, even if the Island government is inclined to throw some assistance our way, which ain't gonna happen since we sided with the opposition, recognise we's gonna get the worst, last, and if the past be any teacher, it's gonna somehow cost us the most."

"You can say dat again, brudder," grumbled Pressflesh.

"To my way of thinking, we's the ones what's got to bring ourselves back, because when it comes down to it, there ain't nobody else gonna do it. But it is gonna take some big sacrifices." He let the words settle and hoped his song still gave them strength.

"For one thing, we've got to start living like we did in the backtime days before electricity, with candles and coal-pots. And we'll have to do without most everything for a while." Then he started to laugh. "Course right now we's doing without, so it gots to git better."

"Das de truth, Brudder," laughed Gitlicks.

"But de most important thing we's got to do is work together. Share our resources, our food, our labor. For *one* of us to recover from what's taken place to us, we *all* must work as One. And for all of us to recover, every individual must pull de line!" His voice and passion had risen to Hallelujah proportions. With his melody still in their ears, they understood both his words and their intent. There was hope in what Fluteman said, and with hope came goals and eventually maybe dreams to be achieved again.

312

"And de first thing we got to do is find out who needs help most. I'd suggest the youths organise themselves into bands and search out all de people who live up and down each of de roads and back-trails of Poppy Dawn." His hand waved in a great arc towards the roads and trails leading away from the Worrystone intersection.

"What else?" He turned to Sambo, who whispered something back. "Oh yes, we must be careful not to create any more problems den we gots. De water could be a real big problem if'n we's not vigilant. So, we must be careful where it comes from. Who knows what dead things might be in de wells and open cisterns? If you have a closed cistern collecting rainwater from your roof, I'd think de source water is fine, you should be safe and share freely. Otherwise, I'd say boil all water."

Again, Sambo whispered something to Fluteman.

"Yes," Fluteman nodded, "another thing what needs for de doing is harvesting what we can before it rots from de salt spray. And, we'll have to butcher what animals is dead before dey turns — sheep, goats and de like.

"Don't know when there'll be electricity for refrigeration, but let's talk of dis after de youths return and each of us goes home to see what we can salvage. There's a job for everyone, so we must have the help of everyone, especially the youths. Them what has a dry roof, give shelter, and dem what has food, share. I won't 'leg' you none, I believe dat de task will be great and most of de suffering is still ahead." There was silence; all became muted by the thought of the work ahead.

"But!" Flute raised both hands. "It is not beyond us! De main thing is keeping de heart strong and not be lading it down with your losses or doubts."

The Liburg Sisters 'hallelujahed' their agreement and parroted "a strong heart" for good measure.

"Praise God for a strong heart," echoed Paulette.

And a strong back!" bellowed Bullo, leaping to his feet.

"AND EARNEST!" Earnest yelled.

313

"So, I ask de youths to pull into groups and each take a different road," Fluteman said. "Search out every person, see who needs help and who can help. If you find dey needs immediate medical attention or some other crisis, send someone to report back here <u>immediately</u>!"

He turned his focus to the rest of the villagers. "Until we know where we stand, I think we should go home and put our own houses in order and come back this afternoon." The young people broke up into four teams and started down the four roads leading away from Poppy Dawn.

The last house that Cusco and Letitia checked on the Estate Road was Aunt Josey's. Both teenagers had known Josey all their lives but only Cusco knew the way to where she lived. Armed with cutlasses, the two hacked their way along a well-worn trail that terminated in a pasture, at the far end of which, tucked into the jungle edge, sat an ancient chattel house. It had no paint nor any sign that it had ever been painted or even occupied. The shutters hung at odd angles to each other with a significant off-plumb skew. The roof that was once sheet metal was now simply rust shaped in a corrugated pattern, yet somehow it repelled the rain. "Somehow" was the operative word to describe the structure, for "somehow" it stood, though its walls were perforated as soft as packing cardboard by generations of termites and prayer. Prayer, Letitia thought, "somehow" it's somehow held together by prayer.

"Aunt Josey!" Cusco called out.

"Zat Youse, Gabriel?" a cheery voice came from the chattel house.

Josey, like Sueky, seemed as old as the Island itself, and like Sueky, she was wizened down to wisdom. But where Sueky was turning to stone and God-form diamond, Josey was an ancient tree, yet equally pure God-form. Her skin was rich ebony, withered to an ironwood trunk and bone-dry limbs. Her roots reached back through generations to the slave era, while her branches of children, "grands"

314

and "great-grands" extended around the world. She was known on-island, by both blood and choice, everyone's "Aunt Josey".

She was on the council of 'smart people', maybe professor emeritus of it. If someone had a difficult problem that either age or wisdom could solve, it was taken to Aunt Josey. She had survived, in her almost ninety years, direct hits by the worst two hurricanes ever recorded in the Caribbean. She had been rattled by enough earthquakes to shake the teeth out of a corpse and had endured for decades a goiter on her neck the size and shape of an eggplant. "Me bump," she called it. "Some does carry der burdens on dey's hearts, but me heart be free of cares cus I carries me toil where de Lord can sees it. Me bump be me passport to Heaven."

"No, Aunt Jose, it's not de Lord, be just us... Cusco and Letitia. You does call me nephew."

"And nephew, who's you friend be?"

"Is me, Letitia, Priscilla's granddaughter."

A wizened woman wearing a faded flower-pattern dress and a thimble-shaped hat appeared at the door. Though her body was frail and her movements slow, one could tell by her eyes that her Spirit was robust.

"For chure!" spoke Annie? "Girl, Youse does grow some. Tells Youse folks not to feed you so much, Aunt Josey don't hardly know'd you." She smiled and looked at the boy and girl. "So, what mischief you doing width dem cutlasses?"

"We come to see if you needs any help. Like maybe de wind tip you's house over. But I sees you's house does stand as straight as ever." Cusco, clucked to himself. Even when Aunt Josey's house was straight, it was only that way for a moment in the tug-of-war between her competing vines and termite colonies. Yet, Aunt Josey lived in complete symphony with all. She slept on monkey time, passing into sleep soon after dusk and rising in the predawn. As the church Choir Director observed, 'Jose is a ... song wrapped in a cocoon of life!"

"No." She looked around her holdings. "I reckon de Lord don't have room for Josey in Heaven dis time. You youths wants for somet'ing cool to drink, jugo *de mango*?"

"Another time. We are on a task and have to report back."

Josey heard but didn't listen as she disappeared around the back of her house, returning with two glasses and a rum bottle with an orange liquid in it. She poured each a full measure of mango juice.

"You should tell dem what needs for food dat me garden is full and overflowing like a ninth-moon woman, and <u>must</u> be harvested. I'll share it all around, but it <u>must</u> be picked soon or de salt gonna turn she all black."

"Aunt Josey," asked Cusco cautiously, looking into his drink of mango juice, "why you think the Lord does do us so?" He hesitated. "It makes no sense to me." He'd been thinking about nothing else all morning, and Aunt Josey would have an answer. "Mean things like punishing de people who have de least. De poor lose all of de little that we gots, whilst de rich and de privileged, what with their insurance and all, they'll be back in business before they's out of business."

Josey smiled, but sat quietly, giving his question respect. "Nephew of mine, it don't serve you for try'n ta figure out de Lord's reasons. Maybe we don't see them now, but dat don't mean He don't have 'um. Remember what de Holy Book say, 'God moves in strange ways.' "

When they'd finished their drinks, the boy and girl rose to leave.

"If'n de phones at Hotel Lemon no be mashed up," said Josey "ask Lucy-she to get a message to Benton in New York, and for him to contact my family there I'd alright. He should also contact Saffron in London width de message dat's me's fine and fit, and so's she Ladyship," the old woman nodded to the pig lying in a mud pit at the base of a eucalyptus tree. The pig turned her dirtiest side to them with royal nonchalance.

"Come de revolution, your Ladyship," Jose looked at the pig, "it's de guillotine for Youse, for chure, for chure," She growled. The pig was ancient, well beyond the eating years, or even making piglets. Her only purpose now was being Aunt Josey's friend.

"Run ahead now tell de Assembly I's a-coming!" she said to the youths.

Chapter 27

"Delbert and the Pirates"

Like everyone else in the Caribbean digging out of the aftermath of Hugo, He-ain't-crazy-ya-know-mon, otherwise known as Delbert, didn't know what to do next. For the first time in his rational life, which was only half his calendar life, he was stymied. His tiny chattel house, tucked behind a shoulder of the volcano had been spared. Even his meager garden, mostly of pumpkins, yams and squash went undamaged except for the salt spray and that wouldn't kill the plants, "Add pepper only, already salted," he'd laugh at his own joke -- at least six times a day.

No, what Delbert felt in his Unofficial Head of State for St Augustine, was priorities. Jabull Rawlins, the father of the children he'd shared half of the hurricane with—gave Delbert a job working in his lumber yard sorting boards. Delbert did it for two full days, one for training that took exactly fifteen minutes, leaving seven hours and forty-five minutes left to do the job which was boring. On the second day he quit in a polite but firm way, teaching his yard master a couple of tricks to ease the labor-load of moving piles of boards from one stack to the next ... one board at a time.

"Pulls d'board back ats you so ta balance, flip she on edge, push down so dat de udder end lifts up, den set she on de next stack. Now, here's de trick, swing da end you's hold'n over to de pile, set she down and 'crab-got-d'monkey's tail' ...you's finished and don't strain Youse back, nor troubles Youse brain."

Working for a 'boss-mon' wasn't a problem, he figured given his job as an Elder Statesman of St Augustine, everyone on Island was his boss in a sense. It was the trappings of the job that he couldn't abide by. "On time... not-later, not-earlier," lunch break wasn't when he was hungry, it was when the clock said he should eat. Also, he found there was no creativity to the work of stacking lumber, not like decorating the town with flowers. Moreover, he had no authority to solve problems. No, without malice he decided a company job didn't fit his style. Mrs. Rawlins saw it too and had him over to dinner in appreciation, and after the meal he told the children about the monkey's secret tunnel to the adjacent Island, but the children had to take an oath never to tell anyone. And that was the end of his gainful employment.

*****

It was two weeks before the first supply ships came into dock. By then the main road arteries were opening up. And suddenly the town came alive again for a brief breath. And for the first time in weeks the sound of truck engines was heard on Island. Many of them had no windshields and sported deep creases in their hoods from fallen trees.

A couple had their frames bent causing the vehicle to travel sideways as much as forward making steering a constant occupation.

No sooner had the dock been opened however, than the traffic jam closed it! Unfortunately, by 10 am. the first morning, all of the open roads were closed again.

The road system to the dock was laid out like the spider's web with the dock in the centre and radials running out into the countryside. The problem was that everyone was coming to pick up building materials... at once! And suddenly St Augustine had its first major traffic jam. The plug-up was Los Angeles quality and it took the rest of the day to untangle the snarl. The boats were coming in continually and they were in a hurry to off-load and move onto the next port. The idea of off-loading directly onto the trucks was soon scrapped because the trucks were stuck in the traffic snarl, so the cargo was simply stacked on the pier to be sorted out later. With the roads plugged, and the docks bulging, tempers flared all along the supply line.

Also, when people realised that there were materials down on the dock, even more Islanders went down to straighten out the situation –adding considerably to the confusion.

At the end of each day they disassembled the jam, but the next morning it happened again and continued for almost a week while the transportation authorities drifted about like loose dinghies without a rudder in a big bay, arriving with no solution. The problem was sorting out an automated system that was designed for donkey carts and carriages.

After studying the mayhem thoroughly, Delbert awoke before dawn of the seventh day refreshed after a long sleep ...and the solution! And the following day, the Islanders themselves awoke to discover that nothing had happened to Delbert, in fact, it was only by his tell-tale signs did people realise he'd been gone.

Obviously, he was alive and well, for not only had he adorned Portstown Square in flowers and palm fronds; but this time there were SIGNS. Twelve of them, half with a bold arrow pointing in one direction and beneath the arrow was written, 'Go-so", and on the other half of the signs there was another arrow pointing in the opposite direction with circle and slash over it, and the words "No-go-so!". They were well placed at all of the critical intersections along the inbound and outbound roads.

"Fuck, Delbert?!" Barked Fulton, the driver of the first truck to arrive at the first sign. "What non-sense Youse up ta now?!" He yelled at Delbert!

"Trust me mon! Jus' Follow de SIgns, **go so** ... you kno'?!"

To make sure the folks recognised his authority, he'd found himself a pair of dark blue pants with yellow stripes down the outside legs, a red whistle, and a green policeman's hat that was actually an old Texaco filling-station cap back when gas station attendants wore a uniform. To add credibility to his already commanding presence, he'd painted a toilet plunger bright day-go pink for his baton. With the baton, Delbert pointed to the truck. "Where ya go when she full?"

320

"Back to Poppy Dawn... if'n ya gits outa d' fuck'n way."

"Jus follow de signs if'n dey say 'No Go', den kno' <u>no</u> go so! Trust me mon!" said Delbert stepping back and plungering the truck through.

"Trust <u>you</u> mon... Youse a crazy mon?! " The driver called back, but still he did follow the signs, because Delbert just might <u>not</u> be crazy. And when the trucker had done the full circuit: reaching the docks, loaded and out of town on a newly formed one-way street running the back home, he arrived in Poppy Dawn with his cargo and temper intact in record time! And raved to everyone how the confusion at the dock had been sorted out by the Crazy Man.

What Delbert had done with the signs was turn all of the threads of the spider web into one ways, alternating one going in and next going out, same with the cross streets turning two way traffic jams into one way flowing arteries like the human circulatory system. Everyone on the south end of the Island came to the docks through Shipwreck Point Street and out through Sweet Cherry Pasture. From the North it was into the docks via Silanders Plantation Lane and out on St.Theresa.

"He ain't crazy ya know mon?!"

"Follow d'signs, mon. Just follow d'signs" became Walter's mantra through the day, and by dusk people had figured it out and it worked fluidly. The following day Walter's presence was only occasionally necessary when someone forgot to "No-go-so".

Free of his traffic controller's responsibilities, he filled his spare time with entertaining the stewards down at the docks. "Mov'n, Mov'n, Keep das roof'n mov'n " was the next message for the day, sang to the theme song of the western television series called, "Rawhide" which he'd seen in Barbados as a youth.

"Clean up, spruce up" he sang the next day covering the Bob Marley lyrics "sit up, git up, stand up for your rights"

Marvin Gay, "Local motion." Was a big hit song the following day when the message morphed into "git de motion-- keep de motion".

"Loco motion! If Youse to ask me." His detractors said, but still they listened to what Delbert said. And just as the Island listened to Delbert.

Delbert's office was situated at the main ventral of the heart of St Augustine, on the steps to the Treasury Building where all passed before him and through his, what some believed," befuddled head'. And the first complaints he heard soon after the transportation problem was solved, was that the merchants of building materials were charging huge mark-ups for poor quality materials. Plywood that wasn't square by three/quarters of an inch on the diagonal, soft nails that bent easily, boards so young and poorly cut that they twisted like spiral spaghetti.

As with all great revolutions, it started with a slogan, in this case a few disjointed words that together make no obvious sense except to He-Aint-Crazy-You-Know.

"Privateers, Pirate-teers, Buchaneers, Bacchanalian-eers dey's a-coming." Filtered through Walter's talents for music, it soon became a calypso song. "Deeee Pirateers jamming down dee docks, second rate goods at triple de cost, soft nails, soft like der cocks, privateers pirate-teers, Buccaneers, Bacchanalian-eers, jam'n up our docks."

The gouging was the same all over the Caribbean, for though there was no shortage of materials in the Northern Hemisphere since it was late fall in North America and not too much demand for concrete, steel, two-by-fours, and plywood.

Drake was the worst of the pirate-teers, having the advantage over his competition of being a pirate from birth. It was hard to say what motivated him except raw, animal survival that later evolved into the rush of the deal, capturing galleons for the sake of the adventure, regardless of their contents.

322

And like the pirates of old, he went to great lengths to acquire his fortune only to bury it in the sand. For Drake, nicknamed after the infamous Captain, he put his holdings in a dodgy bank in Puerto Rico that welcomed pirate money, off-shore banking and drug traffickers. He lived in a rough and rundown cluster of concrete chattel houses that took up lots of space but was itself mainly walls around rooms without a view. He drove a beater Austin Mini-Minor automobile. His wife was silent and wore shabby clothes, unlike those lavished by Drake on Puerto Rican prostitutes. The walls of the house without views had only pictures of Jesus on them, for Drake was not an artsy man, except for portraits that appeared on money, but his wife feared the Lord more than Drake or maybe because of him. He was known around island as a "might be" man, as in "he "might be" a smuggler though no charges were ever laid. The only real charge on his record was cannibalism.

It was said that Drake was the only man in the Caribbean charged with the crime of eating human flesh.

Stoffer Roberts a long time resident of Cottontown claimed to have been there, and likely he was. "It was Christmas and Gage owner of the Hotel Lemon had brought on island a tenor from Dominica to entertain the guests at the Lemon. On New Years Eve, the party spilled out of the Hotel and halfway around the island to a local bar called Merlins. The people of Cottontown took a shine to the tenor, especially Estella, a beautiful fine featured, hip-moving girl that Drake had sights upon, but her's were not on him. When he saw how things went on with the tenor and his lady, Drake took matters into his own hands... or rather mouth.

As it happened, a fight ensued and at one point the tenor had his hand in Drake's mouth, trying to rip his jaw off. He jerked his hand back the instant the upper jaw started to close and he almost got all his fingers out, except for the index that was snapped off clean like a fried chicken wing at the second knuckle!

"Me does see-so me-self." It was a story owned by Southern Cross a roust-about who claimed to have witnessed the fight.

"If you's ask' me opinion," He'd lean forward to his audience. "Me t'inks Drake so drunk dat out of habit of drinking ginger-beer and eating chicken, he not only swallow de finger, he chew she up a bit, den just swallow she down without so much as a second thought.

Drake swore he was innocent. His defense was impeccable "Me no gonna swallow dat man's finger-- no telling where it's been. Probably up he ass."

Still, when he offered a reward to the young neighborhood kids to find the finger where the fight was, where he said he'd spit it out, and yet no one could find the finger though they scoured the grass on hands and knees, it didn't look good for Drake. Still, his supplemental argument was convincing. "Damn dog does take it in d'night"

The judge convicted him because he thought Drake was guilty, and because his second cousin was the Cottontown girl at the heart of the conflict. But mainly Drake was guilty because the judge liked the way the tenor sang. Still, in all charitable conscience, the judge could not impose too much of a fine since there was the matter of the missing evidence. Maybe the singer didn't have all his fingers when he came on island. Oh No! He had all his fingers, testified the Cottontown girl. Drake was fined $1,000 U.S. to be paid to the tenor for his loss, plus a ban from eating meat for ten days.

Drake began traveling the ferry at the age of nine, buying something on one side, selling it for a profit on the other, then doing the same on the return. At first, he specialised in fabrics, buying end-cuts from the upholstery shop or from the seamstress, selling them, then eventually buying whole roles of fabric for the seamstress and the upholsterer.   He worked his way up always improving his lot until he realised that he was spending too much hard-earned capital on ferry tickets, so he bought a boat.

It was a fifth owner, locally built 'lighter', thirty feet long wide at the beam, shallow displacement with a low mast and a long boom like a Nile River boat. Drake was still a teen at the time. Back then everything on island came by 'lighter'. It was a solid craft that could carry cars if they were balanced ahead of time in anticipation of the wind against in the channel. And so, his empire grew.

Finally, he opened a store in a waterfront warehouse with the simple sign *"Drake's, Quality Lumber For Less.* It made no difference that it was neither quality nor cheap, the sign became his banner of business, but not his motto. He served those who needed something now. And after surviving the hurricane, he became a born-again optimist and saw the best in the situation. Realising that as well as the normal profit margin, if he started buying second run, second grade materials, he could charge twice as much. Plus, an additional fee for delivery.

The other two building supply companies had pirate-ering instincts in their histories, though not from birth as the case with Drake, and they raised their prices to his and suddenly the price of plywood went from $30 to $90 per sheet overnight.

Drake was consistent in his dealings with people. He viewed everybody as prey. The only time he looked you in the eye was when he was lying. He spoke with a growl like a grumpy, male lion. Drake had been a physically solid man in his youth, but time and greed had not been good to him, and he commanded the commerce of his empire from an elevated chair on the front step of his store that gave him view of the lumberyard, the street and the cash register. Not a man anxious to pay any wages, he grudgingly settled for hiring a yardman and a delivery man. Settee fitted both job offerings perfectly.

Settee, like Drake was a bully who motivated people with confrontation and humiliation. He too was a large man and his head shaved bullet clean giving him a raw edge. His net worth was in gold chains that he wore around his neck and on his fingers. He was from San Sebastian where "people be rougher dere', more likely to bend d' rules." Over there they were not too worried about the wrath of God or their grandmothers.

"Hey-you , Almost-a-Pirate'" Delbert yelled at Settee who was driving Drake's loaded delivery truck through town. The first day of the protest against the gouging. It was a day when High Court was in session and traffic was slow anyway, giving Delbert lots of time to deliver his rant.

"You gonna walk de plank one day Pirate-boy, and dat day gonna come soon." He sang out to Settee. "Youse a buccaneer "

He chose a calypso to the tune of Yellow Bird. "Profiteer," each word long and protracted like the 'yellow' in "Yellow Bird."

"Pi...rat...eeeer... Buc....caneer... need a boot in d' rear!

Look sharp at what wa ya does, Youse price too high but we got's ta have, so off to de bank we goes, and now we's a roof to cover our beds but no sleep for the debt dat we owe. Profiteer, pi-rat-eer, Buccananeer, Babylonneer coming near!"

He'd composed better calypsos, but this one caught the highlights of the situation and the nerves of people's frustration. And by the time that Delbert had finished the main stanza, Settee had just reached the last intersection of town before a crowd closed off the street in front of him, and, in keeping with Walter's policy of one-way or no-way, he was routed in a180-degree circle back to the lumberyard.

Moreover, he couldn't leave until the police gave the truck "armed" protection -- in that the deputy Chief of Police reached a deal with Drake, if the merchant hired his nephew to ride on the truck, the Policeman would provide the kid with a uniform. No guns, no batons, he could have an empty revolver holster with a radio that didn't work in it. But that was all.

The uniform would have fit a heavyweight contender and the nephew was a bantam-weight, adolescent "sharp-boy" with soft-eyes, and though he looked ridiculous and more like a promotional mascot for Drake's Quality Lumber, leaning more towards vaudeville than authority, the girls his age saw only the eyes behind the costume and flirted outrageously. In response to the "armed guard" a boycott was organised by word of mouth and Drake's business slumped dramatically.

Pleased with the public response, Delbert focused his next rant on the insurance companies, and delivered his rant from the steps of the Treasury Building.

"Dey's nothing more den pirates in plaid suits selling you assurance for a sheltered future. But me friends, das jus' no so! And dey gotta go!"

When Hugo finally moved on, many people sighed with relief that they had insurance. But when they called the Tidal Insurance's main office in Barbados, all they got was a recording, "Don't repair anything until the adjuster looks at it. Keep your receipts, Tidal Insurance will not pay without a receipt. Don't repair anything that isn't essential. An assessment adjuster will contact you."

Delbert suspected it was a stall, in part legitimately because the insurance companies were overloaded with claims. But as the companies started seeing the breath of the hurricane's damage -- essentially the whole of the Caribbean from Trinidad to Florida, the pay-out was going to be far more than they had in reserves including their salaries if they weren't careful, the pressure was put upon the adjustors to keep the claims low.

"Ah's soo sorry Miss Goodwoman," He mimed a smooth-talking suit and tie adjustor, "you''s lovely little wood chattle house was way under-insured so Youse only gets half Youse claim. And Ah's soo sorry Miss Goodwoman, but pigs no covered in Youse policy.... No is d'loss of Youse chickens, or der coop, or Youse goats or de pen," each animal on the Delbert's,

327

adjustor's list drew howls of laughter as more and more people gathered in front of him on the steps of the Treasury Building. Many saw where Delbert was going and laughed in anticipation.

"Miss Goodwoman, Ah'm soo sorry, but de loss of Youse cat is no insured, or even Youse roof cause de cat does sit on it. In fact, not d'walls he rub on neither. None of dat's insured under Youse coverage."

"Nor de roof dat de cat sits on!" repeated a man wailing with laughter. "Das a good'un!"

"And 'not d'walls neither. That's the best!" Said the woman next to him.

"Ah'm sooo sorry, but de room where Youse daughter sleeps ain't covered neither." Delbert amped up his delivery as the crowd grew. "Youse daughter's room is considered an addition, even thou it sits on de same slab as de rest of d'house, and was built with de rest of the house, and even doe dey all shares a common roof and walls. Ah'm so sorry but Youse policy only covers a dwelling "firmly attached" and dat part what takes flight... Youse daughter's room ... was obviously not firmly attached."

"Ah'm <u>soooo</u>..." He drew out the "so", and his audience finished the phrase for him. "...So SORRY!" They yelled.

Again, "Delbert-He-Ain'-crazy"t slipped into the character of the adjustor. "Ah'm soo sorry Mister Gulfstreamjet, tis unfortunate but it's one of dese things dat do happen every so often in de insurance business, but dey does happen sometime.

You see sir, we no realise your house was <u>over</u> insured. Your policy reads," Delbert became very formal as though reading a legal document "replacement value up to, but not exceeding ten million dollars. And though sir, Youse house does been blown away to St. Barts, leaving nothing left but de foundation, in a realistic market its not much value so Youse replacement value is a fraction de claimed amount.

"Usually, we pick out dese problems ahead of time."
Delbert apologised, as though for the parent company
. "Now if'n you wants to cover Youse new house for ten
million dollars, my firm would be happy to accommodate, at a
premium twice your old onentwice preminum. De short of it is
Mrs Gulfstreamjet ....Ah'm so...."

"...Soorrry!" Came the audience response.

"Insurance's no assurance, dat dey pay what dey say!"
Delbert sang.

"I's gonna tell you what insurance be, you's hedging
Youse bets. We's willing to pay someone who says dey gonna to
pay us back if'n we's gets mash-up. Das no a bad t'ing. De 'rub
in de bushes' is dey no gonna pay de full measure of de loss.
Fact, de only t'ing we's be assured of is we's no gonna get full
measure when dey's d'ones what has to pay, simple as dat!"

"Insurance's no assurance dat dey pay what dey say!" he
raised his hands. In his right hand he had a solid metal cylinder
an inch in diameter. In the other a rod of the type used for
playing the triangle, and in one-four time, he started the day's
calypso,

"In-sure-ance no ass-sure-ance dat de pays what de say"
He did a little two-step descending the steps, danced out amongst
the crowd, and finally he led the procession around the corner to
the local branch of the Tidal Global Insurance office -- which
promptly shuttered their windows and locked their doors.

"Wow!" exclaimed a Dutch tourist fresh off the ferry from
San Sebastion to his girlfriend. "That guy's really crazy!"

She laughed."Ya! I hope he's the Premier or somebody
important! I'd vote for him!

Chapter 28

Sueky Found

It was her granddaughter who sounded the alarm that Sueky had disappeared out of the church during the storm. Vanished without a trace. Mrs. Kelly, one of the market women who did not know Sueky well, whispered to all who would listen, that she always thought the old woman was a witch, an Obe' priestess, and maybe it was Sueky who'd caused the storm. Hurricanes have to be beckoned; you know.

"Why would anyone beckon dis?" snapped Brookes, Sueky's neighbour.

"I hears Youse same-self say das you wants ta know a hurricane. Well, maybe she have de power to call 'He' here jus fo' you!"

Lying down in the bamboo forest was a pile of rags. Two people in the search party saw it but no one ventured into the splintered labyrinth of bamboo spears and the corpses of impaled monkeys impaled on them. The island was carpeted with piles of rags and mounds of dead animals.

Sueky awoke, crushed with her knees beneath her chin. Just as she had departed into death, she returned from it. First her hearing, registering the sound of flies. The air smelt and tasted of fresh death, metallic and sweet. Inch by painful inch she slowly unfurled, straightening as best she could against the spines of shattered bamboo. Miraculously, none of the bamboo shoots pierced more than her dress.

Finally, her eyes came into focus, avoiding the brilliance of the long shafts of light piercing the bamboo thicket. She lay head down and tried to come level, but the pain was too much. She lay back, mesmerised by the thrashing of the canes as an ill wind swept through them like they were shafts of wheat. Suddenly she saw them, and then dozens of them, dead monkeys scattered everywhere, impaled on the spears of bamboo, lips curled grotesquely back, teeth exposed in a permanent scream.

She turned her head slightly to the side and jerked back with revulsion, for lying just inches from her face was the face of a dead and distorted monkey. She gasped and scrambled to push herself away, without success. "Lord" she cried, "What hath ye wrought on us?"

"DERE! SHE IS!" cried a sharp-eyed youth, pointing into the maze of shattered and split bamboo... "DERE!!! DERE!"

Fascinated by the dead monkey bodies far down in the ravine, Johnnycake suddenly saw her eyes open in the pile of rags. "Me see she dere! And she see me! Dere!' He tugged on Ursula's sleeve. Look-so!" The boy pointed into the ghaut.

Word went out, and soon both men and women rushed to hack their way with cutlasses down the steep slope of the ghaut, opening a trail of rope lines to carry out the frail form. The spectre of death was so pervasive that the dead and mutilated monkeys and donkeys lost their power of repulsion, and their carcasses were taken up and slung like bags of sand further down the embankment. In the days that followed, the ghauts would become the repositories of the Island's carnage.

Making a makeshift stretcher from bamboo stalks and webbing from the palettes of cement bags, the rescuers gently eased the old woman onto it and, with much yelling and grunting, slipping often on the steep ascent, they finally delivered their cargo to the outside edge of the graveyard.

As they carried her passed the fourth corner post, in spite of the pain from her many cuts and bruises, she sat up a little, turning to the final corner post. Her sight focused.

Tears of relief rolled down her scratched and battered face, for she saw, bold and repellent, the crude mark of the Cross on the cornerstone. Her work was done. "Keep de dead so." She mouthed the message: "Keep de dead so." And suddenly she understood the message,   She lay back, she had done what was asked of her. She *passed* into unconsciousness.   All the souls remained kept in the graveyard -- except for two!

Chapter 29

'Road Through Chaos'

The morning of second day the storm stalled, but it kept spinning with gusts up to one-hundred-miles per hour though its forward movement was less than a mile an hour. Like wet cats fatigued from the fight, Garth, Myah and Bantu sat in silence in the dark back of the cave, confused, exhausted and soaked from the constant spray that filled their cavern from the hurricane's winds upon the waterfalls.

The last twelve hours were a blur that Garth may have hallucinated, or maybe a nightmare he'd dreamt. The white woman in the wedding dress and the younger black woman had elements similar to characters in a peyote trip. But the drug induced experiences, taken with his shaman guide, came to him with sequence, significant lessons, not random and irrational.

He tried to apologise to Myah but she said nothing to him about it and spoke only minimally to Bantu. Most of all, he felt devastated that in his insanity, if that's what it was, he had struck a woman... probably Myah. He had never hit a woman and his humiliation was so great that he would gladly leave then were it not for the storm.

As if to prove the superior force, around mid-morning, the wind struck again with another hard punch to the cliff face, again driving the waterfall back into the cave. The surge came unexpectedly and violently, and again Garth and Myah had to scramble with Bantu to the furthest end of the cavern.

Everything was soaked including their food supplies, only Caraja's herb hanging from the ceiling in the back was dry. The clay floor was slick and muddy and stuck to their skin like breadfruit sap adding to their misery.

"That's it!" Myah screamed that she couldn't sleep in the cave for a second night, so when the storm finally did move to the north, and while Bantu dozed, Myah and Garth slipped out to explore the chattel house as an option.

Trees had fallen around it, but none had fallen <u>on</u> the structure, and it seemed solid. It was dusk by the time they finally cut and cleared an open path through the uprooted mahogany tree that had fallen beside the cottage. Miraculously, it was as though a cone of protection had covered the structure from the fallen tree and its limbs and roots had deflected the wind and the roof seemed intact. The surrounding orchard, however, was a field of downed trees, crushed limbs and broken roots intertwined as though a child-giant had attempted horticultural crossbreeding, splicing banana stalks together with avocados, breadfruit with mangoes, limes with everything.

They cleared the debris from the porch. The front door opened easily and to their relief, they discovered that the roof was in fact solid and watertight, and the inside of the building was dry

With the shutters closed, and the limbs of the tree pinning them shut, it was dark inside and Myah had to light a candle on a side-table. The structure of the house was wood and built a century before. It was the poor man's land-boat in contrast to the great, plantation stone massifs. In contrast to those structures build on the principal of out powering nature -- meeting it head-on with meter thick-walled fortresses; the chattel houses were living, moving, flexing, and though sometimes they tumbled upside down, they stayed together as a unit, a land-locked boat.

The wood in Myah and Caraja's house was hardwood mahogany, six inch by six inch posts framed in with mahogany tongue-and-grove planks. All of the joints were mortise and tendon and pinned with hand-carved dowels. During hard times on St. Augustine when there was peace in the Caribbean and the colonial wars and pirates weren't sinking ships; rather than capturing land, in those times of peace the Island's shipbuilders again turned their skills to building houses. Caraja and Myah had inherited this one from their father, and he from his father before him, etcetera, running back five generations.

The interior walls of the four small rooms were each painted bright pastel. In one bedroom, which Garth assumed was Caraja's, every inch of wall space was a gallery of pictures. Smiling protean faces of school children in uniforms as bright as kites in the sun. Sun faded family portraits, snaps from picnics on the beach. There was a cluster of people huddled together on a busy New York city street city street ...in a snowstorm! Postcards from England, New York, exotic places like Singapore and Uganda. Caraja had also clipped pictures from magazines of places like the Pyramids and Machu Picchu -- destinations where he'd go one day.

Across the room, one wall was reserved for Caraja heroes. All of the Kings of Judea. "Give praise" read two banners. Another, beneath a portrait of Bob Marley there were quotes from the reggae singer. "Give Respect" and "One Love". The largest piece on the wall was a portrait of Che Guevara.

On the wall behind the single bed in the corner, was a collage of pictures of Caraja's friends. Garth recognised a few of the Rasta men, and Daniel Wellington, the Island's most famous cricketer. But one beautiful black girl appeared far more than any other.

"Felicity." Said Myah without further explanation, knowing that Caraja had probably spoke often of her to Garth. Garth assumed that was where Caraja had gone just before the hurricane struck.

The living room had a table along one wall on which a single candle stood were two chairs and a handmade child's chair between them. Garth glanced at Myah's room through the half-closed curtain. It too was a soft blue, but surprisingly barren and void of pictures on the walls.

"I think we should move back here to the house." Said Myah without looking at Garth.

"Would you prefer that I stay in the cave?" Garth was uncertain of his status with Myah. Before the eye of the storm, they seemed to have shared something very intimate. Yet following the calm of the eye, when everything began going crazy again, he would not begrudge her if she felt otherwise.

"It's not a problem, "I'll stay in the cave."" He assured her, though in his heart, it was the last place on the planet he wanted to spend another night

"NO!" She barked and shook her head. Her eyes lifted to his. "No... I *don't* want you to stay in the cave."

She smiled, "It's too dangerous." Then as though reconsidering, she cocked her head slightly off centre. "No, I want you to stay with me and Bantu here in the house. Caves are for animals and bats!"

They transferred as much of the supplies as were salvageable, leaving most of the ganja in the cave since it had survived the surge from the waterfall without getting wet. Neither of them was in a mood for sampling it, especially after having to use it for making the fire following the waterfall's flush into the cavern.

Myah pulled a bag of charcoal from under the house, and two large metal cooking pots. Water wouldn't be a problem. Over the next few weeks, the waterfall in front of the cave would continue to flow with unaltered force, and they were soaked with sweat and rain by the time they'd moved the supplies back to the chattel house. Myah went into Caraja's room returning with a pair of denim pants and a tee-shirt of Caraja's and a hooded pull-over. The pants fit, but the shirt was tight, and the top buttons had to be left undone

After a supper of plantains fried in coconut oil and baked breadfruit, cooked on a coal-pot in the "outside" kitchen (a shed-roof off the back of the house), neither Garth nor Myah spoke about what had happened in the cave. Each knew that if the subject were broached, it would drive them apart. So, they settled for cautious intimacies with their eyes and their silence.

Because Bantu required a lot of holding from both of them, he became their bridge. Bantu was in shock and sat silently on his

336

mother's lap, his eyes dull and lifeless. Events incomprehensible to adults were far beyond the grasp of a two-year-old child. For him everything had melded into one terrible nightmare. At times, he took equal solace in Garth's arms and Myah's, but still Bantu missed Petite, his kitten, terribly. His companion and playmate had simply vanished in the storm.

"There is one thing you must understand!" Myah broke the quiet of the room, her voice was focused with resolve, she looked directly into his eyes, "We can't make love!"

"What?!" Garth blinked, then laughed. It was the furthest thing from his mind.

Garth gave her hand a squeeze and nodded his acceptance, fighting not to smile.

"Ever!" He teased, but she ignored him.

As the three of them lay together on Myah's bed, while Myah and Bantu dozed, Garth thoughts turned reluctantly to his life before the storm. He would have to go home to Wyoming very soon. His tenure was up. And though he still didn't have "Stomp's" stamp, he suspected that it was not significant.

Wyoming seemed so far away, and yet if he made connections to Denver, or Salt Lake, he could be home with his family in a long twenty-four-hour day. St. Augustine to San Juan, Atlanta, Denver, Pocatello and into his brother's truck for the two hour drive out to the ranch and his mother's bannock with goat butter and sage-berry jam.

Still, there was something, in spite of the shame he felt for his behaviour during the hurricane, he realised, part of him did not want to leave. Maybe it was habituation -- ironically now after two years of thinking about the beautiful black girl, he was now with her. And, she seemed to want to be with him. He looked at Bantu, he was awake looking at him in the candlelight as if trying to see what Garth would do -- leave or stay. Garth made binoculars with his thumbs and fore-fingers, and he looked through them at Bantu. The boy smiled, but he would not be detoured.

Garth shrugged that he had no other choice but to leave. The child looked away.

Maybe Garth would be back someday, but for now he <u>had</u> to reach Portstown and try to get a message to his family that he was alive and unharmed.

In the receding storm of the following day, he awoke to see a new fresh light uncluttered with mulch through a crack in the shutter. Quietly he slipped out onto the porch. The swelling sun, obliterated for the previous two days, reflected off the wind-polished trunks of the denuded trees, looking to him like a great backlight cobweb, spun by some giant spider waiting just over the horizon. Mesmerised by the kaleidoscope of light, he watched the sun rise through the spider web, hiding behind skeleton trees, then shooting spears of white lightening through the openings.

He was never so thankful to see a sunrise, for he had wondered if he ever would when the storm was raging full on. At one point in that first night, when he was still lucid, and before the hallucinations of the women in the cave held domain, he believed his death was imminent.

He no longer had a his fear of death after his collision with "Charlie" the bull as a kid when his heart, they said, actually stopped. After that "Death" entered his consciousness only as something else. Maybe what he'd lost early in life was his "fear of losing it. Now, he smiled to himself, he had survived the "Hurricane of the Century" ... and after that, nothing could compare. Correspondingly, never would he ever again be casual about not living each moment, nor tempted to waste any precious time worrying about things beyond his control.

With that awareness, he knew what he had to do. It was time. He slipped back into the small house and collected his things into his daypack. For a long time, he looked at Myah.

Finally, setting aside his fears, he leaned over her and kissed her. He pressed his lips ever so lightly to hers, but her eyes opened, and her lips parted, and they kissed as a couple with a future together would kiss.

"You will be welcome back Cowboy." Was all she said, and quietly drew away from him and smiled.

"Indian." Garth thought of correcting, but knew she was "legging him" and he stood-up quickly and took-up his bag. "You'll be alright?' He asked.

"Caraja will come home soon. He'll help with the mess."

Garth nodded, rose and, with great resolute strides, he walked out of the cottage and off the porch... only to abruptly stop mid-way out in the yard.

"Could I borrow a 'cutlass'?" He called turned back sheepishly, after looking at the wall of tangled trees.

"Borrow or take?" She was standing in the doorway.

"Take." Said Garth with resolution.

"Buy it!"

"How much?"

She thought for a minute, came off the porch and walked up to him in the yard. It was the kiss of a couple who had _no_ future, but still one indelible bond that would last forever.

"That's how much it costs." She whispered, breaking the long kiss, her body still pressed to his. "And if you *do* come back with the cutlass, I'll give you your investment back -- with interest!" She grinned flirtatiously and stepped away. "Remember me," was the last thing she said to him.

Myah returned to the porch and sat down heavily on the top step, watching Garth cut his way into the tangled thicket. Her heart had never felt so heavy as it did then, but she must trust it would be as it was supposed to be. Bantu came out and stood beside her, starring at the yard bewildered by what he saw. His eyes caught sight of Garth's back before the Indian disappeared into the brush, and he started to run down the stairs to join him, but his mother caught his hand.

"He'll be back." She assured Bantu, but she doubted that he would ... nor could she blame him.

The night of the storm had been too confusing in its violence. Myah tried to recall the events of the night in the cave, and her memory was clear until the "apparition".

It <u>was</u> Naomi, the young woman generations back in her bloodline, who had been in charge of a white mistress who had gone insane. Finally, Naomi had taken the life of her mistress and her own. But why had they come to her? Why in the cave?

She remembered it was then that the storm grew more violent until it suddenly became so strong that it pushed the waterfall back <u>into</u> the cave! The apparition vanished and next she remembered was being violently slammed by a wall of water that drove her deep into the cave. Just as suddenly, she was being drug out by the outflow towards the cave's entrance and certainly plunging to her death hundreds of feet below.

She remembered fighting to catch her breath but couldn't get her head above the outflow. Then suddenly, Garth was there and grabbing her arm and holding her solid until the outflow ebbed.

Later, they all moved further into the recesses in the cave where the wave hadn't reached. Bantu slept soundly on a blanket surrounded by a forest of Caraja's drying ganga. Garth built a fire using the dry plants and they huddled together until finally, hours later, the storm died.

Myah knew she'd had a "visitation" that night. It was "Naomi"" and the insane white woman she had cared after centuries before. Sueky had told her of times when circumstances were of such magnitude that the dead could raise from the grave! It scared her more than even the terror of the hurricane, her heart quickened and a shiver ran through her. She knew now a soul, or souls, were loose upon the land of living. Was this the warning that troubled Sueky of late.

Garth said he felt he must apologise, though she could tell he didn't know about what. He thought he'd gone mad. Yet she could not tell him the truth because even she didn't know what had happened. She couldn't even ask him about the events. Why? Because she'd have to explain it all and she would certainly lose him if he discovered her dark secret. She loved him, it was that simple. He'd offered to stay in the cave. But she wanted him right there beside her and Bantu that night, maybe forever but she also knew he too had a culture, a legacy of generations of ancestors, in another place on the planet. And now he was gone, possibly forever.

Maybe he'd understand. He had spoken of the realm of the dead with familiarity, but maybe, whatever had happened during the storm, it was more than even he, she suspected, could comprehend and accept.

But as soon as she felt Garth's muscles tightening preparing to rise from beside her in the morning, she wanted to ask him to stay, but it would only be meaningful if <u>he</u> made the request. And then she felt his lips on hers, cautious, curious, courteous.

"Remember, you <u>borrowed</u> my cutlass?" She called into the canopy of the awaking jungle.

***

It took Garth most of the morning cutting his way down to the Upper Ring Road. Everyone was walking in a daze and at the intersection of the road to Poppy Dawn Village and Remember Me he watched a procession of four men walking in single file with the bowed, stooped walk of beaten warriors, their knuckles almost dragging the ground. Then he began to laugh... the last man was in fact a large male monkey. Hurricanes have a way of equalising primates, he thought to himself.

Near the Anglican Church he saw the albino bellringer sitting on a pile of rubble that once was his house. He had with a hammer in his hands, pulling nails from the fractured lumber-- no piece was longer than a foot.

Meticulously he laid each shattered board in a neat pile and straightened each nail. He spoke to himself, but Garth could not hear what he said. "Hello Mr. Peal". But the albino did not

341

respond, and what Garth first thought was a courageous step to recovery after the disaster, he realised it was just shock.

Garth discovered by the time he got to the main road, that it was far easier to go to the trunk of a fallen tree and crawl over, or under it, then try to cut a straight line through the limbs. The craters left by the roots were immense, especially the breadfruit whose roots ran across the surface rather than down. There was no rhyme nor reason to the carnage. Brand new vehicles were flattened like a beer cans, while "beater-wrecks" that would have been better served to be flattened, went unscratched.

Garth turned in at the Hotel Lemon. Lucy said they had some telephone communication, but it was erratic due to the high volume of traffic coming out of the Caribbean. Garth left his parents number and asked that they contact others in his family that he was safe.

At the old Queen Elizabeth school, where many villagers had weathered the storm inside, there was a congregation of women gathered around an older woman who sat on the stone steps with her head in her hands, sobbing with such a painful wail that it wrenched his heart to hear her. Someone had died, but since he knew no one in the group he didn't inquire. He nodded respectfully.

"Teacher Garth," a boy from his second-grade class came running up to him. "You hear Mistah Swanston be dead so and dey say dey no-can find Cecila Brown and de Grandlady what's named Sueky. Me does go so ta join de search."

"Sueky!" That was Myah's grandmother! He thought about returning to tell Myah the news, but the return trip would take hours and Caraja would pass with the news.

"You alright?" He asked the boy.

"Chure. We hardly takes a lick, but Swany's house down da road from us mash-up pretty bad. "

Then he looked at Garth. "Town go so?"

"Town go so." Garth replied.

Garth joined a party of men and women who were cutting their way towards Portstown, and after a while they collectively opened a tunnel through a great kapok tree. As they worked their way around the hairpin corner on Downing Hill, Garth wondered if his favourite house on St. Augustine was still standing.

Like Caraja's and Myah's, it was an old pasture house the beams and siding-boards had been hand cut with whip saws, yet with the precision of a modern sawmill, though they were sawn more than a century before gasoline engines. Garth imagined that Hugo had crush the rotten wood and termite nests to powder. But to his dismay and delight, the building stood. In fact, stripped of mould, the hardwood structure looked as solid as the day it was constructed a century before.

Cutting his way through the vines, he pushed the front door open and squeezed himself into the single room dwelling. It was as he expected. Abandoned dreams were scattered across the floor, interrupted by death. The melancholia was heavy, but just as Garth started to leave, he heard the faintest squeak coming from a corner of a room that was full of rusted old pots, pans and a broken clay cookery.

There, hidden back in the gloom, Garth saw two small, frightened eyes, their owner alternating between plaintive, helpless cries and an aggressive hiss full of courage. Garth crawled to the opening and sat on his haunches waiting for the animal to make the next move. Pulling his lower lip over his teeth, he made a sucking sound until finally the kitten slowly inched out, terrified, but still drawn by the magnetism of another living being. It was an emaciated thing, fur pocked with dried puss from running soars. Its giant round eyes were red with infection. It wouldn't take much to catch him, Garth thought, but what would he do with it. Still, he couldn't just leave it.

He took a bottle cap from the floor and flipped into the corner behind the kitten, then just at the moment it looked away to the sound, Garth's hand darted out catching the kitten around the belly holding it so the little thing couldn't scratch him. Still, the kitten hissed and spit, and swiped his claws fiercely, spreading his toes like fans, but his tiny paws looked more comical than frightening. Garth smiled and began talking to the small creature in a soft gentle voice, until finally, the kitten relaxed, and Garth began stroking it behind its head. "So little one, you want to live do you. Well, so do I. Maybe we can help each other." He easily caught it and slid the kitten into the front pocket of Caraja's pull-over.

****

It took Garth, by his watch, eight hours to walk from Myah's to the perimeter of town -- normally a two hour walk, or fifteen minutes by trans. There was frantic activity around the Alexander Hamilton Hospital. The roof of the east wing of the hospital had been ripped off and dumped on the West Wing, collapsing that roof and two of the hospital walls .... burying patients who were too ill to be evacuated. Lines of people had formed to pass bricks from one person to the next. A backhoe had been brought up from town but the work was delicate and the best the machine could do was hook onto large pieces with a chain and carefully lift them off to the side. Garth saw Doctor Maynard out in the yard working on a man on a stretcher. Though the doctor hardly acknowledged his presence as she bound a make-shift splint made out of palm ribs around the man's right arm.

"I've some first Aid training." Garth introduced himself. "How can I help?"

The doctor grunted. "Go up where they're digging and help them there," she said still not looking up. "Make sure they're careful moving anyone they find."

Garth nodded at two of the men moving broken cement blocks, he'd taught their children in his third-form class. Nothing was said. Grabbing a block, he swung it to the man behind him, and he to the woman behind him, and on down the line. Another concrete block, another fractured board, until the rhythm of the

344

work became its own relief from the horrible reality of what they were doing.

Suddenly, as Garth mechanically reached down to clasp the next object in his path, he recoiled backwards. It was a hand, a man's hand.

"Here!" He yelled, "There's someone under here." He felt the wrist for a pulse.... there was none! The hand was cold and tallowy. Desperately he flew at the rubble, rolling blocks and throwing boards aside. The arm appeared, but as he exposed it down to the abdomen, Garth released the arm had been grotesquely twisted and dislocated completely from a torso. Finally, he and another man rolled the body over.

"Fuck!" He swore, recoiling backward, slamming into the man behind him. The eyes were wide open in death's frozen stare, the mouth was caught in an eternal scream that would echo through Garth's brain for the rest of his life. Even though the face was contorted, and the tongue lulled to one side, Garth recognised that it was Mister Sutton, the Agricultural Agent who first met Garth at the dock the day he arrived.

******

It was mid-night by the time he finally reached his little house in Portstown. The rain came in a steady downpour now, and though the metal roof over his little three-room dwelling was intact, two galvanised sheets had moved slightly above the bedroom allowing tears of rain to drop upon his mattress. He dragged the bed to the centre of the room out of the leak and collapsed onto it, disregarding that the mattress was soaking wet.

"Ouch!" he exclaimed, sitting bolt upright as the kitten's tiny claws once again asserted its commitment to life.

"So, you're still alive?" Garth held the little cat at arm's length examining the pathetic ball of fur and running soars. "Maybe there was nothing I can do for poor Mister Sutton, but I _can_ help you." He rose and went into the kitchen. On a shelf he found two cans, tuna and corn-beef hash. He lifted the kitten up so it could examine both.

"Good choice," he said, "that was my pick too." Setting the animal on a dishtowel on the table, Garth opened the canned corn-beef, putting a couple of scoops in front of the kitten, saving the rest for himself. The kitten attacked the food as if it had never had anything but corn-beef hash.

When it finished, Garth took some alcohol and dabbed off the crusts around the kitten's main sores. Then, after eating the remainder corn-beef straight from the can, Garth collapsed, once again laying the kitten on his chest. Soon they fell asleep on the wet mattress.

Finally, the persistent discomfort of a full bladder and an empty stomach dragged him grudgingly to consciousness. It was still raining, he looked at his watch 12:17 AM. He'd slept for twelve hours straight! Oh yeah, there's been a hurricane, he grudgingly remembered. He had ventured to a dreamy place where there hadn't been a hurricane, where there was still balance with order, predictability and consistency. Now time was inconsequential against the events of the Hurricane.

He now had to decide. Go back to Wyoming? He would be justified by the end of his tenure. Go and be one less soul to be accommodated.

But 'Go'? Go to what? But if he stayed, he was another mouth to feed. Show his parents that he hadn't perished.. Marry Priscilla and manage the ranch?

On the other side of the argument was the initial decision to try to actually help someplace on the planet. And as he saw it, there was no other place that needed more help than here right now. Ground.zero, but he would become part of the problem, another mouth to feed.

He picked up the kitten and held it facing him. He smiled at the tiny animal. "Once again you're right! We've got to stay and see this one through. "Defiance", that's what I'll call you. You've defied the odds."

Why was Garth so shocked that death and destruction are truly the only democratic events in Creation, treating everything and everybody with equal, indiscriminate measure. Is it because Creation is blind? There is no Divine Plan, only fate and all of the innumerable influencing factors that cause each moment that are merely unpredictable mixings of random combinations.

That was it. The core of his existential angst, specifically the destruction of the hurricane, had shown him that Nature is indiscriminate, random, without purpose or direction. How could he find purpose when there was none even in the Universe?

He had always envisioned his life as pre-ordained, purposeful and ultimately heroic. As a boy driving a tractor, which he thought a Sherman tank -- each windrow was a run through enemy lines taking heavy fire as he breached great stone walls and pushed over trees, unafraid, for that was his scripted destiny. Now, laying on his back, at ground-zero of ruin, he realised, what shocked him the most was not that he would die, nor the proximity of death, but that he could easily die without purpose.

To die without achievement is to be in the control of the *élan vital*, but without purpose is a waste of a life. That's why he'd joined the Peace Corps,

But what had he really done to help? Suddenly, with the sweep of a tropical depression on steroids, all of the work he and Caraja had achieved against eradicating tick fever was of no consequence having lost most of the Island's cattle to the storm.

It is human nature to have purpose or give Nature purpose. Too often, he thought, we need to locate ourselves in the centre of the Universe, to make us its purpose. Asking "Why me God?" is believing that God knows our name well enough to focus attention on us individually. What if, not only is the Universe void of purpose and direction, maybe all human endeavour is ultimately purposeless, hence hopeless.

He lifted his eyes above the floor and looked around the room. His gaze settled on the picture of his parents. They would want to know. They could tell Priscilla, his girlfriend, he hoped she would be concerned.

He knew what must be done. He started to move from the bed but heard a faint mew. The kitten was laying curled up on his chest. Setting the tiny cat in the warm imprint that his body left in the wet mattress, he retrieved his backpack, he began filling it with the edible contents of the kitchen.

Underwear, socks, his other pair of tennis shoes; he went slowly through each room dividing the possessions into take or leave. He set all the plants out in the rain and wedged open the refrigerator for the geckos -- leaving them a 1/2 a loaf of mouldy bread.

Finally, he sat down at the kitchen table and taking his notebook, while sharing the rest of the corn beef hash with the kitten, he began to write.

"Dear Mom and Dad,

I am safe. Not a scratch. But the Island is devastated. I cannot describe the destruction, and I have seen only one small part. There are casualties, but no one knows just how many. The power was shut off just before the storm. It will be months before it is on again. Without electrical current, the pumps don't work, so the island's water system will be down for some time. I heard on a radio earlier in two days that Hugo has hit the U.S. Virgin Islands and Puerto Rico. This little Island will be the last to get help!

For this reason, I have decided <u>*not to terminate*</u> *with the Peace Corps for a few weeks so that I can stay here and help with the recovery. I'm sure you are disappointed, I am too. But I must stay to help, I know you will understand. I am going up to a village called Poppy Dawn, high up the mountain. It is where my school was and I have friends there. It will be the last of the last to recover, though it got hit about as hard as everyone else.*

348

Dad, there is one thing you must do. Contact your friend in the Red Cross in Boise. Tell him this is BIG TIME and we need two things: chainsaws and portable generators (7kw to 12kw). You can contact me through the Hotel Lemon. They have a working phone and radio contact with Antigua. Someone monitors night and day. The Hotel number is (869) 469-2689. Give Gage or Lucy your messages and they will get it to me.

There is much to talk about when I return, but for now I must stay.

(Generators and chainsaws!!!)

Respectfully, Garth

He folded the letter into an envelope, wrote out the address in Wyoming, and his parent's telephone number. Its destination seemed so far away in both distance and conditions, and part of him wished he was going with it, but he also felt he had made the right decision to stay. He smiled, thinking about the letter's journey for he knew it would likely arrive in <u>much</u> the same manner as removing debris and bodies at the Hospital, from hand to hand... and Garth saw that the process began at the dock.

There was seaweed on the steps of the Treasury Building, eight feet above the dock -- which in turn was eight feet above the high-tide line. Most of the goods off-loaded before the storm onto the dock had been swept into the ocean, including heavy things like cars and palates of concrete blocks had sunk to the bottom of the ocean. Interestingly, the ocean surf, normally white was now bright red with a surface of Macintosh apples! bobbing on the white, frothy surface around the Carib Queen.

The inner-Island ferry had survived the storm because its captain, Brother Barkley had rowed out to the ferry with his First Mate. When their dingy was caught in the wind and was swamped, they <u>swam</u> to the anchored ship, started the engines and took the ferry out to deep water, and for twenty-eight hours kept it's bow facing the storm and incoming waves.... miraculously returning it safely to the dock once Hugo had passed.

Garth went out on the port dock. Brother Bart was on the upper deck directing the loading of people on stretchers, many were bandaged in blood-soaked gauze. He also noticed there were a few passengers on crutches being helped on board.

"Where's you going?" Garth called out to Brother on the upper deck.

"Puerto Rico. You want to go?"

For a second the thought was considered. "No, I think I still have a job here." He laughed and waved his hand at the destruction engulfing the Island.

"But I'd like this to go. It's to my parents, it would mean a lot to them to know I'm ok." He held up the letter

"No hay problemo, mon. I does mail she me-self. We all got to pull together. "He disappeared for a moment. "Here," he tossed to Garth a burlap sack used on the ship for crate padding, "Gits some apples before de sea's water turn dem black."

Garth looked down; the ferry was surrounded in rich, red MacKintosh apples!

"You want some?" Garth asked.

"Have-so already." Brother called. "Dey shouldn't go to waste, Tell everyone you meet they can fish out and give dem to whoever needs."

Garth took the bag and retrieved apples until he could barely pull the bag over the edge of dock for its weight. He filled his sweatshirt front pocket with more, nestling around the kitten.

He felt like Johnny Appleseed as he handed out apples en route, telling people to pass the word that they should go to the dock. Gossip travels faster than microwave communication. And, by the time he got up to Remember Me and the cutoff road to Myah's he had only two apples left, one for Bantu and one for his mother.

Chapter 30

"Work Crews"

Fluteman was the unelected, un-appointed, and yet the universally acclaimed leader of the community of Poppy Dawn. As the villagers gathered, he looked intently into each face assessing their wounds both physical, and especially psychological, as they congregated at the concrete slab where once the Domino College stood. It was the untitled, yet all agreed, the centre of the community, the equivalent of the Town Hall.

The Hurricane's toll was written in the faces of all those congregated. No longer civilians, they now looked like worn out warriors that had fought until they no longer knew who the enemy was, nor who won, nor why they fought except survival. Still, Fluteman saw in their faces, that they were prepared for the ultimate engagement.... Recovery!

Fluteman raised his hand, "Does anyone have or know anyone with serious injuries?" He looked into the congregation of bewildered faces. No one responded.

"PRAISE DE LORD!" Someone yelled.

"Agreed! But, if anyone is in need of medical attention, word is that Gage down at the Hotel Lemon has a couple of doctors staying there, and he is going to turn the Hotel into a makeshift Aid Centre." He scanned the congregation, still no one responded.

Earlier, Fluteman had sent out across the community youth reconnaissance parties, that returned to the gathering with reports on the damage.... and there was plenty! Now the question priority!

"I'm guessing that the entire Island is in the same fix as us, and we are going to have to deal with our problems ourselves."

His words settled over the audience. "But!" His voice raised. "we can do it!" Fluteman read their faces. "AND..." He exclaimed. "It isn't going to be enough to just do for ourselves! We got to realise all of us are in the same boat!

He punctuated his words with a look of defiance that touched every set of eyes.

Then suddenly, his voice rang like a revival preacher. "People! From now on, from this moment forward, we have to work together!"

He let his words settle, then barked again. "ONE FOR ALL! " He shouted!

The villagers responded with ecumenical commitment. "ONE FOR ALL!!!".

"And," Fluteman was still on a pulpit before the gathered congregation "We have only ONE problem to contend with..." He paused. "Everything!"

He studied them, then brought the flute to his lips and jumped full force into the song he'd composed in the face of the hurricane full of hope, and defiance; the song of the human will not giving up.

"AMEN Brother!" The response was loud and committed.

"Praise de Lord!" He yelled, then returned to the situation at hand.

"As I see it, we need to break ourselves into work parties, each to their skills. And the first priority will be shelter, and I urge everyone to open your resources to your neighbours, especially if you have a solid foundation, and a dry roof overhead."

"The next consideration is food. I agree that rather than everyone trying to maintain a kitchen that we make a common soup kitchen. And I think it should be right here where we are standing on the floor of the "late," Domino College. It is centrally located, has water and all we need is a new roof. With as many carpenters and loose materials set into flight, this won't be a problem!"

Fluteman let the ideas settle and each figure how they could contribute.

"Obviously the soup kitchen is a priority. Shelter is another thing. If you have room, open your doors... provided you have doors!" Everyone laughed.

"And" he looked around at what was left of the village, "I see many of the chattel houses have just been tipped off their footings, but they're still solid. So, we should form a crew to go around and put them straight on their foundations. Also, if you weren't touched, make room in your homes for those what were, particularly those what have block houses."

"Once we can make do for ourselves and our neighbours, the next priority has to be the roads. My thought is, we form road crews and every man-jack with a cutlass will have to work on them. I expect they're blocked all the way to Portstown."

Then Fluteman thought for a moment, his focus falling upon on Benjam, the man who worked for the Island Water Department. On their side of the Island, he <u>was</u> the Water Department. Poppy Dawn's public water system was fed by a large eight-inch pipe that ran from a pond on the top of the mountain that was kept full by the perpetual cloud on the crown of the peak. Given the vast uprooted jungle, the pipe would have many breaks. Normally it was a one-person job, but following the hurricane, it would require a large crew. Still, clean, uncontaminated water was a high priority.

Eye contact was all that was necessary and Benjam started forming a work crew.

"I'm guessing by all of the trees uprooted and breaking the pipe, that this is going to be a major job and you'll need a <u>big</u> crew." Said Fluteman.

Then, suddenly a thought came to him. "On the subject of water, conserve and collect as much as you can. You'll have to boil it, even if you have cisterns. And if you do have good cisterns, share!"

He paused for a moment. "As I read our situation, we are going to get through, but it means we all have to work together!" He looked into the faces of the congregation.

After the essential priorities, opening up the road network was their next priority. For clearing the transportation arteries, Fluteman studied the gathering, assessing who was left after the construction, water, and the food crews necessary for gathering and running the community kitchen. One source of labor that hadn't been tapped was the young people. Leadership was essential and the Peace Corps teacher would be an excellent resource for the young people. Garth was well liked and respected by them, and he was anxious to help.

"Also, Island electricity is not going to be restored for a long time! So, we are going to have open the roadways before that happens. And we will have to be attentive <u>not</u> to cut <u>any</u> lines, either electrical or telephone lines. We don't want to have to rewire the entire Island."

Soon the first detachments of scouts that Fluteman had sent out to assess the damage returned. The first had alarming news! Sueky Liburd had not been seen since the beginning of the storm, though her house seemed fine but buried beneath two small trees that had uprooted beside it. The structure seemed solid, but the house was empty!

Next came news from Bush, one of the Island's road-clearing crew, that Violet, his partner for as long as any could remember, and the Island account, had disappeared! She was so close to Bush, her disappearance from his sight was an immediate concern.

Still, the final report from the last scouts was even <u>more</u> alarming. Bueno and his <u>entire</u> family of five had disappeared, even though their home too was intact!

Given the news of the unaccounted was the most immediate concern, finding the missing was the <u>first</u> priority.

"Ok, let's form three groups and each look for one of the missing parties!" All agreed.

But suddenly, Worrrymon barked up with uncharacteristic authority. "STOP! It is a waste of time! <u>Aliens grabbed dem!</u> Dat's <u>d'only</u> answer!"

Chapter 31

Aliens

The last to report back from the reconnaissance crews was the most alarming. Three sets of people were <u>missing</u>! Alphonso the beach comber, Violet, Bush's partner, and the <u>entire</u> Bueno family... seven people in total had vanished!

"Aliens!" Concluded Worrymon again, "We looks and not a sign." He looked around the collection of villagers hoping for confirmation of his brilliance. "What other answer could there be?"

Flute smiled indulgently, "Barring Aliens taking everyone up for specimens, I think we have to make the missing our main priority in case someone is trapped some place we haven't checked.

Old Alphonso's house was folded up like a flattened cardboard box -- presumably, they feared, with him inside.

When the Poppy Dawn searchers arrived at Alphonso's, it was as the boy had said, the tiny house had been folded neatly by the hurricane. Then, as though to make sure the box didn't unfold, the roof was flattened on top -- and then, a white-cedar tree toppled on top of the remains. It was not a large tree but Alphonso's house was definitely lightweight; tarpaper over nests of termites that had inhabited it presumably back to the <u>original</u> inhabitants in the nineteenth century.

Though the rescue flew into the job of digging through the wreckage, no one seriously thought he was beneath it alive -- a thought enforced by the fact that not a sound was heard from the rubble when his name was summoned over the debris. Still, carefully, like archeologists excavating back through time, uncovering clues to the intensity of the storm by the debris that it had deposited, possibly on Alphonso, they were careful.

Cautiously the rescuers lifted each piece of the roof in sections for it had broken into six add -on parts none related to the original construction. Carefully they tried to reverse the order of how it was

356

laid down by Hugo. Finally, the roof, all four walls and a door later, they reached the chattel house floor.

Astonishingly though, all they found was a few crushed and broken pieces of furniture salvaged from the seashore, a rolled-up rug, and a few clothes sandwiched between a flat dresser-drawers ... but no Alphonso!

"Where'd he go?" Everyone wondered.

"He never be here in the first place. Dat's the only answer."

"Unless 'aliens does it!"

"Why Alien's wanna snatch a beachcomber who's so lazy he makes he donkey do all the work."

"Don't speak ill of the dead... or gone!" Barked Alphonso's sister, who hadn't spoken to him in ten years.

"How you know he dead, maybe he find some treasure chest exposed by the storm, and he take de treasure and go to New York, or St. Vincent.

"Maybe he finds de treasure and somebody robs and murders he for it"

"No." said Press-flesh, a longshoreman who could lift and carry way better than he could think, "Me t'inks he be sucked-away by de storm. Like Bueno and he family."

"Aliens, I tell you!"

"What would Aliens want with the laziest man on the planet?" Growled Fluteman "No, I think that is the dumbest conclusion I've yet to hear. The answer is right in front of us, only we can't see it."

Benji, a thoughtful man of six years, found on the floor a yoyo and threw himself down on the rug to ponder the problem of untangling the string on his new toy.

But ...no sooner had he landed on the rug than he leapt to his feet as the rug "barked" at him. Scampering to the end of the cylinder, he cautiously peered in!

Less than a foot down the tube, a set of eyes begged for help.

Cautiously they started to unroll the rug, but even that was too much for Alphonso and he screamed anguished cries with each slight shift of his cocoon.

"Me' thinks we should carry him to Hotel Lemon, and de AID Center". Said 'Brother', Alphonso's youngest brother. The idea was considered and concluded that it was the only alternative. Half a dozen men offered to help carry him, and without verbal communication two long poles were cut and a sling made of webbing woven out of downed power wires. But the moment they tried to move the rug to the stretcher, Alphonso screamed in pain.

"Let's fold up the rug and lay it under him." But that solution was also met with more screams of pain.

"Better, let's roll him up again."

Alphonso emphatically grunted that that idea was *his* preference. And so, with much sincere confusion, and commands to do the self-obvious, he was re-rolled. "CAREFUL! ...Ya no wanta kill he!" They pushed, bent, tugged, jabbed, stabbed, folded and finally flopped Alphonso back into his Afghan cocoon. Fortunately for Alphonso, he became unconscious well before they carried him down the mountain to the Hotel.

Another missing person on Island was St. Augustine's Chief Accountant, "Miss Violet" She was Bush's partner for life beginning as children. As with Alphonso, she disappeared without a trace, which to some certainly confirmed Aliens!

Bush, the main roadside maintenance man, cutting the bush back along the roadsides, was beside himself worrying and searching for Violet. He and his road crew had looked every place practical. Their house was in order, but empty. No one had seen her at the Anglican Church. Neither of their two neighbours knew anything.

She was his first and oldest friend. They had been childhood neighbours down in Bachelor Hall, a small cluster of houses built far out onto the parched apron, between the volcano and the ocean shoreline.

His first memory of Violet was carrying a pail of water with her, each gripping a side of the pail's metal handle. Next, he remembered her getting mad at him for some teasing remark and she sloshed the pail of water on his foot. A fight broke out, spilling the rest of the water. Both ended up in detention so they decided to be friends.

School did not suit Bush, but Violet blossomed, and patiently she helped him in the evenings with the basics. Grudgingly, and only because of his mentor, he learnt to read and write and master his sums. Also, they had another thread in their bond which was a 'common enemy'. Their fellow schoolmates teased them constantly about where they lived and how ragged they dressed.

Winds, dry and often relentless, killed their family gardens and necessitated that the houses of Bachelor Hall, constructed of wood instead of the stone had eventually to be abandoned. But there was something else that bonded them, and most of the Island for life.

Their parents had gone to the neighbouring island of San Sebastian for the Saturday-market to sell mason jars of clear "Hammon" a local alcohol cane-drink that their families produced. It would soon be Fall and the money from the sales would be used to buy new school and Sunday clothes for the children.

Then suddenly they were orphaned together when their parents and over two hundred other Islanders sunk to the bottom of the Channel with the doomed ferry, the *Christina*.

They had no other first family on Island and so it was that Violet's distant Aunt Marmalade who raised both children.

One afternoon around the age of twelve they'd gone to the abandoned Bachelor's Hall sugar-mill to discover what was different between the sensations of touching themselves, and someone else doing it. They took off their clothes touched each other, and unsure of what to expect, they fell into hilarious laughter.

When Bush was sixteen, he dropped out of school to go work in construction. Violet excelled in school and wanted to be a teacher and after graduation she attended teacher's college in San Sebastian, returning to teach in the same upper form school where only three years before she'd been a student. Bush was so proud of her, he'd orchestrate his day to walk her home. She would cook a meal and he would clean her yard, but mainly they just sat, happy in the glow to the other's companionship.

It became a routine as predictable as sunrise and sunset, and when she left her sister's home to buy a house of her own on a couple of fertile acres, it was Bush who cleared the land and mixed concrete in the evenings for the foundation and the mortar for laying the building blocks of the house. Accordingly, when the house was finished and painted bright yellow by Bush, it became their cocoon against time.

Next, they built a platform up in the fork of a giant mahogany tree that grew in their backyard. On this deck they placed two chairs facing the ocean. And there they passed each evening in silence, holding hands, each drawing comfort in the other's presence.

Together they grew old with a bond beyond mere love, it was one of inner-dependent souls so intertwined that their silent solitudes filled both receptacles to overflowing -- and that was enough for both.

From her perspective, Bush was the finest man she'd ever met. They'd made their truce early in life and could share a love without gender or sex. He was a man of her family's custom, hardworking, gentle, a force measured against the sea and the sun. Moreover, they found in the other the family each had lost, the companion and partner each needed. He measured himself through her eyes, and she through his and both only saw beauty. Their whole life they'd been together, delivered by the same mid-wife, their childhood houses just across a path from each other. Their mothers shared feeding when the other had to catch trans into town.

Bush felt sure she must be somewhere near to the house, someplace logical for she was a logical kind of woman. Each time he turned onto the path to their house after the hurricane, Bush could feel his heart beating faster though he'd been there alone, and before with the different search teams. The outside of the building had only minor signs of hurricane damage. Inside he found nothing was out of place, the dishes washed, the beds made.

Where could she have gone, no one saw her after the hurricane began, though Mrs. Liburg had spoken to her that night trying to persuade Violet to take refuge in the Anglican church. But Violet said she expected Bush to come home soon and he would be concerned if she were not there.

When he heard this, Bush hung his head with shame for he had promised her... but he left town for home too late and the trans had all gone home and he had to walk getting no further than Government House where he had to take shelter when Hugo's full fury hit.

Once more Bush looked everywhere, and though it had been three days, he called her name until his voice cracked with anxiety. Someplace logical... he opened the back door. And though the house had escaped damage, the giant mahogany tree behind had been uprooted then crushed to the earth with such force that most of its limbs had snapped and were teepeed around the thick trunk with a pyre of debris reaching far higher than the roof of their house.

He could no longer contain his heart as it raced like the first lunge of a racehorse, and he attacked the formless heap of limbs with his cutlass. Two hours slid by and though his arms throbbed, the thought that Violet could be in there fed his fury further.

Then, suddenly he saw it ... a short length of yellow nylon rope and though he could see neither its source nor terminus, his heart stopped for he knew the rope had not been there before the storm.

Wildly he cut his way into the fork where the platform had once sat. It was crushed into splinters, the chairs mashed flat, their tiny coal-pot in pieces.

"Oh Lord!" he screamed, "Where is she?" He arched back looking up through the thicket at the humid sun... then gasped -- he saw her high above him, hanging, suspended at the waist like a dishrag hung on a hook, suspended by the yellow rope!

Fearing her house would not survive the storm, she had gone outside and tied herself to their platform in the ancient tree, likely reasoning that since the monarch had withstood three centuries of hurricanes, it was the safest place to be.

Tears blinded his vision as he climbed to the body and tried to untie her knots. But they'd been stretched so taut and they couldn't be untied. Finally in desperation he swung his cutlass into the nylon rope and bringing his shoulder beneath her body, he carefully carried her from the tree and lay her on her bed in their house. Only then did he look into her eyes.

He recoiled at the visage that would plague him for the rest of his life! What he saw in her eyes was the unbearable fright she'd known in her last moments. His cry would haunt all those who heard it for the rest of their lives!

"Take me Jesus!" he pleaded, collapsing beside her body as the magnitude of his loss surged over him. "Take me too!" He cried, and it was a wail that circled the Island with such sadness it awoke all to their own losses.

A search team continued looking for Violet, and subsequently found him beside his lifelong love. It was hard to persuaded him to leave her side, and even then, he kept one callused hand upon her cold velvet arm as they carried her body down the mountain.

******

"Lord be de Infant God!" screamed Paulette sending the chicks that ambled around her yard flying to the shelter of a wall. All night long she'd been thinking about her Grand Eva's words... "Dey's right in front of our eyes."

Then suddenly they made sense. "I know where they be!" She jerked bolt upright in front of the outside wash basin. She'd been washing dishes and looking absently up the mountain when it hit her. Right in front of her eyes. She could see just a corner of the new house Bueno had been constructing for his family. "That's where they be!"

"Boyo!" she yelled to her grandson. "Run quick and call the Elders to the Worry Stone. I know where Bueno and Rebecca be! I know where dey all be'd all along!!!"

It had been seven days since the hurricane, since no-one had seen the missing family. At first everyone in the village set aside their own problems and searched, but no trace was found and finally the missing family became just one more bewildering mystery wrought by Hugo.

Rumours abounded including a dream Priscilla, Bueno's mother had that they were in England.... swept up by Hugo and, by her reckoning, England was on the opposite side of the planet and thus the obvious depository for Hugo's carnage.

The longer the lapse, the more outrageous the rumours became!

An entire family missing was a significant event on the Island, and after the third day, the Island Government organised a search party with soldiers from Antigua and a command post in a room at the Red Cross building. They had an antenna set up for Island wide communication, but it only reported failure.

A team of rock climbers descended into the vertical "Remember Me" ghaut and searched it all the way to the sea. They found a human skull and a femur but they were ancient, maybe dating back to the 18th century. Dogs were offered from Barbados, but the boat carrying them had to turn back because the Caribbean Sea was still in a state of chaos as the storm slowly beat it's way north through the Leeward chain to Puerto Rico, then west to Cuba, Jamaica, Haiti, then East again to take a shot at Florida. No island north of Barbados was spared.

Speculation grew beyond reason as the duration of the family's disappearance increased, until finally it became an International conundrum. Even the National Enquirer reported that a "Highly credible unnamed source" that a St. Augustine family had been abducted by <u>aliens</u> to work as "Laboroids" in the Palladian Galaxy.

"Why dey <u>always</u> takes black folk when deys need'n slaves? Growled Pickens the plumber, "Das what I really wants to know."

Not bothering to take off her apron, Paulette rushed through the community pasture towards the Worry Stone. "I know where dey be!." She yelled to Calvin who was pulling dying plants from his bean patch. She didn't stop to explain. He didn't catch her words, but curious about what could move a woman of Paulette's size to hurry so, he lay down his spade and ran after her. Mrs. Carlton was in the adjacent garden pulling up the few carrots the monkeys had left from a raid the night before. She looked up just in time to catch Paulette passing the wall, then her husband in chase. "Old Fool" she muttered thinking the old man might have softened his mind and harden other parts.

"Paulette take de fits!" he called to her. And not sure which variety of fits she'd taken, Mrs. Carlton joined the procession

Most of the villagers were already there at the Domino College when she arrived panting, her hair wild with bush and sweat, her eyes round and urgent. "Yes, yes," she gasped as her neighbours pelted her with questions, "I tells all but I must catch me breath."

At last she drew a deep breath and pulled up her apron to wipe her face. "Dey's in dat <u>new</u> house Bueno was building for he-self!" she exclaimed. "D' one way up above Sista' Shauna." With the discovery of the body of Violet lashed to a gum tree, no one had thought to look further up the mountain. It was a new house under construction only the first floor finished but it had water, a working toilet, a gas stove <u>with</u> gas.

"Of course!" Exclaimed Fluteman. "The most obviously place. But I'd totally forgotten that he was building it.... And it is so overgrown and packed from mash-up, we've been walking by it all along."

" For chure das where dey be. Why we no think o dat sooner."

"What did she say?" asked a little boy in the back of the crowd?

"She say she see Bueno and Rebecca in a vision." Replied an older boy trying to sound more informed than he was.

"What dey doing so long?" asked the younger one.

"Lingering, me suspects." Calton's voice rose above the confusion. "But why dey no come so after d' storm?

"May be dey can't, maybe dey's trapped!" Fluteman thought out loud.

"Or dead!" Someone else thought, also aloud, sending a gasp through the crowd,

"Or maybe dey's being held prisoner." It was the last straw causing Pricilla to shriek, her heavy legs weakened and she collapsed to the ground.

Six men with cutlasses stood in front of a wall of fallen trees, none imagining how Bueno and Rebecca could have forged their way through the impossible maze. Not thinking that at the beginning of the storm, the land was clear! Flute found traces of cutting, but it was not certain if it was recent.

"Me can no see how dey gets dere? Me think dis a waste of time." Someone said.

"You think it's better to go looking for 'Aliens?" asked Fluteman. " Der's no way we's gonna find out until we do it." And he began attacking the nearest limb of the maze. For three hours they cut away at the snarl, taking individual breaks, allowing a rested man to move into the position vacated in the chain. Occasionally someone thought they heard shouting but never twice in a row.

"Bueno! You in there?" Fluteman called as they finally reached the building.

There was a long silence followed by giggling!

"GO AWAY!!!" Came a callback from inside the structure. More giggling in the background.

"Depends on who's asking." Came Bueno's baritone bellow. "If I owes you money, d' answer's 'No!.'"

"Bueno?!" Fluteman called back.

"Maybe... what's you's selling?" There was a pause. ..."Naw ... come to think of it, we don't need nothing! Go away!"

"Stand back! Give us room," Fluteman commanded. And soon with Bueno pushing from the inside and the rescuers pulling. the door, badly bent by the tree that had fallen against it... it creaked open.

When they appeared, it was not a family of forgotten souls desperate to escape for the last seven days!

Rather it was a family sitting around a saw-horse construction table playing cards. reading books, colouring.   But ... they could hold back no longer, and the family started laughing at the startled faces of their rescuers.

Later Bueno confessed; they were absolutely trapped. He'd checked all the possibilities long ago, but the fallen trees had pinned them inside. Resigned, they did as their family did normally, ate, slept, played games and well.... took a vacation. Plenty of food, good company, no alarm clocks. Surely someone would put the clues together and come rescue them. No! It was a family vacation!

Bueno was the first to appear. Immediately he turned to his family, and like a preacher after a church service, he shook each member's hand as they stepped out into freedom. "Congratulations!" He said to each. "You conducted yourself proud."

"How was it?" Somebody asked.

"Great," said Bueno without sarcasm, "Longest holiday I've had in years.... maybe ever!". He grinned. "In fact, we're planning our get-a-way for next year... possibly a cruise ship!"

No sooner had they been rescued than a boy named Calamari, took off at a run to carry the news. At the Domino College, where most of the village gathered for information, he yelled out. "Dey's found! De aliens hid dem in dey's own house."

"Just as I thought!" said Paulette. "And right in plain sight!"

Chapter 32

"Smokehouse"

Bantu was ecstatic to see Garth, and overjoyed when he saw the apples in the Indian's hands. But when Garth took the kitten out of his jacket pocket, the boy just stared in disbelief. Ever so cautiously he reached for the kitten. Nothing was going to happen to this one — Bantu was not going to let it out of his sight, ever!

Myah, too, was happy to see Garth -- though she tried to hide it. Still, through the mask and the quiet joy, there was also uncertainty in her eyes.

"I brought you something all the way from the United States." He handed her the apples.

"You go so far... so soon," she smiled, accepting them.

Garth stepped beside her and touched the back of her hand. She did not respond, but when he started to remove it, her fingers arched and wrapped around his, though still she kept her eyes averted from his.

"I thought you might need some help," he said cautiously. "Have you heard from Caraja? Did he deliver his hurricane?"

Myah shook her head. "I've heard nothing. I'm told that the road off the Ring Road to Remember Me has been washed out and that the ghaut between Poppy Dawn and Remember Me is a raging torrent." Finally, she smiled. "But Caraja is all right and if it were, otherwise I would feel it."

"Apples and a can of tuna that I shared with Defiance."

"Who?" she asked. Garth pointed to the kitten.

"That's what I called him since he has defied all the forces of Nature gone sideways, to live."

"That's an awful name 'Defiance' for such a tiny little thing."

"Nogo!" Bantu said clearly. "Nogo."

Myah laughed. " No, he's not going to go. That's a great name…Nogo."

They sat that night in the house, across from each other at the kitchen table. In the candlelight they studied each other's eyes.

"Do you need me?" Garth's question stunned her. "No, I didn't mean it that way, he said, seeing her consternation. "I meant that if you didn't need me here to clean up around the property, I'd go down and work with the cleanup crews in the village during the day."

She laughed at her misunderstanding, but then a frown creased her face. "And stay down there?"

"Well," There was a long pause. "I thought… well, I'd like to come back here at night." He smiled sheepishly, a little fearful that she might not want him around.

"That would be all right." Myah gave his fingers a slight squeeze. "You could stay in Caraja's room."

"I could stay in the Cave, if you preferred."

"No!" She jerked her hand away. "You must never go at night to the Cave!" she exclaimed, her eyes flaring in the candlelight, fixing his eyes with hers. "Never!"

"Jumbies?" he smiled casually, but it was the wrong thing to say.

"And more," she stood up, the words hanging in midair. Then she turned abruptly and stepped out onto the porch.

Puzzled, Garth let the subject drop. Myah returned wiping her eyes. "Come," she said to Bantu. "Bring Nogo. It's time for bed." Taking the boy's free hand while his other clutched the kitten, which didn't mind being squeezed like a water balloon, she led him into her bedroom.

She came back into the kitchen but said nothing as she filled a small pan of water and picked up a washcloth. Soon Garth heard her singing a soft lullaby to Bantu in a language that the Indian didn't recognise. It was a song that drifted between the conscious and beyond consciousness.

He loved this woman, and to "fuck" her, as she had put it, would be a blasphemy of his feelings. His Grand held 'moderate celibacy' in high regard because she believed that premature sex would dull the ecstasy of lovers' first love together.

Finally, after a long silence, Myah came back into the main room and motioned for Garth to come see. In the candle glow in the bedroom, Bantu lay flat on his back asleep, the kitten sprawled on his chest, also asleep, heart to heart, assured that they'd been found.

Myah turned toward Garth and looked into his face, smiling. Then she reached up and, taking him by the earlobes, drew him forward and kissed his lips, lightly at first and then in earnest. Garth was so startled he could only respond by kissing her back.

"Goodnight," she whispered, "I'm glad you are here."

It was still dark when Garth awoke to the sound of Myah humming and banging pans. He put on his pants and walked out into the kitchen, where he saw Myah busying herself at the counter. "Breakfast?" he asked.

She nodded, "And lunch. You can't do a day's work without a good breakfast <u>and</u> lunch."

"You Blackfoot?" He asked.

"All black, remember?! Why?"

"Because you sound surprisingly like my grandmother 'Mor'se'ya'.

"That's what she always said. And don't you know, I had the biggest lunches of any kid in school. Everyone wanted to trade their peanut butter and jam sandwiches with me because mine were always elk salami sandwiches, and smoked jerky, and huge pieces of berry pie." Garth shook his head, grinning.

"Funny, even though Dad raised cattle, Grandma Mor'se'ya never ate beef. Said it had no character, tasted bland and kinda stupid like a cow. I guess a diet of wild game didn't hurt her any, she's still with us."

"Ancestors are always with us, even when they are not. How old is she?"

369

"Ninety-seven, according to the government, ninety-four is what she claims, but that could be vanity," he smirked. "Truth is, who knows, her generation didn't mark time the way we do."

When Garth arrived in Poppy Dawn the following morning, the entire village and many of the families from the surrounding farms were already at the Perch slab. A grey drizzle filled the air. Some people wore plastic garbage bags with a hole slit in the top for their heads, but most were stripped down to the bare essentials.

The women had separated themselves from the men and were discussing what they'd need for a communal kitchen. It wouldn't be enough to just make meals, they were going to have to preserve as much as they could before it rotted.

Mister Douglas, the white man up on the ridge, had offered his kitchen and, his cisterns were full, and they'd accepted. But the women figured he probably didn't have enough pots and pans for a big operation. They would have to collect some. Bana was staying up there for the time being. Rumour had it that her parents' house had blown away, down to the foundation, and that Lottie was staying at the St. Jude Anglican.

The children under the age of eleven or twelve would remain in the village, scouring the gardens and orchards for fruit and vegetables.

One immediate problem, however, there were a lot of animals that had to be butchered and cooked into stews and canned or bottled. Garth suggested they smoke the meat .... It was a novel idea that bewildered many since, no one on-island had ever smoked meat.

Jokes were made that it is like Ganga and make you foolish. Or where would you find rolling papers big enough for a goat roast.

For the first few days following the hurricane, Garth and two of his older students dug a crater into an exposed embankment and made smokehouses out of old refrigerators ... stripping them of their

370

motors and wiring. Then, cutting into each two holes the diameter of 6" stovepipe, they connected them in a line, one pipe at the bottom, another out at the top for the smoke to go into the next refrigerator.

Beside the first fridge they built a firebox to provide the smoke for the system, with the smoke passing from one unit to the next and finally out a chimney in the last refrigerator.

Between the rising heat and the pull of the chimney draft, smoke moved easily though the piping; and filled the inner chambers with fresh hickory smoke that lingered around the meat on trays in the refrigerators.

The trick with smokehouses, Garth had learned as a child saddled with the responsibility of tending the fire, was to keep the smoke cool, meaning a low, smouldering, fire. The idea was not to cook the meat, but to dry it out with the smoke, flavouring it in the process. It was an ingenious process of low fire and green wood, of which was there was now an abundance.

He showed Benton the butcher how to slice the meat and cut it with the grain into strips and thin fillets for smoking. Too thick and it turned to shoe leather' or crumbled like burnt bacon. The regular standard issue refrigerator trays made perfect drying racks and they could be easily rotated top to bottom, back to front equalising the smoke-curing process. Once the smokehouses were in the hill and working, Garth began to experiment with different woods for different flavours.

In one batch, he salted the fire regularly with green bay leaves, giving the meat a soft cinnamon taste. The hickory seemed even more flavourful than he remembered back home. Of course, back home the trees were desert-tough imports. Likely the hickory on St. Augustine was brought by colonialists.

Then one evening, Garth, who stoked the fires twice a day between work the road-crews, announced that the meats were ready for a taste trial. Since the crews were coming home via "smoke hill" and its enclave of statuesque refrigerators, looking very much like Easter Island, they were the first stop.

" Who's going to be the first victim?" Garth called out that the initial batch of smoked meat was ready for public opinion. It had taken a week of smoking, and the curiosity level of the villagers had risen until it spilled over into rampant rumours about the outcome of the first batch. One authority claimed he'd opened a smokehouse door and stolen a piece of beef from one of the trays. He reported that it tasted like a "bicycle inner-tube".

"How you know de taste of tire-rubber?" Someone asked.

"Seems so to me," the storyteller shrugged.

Fluteman stepped forward, took the first piece, bit off a chunk and chewed it with an expressionless face, savouring the tension amongst the gathering. He then looked to the heavens, not wanting to be distracted as his mouth analysed the taste judiciously. Suddenly his face puckered as though he'd eaten an entire bitter lemon.

"Firestone rubber," he blurted, as though the words could no longer be contained by good manners and had to be expelled regardless of their consequences. A gasp ran through the villagers.

Then, just as suddenly, a grin swept his face and Fluteman laughed and laughed while he chewed the jerky with delight. "No, mon, she taste like she fresh off de coal pot.... Even better!" Everyone sighed, then laughed; they liked Garth and they wanted his smokehouses to be a success.

For two years, he had taught in the primary school and coached soccer in the senior secondary, as well as working mornings down at the government farm. He had always felt an outsider but wasn't too concerned; he really wanted nothing more than to be received. He was close to his students and knew some of the parents, such as Bueno, and there was mutual respect between him and the men he worked with at the farm, but they never invited him into their lives and he didn't have one to share with them. But all of that had changed since the hurricane.

Fluteman put his arm on Garth's shoulder, looking at him and then at the assemblage happily enjoying their first taste of smoked meat. "You's one of us now, mon," Fluteman assured him.

Everyone agreed that his smoked meat was better than any fresh off the coal pot, and a lot better than monkey, even soaked in brine. One of the Garth's older students stepped beside Garth and, raising his hand high as though holding a bottle of beer in toast, he cried, "Garth Longgrass!"

"Mistah Long!" echoed Garth's students, while the rest of the people clapped and went through the motions of holding imaginary beers on high. In a strange way, it was a tribal rite of passage, his baptism into their life. He had come of age in an ageless place.

Chapter 33

"Fife: A Traveling Man"

Garth's crew, with the advantage of youth, was the most effective of all the clearing crews on Island, as one would expect, since Garth was both the most popular teacher on the Secondary campus, the coach of the soccer team at the Poppy Dawn Senior Secondary... and he welcomed girls on the crew provoking the boys to work harder. They had cleared the road from Poppy Dawn down to the main Ring Road where they joined other villagers opening the Ring Road the rest of the way to town. Competition among teams, combined with mixed gender; Garth's team arrived in Portstown first! And just as the dock was finally being opened for delivery of everything from treated electrical poles to great spools of wire. The timing was perfect and immediately Garth's crew was assigned to work exclusively with the electrical restoration team.

The "Sixers" were an international team, sponsored by the United Nations, and composed of highly trained electrical technicians that traveled the world repairing systems after natural disasters. The name "Sixers" was derived from their work habits... starting working at 6:00am, finishing at 6:00 pm -- six days a week!

Fife was Flute's grandson and as his name implied, he played the Fife in the Flute's the Honeybees. Because Flute's band of musicians popularity, they played in venues around the Island, and Fife was well known Island-wide. Also because of his stature for his age, and willingness to work hard, he was on Garth's crew. In fact, two of the Sixers had adopted him to work the ground while they were up the electrical poles. His job was to fetch grounded tools and supplies and feed the tools up to them via a pulley attached to their belts.

For reasons no one could explain on the fateful morning Fife decided to expand his job description and lift, with a metal pole, the end of a neutral line which they would soon need above. Unfortunately, Fife didn't plan for the wind that was coming in gusts, and suddenly when his pole was extended out fully, a gust caught it and pushed the aluminium pole against a cluster of electrified lines.

The explosive "Bang!" from the grounded voltage was deafening, and Fife convulsed backward. The linesmen tried to revive him but he was dead!

****

Usually, Alberto looked regal riding his donkey Asuwink to a funeral service. His black suit clean. His stiff, high-collared shirt holding his head erect. The rim of his fedora crisply curled yet shading his ancient face. But not this time.

His suit was crumpled, and on one sleeve a milky green stain of mildew had been washed with vinegar to no avail. His collar was limp, allowing the old man's head to slump forward, his fedora sagged sadly.

Alberto rode Asuwink sideways, both legs on the same side, no saddle, just balanced on a blanket to pad the donkey's sawtooth back. Asuwink had to thread his way through the narrow path of downed trees and debris from the storm, as Alberto's mind wandered. Back in time — how similar the devastation was between the last real hurricane and Hugo, in spite of electricity, good roads, and accessible water. Before him, everything was yellow. The green had been blown away, like the animal pens and the birds' nests. Hugo had pulled the green even out of the tough coconut palms. The sky, too, seemed to have had the color sucked from its heart, turning into a uniform grey.

He spoke to everyone he passed on the way to the funeral, but there was no life in it.

"And how you does for dis sad of sad days?" he would be asked as he'd venture past.

When he was asked, he say "Good enough ... considering." he'd answer for himself, never venturing anything more except to repeat himself. Even the babies only stared at him with uncertain eyes.

Alberto and Asuwink arrived at the graveyard early, which was their custom. The old man had neither radio nor television, only age, but that was enough to provide his quiet life with an abundance of excitement. Funerals were about all that was left for him, but they were enough. And he didn't miss any. Asuwink knew the way to and from the churchyard as well as he knew the way from home to the rum shop and back. Arching his neck and back, his head held high, normally he'd let out a loud, proud bray, paying respects to the rest of the donkeys tethered outside the churchyard wall, but this time he didn't, sensing his owner's sorrow.

Alberto knew the name of everyone that had ever been born or died in Poppy Dawn. He'd never been to a birth except his own, so funerals were important social events. Funerals, Sunday church services, and a Heineken at the market shop Saturdays before supper — these were his reprieve from the isolation of his fields, but they were enough.

Alberto heard everything and repeated nothing, unless it was simply to give affirmation to common knowledge and to hold his place in the conversation. "Yep, das so," he'd say and nod, or wag his head, "No so," according to what was expected of him. He was a man who spoke seldom in public, but alone with his crops he was the village crier, sharing all the news as he saw it with the pumpkins and carrots, rutabagas and squash. In turn, Alberto was always welcome wherever he went. He was a good "Amen'er!" with a deep baritone voice that many thought mirrored the Lord's. His expressive eyes always carried the right measure of sympathy, empathy, comfort, and occasionally wisdom. But most of all, in spite of saying only few words, he always spoke well of the dead.

Mrs. Wade came early. She had not heard how Fife had died, and hoped to discover all from Peale, the church custodian and bellringer, but he was not at his usual station by the gate. Neither was he in the church preparing the altar, nor in his stead in the bell tower. A boy she didn't recognise was untying the bell ropes from their wall hooks. "Where's Peale?" she asked?

The boy shrugged. "Me no-know, me doesn't sees 'im fo' de day."

Strange, she thought as she returned to the gatepost at the entrance. She hadn't seen him since the night of the hurricane when he was huddled in the church like everybody else.

"Best of the morning, Mrs. Livingston." She spoke to a woman approaching in a black dress, black shoes, hat, purse and even gloves. "And a sad day she be," Mrs. Wade said casually to Mrs. Livingston, trying not to betray that she had no gossip to feed her neighbor. "Peale does not seem to be at his station."

"Don't you hear so?" Mrs. Livingston replied with a superior note in her voice. For once, she knew more than her neighbour to the North. "The storm took his mind. Lost everything, his house, clothes, even dem special dark glasses of his."

"How do you mean… 'took his mind?'"

"Dey say for the last few days since Hugo come-so," interjected the farm girl, Caloo as she came up behind Mrs. Livingston, "he just sit in he house rubble talking to himself all sorts of crazy talk. Nobody what goes by he can figure jus' wha' he say, or what to say back to him. The Anglican thought he might be speaking in tongues, but after he go to see de mon, he understands Peale be in a state of devil tongue, wha's gonna takes de Bishop to exorcise. Can you imagine, de Bishop here to cast out Peale's deamons!"

"Everything gone?"

"Seems so."

"Seems like he weren't so close to the Lord as he make out to be!" Mrs. Wade said with a pious smirk. She had never trusted Peale. If he ever said anything sweet to her, she knew he was also talking behind her back with a hard tongue. And if she slipped too much information about herself and family, it would be passed to the next person who came by his post at the gate. She'd much rather keep her affairs tidy. Also, she didn't like the way he looked over the girls. It was especially apparent when the jungle woman Myah came to church in her cotton dresses.

Mrs. Livingston shook her head in agreement. "What's I wonder is, what did the mon do to deserve that punishment? You-know-so?! He is a man of the Church."

"I does seem to remember hearing one time dat he has an eye for de young ladies what help with the choir."

"Well!" declared Miss Stanley in a muffled a tone, waving the gathering of women closer with her hand knotted around a hanky. "You must tell no ones. I does hear from a small boy who saw it for himself, and you know de youth must speak de truth."

The half-dozen women all nodded. "Well, seems Peale calls up de devil one night here in de graveyard, when de youths walking by! And he does hear Mr. Peale making bargain with de devil." Her voice danced with expectation yet paused for the anticipation to build.

"Bargain for what?"

"Well," Miss Stanley whispered, "de boy don't hear dat, but next thing he knows, Peale is not alone... Myah's with him." She paused again, this time out of breath. "And he was _having_ her!"

"I'd know'd it!" exclaimed Mrs. Wade. "I'd know'd as much for a long spell, but I don't say nothing," she boasted, though no one paid her any attention.

"Me thinks he does trade he soul to de Devil for that woman to go with him. That's why the Lord does deal with him so."

"Girl!" barked Ellen Walters, "that's just foolish talk!" Peale's next-door neighbor spoke from the back of the sisterhood that had formed.

"Accidents is just that and it doesn't make any sense turning them out to have more weight than they can carry. Peale's only sin was putting his house where he did, and not ten feet over towards me!

" No... the way you go on about him does disgust me. And pulling Myah into this is just you's green envy showing cus you's

378

sexes is wizened and dried-dead! Even the Devil couldn't persuade Myah into He bed!"

"Everything is the will of the Lord!" Mrs. Livingston bristled back. "Maybe you should ask what's in your life to made God take a part of your roof."

"And what about Fife?" Mrs. Walters snapped at her. "What sin did that poor innocent youth do to God? Maybe you think he had his way with Myah too! " She glared. ""You disgust me!"

"And what about the Anglican's wife?" She continued. "Poor thing, she mind so mixed that she don't even know the Anglican to he face?!. They say she so afraid of her dreams that she doesn't ever go to sleep. What sin did she commit? Sisters, you does disgust me!" She glared hymnal and scarf and abruptly turned away.

"Oh, my goodness," Mrs. Wade gasped, looking towards the gate.

Myah stood in the graveyard gates in a soft, contouring cotton dress, jungle-flower bright. Her hair was braided into long plaits that were then curled back onto her head in a tribal turban reminiscent of an African queen.

More shocking, beside her stood the Peace Corps teacher, tall and proud in slacks and a clean tan shirt. They stood side by side, one of his fingers lightly touching the back of her right hand. The gesture was seen and noted by all of the sisterhood. And secretly each grudgingly grumbled at what an elegant couple they made.

As they passed the corner post, Myah's eyes fell upon the small cross painted on each gatepost. It was just a glance, but when she realised what it was, she gave a short angry gasp and clutched Garth's arm.

"Oh my God!" she whispered again and again, her eyes welling with tears as she stopped in front of the Main Gate post, her fingers lightly tracing a crudely drawn cross. They could be smears of stone lichen as though something had rubbed against the post. Few would notice unless they looked to see the primitive paint, the claw marks forming. Nor would they know the story.

Her thoughts flew back to that night. She knew Sueky had been there. She knew as soon as the message came that her grandmother was going to take refuge in the Anglican church. And she also knew in her core that she was not supposed to go with her grandmother that night.

Myah did not want 'The Knowledge," she feared its power inadvertently even more than its source. Even if it were never used, just having it had influence. Surely her grandmother was silently blamed for her enemies' ailments, feared secretly even by her closest intimates. Sueky kept herself beyond its influence of public opinion. upon her life.

She did not try to impress, but too many people had projected everything from hip displacements to hurricanes on her. But Sueky was devoutly Anglican and seemingly with the Anglican Priest's blessing, though he had heard rumours. Myah had much respect for her grandmother's gift, but Myah found little actual application in Sueky's power. When Myah did attend church, it was for the fellowship of Sueky and, in this case, respect for the family of the dead.

She realised when Sueky warned her in a dream that a calamity would fall upon the land, and that Myah must prepare herself for a "visitation". She suspected that Sueky had been asked to perform a related rite, but she didn't know what, nor where. Myah also understood from the vision that she wasn't supposed to be there with her grandmother at the graveyard that night! She was supposed to be exactly where she was, there on the mountain, in a cave with her child and... her man and the storm.

As soon as Myah's hand touched the graveyard corner post, she felt afresh the chaos of that night. She closed her eyes and her heart raced as she felt the frail weightless skeleton of Sueky in the storm. There was more weight to the rags she wore than the woman who wore them. Crawling from corner-stone to corner-stone, from grave to grave for shelter, holding desperately to them with all her strength to keep from being ripped away by the rogue' cyclones.

Myah grew cold as she felt the claws of the dead ripping at the old woman ... their shrieks wailing in Sueky's ears. Myah could see their marks on the corner stone, trying to erase Sueky's crosses.

"Keep de dead be so." She heard Sueky's scream, over and over again. And in her head, she too yelled as she heard the old woman yelling.

"Keep d' wind at your back!" was all that Sueky said about the experience. Myah felt humbled by Sueky's faith, and what the old woman had endured. Her eyes burned, but Myah would not let the cluster of hens see her as other than a young, beautiful woman ...in love.

"Stand up, girl," Garth whispered, "people'll think you's drunk." And immediately she smirked, then smiled at him lovingly.

"Oh, Garth, it was so horrible what she went through that night." He watched as Myah's fingers mimic each brushstroke of the Cross on each corner post. "Soon you must meet Sueky."

She looked for Sueky in the gathering, but there was no need, for everyone else was looking either at her or at Sueky. The old woman pulled her pretzeled frame as straight as her bent bones would allow and beamed at her regal granddaughter. What caught the moment, however, was the way Myah looked, as she approached her grandmother. No longer did she carry the edge of anger, but rather a soft embracing gaze of someone in love.

Accordingly, the gathering parted as the woman and her man approach Sueky

The first to speak at the service was Fife's father, Felix. "Everyone knew Fife," said Felix resolved to speak overshadowing his grief and natural shyness.

"'You's Felix's boy?' or 'You's Flute and Tasco's grand?" People would ask of him.

"No sir. De's my relatives, I'm my own man Fife was his own man. Right from de first measure, you could tell dat he was somet'ing else. Always grinning, watching, learning. Ever new lesson was like a fresh door to freedom for dat boy." His strong voice became thin, and he had to pause.

"I'll say Amen to that," said the Anglican, seeing Felix falter for a moment. The congregation repeated amens and hallelujahs.

Felix regained himself. "I remember him at de market with he mother. He'd go right up to complete strangers and start discussing whatever was on his mind. And if dere was a door open, he was through it." Felix laughed. "Mon, many was de time when he'd come back from market separate from us, after having a fine adventure with whoever's car he'd crawled into."

"I made him learned his name, and first words. That and "Poppy Village," cuz I know'd we'd never break his spirit to explore. Just full to the top with curiosity." He laughed, reflecting, "And Fife understood dat it was his license to move, and he became a far traveling mon!"

"In fact," Felix laughed, "that boy's been to West Zion, Hardtimes and even Matchman, where even me and his mother have never been." The congregation laughed.

"But always come home, well fed and entertained. Sometimes it would be in a tap-tap, or in somebody's car."

"Fact of the matter is..., once he came home in de front seat of the Premier's car with the Premier driving. We asked him where the car was parked when he got in, but he wouldn't say."

"Always smart, dat," said Fife's Uncle Tennyson.

"I knew Fife as a gentle boy in school," said Mrs. Inez, the headmistress of his lower school. The people of Poppy liked to listen to Teacher Inez, because she had won awards for speech all across the Caribbean, and she was one of theirs. She spoke with precision and elegance, a debating champion, on subjects they'd discuss if they had the gift. Traveled as far as Trinidad and north to Puerto Rico with her skills.

"Fife was only in trouble once, and that was for trying to stop a fight. Turned out the boys were brothers, and when Fife got involved, they did stop fighting but then teaming up on him!" she laughed.

"'What is the lesson we can learn from this?' I asked Fife," continued Mrs. Inez. Her voice had the resonance of a preacher asking a rhetorical question of his congregation. "And he looked me right in the eye and said, 'Brothers are like fighting dogs... they got'a do it!,' he said proudly, 'So just let them go accordingly.'"

"Accordingly!" exclaimed the Anglican as Teacher Inez finished. "That was Fife's way of saying 'according to God's plan'. Accordingly.... According.... According to the preordained plan... in other words, as God would have it. **Accordingly**," his voice raised significantly.

"Fife was taken from us by God. And it is not for us to know why," His voice began to raise in tenor and the predictable tone and passion! BUT!" He roared. "We must have faith in the reassurance that Jesus rose from the dead and his resurrection is our salvation from eternal damnation, and we must have faith that there is a reason behind all things within his holy domain. Glory be to God."

"Glory be to God," the congregation repeated.

The little boy Sugarfoot slipped through the congregation and up to Alphonso. He tugged on the old man's trousers. "You must come so to de gate," he whispered. "HE CALL FOR...YOU!" And with that he slipped away.

Even with his dark glasses and new black hat, his black suit pressed razor sharp, Alberto immediately recognised Fluteman, standing behind the people in the back. His old friend Calvin was there, as was Josey Freeman, his sister.

"Walk beside me, old friend?" Fluteman asked.

"Right beside you," Alberto said proudly, then a cloud came into his face, "but not so fast I can't keep pace, de knees, you know, de knees."

"Just regular," Flute assured him with a smile.

383

The people parted as news ran through the gathering. The Anglican had just called for a hymn when word reached him that Fluteman was present. He stopped, raising his hands for people to let Fluteman pass. Like a zombie suspended between life and death, the man who danced in their hearts was bent with grief's burden. He walked to the edge of the grave. No one made a sound, waiting to hear what Fluteman would say, and for a long time, only the braying of a distant displeased donkey broke the silence.

Then with resolve, Fluteman hand reached inside his jacket and he pulled out his flute. He squared his shoulders, his weight shifted ever so slightly, and he drew the flute to his lips.

There was no warm-up, no riff. It was a single note, long and hollow, clear and delicate, so poignant that people would talk about it long after. It was a note of infinite sadness, and when his heart could take no more, he slid into the second note, and finally the song followed. It was a bird in flight without effort, a living kite caught in an evening updraft. Slowly the melody formed into a song that all recognised. It was Fife's favourite song, "Yellow Bird". Fife learned to play it when he was but six years old. Flute played it through solo, then turned to Alberto. On the second playing, Alberto sang. "Yellowbird." And his great baritone voice rushed from beneath his lips. When he'd reached "fly away," everyone was crying. Just as the singing was through, David caught the first note again and sent it out to Montserrat, beyond to Guadeloupe, — carrying everyone with it.

Then, suddenly, he called the note back and stopped. Taking the flute from his lips, he bent over the grave and dropped the musical instrument into the pit. It clattered on the coffin lid. Those in the front gasped, word passed rapidly about what had happened. The villagers parted to let Flute pass, then rushed forward to see if it were true. There, lying on the coffin, was the magic flute, its silver polished, its wood well shined. The flute that had held them together through so much was gone.

"Who's to play for the masquerade?" Paco asked.

"Who's to play for our souls?" Sally whispered, and many around her nodded in accord.

"Anyone can learn to play the flute," Ellen Walters spoke up. "But, Flute, you taught Fife how to paint with music, a picture of happiness. You taught him how to reach inside of himself and call up any note to match the color of the moment." All turned to Fluteman. He turned and walked away.

The Anglican said some words that no one heard, and then as if choreographed, each caught in his own sad thoughts passed and threw a handful of dirt into the grave as was the custom,. Suddenly there was a yell and a young boy, Fife's younger brother, Felix's youngest, slipped and fell face first into the pit. The rescue was uneventful and the boy immediately ran away unhurt, but embarrassed.

Calvin, Alberto and David walked out of the graveyard together and down the road aways and with Calvin in the lead, they turned up a trail leading to a ridge above the village. They stopped beneath an ancient mahogany tree looking out over a pirate sea and a pasture where they had grazed their goats as youths -- where Calvin, eight years Fluteman's senior, had taught him to play the flute, and it wasn't long before the student became the teacher.

Calvin and Alberto sat down on roots, Flute squatted against a rock. From under the root that he sat upon, Alberto took out a mason jar of Hammon homemade, unscrewed the lid and passed the home-distilled alcohol to Fluteman then Calvin. Each took a long pull.

"Flute," Calvin said after a long silence, "I does take you on when you was jus' Fife's age, so I know'd something bout de love and de dreams you held for him. But, me say to you true, love is just a flame what gets passed from candle to candle. Sometimes de wick gets snuffed out before de candle give hardly any light... and sometimes... well, sometimes de candle burn down to a nub dat don't have much flame left, like me and Alberto.

385

But here's what I say to you ... as long as you gots de flame, you gots to share it while you can. Dat's what we's supposed to do here on dis earth, share de flame." Alberto grunted in agreement. "You know-so..." He stared hard at his old friend, "You know-so whas' he says be true."

Fluteman said nothing.

"People of Poppy does take some bad licks," said Calvin, "and dey's studying it hard to see if dey's got de strength to go on. You and dat flute give dem hope. But when dey see you throw it away, well, maybe dey's thinking of giving up too! Understand whas me say?"

Fluteman pushed himself away from the rock, "I'll make my peace when de time-she full," he said quietly. "When de time is right, I does accordingly."

"Mr. Fluteman...: a little boy stood in his way with his hands behind his back. He stepped nervously onto the trail in front of Fluteman, blocking his way. He started to speak but paused once more, then blurted out... "Mr. Fluteman." He choked unable to proceed for a moment. "Mister Fluteman would you teach me to play? " It was the boy who had fallen into the grave and in his hand was Fluteman's flute. "Will you? Will you teach me to play?"

Flute looked hard at the boy, his shoulders sagged and started around the youth.

Then, just as suddenly, he reached for the flute, slowly brought it to his lips and immediately sparked into a series of short riffs of final acceptance of what had happened. Another long silence... then runs full of both passion, of sorrow, of bottomless grief, of birth and finally the full joy of life.

When he finished, he stuck out his hand with the flute and gave it back to the boy. "You best pay attention, o' Youse down d'road." He smiled at the boy.

Chapter 34

"Survivors' Celebration"

It was Jonathan who suggested the party. A 'Survivors' Celebration!'

Danielle liked the idea and thought that everyone should wear the clothes they had on for Hugo. But on second thought, considering their own attire, worn, continuously for three days, filthy and torn from the ordeal, they decided that the better dress would be what they <u>wanted</u> to be wearing one year later.

Jonathan was amazed by the diverse number of characters who'd accepted Danielle's invitation. There were politicians including the Premier ... and the leader of the opposition party.

Boat people who had either taken their craft out to sea, to those who had lost their boats completely anchored offshore in front of Portstown. One boat had been lifted clear across the Ring Road and deposited in a field of sea-island cotton.

Musicians, Rastafarians, a Catholic Priest, an Anglican Priest, and Judas Priest, a stonemason who had worked on Jonathan's house many years before. Though a couple of the Christian fundamentalist ministers had been invited, upon hearing that the hotelier Gage would be in attendance, and the Madam Ruthie, they declined though most of their congregations accepted with pleasure.

But, most of all, the party was for the villagers. Jonathan and Danielle, because of Hugo, had become part of the Island's history and they in theirs.

Many of the women in attendance knew the house well, having spent days there canning, pickling and drying food for the future following the hurricane. In fact, at one time the entire kitchen was full of the canning crew, visiting, laughing, each adding their take to some mutual adventure.... Each story taking on energy unbounded by memory or fact.

Sueky came in a dark blue print dress, saved from the sun for years for very special occasions. The dress hung on her a little like a tent but it was not a burdensome one, light polyester, though she did bring her store-bought, adjustable cane, and not the bamboo staff she'd known all her life. With Aunt Josie came an entourage of her spacious family -- all shy, watching Josie for leadership on how to act in a white-man's' house.

Sueky, after a tour through the gathering of giving "bestess" to the hostess and host, gravitated to a side wall with a comfortable chair from which she could see all. Two very shy great-grands happily sat by her side as everyone gravitated at sometime to pay their respects to Sueky, ... many acknowledging what she had done on that terrible night.

Myah came in a chic dress, borrowed from Bana that accentuated not only her beauty but that wild exotic allure of one who had lived in her thoughts alone with the jungle. That was the charm of all three of the girls; Myah, Ruthie and Dannielle. They all carried the Island in them and radiated its energy without effort, yet all wearing different shoes and memories.

The expensively chic dress Myah wore was given to Bana by a New York designer after a photoshoot. Myah had accepted it doubting at the time if she would ever wear it. Garth, though clearly shy, wore suit pants and a white shirt with a starched collar he'd borrowed from Caraja, who'd inherited the ensemble from his father, and he from his.

Danielle dressed in one of her 'Bana Designs' that was light, loose, bright and brimming with Rousseau jungle scenes of panthers, toucans and birds-of-paradise peeking out from the fabric and contours.

Ruthie, on the other hand wore a conservative two-piece, grey dress and jacket. She'd bought it for an ad hoc funeral for Princess Diana in New York.

"Hello." A large white-man extended his hand to Ruthie, "My name is Jonathan Douglas, I'm a friend of Danielle's." He smiled knowing the woman knew exactly who he was, though he hadn't any idea who she was. "I think you call her 'Bana'". He smiled knowing she knew exactly who he was and that the party was in his house.

"I too am a friend of her's" playing to Jonathan's joke., "But I knew her as "Sling" ... kid's name."

Jonathan had a brief questioning look. "And not Bana?"

It had to do with catapults and monkeys." Ruthie replied with the hint of a smile. She had heard much about Jonathan, Island talk, all good, but nothing from Danielle, which she hoped to rectify as soon as she could get Bana alone.

"What did she call you when you were kids?" asked Jonathan still trying to place Ruthie.

"Same as they do now." She said without giving more.

"And what name would that be?" Jonathan asked innocently.

"Ruthie."

"And what do you do Miss Ruthie?"

"I'm an organist," Ruthie replied without hesitation, watching his eyes scan her to see how an organist dresses. His eyes concluded she was as she claimed, and the same on Sunday in church.

"Which congregation?" Jonathan asked innocently.

Ruthie smiled, but let the question drop without answer for shyness. He would find out soon enough from Bana or Myah.

As soon as Danielle saw that the party had reached a self-perpetuating running-speed, and Jonathan was being the charming host, the three girls slipped away and went out into the garden by the jacuzzi and sat down in pool chairs. Danielle, Ruthie and Myah hadn't been together since the hurricane, and now that the road was open all the way to Jonathan's, Bana wanted to see them dearly. But she also wanted them to meet Jonathan, and she wanted to meet Garth. She knew he must be special since Myah had never taken up with a man except the Columbia University student, which Danielle suspected was solely for the purpose of making her baby Bantu.

"The smell is heavenly here." Ruthie took a long deep breath through her nose, caressing her olfactory sensors with the smell of Jasmine, gardenia and ylang ylang. She rose, stood by the Jacuzzi, took off her shoes, pulled up her dress and sat down on the side with her feet in the water.

"Nothing changes." Myah laughed at her friend's disregard for the decorum of her church-attending outfit. She too removed her shoes rose and sat down putting her feet in the pool. Danielle joined them. Soon they were kicking water at each other laughing as children, but finally they sat quietly as adults simply enjoying the others' company.

"What do you mean, nothing changes?" Said Ruthie. "You guys have changed that's for sure. Both of you. Tell me what's happening in your lives?"

Myah and Danielle looked at each other and seeing that the other knew exactly what that "something" was, they broke out laughing.

"What?" Ruthie asked growing a little angry, being excluded from the joke. "What's so funny."

"She's in love?!" They both said it simultaneously, pointing at the other, which served to send them into hysterical fits of laughter

"So? On a good week in New York, I was in love three times. What's the big deal?" But her question was met with side-long glances and then silence.

"So?" Ruthie press on. "What is it like making love to a full-blooded Indian."

"Ruthie!" Myah splashed on Ruthie, who threatened to retaliate had Danielle not been in the middle and interceded. "You're disgusting!"

Still Ruthie looked at Garth through the kitchen window as he talked with the hotelier Gage. "He's really a hunk. What's he like in bed?"

But Myah wasn't going to bite. "Oh, come on now, Myah, you can tell Youse Auntie Ruthie. May me tongue be tied till it turns

390

black and festers if'n I ever repeats a word." Ruthie teased. It was a meaningless vow they used as children sharing secrets.

"Your tongue is already black." Myah replied. "Fair, okay good", She paused for a minute. "Oh Hell... he's very good!" and started laughing.

There was a moment of silence, then Myah confessed softly, "I love him more than I've ever thought possible. Bantu and his sister worship him." She reflected for a moment in silence, "You know -- I'm really happy."

"Wow, that's wonderful." Ruthie said sincerely, putting her arm around her friend. "For me, happiness is a moving target between spells of lust and acute boredom."

"Where did you spend the hurricane?" Ruthie asked Myah further.

"In the cave behind my cottage. There where Caraja keeps his herb."

"Oh God!" Exclaimed Ruthie. "With all the bats and lizards?"

"Not so bad." Myah answered though her eyes fixed on her feet.

"And ...?"

Myah took a deep breath. There was no sense trying to keep a secret from her two best friends. "Everything was wonderful that first night. Garth played with Bantu, and we talked for hours from our hearts. Garth is very much into his Native Indian culture and I believe one day he might be a great Shaman." She let the sentence settle, then arched her head back looking at the sky of stars.

"And I thought at last I have someone who would understand. But..." her words chocked in her throat. "But... sometime soon after the eye of the storm came through, something went terribly wrong." She was on the verge of tears and her sisters each held her hands, waiting patiently for her to recover.

"I... I had a 'Visitation!'"

As children, Ruthie and Danielle accepted that Myah was different and were even a little envious, but as adolescents they saw it as a curse verging on the insane. To them voodoo was an old-time superstition that had no place in the modern world ... except for the Rolling Stones and the *"Voodoo Cafe"*. "Obeism" had been an underlying current of their culture, and they respected it as part of their past history, but not the present, and certainly not the future.

"What happened?" Asked Ruthie feeling her friend's trepidation.

"To tell you the truth... I don't know. I had fallen asleep in Garth's arms. Bantu lay curled up asleep between us..." She frowned, her thoughts trailing off. "And then... I don't know... I don't really remember...! All I'm sure of is that I was afraid. There was 'something' or 'someone' in the cave... and only then did I realise 'They" were there!."

"They? Edan and Naomi?" Asked Ruthie who didn't believe in the stories and the superstition that plagued her friend.

Myah nodded but remained silent.

"Then suddenly..." She spoke again, "I was knocked flat onto the cave floor by a giant wave of water that crashed through the entrance and threw me further into the cave. I grabbed for anything ... but the wave immediately changed directions and started dragging me out towards the waterfall!"

"I remember fighting against the current." She shuddered thinking about it. "And then, just as I felt I could not overcome the torrent. Garth grabbed me by the arm and pulled me back from the edge!" She shuddered with the memory.

"I can't tell you anymore because I just don't remember. In fact, for a long time during the remainder of the storm, I thought, or rather, prayed it was just a nightmare... but it was real... all of it... the wave, Edan and Naomi... and... I knew there had been a "visitation"."

They sat there with their feet still in the pool, staring at the reflection of the stars in the water, but saying nothing. Myah's friends were torn. Was it a seizure of insanity, or... was their friend as they believed since childhood, one of the "chosen" by her ancestors to settle past injustices.

Quickly, Ruthie changed the subject. "And you?" Ruthie asked Danielle. "Did you stay at your parents' house?"

"The Bamboo Manor is no more!" She sighed. Startled, both Myah and Ruthie looked at her in disbelief, though both had heard it rumoured on Island, it was hard to accept that one of the foundations of their youth was gone. They remembered so many nights sitting out on the bamboo veranda planning how life would be for them. The Bordeaux family was loved by the Islanders, and the loss of "Doc Bordo's" home was a personal loss for each.

"Lottie had a premonition that it would happen and wanted me to go to the Figtree Shelter with her, but Jonathan offered his house, so I decided to come here."

"And...?"

"No Ruthie, we did not make love, if that is what you're asking. ... You have such a one-track mind." And Danielle relished that secrets from her friends were not long kept. "In fact, Jonathan and I still are not lovers."

"But...' she confessed, "I believe it will be ... soon if I have any say." She said it quietly.

"Still, I'll tell you one thing," her voice had conviction, "I saw a lot of the character in that man during the hurricane."

Ruthie looked long at her friends. It was clear to her that both Danielle and Myah each had a man who had captured their hearts. She had suspected it watching them earlier that evening as each tried to hide their feelings. She saw the hidden signs of closeness between each couple. Little things like how Myah and Garth were unconsciously aware of where and how their partner was at any given moment. Adoring looks when they supposed no one was watching, downcast eyes should their partner catch them looking at them with wonderment... knowing what the other would say before it was said.

And Myah? Wondered Ruthie. Why did she try to act so indifferent about Garth. There was certainly nothing wrong with him. He was incredibly handsome, neither black, nor white, but a blend -- bronze. He walked well in both worlds. But the thing that mystified Ruthie the most was that neither of her friends discussed consummating their relationships.

"It is a blasphemy against God," Ruthie said finally, "Not to indulge in His gifts! It is a Sin! And besides that," she looked at her companions. "It isn't healthy! In my opinion," she laughed, "celibacy is the number one cause of cancer, pimples, and poor eye sight."

"I don't see that!" Laughed Myah.

"My point proven." Ruthie grinned at them.

"What about you, Ruthie dear?" Danielle asked trying to change the topic, "Where were you during the hurricane?"

"Ya, where were you? What mischief were you up to." Myah coaxed.

"Ya! For all your questions, you've been inordinately quiet about your antics. Did you have any clients? Throw a big party. An orgy?"

"Ya right," Ruthie snorted. "A party of just me alone. I sent all the girls to the Episcopal Church and told them to repent for there wasn't going to be any paying work for a long time after the storm. Brando -- you know my bouncer-- he wanted to stay, he's so loyal, but I sent him to the Episcopal church to make sure the girls were welcomed into the fold."

"And then..." She hesitated and then decided to confess.

"And then, you know what I did? I printed a sign for the front door of the Snackette, for clients seeking shelter and solace, "Closed for Hurricane… Beat it!"

"You didn't?!" Danielle squealed with laughter

"Yes, I did. I'm told it is the oldest joke in the world but given the circumstances it was all that came to mind."

"So? What did you do? Weren't you afraid all alone?"

"Afraid of what? Either things were going to go badly, or they wouldn't, and all the fussing and vexing wasn't going to change that. So, I went upstairs to my apartment with a bottle of scotch. Lit a couple of candles, rolled a joint, and spread out on the bed." Ruthie stopped talking as though that was the end of her narrative.

"And then? What did you do to occupy yourself?" Asked Myah after a long moment.

Ruthie looked out across the roofs of the villages far below.

"Well?" Myah prodded. "Tie me tongue 'til it blackens and festers if'n me repeats a word."

Still Ruthie offered no response, but there was a detectable smirk on her face. Her friends looked at each other perplexed, then Danielle caught onto what she did.

"Oh my God!" Exclaimed Danielle and she broke out in hysterical laugher. "You didn't!"

Myah still didn't understand. Danielle whispered in her ear causing Myah's eyes to open wide in astonishment. Then she too began laughing.

"Ruthie, Ruthie," she gave her friend's hand a squeeze. Ruthie nodded that it was true!"

"All the time?!" Danielle asked.

"Cept when I slept." Ruthie said in her defence. "So?! So What?!" Ruthie said defiantly in her own defence. "It worked didn't it. I wore Hugo out didn't I?!'"

"Lobetojesus! Our very own hedonist heroine! They're going to build shrines to you when the word gets out! 'The girl who saved St. Augustine from the' 'Hurricane of the Century!'" Teased Danielle

"I just hope I'm not addicted to the experience, or worse… in love." Ruthie kicked her feet happily in the water with her own joke.

"What were you thinking?" Myah asked Ruthie. "Was it to block the fear?"

This made Ruthie laugh even harder. "Mon, mes jus gits fetched-up in He energy an t'ings jus' gits outa hand."

"... So to speak." Danielle teased.

"I may never go back to men. I mean, after you've had sex with a hurricane, men are going to seem a pretty tame."

The three women were still laughing when they returned to the party arm in arm. Both Jonathan and Garth were relieved to see them ... though Jonathan wasn't sure about the tie between Danielle and Myah with the 'church lady'.

"What's the joke?" He asked.

"One you'll never know." Danielle smiled.

The party ended early. Ruthie had to get back to the Snackette before the girls "looted the 'till' and emptied the bar", though there was no business, and Brando would never let it happen anyway.

Myah and Garth had walked over to the Douglas house which was also high on the mountain and close to Myah's cottage on a horizontal line. Bantu and his sister had spent the night with Myah's cousin, Arabelle, they would pick him up the next morning.

Danielle and Jonathan cleared the dishes, neither spoke, a habit they'd grown accustomed to, both happy to be alone with the other.

Danielle was lost in thought about what Ruthie had said. What was she afraid of. It wasn't as Danielle claimed, an age difference, for she knew she and Jonathan had found a common meeting place that was ageless. She had never met anyone like him and through it all, the hurricane, the recovery and turning his house over to the village women for a kitchen, he had unaware become a fibre in the weave of the community.

When they first met, and their friendship romped in the abandonment of safety and newness, and she felt free to feel all her sorrow for her parents passing and he for the loss of his wife. But now there was something else.

Suddenly she knew its cause. It was a phone call Jonathan had made to his family. He'd used the word "We".

"We will be alright" he'd said and hung up the phone and didn't answer it when his daughter called back. A cold chill ran down her back, was he ashamed of her? He'd said that his children had encouraged him to meet other women, and the first night she and Jonathan met at Miss June's dinner. And back then, what was there to explain, anyway? Friends bonded by mutual losses?

Her heart sank for suddenly she saw that it was her fear of being relegated to friendship. Even so why would that matter? She stopped washing the dishes and stared out the kitchen window into the night and the curtain of stars outlining the volcano's silhouette. She loved this man. Loved him more than she'd loved before, more than she thought possible. She had pushed it so deep down that its force, when it surfaced, made her cry. Standing over the sink she didn't try to stop her tears from running down her cheeks and into the dishwater. Friendship? Suddenly she couldn't stand the thought.

Finally, when she heard Jonathan come in from the verandah with more dishes, she drew in a deep breath and wiped her eyes with the back of her hand. She remembered what Ruthie had said about being afraid, and making the thing feared-most, happen by running away from it.

They finished the dishes. Jonathan put on a CD of an Italian tenor named Bocelli. Danielle knew the singer and his family well. And when she was in Rome, she spent a long weekend at the family villa in Pisa.

From Jonathan's perspective the music no longer took him into memories of Mallory. It held new meaning, a celebration of love's essence, unbound pure potentiality. He lit a candle on the table on the verandah and turned off the lights. In the absence masked by the house's incandescence, the stars rushed into the void dwarfing even the village lights, rendering the planet and all of humanity down to a footnote in their vastness.

Danielle lay her hand on his shoulder, "I will be right back." Her footsteps receding down the hall to her suite.

Now was the time, he had no more excuses, he would tell her tonight. It could be the end of all that they shared. Still all of the arguments he'd presented before his court of reason were old and thread bare. The age difference, different backgrounds, Mallory... they were like cliché's that no longer served to describe the situation and held no further intrigue except for their habituation and tautological poetry; all fell away.

The age difference was the first to be forgotten for she made him younger, and in her presence, he saw how his previous life was grounded upon the senior-statesman persona; conservative, cautious, a planner for the future. With her, he felt himself adventuresome, willing to take chances, immersed in the present. Their backgrounds too had disappeared. Since Hugo all there was, was the 'Now'!

Island life and the will to recover and rebuild had changed him. Even the loss of Mallory had found its balance. Music, smells that before sent him reeling in a downward spiral of sorrow, now took on their own character, void of memories of the past, full of fantasies of a future. He sighed, accepting the truth -- but how could he be in love?

She was so beautiful, and probably she was tired of men telling her that they loved her. Part of him warned that he didn't deserve more than to admire her. But again, since the hurricane, he came to realise that her true beauty was not physical. He saw it in the eyes of the Islanders. Everyone loved Bana, not because of her celebrity, but because of who she was. Why should he be different? He would tell her tonight.

When she returned, she was wrapped in a silk wrap lightly defining her body. No longer afraid to study her as he had avoided that first day that they swam naked in the family's primeval lily-pad pond... now his eyes feasted on her beauty, her grace, and most of all <u>her</u> eyes. And as the music swelled in his ears, the Universe, just minutes before vast and overwhelming, shrunk to a pinpoint occupied by only two souls.

She said nothing, but stepped close to him, her perfume was merely jasmine petals from the garden crushed and rubbed into her skin. One hand touched his cheek, her eyes held his with clarity. Drawing close to his face, she kissed his lips lightly and whispered something. Unsure he heard right, he drew back, looking into her face.

"I love you," she repeated. Stunned, he stared overwhelmed, he had never considered that she might feel the same for him as he did for her.

"Dance with me." She said, letting the sarong fall to the floor.

"Are you sure?" He asked, still not believing what was happening.

"I have never been more sure."

He took her face in his hands and returned her kiss, at first timidly but soon his shyness was swept away like morning mist to reveal a new day full of life with unrestrained possibility. "I have something to tell you!" Then he realised she already knew!

It was a night without beginning or end, without duration or place in space. Children at play in the fields of the Gods.

Chapter 35

"Coconut Walk"

Caraja had moved from the cabin he shared with Myah and Bantu to the village of Remember Me and his new family. Garth, because of his work on the road-clearing crews moved up from his Peace Corps house in town, and at Myah's invitation into Caraja's room.

Though they both felt strongly the attraction they had for each other, they kept a defined distance. Finally, after Myah had gone to see Sueky and at, the old woman's insistence for Myah to tell Garth all about the night of the hurricane, the visitations in the cave, and the history leading to them; Myah reached a decision, she had to tell Garth everything.

The day's chorus of doves that had began at dawn dwindled to an occasional call of a lone male as evening settled over the Island. It was a time of peace that the Island had not known since the hurricane first struck. The full moon would soon rise out of the Atlantic pushing the sun into the Caribbean.

Garth and Myah sat on the front porch of Myah's cottage, watching the day's pastels dissolve into indigoes signalling the advancing moon.

. Bantu played in the front yard with the rescued kitten Nogo. He had a long string with a ball of tinfoil on the end, and when he ran, the kitten galloped with long reaching strides, easily catching the boy. When the kitten got bored, all Bantu had to do was kneel down and call "Nogo" and astonishingly the cat would come like a pet dog, often stopping just short of the boy, hissing, then, for reasons known only to cats, jump back and take off running with Bantu in pursuit.

"That boy needs a dog." Garth laughed.

"Shush, Nogo thinks it is a dog."

For a long time they sat silently in the evening symphony.

"Even if you don't admit it, you will soon have to go home to Wyoming." Myah suddenly broke the quiet. "I sense you have too many questions unanswered about your family. And you know, by the fact that the Island now has the generators and chainsaws, that your letter with the request got through to them."

For a long time, the couple sat silently. Garth had never been happier, but he also knew, she was right, he had a fundamental obligation back in Wyoming that needed to be resolved.

"Garth," Myah spoke breaking his thoughts. "I went to see my grandmother Sueky and..." She hesitated, "...and she councils that there is something I must share with you. Something about me, about who I am... what I am ... something that has been passed on in my family for generations." She looked away from his eyes. "Something I carry in my core, ... something that may drive you away and keep you from ever returning when you hear it!" Tears welled in her eyes. "Sueky says I can't wait no longer. And... I know she is right. But…".

"But what?" he asked cautiously, anticipating something he didn't want to hear.

Her hand touched his, "I don't know if you will understand. In fact, it is something that even I don't understand. And to-tell-you true, well … I am afraid of losing you because of it!"

He laughed and squeezed her hand. "Not very likely." He smiled radiantly, "I think you will have me with you for a long, long time."

"It has to do with the type things you probably learned from your 'Shaman guide.... Goto?"

Garth was thoroughly confused for he had intentionally not spoken of his 'Tribal Education" for fear of scaring <u>her</u> away.

"Do remember the night of Hugo when you saw..." She paused picking her words... "the 'apparitions'? ... The young black girl in the fire and the woman in the wedding dress?"

He nodded.

"Well, they weren't apparitions from <u>your</u> imagination... they are a 'legacy' from my family's past! They were ... no ... they <u>are</u> real!" She burst into tears.

Finally, taking his hand firmly again, and committed to pursue her initial resolve, she spoke. "Sueky says if we are to grow in our relationship, I must tell you all .... and <u>now,</u> before you leave.l"

" You see, I carry a family 'scar'" she began "... no, a 'burden',,' a "'legacy'" from generations gone past ... as does Sueky!   In fact, it has been a scar in my heritage for generations!"

She studied his face. "You have shared with me openly that you have witnessed the powers and insights of your Shaman Goto." She paused once again.

"Well Well," ... "she looked hard into his eyes, "well I too have those insights!" She paused.

" And now I must share with you something that has inhabited my ancestry for hundreds of years!" She could no longer look in his eyes.

"Inhabit?" Garth frowned at her choice of words.

"Exactly!" She said, "It is a part of an ancestry ... maybe a 'curse' that now must be exorcised!"   She thought for a moment. "Historical baggage! Heredity baggage that can't be left in the luggage-rack any longer if you and I are to... are to..." Her words trailed off, leaving the sentence unfinished.

Bewildered, Garth stared, searching her eyes.

"Sueky believes you have been put in my life for a purpose and if we are to move on, it is time to leave this baggage behind."

They sat in silence watching Nogo play with the string and the aluminium ball

"Sueky says that you must remember that I too understand the knowledge we carry from our ancestors and it is an <u>honour</u> for us to be a chosen to hold it. But she also believes". Myah paused, picking her words, "... She believes we must also do what is asked of us by them, regardless of the consequences...!"

Garth frowned. Myah spoke again. "I guess I must start with the night of the hurricane in the cave and the two 'phantoms'.

"First," He held up his hand cutting her off. "She is correct, I too have heard and spoken with the Spirits of the Dead, and sometimes I too have done their bidding." He said it openly.

"My Uncle Goto, the Shaman, councils that their knowledge can only help us, and though it may be a burden over the simplicity of ignorance... we are never given more than we can carry."

He looked into her eyes. "And, if there is something that we don't understand, we must trust that one day we will."

"I pray so daily." She smiled but said nothing more for a long time.

Then, after the long period of silence sorting out her words, Myah spoke again.

"Our union has been destined.... But it is not fully complete. Before you leave... and I so hope, you will 'return'..." She took his hand, "it is time to remove these final barriers."

"It has not been my choice that we should lay apart each night; and now the time has come for us to move on! ... But," she said abruptly, "the price may be very high!" She looked into his eyes. Hers were full of fear. "Maybe the highest... maybe losing each other forever!"

Garth flinched.

"Garth." She took now both of his hands into hers and looked intently at them, avoiding his eyes. "Suppose I were to tell you that the things that happened in the cave were not of your imagination. That the two apparitions are part of my past... even my heritage."

Garth looked at her bewildered, he understood nothing of what she was saying.

"For you to understand, I would like to take you tomorrow, with the full moon to a plantation on the West Coast. There I can tell you all, even <u>show</u> you and you will hopefully understand!'"

He looked at her without flinching. With Gotoshaman, Aishen, he had passed into even the realm of his dead ancestors with ease ......it was a journey always with purpose! Was there a purpose now, he looked into her eyes searching. He trusted that this was of such importance that she would risk losing him, and took both her hands, smiled intently into her eyes.

"Vamanos! Let's go!"

****

On the morning of the eve of the full moon, the couple walked down the mountain, out across the long volcanic apron of abandoned pastures, on an animal path that led to a set of ruins, close to the sea. It was there the Atlantic storms struck first, and now the once sandy beaches had been eaten away leaving a shoreline of breadfruit sized boulders worn round from rolling back and forth in the heavy seas. Though it was mid-morning when they left the cottage on the mountain; after taking Bantu to Sueky's, dusk was descending over the Island and finally the fierce sun of day slipped quietly behind the western shoulder of the volcano, throwing in turn bright orange spears over the Atlantic horizon, piercing the gauzy clouds that wrapped the mountain's top, turning them to gold... a 'Golden Rock' as the mountain was called by locals.

Garth and Myah turned off the main Ring-road around the Island onto a goat path that was a well-kept roadway complete with two great gate-posts once guarding the entrance to the Fontaine Plantation. The long driveway that descended towards the Coast was lined with flamboyant trees. Their branches that once reached over the driveway and one time a beautiful flowered road, had been pruned by Hugo and four centuries of hurricanes before; leaving two walls of armless stumps, impotent guards left to

404

protect the abandoned plantation. -- They seemed to Garth to remain out of loyalty more than service.

Off to the sides of the road, where once fine carriages from England rattled over the cobblestone lanes to the entrance of the great house, were now only goat trails laced into thickets of spiny scrub bush.

Myah grew anxious as they approached the manor house. Garth, a man raised in the prairie where once his ancestors lived in animal-skin teepees, he was in awe by its size and stone construction. It was obvious that once it had been a rich West Indian plantation.

The manor house had a great staircase, that fanned out across the front of the building curving into a wide double-door entrance. Above it there was a keystone arch, "E.H 1798" was chiselled into the keystone.

Garth was, in awe of the flawless construction and wondered how many hurricanes the manor house had withstood. How many generations of antebellum women in flowing dresses and gentleman in coats with tails and starched collars had passed thorough them. He smiled again thinking of the mobile animal skin teepees of his ancestry.

Myah took his hand and led him up the staircase, and then over to one particular arched window facing out over a once elegant courtyard garden.

"I am going to tell you a story that happened there." She pointed to the now overgrown lawn.

"It happened almost three hundred years ago, and yet the events have changed my families lives for generations ... even mine!"

"History and hurricane leave lots of casualties besides buildings," Myah reflected --, there was a deep sadness in her voice.

"Back when rum and sugar cane were the main commodity of trade between the West Indies and Europe, the two adjacent

405

plantations produced most of the rum exported out of St. Augustine. And while the families were friends, the two sons of the same age, both had an interest in the same 'dusty'" maiden... a young slave girl, still a virgin, named Naomi."

"Of course, the men's mutual interest was not known to Naomi who was still too young for sexual encounters, and certainly not to her mistress, a woman named Edan Braun. And, as was expected by both families, one of the men asked for the hand in marriage to his friend's sister, the beautiful Edan.

As the story goes on the eve of the wedding, at the groom's bachelor party, the men got drunk, and an argument erupted that festered over who now had claim to the young Naomi. One friend challenged the other to a duel over her -- to be held with the morning sun of the wedding.

"The duel was there in that glade," Again Myah pointed out to the lawn. "And, as the story goes, with both bride and her handmaiden Naomi watching from this window, the two men turned and fired at the same time! Both were excellent shots -- and both men died simultaneously ... right before the women's eyes!"

Myah shuddered and fell silent for a long moment. "They say Edan, started screaming... and she never stopped!"

Garth looked at her in shock, and wondered why she told the story, and was so affected by it.

"Come." She took his and led him away from the window. "I want to show you another place and maybe you'll understand." She led him out of the great house around to the back of the mansion. There, attached to the kitchen, was a dark chamber no more than twenty feet square. The room was dark and latticed thick with cobwebs, the floor covered was with centuries by that of rat faeces.

"See that room," she pointed inside but made no move to enter. It was dark and the only window was against a side wall. It was barred with heavily rusted iron bars.

"That's where they were kept in their 'final' days."

406

Myah's eyes shot past him, away, towards the sea. They were full of tears.

"That is where the Edan and Naomi were imprisoned." She nodded back to the vault. "And though they brought her food and other necessities from the kitchen, Naomi was her Madam's sole source to the outside living world... and even that was not enough and, Edan screamed continually for Naomi to let her die!"

Myah fell silent and then began again.

"Finally, Naomi succumbed to her mistress's pleas ... and she had a cousin, a fisherman, bring them fish from the copper deposit banks off Redonda Island... Her excuse was to kill rats that had inhabited their cell."

Myah then took Garth's hand and held it tightly. "She prepared their last dinner and, so loyal her service... they died together!"

Myah was silent for a long time. And then she spoke again. 'Sueky says I must tell you all, but first I must tell you about Sueky."

"The '"apparitions' that came to the cave the night of the hurricane..." She began, then fell silent for a long time then blurted out ... "they were Edan Braun and Naomi!" She shuddered and said nothing more.

"I don't understand. What did they have to do with us?"

Myah said nothing, then grasped Garth's hand tightly and looked into his eyes. "Sueky... is my grandmother. She is the best farmer on the Island. She is Bantu's great grandmother and she is a devout Anglican Christian. But she is also an Obis, a practitioner of Obism!'"

Garth knew her grandmother Sueky but not the expression Obi.

"She is both a Christian and devote practitioner of the Obism... a 'Voodooist' in your in your words!"

She studied his face. "I know that seems contradictory, a Christian and a Voodooist. But in truth they are quite compatible."

(("Most people think that the Voodooism and the Christian doctrines are mutually exclusively. But they are not. Voodooism is a "perspective" not a religion. Christianity is simply the practicing of multiple facets of the same encompassing parent perspective. They are not contradictory nor incompatible.)) She is both a Christian and an Obihist."

Garth knew Sueky well, and she certainly was not a witch.

"She is a... " Myah began again, "a follower of an ancient practice, called Obihism -- a primitive variant of 'Voodism.'". But, in fact, it is a way of seeing things", a perspective, rather than a way of viewing God.

Seeing Garth's confusion, she continued. "I suspect you were raised with these two perspectives yourself but didn't see them as such. In your case, Christianity and the teachings of your Shaman Goto, which you might call "Naturalism".

"Think of Sueky and your Gotoshaman as two shamans, as two teachers of non-conflicting perspectives.".

Still unsure, but Garth nodded.

"The full story is while Sueky was herding her goats, a few days before the hurricane she received a message. "Keep the Dead So."

"Now, from her perspective as an Obeist, the wall between the living and dead is thin and that in times of great upheaval that the wall can dissolve... and the dead can in certain situations join the living and become alive!"

"So, following the directives Sueky was given, she made a potion, a special salve from manchineel roots and cactus pulp for the purpose of keeping the dead confined ... specifically to keep the dead buried in the Anglican graveyard, and keep them from frequenting the realm of the living. At the height of the hurricane she was to use the salve to paint on all of the corner posts of the graveyard the sign of the cross thus confining the souls of those buried there until the upheaval passed."

" This she did, before being grabbed by the wind and thrown into the tangle of the ravine beyond the bounds of the Church yard.

Garth still didn't understand the relationship of Sukey's ordeal and the apparitions they experienced in the cave.

"As I said, isolation didn't help Edan Braun's madness and finally Naomi gave in to her mistress's wishes for death."

"The Priest at the time of their deaths ruled Edan and Naomi's deaths were 'suicides'" -- a "Mortal Sin,", and refused them burial in the Church graveyard. And, as a consequence, their bodies were interned just outside the church's boundaries!"

Garth sat silent. Shocked by the story -- suspecting it to be true.

"But why the incident in the 'cave?" Garth asked bewildered.

"I've told you I carry a heavy historical, family burden." She said offering no more answer.

"Even Sueky doesn't know exactly why they came to us in the cave. But something you should know, and Sueky pointed this out," She grasped his hand violently. Finally, releasing it and taking a deep breath. "Beside Sueky... "She looked deep into his face… "I am the last living relative in the bloodline of Naomi!"

She stood abruptly. "Come," Myah grasped his hand, "Come away, we must leave this place!" She said. "Come!"" And led him away from the dungeon, away from the Manor House .... away from its histories.

"I will take you to a place of happiness... for me and my back time childhood memories." She took his hand, and as they walked down the road through the coconut groves towards the ocean, he could feel the history of the manor shed away and a lightness of joy replace the tempo of her step.

Soon they passed a cluster of the remains of old, wooden pasture houses. "Naomi's family came from there," she pointed to one of the collapsed chattel houses.

"After emancipation, my father's great- great-grandfather was given the piece of land high up on the ridge where Caraja and I now live.

As they walked, with each stride Myah recounted happy memories from her childhood as they swept over her like the incoming waves of the ocean ahead.

"One of our responsibilities as a youth for me and my friends was to come down to the beach with baskets and hard-soled sandals and walk out in the ocean on the coral. And, while the men went far out into the surf with long iron poles, standing waste deep facing incoming waves, they'd pry off pieces of coral free from their colonies and then send them rolling towards shore."

"Our task was to collect them in baskets, and carry them to shore, then dump them on the beach to dry."

Myah was smiling, for the first time since they left the mountain, Myah smiled.

"This process went on for a few weeks, collecting, sunning the chunks of coral on the high sand until they were dry, then we'd carry them inland to that large round building." She pointed to a large cone shaped building, tampered upward, but with no top.

Myah explained that the structure was a giant incinerator for burning the coral until it was brittle-dry and then would be then crushed into lime powder for making construction-cement strong. The building was open at the top. A tapered amphitheater that telescoped up to the heavens.

"Come!" Myah said, pushed the pack she'd been carrying from the mountain house through the doorway of the building and then she ducked inside an archway facing the ocean.

The empty inside of the chamber was lavender in the setting sun. Taking an old handmade broom leaning against the wall by the doorway that had been used for sweeping the floor after the incineration burns ----- Myah collected the sweepings into the middle of the amphitheater and with dry driftwood from outside the doors she started a small fire in the middle of the chamber. The smoke rose straight up into the sky as it had for centuries.

Near the fire she rolled out two mats side by side and facing the entrance, out towards the white froth ocean beyond, and the full moon rising out of the ocean. She sat down on the mats and motioned for Garth to sit beside her.

For a long time, she looked at Garth then finally following a deep breath she spoke. "You know the story I told you at the Manor House... about the Edan, the bride to be, and her hand-madden, the duel, and the suicides?"

"Not easily forgotten!" Garth nodded.

"Well... there is more you should know." She paused for a long silence then spoke again. "Sueky believes, no... I too believe, that the death of the body is not the death of the soul. And in some circumstances the soul can return to frequent the land of the living! That was what Sueky was charged with doing, confining the souls to the graveyard!

"But... under certain circumstances," she continued, "in this case a storm of such power and violence, the dead have open portals they can use!" She looked hard at Garth... and he saw in her eyes, it was not a statement to question, but a fact!

"Naomi and Edan were buried <u>outside</u> the containment of the cemetery!"

"You said that before." Garth nodded.

"What I didn't tell you is... I am Naomi's <u>last</u> living relative... the last of her bloodline!" She looked directly at Garth wondering if he understood. "The Spirits in the cave were the Madame ... and Naomi!"

Her voice was strong and defiant as if preparing for a response. But it didn't come.

"<u>That</u> is the curse of my bloodline... for six generations.... Offspring of a murderer...!" She could no longer hold it back and started to weep, then sob!

411

"And...?" Garth said quietly. "That is your secret? That is why you have pulled away from me ... from us for so long?" He put his arms around her and for the first time, he held her close, feeling their complete oneness.

As the full moon slowly rose from the sea, the chamber echoed her tears.

"It's over." Garth said quietly. "Maybe that is why they came to us in the Cave... to say goodbye!"

Myah looked up into his face, strong and reassuring. He was right, it was over, it was time to let go! Events from the distant past only have hold if we let them, she finally realised and folded into his arms

For hours they lay on the mats looking upwards into the heavens above telescoped through the open roof. Shooting stars raced across the sky in a galactic war maybe millions of years ago, resulting in a silent big bang light years in the past, rocketing into the future.

And, as galaxies collapsed into the ethereal darkness only to emerge as brilliant new solar systems, the couple finally shared finally as a single being. For the first time, they lay as one, breathed as one, relinquished themselves as one, shared their bodies as one, and grew together as one.

****

She was gone! When he awoke to the soft dawn, he was naked and alone. Myah was no longer beside him, nor in the chamber. The sun, following the moon, was raising out of the Eastern Sea, igniting the day with shafts of fire through the clouds, streaking over the Island from an indigo ocean.

Garth scrambled to come awake as though from an aphrodisiac trance.

She was not in the chamber, nor outside its entrance. Then, far down by the shore he saw her, naked, her arms folded around her knees, starring out to sea.

"Private meditation?" He asked when he joined her, then sitting beside her, he putting his arms around her.

"You must leave!" She whispered holding back her tears. "If we are to have a future together, you must resolve your past." She shuddered but did not speak more.

He was devastated!

"You must go!" She whispered finally as though if she spoke with more strength, she would break down... shatter.

Garth said nothing for he knew she was right.

"I tried to avoid you for so long!" She snapped around glaring at him with the eyes of a panther. "For two years I tried to stay away from you... because I knew this moment would one day come... though I didn't know how or why." She looked at him, but fell silent

"You must go back to your life in Wyoming... to your family... your... your fucking girlfriend.!" Her voice had force, but then softened "Before... before we could ever be as one... you must go back."

Garth was silent. He knew she was right.

She suddenly grabbed his hand as he started to get up. Looking into his eyes, "One.," she said. "We are as One!"

"One." He repeated.

******

He was off the Island that night and on a red-eye special from Antigua to Chicago, missing deeply her laugh in Denver, tears came to his eyes, but dried by years of maturity while waiting for a sage-hopper to take him to Cheyenne where his brother would drive from the ranch to meet him!

Twenty-eight hours and four time zones he was standing at the horse corrals on his family's ranch, saddling Bolero, joYouse

413

to be home, though ever so angry, defiled, crushed, humiliated, confused, saddened and yet, very much in love!

Only at that moment, a thought grabbed him, he may have to go back to the Island of Saint Augustine... he still didn't have Stomp's "Exit-visa!"!

Chapter 36

Ruthie and the Second Coming

In the two years since Garth left, prosperity had come to the Island; new buildings; new roofs, windows, and bright new paint on the old structures. The ancient wooden dock had been replaced with a concrete pier. The breakwater in front of Portstown was now gift-wrapped with boulders the size of Volkswagen "Beetles", and it extended far out into the bay to accommodate two lanes of traffic and multiple boats on either side.

Along the dock, there was organised cargo-space, far different from the wreckage that he last saw as he left Island when chaos ruled. All of the stores had added new wooden stories to the one level, 17th century, foundations, and bright paint, pastel colours with fresh gingerbread trim. Boutiques and tourist shops replaced the pragmatic hardware and cloth stores.

A large cruise ship lay anchored offshore and a mini-fleet of five long boats shuttled passengers off the ship to the waiting taxi-vans for a tour of the Island. Some tourists shopped around Portstown, while still others set their sights on the sand for a beach-bar afternoon. Rainbow's was packed, drawn by the owner's reputation and the rumours of the sting of his "Killer Bees".

Garth waited on the upper deck of the ferry for the crush of passengers to debark before getting off the ship. Except for a wave of recognition from Captain Bart and, an exchange of short greetings with some of the crew, Garth saw no one he knew and that was the way he wanted it. Until he understood why he'd come back, he wanted to pass unnoticed amongst the crowd moving down the dock.

Except for the deck crewman Bantileg, no one paid him any attention.

"Wash Youse feet Mistah Garth." Bantileg cautioned.

Garth laughed as he stepped onto the dock. "I does wash my feet dis morning." He replied, but the joke was lost.

Garth had not gone far down the pier when he heard a woman yell "<u>Geronimo!</u>" from behind him. He knew the voice and it made his heart happy.

"How'd you know I come so?" He called out not looking back.

When he got no reply, he turned, but did not see Ruthie in the crowd. He looked ahead and again he heard her.

"Geronimo, <u>everyone</u> knows by now you's sneak'n home."

"Visiting!" he called back over his shoulder.

The woman grabbed his butt from behind and laughingly spun him around. Ruthie's face was full of sparkle. She hugged him, giving him a peck on the cheek, drawing him back for a second look, and then threw her arms around him and gave him a full kiss on the mouth, something Aunt Ruthie <u>never</u> had done-- a gesture saved for someone special, but never for clients.

"New man Ruthie?" one of the dock stevedores clucked pushing a flat-deck wheel-borrow in the opposite direction. Then recognising Garth, he grinned. "Dat be you so Geronimo?"

"No!" Garth assured him, A little embarrassed he drew back from Ruthie's hold. "Is me brother."

"Times so hard you're working the docks." He teased Ruthie.

"Mon, don't you be causing no trouble now. Times are good, <u>real</u> <u>good!</u> I doesn't do the heavy lifting anymore. I have staff now. I'm in management."

"Please tell me that 'Auntie Ruthie's Snackette' didn't die an Earthly death or was finally busted by the police!"

"Naw mon, I'm far into the future. Now she be 'Aunt Ruthie's Lounge <u>and</u> Internet Bistro!" She looked at him appreciating his expression. "What do you think o'dose mangoes?". "Lots of boat people. Sailors after a long Atlantic voyage... they're the best. We offer them everything their hearts desire... except tattoos." She leaned over and took one handle of his duffle, Garth carried the other.

416

"Qué tienes aquí?"

"Rocks!" He said with a straight face.

"Mon, you'se bringing rocks to the Rock?!"

"Presents."

"Oowee" she cooed, "I like presents."

"Only for bad little girls." He teased.

"Guess that leaves me out." They walked in silence happy to be in the other's company. Garth was especially proud, Ruthie had always been a class act, and he was no longer a lowly Peace Corps Volunteer and could now partake in her services were he not otherwise distracted.

As they entered the old, and even more elegant Portstown Bank building, Garth saw that Ruthie certainly had come up in the world. "Aunt Ruthie's Lounge and Internet Bistro" was actually elegant. Ruthie had moved into the 18th century stone bank building that was first built in 1789 by the London Tea and Spice company. The cut-stone edifice was two stories, surrounded by a wide veranda and a courtyard in the back filled with tables made intimate by large, exotic potted plants.

The first floor was divided between a restaurant, an internet "lounge" and a beautiful purple-heart hardwood bar with a dark mahogany pool table along one side. The place was certainly much classier than its money-changer past of pirate days, Garth noted, down to the doorman dressed in shipboard whites. The interiors of the private eddies were fresh pastel colors, original art on the walls, and a discrete VISA or Master Card decal on the side of the antique cash register.

"Two Caribs," she said to the pretty girl behind the bar.

"Jasmine? That you?" Asked Garth.

"In de flesh and blood! So how you be cowboy?"

"Indian," he corrected.

"Oh das roight, I gets confused with all Youse comm'n and go'n."

417

Ruthie moved the duffle down by the side of the stairs and guided Garth upstairs and out onto the veranda overlooking the street, the port and the blue Caribbean beyond. The beers arrived with two chilled glasses. "Pretty classy," Garth smiled.

"Lots of changes on Island since you left. Attitudes mainly and for the better, I think. Unfortunately, the youths's hands 'don't dirt' anymore. Only the elders and the Rastas do the planting and gardening and the result is that we are now a net importer of food when just a few years ago we were exporting.

She sipped her beer. "You remember, Garth, how our Island used to be self-sufficient? Now we are just as dependent upon the third World and agro-business as the First World. The only difference, we don't have a land-based income anymore."

Garth had noticed that there were a lot more automobiles on the street, and a lot more ladies in chic clothes, men wearing ties though he saw no one in business suits except for foreigners attracted by the newly legislated offshore banking businesses.

"Of course, the cost of everything is going up, food, trans, taxes. Big villas springing up everywhere, and you watch, it won't be long before we can't afford our own Island-- just like the rest of the Caribbean."

"Funny, but of all the Islands that got smacked by Mr. Hugo, everyone figured we'd be de last to recover since we were no longer a protectorate of England, and a newly established, independent nation.

"But don't you know, we were the FIRST to come back! We were the first to get the roads opened, the power on, the hospital functioning – with no looting, nor crime!"

"And, you know why?" Ruthie asked rhetorically. "We were still a "WE" society. We look after each other. Nobody goes hungry on St. Augustine. You want for something that I have, it's yours. Somewhere in our history when the rest of the world joined the twentieth century, little St. Augustine decided that the 18th century was good enough!"

418

"And when all the rest of the Caribbean joined the twenty first century and became just like the rest of the World, a "ME Society", we remained in place. Elsewhere everything was about ME. And as a consequence, when turmoil comes everyone looks after themselves first, and out comes the looting, break-ins; the army to protect the populace. But not here!

"And as you saw, when they sent the Army over from Antigua to protect the peace after the hurricane... you remember, we, instead put them to work rebuilding the hospital and the schools.

"Mind-you we are not without the influence of the outside. Sure, we have Internet, but the hurricane also brought with it new diseases to our plants and new species of insects never before known here. Crime rate never was worth figuring, now we have the beginning of crime and violence; guns, even one murder... can you imagine!

"So, how about you?" Garth asked. "How did you fair from the blow-back?"

"Good, real good. Insurance finally came through on the Snackette and I put it back into this place."

"You own the building?"

"I do!" she said pleased. 'No... I'm doing very well ...even have a man... sometimes."

"Yea? I thought you were going to wait for me," Garth smiled, "I'm not in the Peace Corps any more.... But I still don't have any money." He laughed.

"Too bad! You'll just have to beat it."

Garth groaned at the ageless joke. She gave him a condescending smile.

"So, who's your squeeze?"

Ruthie smiled, watching for Garth's reaction. "Captain Crunch!" She boasted, anticipating a response.

"Oh MY GOD!" Garth barked. 'Mike?! He's still alive?"?" Garth shook his head astonished, "I figured that after his boat got mashed-up in the hurricane he'd move onto a better harbour."

419

"Mon, der be <u>no</u> <u>better</u> harbour den ME!!" Ruth teased. "Baby, I'm the best harbour der be!"

"What I meant was, you're a class act and Crunch is ... well... a sailor! The last I saw him was that New Years night when the bunch of us sailed over to San Sebastian and in the middle of the night when we came back, we had to land at Backwash Bay because the sea was so rough. Remember the surf was running six-to-seven-foot beach-breakers. Remember that?" He turned to Ruthie.

"What I remember", she said, "there were three little kids along, two professional football players... ten of us in all, and a four-person dingy. We had to land in shifts -- the big guys first, then kids and cowards in the last boat." Garth grinned and nodded.

"Remember how the first two runs were disasters with the dingy getting swept sideways and then flipped into the curl, sending everyone scrambling for shore? I was in one of them." She said.

Then we had to bail the dingy out and line it back again for you in the Crunchette.... Remember that's what he called his boat after its first accident off Lover's Point?"

"Of course, I remember. I was in the last run."   "Oh, that's right, but I forget how you got into shore with the children?"

"Great Story" Garth mused. "I had the littlest kid under my left arm, and the other two hanging onto my belt, and I was figuring to jump for shore just before the boat capsized!"

"According to plan, Crunch cranked up the motor, but a wave caught the dingy early and started to swing us sideways, tittering on the edge of capsizing in front of it, when suddenly we stalled in the water with the bow still pointing to shore! And ... somehow the wave swept <u>under</u> us, flushed beneath the dingy without flipping us and we suddenly started moving again <u>on</u> the tail of the wave upright and rode it right up onto the beach without flipping!"

"Yea, I remember... and I remember how?" She sparkled. "What had happened was that two of the professional footballers stood out in the   surf, waist deep, caught the dingy and held it solid while the wave rolled under you guys... and then they let her slide right up to shore!"

"So, <u>where</u> is Crunch now?"

"Sailing! Taking an eighty-footer down through the Canal to New Zealand. Says in his emails that he will be home soon ... but I also heard, he was going around world to get here! Who knows?"

"And Bueno and Rebecca? How are they? Did they recover from their hurricane forced vacation?" Garth asked.

"Tightest family you've ever known, even today all of the family lives under the same roof. They do everything together, farming, fishing. hard workers. The kids went on to use their brains. One works in the Bank, one works on a private fishing ship. No, their forced isolation has made them closer than ever. In fact, they are planning a vacation together... get this... she smiled. "Get this, ... to Hawaii!"

"And what about Fluteman? How is he doing after the death of Fife? The last time we spoke was at Fife's funeral. My heart cried for that man that day."

"Well as they say on-island, 'Life follows life'. It was really hard for him at first and many people thought he'd stop playing all together. But now he has a new protégé, a younger cousin of Fife's that has taken up the flute. And from what I hear, he has a lot of potential. However, sometimes I worry about Mrs. Flute, she smiles and all, but I think she still suffers hard from their loss.

"And Delbert, 'He Ain't Crazy You Know, Mon'?"

"Well, he's still 'Ain't crazy you know mon'. Same as usual, turning the Portsmouth's garbage into works of art. Keeping the island smiling and the government on course. One funny thing did happen while you were away. A politician from Hickman Parish started verbally abusing Delbert for writing a calypso about him."

"The guy got so mad that he began punching and kicking Delbert. Can you imagine?! Course, everyone got in there and stopped the guy before he could do any damage, but the case went to court.   And the politician argued his character had been assassinated."

"However, the judge ruled in Delbert's favour, telling the politician that Delbert was more of a public asset to the people of St. Augustine and Portstown, then the plaintiff would be if he were elected Premier.

Delbert was so pleased he wore his Texaco uniform around for a week and wrote a new calypso about the man and the trial, and it was more defamatory than the first offense. But what could the Hickman politico do, Delbert had him boxed in. 'He ain't crazy you know, mon!'"

Garth laughed and laughed. He loved Delbert, everyone did, he was the levity in the Island's soul. "We should build a monument to him in Chaos Park" he said, "something like a bronze statue of him there on the steps of the Treasury where he sat in the afternoons."

"We? How long you back for?" Ruthie asked the question she'd been wondering about since he stepped onto the dock.

Garth hadn't realised what he had said. Force of habit, he figured. When he was here during the recovery, everything was 'we'. "We gonna git tru mon!" as the Wretched Wrecks work crew would say.

He shrugged. "A day, maybe two, I'm on my way to South America. I going to have a job interview with UNESCO working with the Oltovalo Indians in the Ecuadorean Andes. Thought I'd stop here on my way down."

"On your way!" Ruthie smirked. "St. Augustine is a long way out of your way from Wyoming to Ecuador ... isn't it?"

Garth said nothing more, Ruthie didn't press it.

"Caraja and Felicity have a second child on the way." she added into the void. Their son "Hugo" will be two year come October. Caraja is still working for the Government but has moved in full time with Felicity... now his legal wife... at <u>his</u> insistence!"

"Oh!" Ruthie exclaimed. "Do you remember Jonathan, the white lawyer from the States, and my dear friend Danielle ... better known as "Bana". She was the super model? Well, they have a baby... a very cute little girl!"

Finally, when the catch-up history lesson was over, blatantly avoiding the one subject Garth hoped would come up -- as did Ruthie. She suggested they walk down the beach to Rainbow's, have a "Killer Bee" and supper.

As they walked, they discussed everyone else on Island except the one person he wanted to know most about... Myah. Ruthie knew that too but didn't volunteer any information until he asked.

Rainbow was delighted to see Garth. He gave them a table away from some Americans that were talking loudly from the sting of too many killer Bees.

They ate in silence, though both knew they should be addressing the elephantine question that was on both of their minds.

Finally, he could wait no longer. "And Myah? How is she? And Bantu?" he tried to sound casual. "He must be all grown-up, how old is he? Four plus some?

"He's wonderful. Really happy little guy. His mother is more beautiful than ever. But I'm afraid after you left, she's became even more jungled-up -- if that's possible. No one sees her much. But Bantu's starting school soon so I guess we'll be seeing more of her then."

Silence settled between them. Finally, Ruthie spoke. "Why did you leave for so long? Two full years?"

"Complicated," he said looking out towards the setting sun. "I hadn't seen my parents since I left for the Peace Corps, and then the hurricane came. The ranch in Wyoming is doing well thanks to my very capable younger brother. In truth the days passed so fast on Wyoming, yet you never see them go. Rise with the sun, and the next thing you know it is setting.

He thought for a long minute, ...and, I guess I felt useless.

"Also, there was another expectation on me, or so I thought. I doubt if my tour with the Peace Corps ever had made much difference in the state of the world, or even St. Augustine. In fact, it was only after Hugo that I felt like I was really involved and making a difference. And that was over."

"But," he hesitated, "there was another reason I had to go back. And I am not sure you'll understand this, but since my early youth I was being groomed in a different direction."

He paused. "There was a special issue I had to deal with". He decided to tell Ruthie it all, though she likely wouldn't understand.

"When I was young, a Shaman.... A spiritual leader came out to the ranch to buy horses, or so he said. His name, in my native Culture of Shoshone is "Natia Goto" or "Wise Owl". He is what you would call a "Medicine Man". One of very high esteem throughout the Shoshone Nation.

He said that he wanted to buy a horse, but my folks suspected he was there to see about my spiritual education. It was a great honour but nothing was said outright." Garth laughed, "You see, the Shoshone people tend talk not in the words, but in the silences between them."

"This idea that I had special powers was further supported on the first day, when we had gone into the high alpine where the horses range in the summer, and Goto made no reference to the horses. "

"For three days I sat with the old Indian Shaman without food or even water, in silence. Often, I saw many things but was never sure if they came from inside of me or the 'other source'".

"Once as we sat there, an elk walked within yards of us. Neither of us moved, but I sensed that it would have made no difference. We were invisible! In fact, the bull elk, majestic in his scrubbed summer antlers, looked directly at me, then through me and walked so close his hoof fell just inches from my hand as though I were not there.

Finally, on the third day old Goto rose, there had been no mention of horses. "You have strong Indian medicine' he said. "It is your gift, but with it comes responsibility. Use it wisely!"

That was all that was said. And from then on Goto became my guide." He paused, but Ruthie sensed he was not finished

"It was a great honour and privilege. But in the real world at the time, my choices were two... one, the Peace Corps ... or Vietnam. Shamanism was not a choice according to the United States Government!"

"So, you see, when my tour with the Peace Corps ended and my efforts helping the Island recover from Hugo were no longer needed, my Shoshone responsibility to Natia Goto weighed heavily upon me."

"For two years I worked closely with the Old Shaman and learned much. But, I was deluding myself and Natia Goto being the wise owl, finally confronted me with what I was denying in myself. Finally, he said, "You will find what I have taught you has a home in another place, with people who are not of your kind. I believe that is your destiny!"

"I too had felt this, but it was such an honour to be chosen I'd closed my heart to the message."

"Go." He counselled me. "I feel you are not the only one close in your life who has the gift".

"Turning the ranch over to the management of my younger brother was easy. Trying to let go of the responsibilities that came with Goto's teachings was not as easy for I felt I was abandoning my destiny. But, in his wisdom, he was right. But then came the reality that I may not be welcome back here, after all, Myah had told me to leave."

"No! That's NOT true!" Ruthie barked so loud that even Rainbow turned.

Ruthie ignored their looks and stared hard into his eyes. "It was your situation. You hadn't been home since before Hugo, and she knew you had to resolve things back in Wyoming before you could forge something here...!" She glared at him. "Simple as that!" Her looked softened.

"When she said that you must leave Island, she simply knew that you had first to find resolution back in Wyoming! And whether you admit it or not, she was right! If you then came back, it was your decision...free of other magnetic pulls... but you <u>didn't</u>!"

Ruthie looked out over the sun setting on the ocean and said nothing more on the subject. Finally, she asked him a second question. "Do you still love her?"

It was a question he asked himself daily over the last two years. The response was always the same answer... but now there was a second issue he must face. He had been gone so long without contact; how could he now parachute back into her life.

Garth sat there in silence. It was a bad idea to have come back. After the initial homecoming in Wyoming, he realised life on the ranch was as it should be... but he was not, though he tried hard.

The Island was fresh and vibrantly alive. The place that was supposed to be the last to recover from the hurricane, was, in fact, <u>the first</u>! Myah too. She too would have gone on with her life, and for the better. No, he could not suddenly just drop into it.

"Fuck You!!" Ruthie slashed into the silence "You <u>can't</u> leave before seeing her!" Ruthie snapped and again all of the attention in Rainbow's fell upon them.

Following a sleepless night on Ruthie's couch, he decided he <u>would</u> stay long enough to at least see Caraja and meet his friend's son, named Hugo.

He would go up the mountain at dawn and be back to Portstown in time for the midday ferry... then the afternoon flight back to Miami, and from there to the interview in Ecuador.

"You <u>have</u> to go up the mountain." Ruthie barged into her dressing room at dawn. "It is not a fuck'n matter of choice!"

There was a long silence... both knowing she was right.

"Why did you <u>really</u> leave here!" Her voice was hard and demanding an answer.

"How much did she tell you?"

"Everything! But I want to hear it in <u>your</u> words"

Garth knew she knew Myah's version, but he had so blocked out that night he was fearful of opening the door... but he knew now he must.

Myah and I are... maybe, <u>were</u> deeply in love, but I knew there was something she carried from her past, some tragedy that went far back in her history... her family's history".

"I also knew it was important for her to explain and for that she'd suggested that we go to the abandoned Fontaine plantation. There was something there she must share."

"Myah knew it too because she too has the gift of communication with her ancestors." Ruthie said, then fell silent letting her words settle upon Garth.

"But... Myah also carries a 'burden' from her past -- and it is a legacy written into her heritage ...her's and Sueky's, her grandmother's ..., that goes back back to the slave girl Naomi!"

"That is why she took you to the Fontaine Plantation and told you the full story of the duel and the terrible consequences that followed, ending with the tragic deaths of two damaged women."

"You talked with her about our trip to the plantation... all of it?!" He asked, feeling a little betrayed

Ruth looked at him hard before continuing. "Even before... she also told me of the "visitation" in the cave.

"Good Hell!" Garth, barked. "How <u>much</u> did she tell you about the that night in the cave?!" He, in his mind had written the events off to fear from the storm -- a hallucination, never considering, in Ruthie's words, an actual "Visitation"

"She told me everything!" Said Ruthie in a way that marked that the subject as over. They sat in silence. Then.

"What Naomi was asked to commit was the ultimate sacrifice. You know, I really think Myah would give up her life rather than hurt you. But she <u>had</u> to do what she did ... there was no choice. She was chosen and for those with <u>the</u> power they can't be unchosen."

Garth still said nothing.

Ruthie looked away and then back at Garth. "After what you told me, you of all people should understand what it means when your ancestors speak." But…..I guess not!"

"But even with the trip to the Fontaine Plantation and our night together, I never did believe Myah would understand that I was being trained as a "medicine man". He fell silent a moment, then gave a short laugh. "She must have had the same fears.

The conversation ended, but Garth carried it on in his head, remembering Myah's parting words. "When you've cleared yourself of your duties, I will be here should you come back!"

Garth also remembered his last words as he walked from the beach, following a night of such beauty "I love you!"

With a deep sigh, Garth resolved to face the present. He'd catch a bus to Poppy Dawn, call out for Caraja. He envisioned him carrying his son on his back while weeding his garden.

When he got there, he was fully prepared to walk to the village of Remember Me and on to Caraja's farm. But the bus doors burst open on a great grin that radiated against the lush green jungle it was Caraja standing there ... but he carried no child on his back!

"What took you so long to come home?" Caraja challenged.

"Just visiting." The two men hugged. "I'm on my way to a job interview in Quito!" He said, trying to sound convincing. "Where's Hugo. I thought he'd be in a sling on your back."

"Hugo?! Mon, you've been gone too long! Too long!" Caraja broke into his gatling machine-gun bursts of laughter. "He's standing right behind you!"

Garth turned and there holding onto Garth's right pant leg stood a young boy starring up at him and with round walnut eyes and a great Caraja's grin.

"I got the news on the jungle-internet." He looked at Garth. "Actually Mon, I got a text from Ruthie."

"Oh my God!" Garth exclaimed. "I never thought I'd see the day you, of all people, would be on the Internet!"

"Not there yet.: He laughed. "Bo-Bo Johnny saw Ruthie's message to me on his phone and he passed it on to Worrymon that you's coming, and he passed it along the village network and finally to me."

Caraja laughed and lifted his friend's duffel and was surprised by the weight. "Mon whas in here? Rocks? You bring rocks to the Rock?!"

"Ruthie said the same thing."

"The rocks are headed for Ecuador". He smiled, seeing his friend needing more explanation. "My Shaman, Goto, my spiritual guide said I'd make the transition to a new life smooth, if I didn't let go completely of what I'd left behind."

"Mon, dat's de dumbest idea I've ever heard. "Rocks to the Rock" Caraja laughed. Even his son was caught by his father's merriment and started to laugh.

"Hey Mon" Garth shifted to the language of the location. "Youse jus de same!"

He pointed to the duffle. "It's my rock collection. Mainly arrow and spear heads. Treasures from my youth... my heritage. I'm Indian you know." Garth smiled. "Cool stuff I'd gathered as a kid."

"I understand dat mon, but enough be enough. You got to let go of you's baggage."

"You don't understand, I'm going to an interview to teach in an Indian village high in the Andes. I figure I could use my fossil collection to show how "Original people"... as youth now call Indians, lived on the other side of the planet a thousand of years ago.

"These rocks are not just 'pick-up-off-the-trail' rocks, they're lesson books about my heritage! Besides, My Guide says, "Where the duffle sleeps there is my destiny."

Caraja huffed, paid no attention and swung the duffel over his shoulder, extending an index finger for Hugo to hold onto. "Time to go meet your destiny!"

"What does that mean?!" Garth looked at him. "I'm a moving target. I'll be learning a new language this time next week! That is my destiny." He said hoping his friend would accept his decision maybe even reinforce it. But Caraja only 'humphed' and started up the jungle road, with Hugo happily swinging on the extended finger.

For half an hour they talked about changes in the village since the hurricane, the births, deaths. But after the hurricane, Caraja noted, gossip was no longer an art, nor sport. It was a <u>blasphemy</u> in which no one indulged. Everyone still <u>needed</u> each other.

Finally, they came to an intersection in the path where the trail to Caraja's farm turned off from Myah's trail. Caraja set down the duffle.   "This is your stop cowboy!" He smiled. "Remember, she's not connected to the pine-cone telephone... she doesn't know that you are on Island.

"Be gentle." Caraja said in parting, "she too is wounded!" And with a wave of his free hand, he and his son turned from Myah's junction and started onto the trail to his farm.

Chapter 37

"Garth Returns"

As he walked up the trail to Myah that he had tread twice daily, Garth smiled remembering coming back each evening after an exhausting day of working with the recovery crews. Exhausted, but so happy to be back.

The jungle seemed the same; the cottage snuggled into the arm of the lush volcanic mountain towering above. All seemed the same as returning from work on the road crew. Even Bantu on the cottage steps reading a book to Nogo was the same as two years before. But, as he got closer, he saw it was not the cat he read to but a child, a little girl.

They stared at each other frozen in the other's eyes. Bantu was no longer a child, for now it was he who read to a child. Startled by the squawk of a yard-chicken that there was a newcomer amongst them, Bantu looked up.

At first Bantu didn't recognise the man. His hair was long, straight, black, though still the face was familiar.

The child, a little girl was roughly two years old -- Bantu's age when he left, but her hair was long, and straight, her skin more golden than black and her eyes more the colour of walnuts than obsidian. Absorbed in the story, the little girl was unaware of the man, she held a cat, presumably Nogo draped in her arms, folded contently like two halves of a water balloon.

.   Myah looked up from shucking the ears of corn in her lap to see the source of the commotion caused by Bantu's yelp.

At first it was just a dark figure at the bottom on the garden, but she thought she recognised a certain stride in his step and the silhouette of his shadow was familiar. Then suddenly, she knew who it was!

Oh My God!" She screamed suddenly recognising him, scaring a flight of nesting egrets out of the surrounding jungle canopy.

"Oh My God!" she yelped again. Jumping to her feet, dropping the corn, she leapt off the porch and ran down the yard towards Garth, throwing her arms around his neck!

"Oh My God," she studied him with disbelief, grabbed his ponytail with both her hands, looked with disbelief and pulled his head back, studied his face for a few seconds, then kissed him. To the children's bewilderment, they continued to kiss and hug each other and laugh.

Garth dropped the duffle.

Equally excited the children rushed down the yard, Bantu throwing himself around one leg, the little girl, imitating her brother, grabbed the other.

Of course, Bantu had never forgotten Garth, but his sister was bewildered. Myah had raised her in the jungle and strangers were rare.

"Oh my God!" Myah exclaimed, seeing the source of the little girl's bewilderment.

"Are you here for dinner?". Myah asked.

Garth answered "Yes." without credence to the story he had woven about the Indians of the Andes.

"Wonderful!" She smiled, taking the duffle from him and promptly dropping it.

"What's in it, rocks?"

"Exactly! Bring rocks to the Rock!" He smiled pre-empting her response.

The four of them ascended finally to the cabin, holding hands and laughing without reason other than happiness. Near the house she instructed the children to pick up the ears of corn that had been scattered across the lawn. "Then" she smiled, "fetch water for supper."

432

"Why don't you go with the children." She smiled. "I assume you remember where the water-well is". She studied Garth and immediately her face lit-up for she knew, though maybe he didn't, that he had landed!

The troupe disappeared with water bottles in a mesh basket into the ravine to get water from the stream below where Garth and Caraja had swung on vines years before. Now it was just a beautiful stream of mountain water tumbling over a twenty-foot ledge into a swimming pool basin. And it wasn't long before they were splashing away, the little girl the most enthusiastic. Finally, when they were thoroughly soaked and gasping with laughter, they filled their pails and started for home.

Myah smiled but said nothing to the wet rats, but she couldn't help smiling. On the porch Myah had pulled together two chairs and set down a handbasket of corn-ears, and another one for husks and a boiling pot for super.

Garth took the children to the duffle and carefully showed them the artefacts of his childhood. Immediately they were mesmerised and leaving them with the duffle of artefacts, he returned to Myah.

At supper, Myah asked about Garth's return to his home in Wyoming. " Did they know you were coming back?"

"My Brother, Jake, 'De'de Babu' is his Shoshone name, came to Denver and we drove back together in his pickup. Obviously, he speaks fluent Shoshone ... probably better than me and we rattled down the road like a couple of wild Indians fresh off the reservation!" He laughed.

'What did you tell him about us?"

"*Pihwa-ppyh biha*" he said.

"Meaning?" She asked.

Garth smiled, "Broken Heart." Then laughed. "No, I told him that I had fallen in love with you, but the hurricane had scrambled our lives."

"How do you say your name in Shoshone?" Myah asked.

"Listen closely." He leaned forward near her ear.

"Garth! "Garth with a G", he teased'

She lightly punched his shoulder.

"Dede Babeau.... Little fox.... Dede Babeau

They sat in silence, both relishing that they were finally together again. Garth spoke at last.

"You were right sending me packing back to Wyoming. Too many loose ends needed to be dealt with." He nodded and touched her hand. "Way too many loose ends!" Myah looked away on the threshold of tears, and quickly she changed the subject.

"What did your mother say when she saw you? Myah asked.

"When I walked through the door, she screamed, hugged me, then started to thank every deity in the Shoshone language, finishing with Jehovah just in case God is Catholic!"

"No, when they got my letter that I was staying to help with the recovery, they relaxed and trusted I could take care of myself."

"And now?

"I think they see I have changed and that I wouldn't be at peace living out my days ranching, surrounded with sagebrush and rattle snakes." He smiled and nodded, "In fact, I think they were relieved ... the ranch is running smoothly with Jake at the helm. And turning a profit for the first time in years."

For a moment he sat in silence then spoke again. "Before I joined the Peace Corps, things were rough between Jake and me, and a couple of times we got into "tooth and claw" fights like two wolverines. In fact, once I got a broken nose and he a broken wrist from hitting the ground instead of my face for a second time!"

Garth fell silent for a while. "No. He is very keen on the working ranch, and I guess I suffer from wanderlust."

Myah smiled. "Rather than just 'lust'?!" Myah teased.

After supper, Garth told the children Indian stories until their brains could hold no more and they resorted to dreams of their own making.

Math and Garth went down to where the duffle was dropped.

"Just rocks." He said sheepishly. "It is my rock-collection. Special rocks that I found, arrowheads mainly, half a dozen full spear heads." He bent down and unzipped the bag, and after routing around for long enough that Bantu became curious and soon he too was looking with awe at the beautiful rocks carved into arrowheads.

In the quiet of the other's company and the evening symphony of the jungle, there was one question that nagged at Garth. As they shucked corn Garth became braver to broach the question that had risen when he first saw Bantu reading to the little girl.

"She's ours you damn foo!" Laughed Mayh reading his mind. In fact, can't you see her features alone are more Shoshone Indian than West Indian! She _is_ ours!"

Garth's breath caught short. He'd never thought of being a father by example to his niece and nephews though he'd often shown himself that he'd be a good one,. He smiled. She was a beautiful, a happy child in paradise.

After supper, Garth had a tussle with the children, something they'd shared with their mother, but she didn't have the skills of wrestling.

"Time for bed." Myah said.

But no sooner were the children tucked in their own beds, and Myah and Garth retired to Myah's room, that the bed was full with the whole family. And so, it remained for the rest of the night. And when the children were confident that Garth wouldn't bolt, they returned to their own beds. And for the first time since the night in the old sugarcane mill, Myah and Garth held each other intimately.

"How long are you here?" Myah asked with trepidation.

Garth looked at the duffle still in the front yard and thought about what Shaman Goto said about finding one's spot on the planet.

"You ought to bring it in, here is where it is supposed be ... even the dumb bag knows that!" She laughed.

She then turned and looked at him. " How long 'are' you here for?

Garth adopted an inscrutable Native look.

435

"A lifetime if you'll have me! "

Chapter 38

"Final Catch"

With the only working telephone on the Poppy Dawn side of the Island, coupled with the fact that the Hotel Lemon plantation had gone through the storm without major damage; the Hotel was a central hub for the recovery effort. Gage immediately cancelled all future reservations and turned the rooms over to an international team of electrical lineman whose lives were going from one disaster site to another around the Planet. The manor house had become an ad hoc hospital, a drop-in medical clinic, and soup kitchen for villagers and expats whose houses were damaged... and a morgue!

There was a day-care in the Hotel garden so parents could turn their attention to the damage to their homes. But the main attraction was the telephone and fax thread of communication with the outside world for half the Island. Lucy handled the traffic, assigning times when Islanders could use the phone, while other times the lines were kept open for communication related to the relief effort.

The hotel had become a place of lines; people waiting in line for the phone, waiting in line to draw water from one of the hotel's two cisterns. Line-ups to see the doctor, line ups to get shots. Necessity and hardship make humans more humane and waiting in lines served to weld everyone with a common resolve. "We gonna get tru! For chure, mon." became the phrase often repeated.

The electrical line crew were a happy lot, though they were seldom around, working from six in the morning to six in the evening, six days a week. Most were bachelors; many divorced after failed attempts to hold together a marriage while being sent around the world following Nature's unending trail of disasters.

Sixteen men complete with rigging-trucks and high-lifts, spools of cable and transformers. What they didn't have were poles, which were sitting on the dock in sight of their destination but across the channel from St. Augustine, being held by neighbouring San Sebastian Customs by politics.

Sent by the World Red Cross, Mrs. Sutter had become a big part of the operation. "Doctor Linda", as she was known, ran daily outpatient clinics, while Richard Sutter, sent there by the UN World Relief, worked on keeping the pipeline for disaster-aid open. Jonathan Douglas helped with the legalities of moving agreements among countries... not so much getting things into St Augustine but getting them out of their source country, especially the United States. The problem was, the US had conscripted most of the available merchant vessels for carrying building materials and medical supplies to their interests in the US Virgin Islands. This meant for Sutter and Jonathan, working with other International aid sources, to do end runs around the American supply lines. Soon their efforts were so effective that hospitals in the Leeward Islands began contacting the Hotel Lemon when they ran out of emergency supplies.

But, as time passed, the Hotel began to slow down, and six weeks after Hugo, the Sutters returned to their lives with the Red Cross." In fact, when the electrical line crews were out working during the day, the Hotel was actually summer-quiet and one mid-week day around Christmas, Garth went fishing with Pali, Captain of the *Le Petite Lemon, and* Jonathan. Jonathan, who had never been deep sea fishing but became addicted when he hooked a large tuna, only to lose it after an hour's fight.

Soon after, Gage hooked a huge marlin that breached high into the air with a fury Jonathan never thought possible for a fish. Strapped into the landing chair, Gage fought with the marlin in a give and take battle that lasted over an hour.

Twice the giant fish was drawn close to Petite, but each time it tapped a reserve of strength and anger, and again the drag on the reel screamed and the windings grew hot from the friction.

"Run with him!" Gage yelled to Pali, "I'm almost out of line." When the boat started chasing it, Gage wound in line as fast as he could.

"Pali! You're going too fast, God Dam It! you're going to go over him!"

"Chinca tu!" Pali cursed but cut the throttle back.

"Damn! You're still going to go over him! Watch the line, damn it" Gage raged into the wind, keeping his concentration on the direction of the fishing line.

"If you cut my line with the prop, you're fired!"

"Chinca de Madre Dios!" Pali growled and steered the bow downwind to starboard and gunned the giant engines causing the boat to set up and turn a tight one hundred and eighty degrees in a circumference of a few yards -- the starboard gunnel was but inches above waterline. Jonathan had to grab Gage's chair to remain on the ship, fortunately it was bolted to the deck.

"Okay, that's great." Gage yelled and pointed. "He's lining-out this way." Pali cut the engines and the wake from their tight turn surged under them.

"Try to turn him." This time Pali didn't swear but brought the engines to just a purr -- his concentration focused on the intersection of surface and ocean's swell. Jonathan was aware that something exciting was going on. Neither man spoke, both intent on a single point in the ocean and the bend of the rod into it. With feathered-touch Pali cautiously eased the boat slightly off the fish's course.

"Easy … easy… "whispered Gage, "he feels the line now!"

"Watch over there!" Gage spoke quietly but quickly to Jonathan. "He's going to breach…"

Suddenly the drag on the fishing reel started to sing again in a furious match between predator and prey.

It was more than two hours before Gage was able to bring the great fish up against Le *Petite.* Pali stopped the engines and vaulted down the stairs from the tower to the deck. He started to grab the gaff and the machete to kill the great fish, but when he looked in

Gage's eyes for assurance to kill it, his eyes engaged Gage's. His first read was correct, but he couldn't accept it. He looked again.

"Madre de Dios!" Pali swore, he looked away then back wondering that he read the Gage's intent correctly. Again, he swore.

Assured he'd read Gage right, the Cuban Captain took up a set of side-cutter pliers, bent over the rail, and reaching with a leather-gloved hand, he slid the pliers down the line, tight to the fish's huge jaw, and cut the barb free .... the eye blinked, and with an explosion of renewed energy and the smell of freedom, it was gone!

"Dat's it!" Pali exclaimed. "Me's gonna quit you soon as we dock!

"Ustedes es muy loco, hombre, muy muy loco! Even mi Junita say so!" Pali growled at Gage, as he walked past him on his way to switch over the rudder to deck control. He was still muttering under his breath, when he emerged from the gallery carrying a tray with a bottle of Glen Dronach Scotch, a pail of ice and three glasses.

"Heilo?" he asked Jonathan.

"Si claro. Gracias."

"Habla Espenol Senior Jon."

"*Un poquito. Pero yo comprendo "Chinca."*

"*Muy Bueno!*" Laughed the Cuban as he added ice to the glasses. "*Yo hablo Espaniol muy bien!" !*"

Gage cracked the seal on the bottle, twisted off the cap and threw it into the ocean. "Nothing sadder than a crippled soldier." He said.

"Crippled soldier?" Jonathan looked puzzled.

"An open booze bottle half-finished." Gage grinned, obviously set on finishing the bottle of scotch before they docked.

"*Attencion.*" Pali held his glass to toast, "*Pez magnifico pascado* .... may he replenish de sea... though my belly goes hungry."

"*Magnifico pescado.*" Gage's arms were so tired that he had to hold the glass with both hands.

440

The rods were stripped down and put away. They had officially stopped fishing and bobbed on the sea slowly killing the wounded scotch warrior.

"Pali thinks I'm getting soft," Gage said looking at Pali. "No longer a man who was once known on the docks as a great fisherman. Old age has weakened me." Pali mumbled a curse, but still, he was also saddened by the picture Gage was painting.

"Now when we come home it is only stories. No pictures in the paper of captain, crew and client. No weigh-scales recording as yet another triumph over the sea. No name on a plaque on a trophy at the Ballyhoo Yacht Club. Right?"

Pali nodded that it was exactly right and there was more he could add.

"I'll tell you what it was about <u>that</u> fish. I could tell in the first few minutes that it was not his time. You can feel their will. His was strong. If you land a fish like that, killing the 'will' does nothing. It's not the killing that holds the intrigue, it is our dance with the sea. Two beings tied together by a single thread so sensitive I could almost feel what he was thinking. Hell, I <u>could</u> feel it. Remember when I felt him coming up to breach?"

"With Pali it is much less circumspect. Fishing is a thing you do to feed yourself and family.'

"When a fish gets old and no longer has the will to fight for his life, then it is a different matter. Then I'll harvest the fish and dine happily on its fillets." Gage took another drink of scotch.

"Agh!" Gage twisted his shoulders from side to side undoing the knotted muscles that were starting to tighten up. "I'm getting too old for fighting big fish,"

"It's sad," he said without remorse, "I'm too old for young women, too jaded for idealism, and too soft for fighting big fish." He sighed, but his eyes still twinkled. "My sole passion now is teasing death with life, and even that meagre joy will one day be taken from me."

441

When the wounded soldier was finally killed and given a proper burial at sea, Pali started the boat's engines and pointed the bow towards a distance glimmer against the northern horizon.

Gage stared for a long time in the direction of where the swordfish was released. "I think I should start thinking about my legacy."

"Jonathan, I want you to come down to the hotel sometime soon and help me start untangling my estate. I'm afraid it is a bit like a knotted ball of fishing- line right now."

The effects of Jonathan's help to killing the wounded soldier made him philosophical and when Gage and Pali fell into drunken fits of laughter at the memory of an adventure running contraband guns from Panama into Nicaragua, Jonathan sat down in the landing chair letting his thoughts drift.

He had heard that ring of resignation in other clients who suddenly felt the need to wind down their affairs. It was funny how the hurricane had turned Gage towards cleaning up his house and reliving the past without much consideration for the future. While he, Jonathan, had never felt more excited about what life held ahead with Bana.

Chapter 39

"Burial at Sea"

It was Lucy who noticed something had changed in Gage. He started taking longer naps, shorter walks, and told condensed stories with faster punch lines. He drank seldom, smoked infrequently, and yet he was still short of wind climbing the stairs to his residence in the plantation's main sugar-mill. Most wouldn't see it for when he was behind the bar, he was still gregarious and vibrant, but in the private times when he wasn't on duty, he felt chronically tired, not bored, but exhausted by even simple delights. Finally, Lucy confided her suspicions to Bana, and she to Jonathan; and he spoke with Gage about going to Walter Reed hospital for a check-up.

When he returned five weeks later, he had a pacemaker in his heart.

"It's the only pacemaker in the world that runs on alcohol," Gage said at his welcome home party, "and I'm not sure they have perfected the technology. So, I've come home to the best heart specialists in the world... friends and fuel."

Jonathan had done wonders untangling Gage's affairs. And when the hotelier got home, all that was left was the signing of the papers. Surgery of that magnitude is bound to knock a person back, but Jonathan noticed that even so, there was something missing. It was his "Will".

"I've got some things to attend to around here, Jonathan. Come Saturday and we'll go over your labours."

***

"You check with the government to see if they have any problems with the bequest?" Gage asked as they sat on the verandah of his private residence in the plantation's sugar-mill. Before them, towering cumulus clouds faded through a pallet of brilliant pastels in the setting sun. Jonathan nodded affirmatively.

"And the stuff in Nicaragua? You'll sort that out?" Again, Jonathan nodded. "Pali still has some problems with the US Feds about the guns, but they have no evidence. See if there is anything you can do to straighten that out. I mean Hell, the Gringos are just sore losers because the Sandinistas won and the gringos can't admit it!'

"Consider it done." Jonathan nodded, smiling. ... that was the problem... the Sandinista won.

Gage released a sigh of fatigue and lit a Benson and Hedges cigarette. "So, I hear all the way to Walter Reed that you and Bana Bordeaux are a couple." He studied Jonathan's face. "Hell, I saw that the first night you two came to supper. And I thought then, what does a middle-aged widower see in a beautiful, ravaging, intelligent woman like her?"

Jonathan laughed, "Love's blind, they say."

"Apparently."

"Remember Mallory?" Jonathan asked.

"Of course I do."

"She too was a fine woman. In fact, back in those days I saw more of Mallory and your kids than you did."

"I know, and I'll always be in your debt. Teaching them to fish, and ride horses."

"<u>And</u> swear, and mix martinis, don't forget that." Gage interjected. "Anyway, why did you ask me if I remembered Mallory?"

"Well, one time Mallory called me an 'arrogant asshole! And I wonder where she got that?"

Gage shrugged. "You know how it is when words get to flying around on the open seas!"

They sat for some time enjoying each other's company and the afternoon sounds of the village. "You know, my life has been a series of memorable moments any one of them so full that it alone would have made my life complete."

There was a long pause. "But remembering back during the War, I still have hard memories that will always be burned into my brain." He paused for a moment. "I told you I was a pilot in the RAF because America wasn't in the War then, so I went to Canada and enlisted. Eighteen years old. At first, I was detached from the War dropping bombs from high above on enemy installations on a map.

"But then when the Germans started bombing London and the countryside, and I'd come back from flying missions over Europe to find the carnage they'd wrecked on us, it was suddenly like 'I' had done it.

"Suddenly, all those bombs we dropped had real consequences, and all the agony and mutilation came home to roost. I never talked about it, maybe that's why I still carry the shame with me even today." He wiped the edge of his eyes with the back of his hand.

Jonathan sensed in the pursuing silence that it was over. They'd finished their business and Gage had said all he had to say. There was no more that Jonathan could add.

Gage rose. "Well, my friend this is my station. Give my regards to that stunning woman you have at home. You'll put together those things we talked about?" Jonathan nodded assuring him it would be done.

Gage extended his hand and when they shook, their eyes said goodbye as they still held hands reluctant to acknowledge the final parting. At last, Jonathan gave Gage a firm squeeze as one might a brother who's catching a train for a new adventure.

Jonathan was halfway up the hill towards his home when he heard the shot. He had been expecting it with each footstep.

The island wept that night.

The following morning, preparations were made for his funeral. Fortunately, Gage had left detailed instructions with Jonathan about the service. But first, Jonathan had to intercept the examining doctor and coax him to simplifying the cause of death to *Contusion to the skull suffered during a household accident*". Causes: "Natural."

445

Insurance companies don't like suicides, and of course, Gage never had much use for insurance companies' rights.

*****

Gage had also spent some time planning his funeral. First, he wanted to be buried at sea, something that never been done on St. Augustine since pirate days. Gage planned two services, the shore party and the boat service, which was to be more intimate and presumably sedate. The main send-off party would be held on shore at the Rookery Nook with the body in attendance. The Nook was a Portstown bar with a courtyard in the back that over-looked the Caribbean horizon. The logistics of the shore party was planned by the Hotel Lemon staff, but the actual tending bar, food, catering was done by the staff from another hotel so the Lemon crew could participate in their boss's funeral.

Brother Bart's boat could legally carry twenty-five passengers. Staff from the hotel (twelve), close friends including Danielle and Jonathan (twenty-six), family ...including six grandchildren from, and including, three daughters and husbands who came from far corners of the world (nine). Island dignitaries who threatened to scuttle the sea burial if not allowed onboard (six). Captain, crew and Miss. Furgeson the undertaker (five) and of course, the undertaken (one).

Miss Furgeson was the Island's mortician, and she took her job very seriously as the job demanded! And though her deeply bereaved face lacked any real core compassion, she could accommodate a thespian's sympathy mood that was sufficient. Miss Furgeson's funeral parlour shared a wall next door to her brother's woodworking shop. And many assumed that if she performed her job with the craftsmanship of her brother, then the deceased would be preserved for a long time.

Gage was very popular and all the shops except the rum shops shut down a half day for his funeral. The beach was crowded with an eclectic cross-section of the Caribbean from preachers, pirates,

446

ladies in waiting, ladies arrived... and a number of not-so ladies at all!

Church children dressed in their Sunday best, their collars tight as their shoes, squirmed and watched with envious eyes the tourist kids swimming and splashing in the surf. And far down the beach, the Zion Pentecostal Church was holding a mass baptism in their white robes, standing waist- deep out in the ocean.

The baptism wasn't scheduled to happen until the following week, but when Reverend Pinesette heard of Gage's passing, he saw it as a sign from God to test his congregation and draw them away from the Devil and the funeral of the Heathen. Unfortunately, there were way more sinners than saved!

As things got rolling, the Reverend didn't want to conclude that more people wanted to go to Hell than Heaven judging by Gage's gathering. In fact, he assisted only three lambs into the arms of Jesus the Shepherd, and with attending family and friends there were only a dozen people present for the baptism. While up the beach -- the music was so loud that he had to yell at the lambs before submerging them—Gage's funeral was a pagan ritual of the magnitude of Sodom and Gomorrah, and an attendance of near two hundred.

The funeral's pulpit was four pieces of plywood cross braced laid flat and elevated on cinder blocks. On it there was a microphone complete with two huge speakers and a large amplifier. Near to the platform stood a tent and awning covering fifty plastic chairs. Fluteman was the master of ceremonies, and his band, the Hornets provided "Rock a Jesus" background music until the hearse arrived and the six pall-bearers lined up behind it.

Then, Johnny Sinclair and his "All Brass Trio" did a very credible "When the Saints Go Marching In." that soon got people to bobbing and clapping while the pallbearers carried the casket from the hearse down to the beach and rested it on two chairs set on the sand. Since the service was non-denominational, in fact, non-

447

religional in any form, Fluteman's sister, Poinsettia sang a freedom song which was as close to an open prayer as Gage would allow.

As is the custom, members of Gage's family spoke first. Both former wives were there but declined to say anything, as did a mystery women from California. His blood family were his daughters and grandchildren. And the three girls took turns talking about their Dad and what they learned from him.

"Dad used to say we wouldn't have him one-hundred percent of the time, but when we were with him he was a hundred percent there."

"Amen child!" cried Patsy who helped raise them at the Hotel when Gage wasn't there.

Dad could smooze his way into anywhere and out of anything. Remembered the time he was caught speeding in Miami, and by the time it was over, he had gotten the officer's mailing address and sent him Christmas cards for years!"

"In fact, Dad's probably right now smoozing he way into Heaven." Laughed the oldest daughter.

The family memories were followed by a coral group from the "Church of the Blessed Lamb" congregation, a rock-a-Jesus group that used to come to the Hotel Lemon on Christmas Eve to serenade the guests with Calypso Christmas carols. They did to gospel, what Elvis did to jazz.

The next set of tributes were from the Hotel staff. Fluteman spoke about Gage's qualities and how they inspired others to see the same qualities in themselves. "He always spoke with respect. Old, young, friend or enemy ... He always addressed them with respect."

"Youse can say das again!" someone spoke up.

"Amen!" Affirmed the Director from the Rock-a-Jesus choir.

"He never took life too seriously and didn't have patience for those who did. I guess that was because of his time in World War II."

Lucy began to speak as well, telling about how Gage entertained the Hotel guests during Hugo, mainly the children and how he made it such a special event that some were disappointed when the storm was over.

But she got only part way through describing Gage teaching the staff's kids poker when she started to weep. After a pause to recover she resumed but this time didn't get but a few words before she started outright crying with such abandonment that finally many others started to cry!

Sensing disaster Fluteman cued Johnny Sinclair and his "All Brass Trio" on shore and they did a hot *Tijuana Taxi* over the 'two-way' from the beach that changed the mood yet again.

Miss Furgeson started getting nervous about the length of time Gage's body had been sitting in the sun and whispered as much to Fluteman. He looked out across the gathering for one last person who had not spoken, his eyes fell upon Pali.

Shyly, the Captain of Le Petite approached reluctantly the microphone that Flutemon held out for him. He stepped up on the platform and a hush settled over the congregation, each anxious to hear the inside story about the "edgy" side of the deceased's life that only Pali and Gage shared. There had been so many rumours of guns to the Contras in Nicaragua. A close call in the US Virgin Islands with the *Federal Bureau.* Smuggling a tin-pot dictator into exile from his island fiefdom.

A quiet of anticipation held the audience. Pali looked awkward and starred at the mic for some time. "*Madre de Dios,*" he swore not knowing the volume had been turned up high. When the laugher settled he tried again. "Gage... " he said and adjusted himself to the microphone. "Gage ..." again he changed his position, "*Gage fue un grande hombre!*" Miraculously, his tenor had the delivery of Che Cuevara giving his famous "*Cinco de Mayo*" speech in Havana which Pali had attended.

"*Gage fue un grande hombre!*" He repeated raising one a fist in the air as though he were "Che Quevera El Comnadante" His eyes surveying the audience for the effect of his speech, "Gage was a real man!" He translated slowly and clearly for the gringos.

Then, after a number of "Amens" and "You's right der mon" from his listeners, he drew himself erect and as tall as his short frame would allow. Everyone listened for him to begin some great saga of high seas adventure, maybe an explanation for the bullet hole in the front windscreen on *Le Petite*. Now with Gage gone, surely, he would tell them all!

"*Gracias*." He said, bowed elegantly and stepped off the platform, smiling from ear to ear at how well his speech had gone. Leaving his bewildered audience, as he walked to the beach, up the gangplank onto the back of Brother's boat turned to his people and bowed.

Miss Furgeson waited with the body until the last. She saw her primary allegiance was to the deceased's remains and the hot sun was making her anxious. Once she was on board, the pallbearers laboured the casket to the back of the boat. It seemed heavier than they'd have thought, each man straining to carry his share. And lifting the coffin over the transom took some effort and required the help of a number of hands from the deck.

There was a congregational singing of "Do Lord" that seeped into the cellular memory of all who attended and remained in their subconscience through the rest of the day. Fluteman thanked everyone for coming, and the "*Hornets*" started once again the songs they played so many times at Gage's Hotel Lemon.

Using the ship-to-shore radio, the boat people could hear the amplified the festivities on shore. More importantly, when it came time, the people back at the wake could hear what was said at sea. The celebration had splashed over into the boat before departing, and the trip out to the banks was a non-stop party of toasts and funny memories about Gage -- all were laughing hysterically except for Miss Furgeson who would have rather been at her niece's baptism just down the beach.

Finally, Brother's ferry crossed the edge of the deep-water shelf where the ocean floor dropped away for a hundred meters, Brother cut the engines. Only then did the gaiety subside to a level of propriety and respect warranted by the occasion of a final parting.

"So much has been said of Gage this afternoon," Jonathan spoke -- as was Gage's wish, "that I won't try to add more. I will simply say that Gage was a dreamer, a romantic, a child, and at times, more adult than any of us here may ever have had to endure.'

'But the one thing I will always remember about Gage was he made his dreams into realities. He saw in a ruined plantation one of the finest, exclusive hotels in the Caribbean. And I'm told that in Wyoming he resurrected a dying cattle ranch, transforming it into a thriving 'Guest Ranch". So, in keeping with this sentiment, it was Gage's wish that I read his last words.

> *'My Loved Ones*
> *Where's the gain to be a romantic without love, to be an idealist without the conviction to commit, or to want something without the desire to risk everything for its sake.*
>
> *Where is the gain to be fearful of death -- without having lived life to its fullest. Thank you, my friends, for the abundance, commitment, loyalty, respect humour and most of all love you have given me. I wish you all joy and safe passage."*
>
> *Gage*

Lucy couldn't hold back anymore and she sobbed outwardly and loudly once again.

Brother had made a teeter-totter ramp off the transom so the casket could be loaded on one end then tilted to the seaside allowing the casket to slide down the ramp into the water. He checked his longitude and latitude to note where the body was buried. A St Augustine Flag was draped over the casket with a beautiful homemade wreath of the Island flowers laid on top.

The pall-bears lifted the casket-end of the teeter and as they tilted it, the enclosed body of Gage slid into the ocean without a splash -- the wreath floating to the surface. Perfect as planned.

However, to everyone's amazement, the casket came shooting out of the water like a sounding whale!

Some screamed, many gasped, most were awe struck with the miracle. Instead of sinking to the ocean's floor, the coffin floated to the surface!!

Then the casket crashed back to sea as though to go beneath the surface, but instead it floated contentedly on the surface like a cork!

Amazement turned to speculation and finally celebration of the inexplicable supernatural miracle! Everyone waited for bubbles to surface and the coffin slip from sight... but it didn't!

"You can wait 'til de monkey shit smell like jasmine, he no gonna sink." Said Captain Brother, taking up the ship to shore radio, "Ya, dis Captain Brother, me needs to talk with Mistah Furgeson."

A horrified Miss Furgeson came into the cockpit, reaching for the microphone. "Brother o'mine, here' de problem, he no wanna sink. You put too much air in de casket." She scolded.

"Sister o'mine , I put no air den de casket! Maybe he been sitting in de sun too long!

"Well, we gotta let out the air, and the water in. Did you put holes in he coffin?" The mortician asked.

"Why for?! Me makes me caskets water-tight for eternity."

"Why for? You FOOL!. We want it to sink!" Yelled Miss Furgeson.

"He gonna sink all right, I puts near to a fifty-kilos of deep water fishing weights in der width he. " The carpenter said, pleased with his work, and his brilliance,

"And, me make he to ride upright with deep water weights laid into de coffin's bottom. And, me do dat so Mistah Gage gonna rest flat on de ocean floor look'n up. See, me does t'ink dis t'ing tru."

"Obviously, brother o'mine, Youse didn't use enough thinking power because we's got a very big problem!"

Captain Brother took the microphone. "Ya, dis Captain Brother. Do you have any suggestions on how to let the air out, and the water in?"

"No problem, mon. Simple, simple. All's you gotta do is pull he up alongside Youse boat and take Youse brace'n'bit and drill maybe half dozen holes in de lid. Not too high to de top, you no wanna drill into he face!"

There was a long silence. "We don't have a brace-n- bit, this is a boat... not a bloody carpentry shop."

"Should I go get mine?" Furgeson offered. "Could take some time cus me no sure cousin Benny didn't take she up las week."

Actually, the polished mahogany casket with real brass handles was a beautiful sight floating with the current and wind on the rich Caribbean sea. One of Gage's daughters suggested just letting him go to follow the wind."

"Don't know how that is going to work when he washes up on a foreign shore. He could end up getting buried someplace he no wanna go... like de Virgin Islands or Saint Thomas."

"Okay, let's discuss it." Brother turned to the family. "What are our options?

"Do you have a gun on board?" Asked one of the son-in-laws.

Great Idea! Everyone agreed except Miss Furgeson who was horrified at the idea so shooting holes in her masterpiece. There were certain codes of propriety in the burying business that had to be followed. In fact, it might be against the law shooting a dead person!"

Brother rolled his eyes and asked for other ideas. Why not go get the coffin and just unscrew the lid?

Eyes rolled... bad idea.

Frustrated, Captain Brother asked, "More ideas?"

"No?!" He asked when no one replied. "Well, I have an idea, but we must catch the coffin," he said.

It was not an easy task, and from the shore they suddenly saw the funeral boat tracking back and forth across the horizon. They tried to call from shore to hear what the problem was, but nobody answered. All the people on the beach could hear was people yelling orders to each other, and swearing, and a lot of laughing.

"Do you have a fire axe?" Someone asked Brother

But again, Miss Furgeson complained about chopping up her masterpiece. Finally, she decided that if the coffin were attacked at the foot end, it would be acceptable. What's a couple of toes in comparison to say ...a nose or an ear.

They were having some success chopping into the coffin until the axe got stuck and pulling it free, it slipped and, unlike the casket, the axe sank to the bottom of the ocean.

Finally, the idea of a Viking funeral where the body was placed in a boat that was set on fire and pushed out to sea, was purposed and it set well! Immediately everyone contributed some article of clothing for the funeral pyre.

For many like Jonathan it was his socks, Danielle, her shoes since other than the dress, that was all she had on. Back, in the shadows, Jonathan noticed the mystery woman slipped off her panties, and discretely slide them into the pile.

Brother took one of the flower vases, placed the flowers to the pyre, emptied the vase-water into the ocean and filled it with a "special" diesel.

Once the pile of clothing, flags, undergarments and sentiments was tied down with a rope strung through the handles of the casket, the last earthly remains of Gage were push away from the boat

"*Hasta Luego Amigo.*" Said Palis saluting the coffin.

When it was ten meters away, Brother shot it with a flare. The explosion was more than anyone expected, including Brother, sending a shower of phosphorus sparks flying towards the congregation making everyone duck for shelter as the coffin exploded in flames.

"Do you realise we are witnessing a cremation at sea. Not many can say that!" Danielle said to Jonathan.

"I cannot imagine a better send off for Gage than this. It was as though he'd scripted it!"

Suddenly, Lucy shrieked with laughter.

"What?" asked Brother, looking away from the receding coffin. Everyone turned, ready for some merriment.

"I can't." She gasped, wiping the tears from her eyes... then reconsidered.

"Well... if Gage were here looking at this scene what would he say..." She began laughing again, -- "he'd say, 'Too bad nobody brought marshmallows!"

Even Miss Furgeson had to laugh.

It was deep dusk when the "grieving" abandoned their vigilance and turned towards shore. The casket and its cargo continued to burn without signs of being extinguished, and when it was but a dwindling beacon on the horizon, it was going south by southwest towards Nicaragua.

Jonathan was pensive on the trip back,. He knew when Gage cut the marlin free that experiencing a hurricane of the magnitude of Hugo, navigating his Hotel and occupants safely through the storm was Gage's last adventure. The hand felt by old age was not in his cards!

Chapter 40

"Second Litter"

Jonathan sat cross-legged at the water's edge and the long stretch of isolated beach in either direction. Beside him sat a two-year old girl engulfed in the mysteries of the disappearing hole she had dug in the sand, only to vanish with the advancing and retracting ocean surge. For no sooner did she dig one hole than a wave no bigger than a bathtub-slosh rolled over it, taking the hole with it as it receded --leaving a smooth sand surface. Mystified, but undaunted the little girl gave it some thought -- then began again.

"Ah, the curious mind will never be bored," Jonathan thought of his own conversion to a lifestyle that allowed both curiosity and considerable time to ponder the answers. He was never bored since the "Storm of the Century" twisted his life back upon itself. Watching his daughter, Andrea a case in point. Before he and Bana were married, he'd sit on a beach hardly aware of his children playing in the water, his sole focus at the time was the work he'd brought to the Island in a well-worn briefcase.

Now as he sat there watching his daughter, he marvelled at the unfathomable complex route of the mind to develop from blank slate, "tabula rasa" of infancy to total curiosity. It was a theatre of the most complicated script written in an as yet undiscovered language. Everything happens sequentially, at a set rate, consistently. Hole--No Hole? It is the evolution of the human consciousness. Curiosity is the cutting edge of knowledge emerging from the uncertainty of ignorance.

Jonathan felt a pang, "moments-lost, as he thought about his neglect of his first children's pursuit of the curious. Children are justification for adults to act like children, he smiled. Back then when his family was young, his world was too important for play. Now he realised that the world was too unimportant to be taken seriously. He chuckled and began digging a hole beside Andrea's.

It seemed incredulous that once his life was full of certainty, his decisions well-crafted for predictable outcomes... and rich people paid him for his decisiveness. Now events flowed over him easily, one to the next without his help. He never returned to his Manhattan office. He had retired from his firm in absentia, leaving his eldest son to assume the "Chairmanship of the Board".

Jonathan smiled thinking how his house in Connecticut had sold immediately in a bull market for a cash settlement well above the listing price, while the St. Augustine house that he'd intended to sell before the storm was never listed and was now the base for a new family and a second chance to mend the errors of the past. A chance to pursue the curiosity of a child chasing holes in the sand. Still, he was a little anxious. His adult-children were coming down to the Island in a week and he wondered how they would accept his conversion.

Looking up from his labours with the sand, he saw a long silhouette coming towards them from far down the town side of isolated beach. Even at a distance, he could tell that the figure was Danielle by her strides across the hot sand -- her strides as graceful and as casual as a cat on cool moss. While balancing a bundle on her head, she moved with the stately stature of a Zulu queen... as statuesque as the first-time time they'd met at the Longstone Bar ... as statuesque as the Dior model on the poster behind Rainbow's bar.

She too had come a long way in the three years since the storm -- the consequence, he mused, of Hugo, of himself, and most of all Andrea. Out of the destruction of the hurricane, Andrea was born. 'A Phoenix.'

In the end the name "Andrea" was chosen because of its neutrality, neither judicial nor jungle. Besides both parents realised that her 'given' name had little consequence, except on documents. And during her Island life, she would go through a vast array of nicknames. Already she was called "Bunches" by all except her parents, 'Bana Bunches' was the census in their village and soon it circled the Island.

By a curious chain of events, Bana Designs had suddenly taken off in spite of Danielle's neglect of her Company. After Hugo, Danielle's life became exclusively focused upon the present and the recovery efforts on Island, putting dreams of another future on a back-shelf for another time. As a consequence, Bana designs was reduced to a beautiful website that hadn't been updated in months, and a faded sign that hung on Jonathan's front gate.

Then, either by chance or ordination (as Danielle believed) "Vanity Fair" sent a writer and photographer to the Island to do a story on Bana after the hurricane. Rumour had it that she had lost everything in the disaster and was left indigent. What they found instead was a well-grounded, happy woman, the centre of a vibrant community, caught in a collective effort to rebuild their lives.

"One Jar of Mangoes' at a Time" was the title of the article. It was a quote Bana had made in the community kitchen (her house, by day). The journalist asked about her dreams of designing her own line of clothes.

The writer wrote, "She turned from her hot stove each burner simmering fruit preserves and sterilised jars.

"'Dreams?'" she humphed wiping the curl from her forehead with the back of her wrist." The writer observed.

"Mon. Now days I just go one jar of mangoes at a time.' The article went on to paint her as a champion of the people of her village. Unfortunately, it was, a cross between a Sister Theresa and Che Guevara.

Fortunately, the journal was never read on the Islands.

"It is not communism, it is communalism." She was quoted. "Right now we are an Ad Hoc collective of individuals doing together what we can't do alone. It is not communism, it is communalism." She was quoted.

"Is it correct to say you're a socialist?" The writer asked.?

"Socialism implies a government. But right now, we are the government. We're getting no help from the outside, neither from the Island government, which is in disarray, and certainly not from

458

the outside. We're governed by a common objective and mutual respect. We have no crime, the kids still have school, but it is under a breadfruit tree instead of a roof. And no one is going to bed hungry! If disasters like Hugo become more frequent, we may be the model for the future of World! Community-ism!"

It helped that the photographer was very good, capturing both the model and the role-model. Unconscious poses, which at first glances were the taught lines of the super-model, when in truth, Daniel was stretching her aching muscles while she worked. Her beauty and her passion for life showed through the series, though her pregnancy with Andrea was still hidden. In two pictures that made it into the article, Jonathan was seen in the deep background with an identification tag, "Fellow Survivor".

The article went on to become a sensation and the dormant 'Bana Designs', the last thing on Danielle's mind, suddenly became a "cause de promo". What few designs she had on the internet now had large orders for them. And as the Island community emerged to once again self-sufficiency... and her kitchen duties became less necessary, Bana started rebuilding the company.

Within two weeks after shutting down the cannery, Bana had pulled together six sewing machines to start filling orders. Still, even with six seamstresses and four women for cutting out patterns, it was slow making dresses especially since her primary focus was on quality. But, as she soon discovered, there was a demand market that commanded substantive prices.

Jonathan started taking long walks that sometimes-had purpose but often as not they didn't. Trips of discovery. Where does this trail lead? What is this plant... that bird? Who is that, and putting names to faces was easy since they had all shared indelible histories together. What initially he lacked was understanding the local language, but he trusted their intent and simply let the words wash over him like arias in an opera sang in Latin. Still, he soon noticed that either people were slowing down their speech, or he had quickened his ear as he discovered that in fact, he understood far more *beach beside him, Andrea and her sand vanishing holes?*than he thought and his writing, which was now his primary focus, began mirroring his growing immersion into the Island culture.

"You want me to take over?" Danielle asked, kneeling down on the

"Fat chance!" He said. "But I'll share the workload."

"Andrea! Come so," Danielle pointed to the sand beyond the gentle surf's edge. "D'wave does eat you's work." She laughed. The little girl lifted her head to the sound of her mother's voice and let the surf take once again her labours.

"My strategy exactly!" Jonathan smirked with barristerial smugness,

"Humph!" Danielle humphed. "Andrea, come to me and let Mommie wipe the sand off your face." It was only when Danielle got to her feet and moved to retrieve the child, that Andrea slowly crawled away from the water's edge, and frowned severely at her mother.

"She's going to be a strong-willed woman... just like her mother." Jonathan laughed.

"Mon, you're in my bad book for letting her spoil her supper with sand."

They sat in silence watching the toddler. "You nervous about my children coming down next week?" Jonathan asked.

"Yea, a little I guess." She said giving Andrea's mouth a brisk brushing before releasing her. "I'm assuming they are pretty New England-ish ... so they may not take it well that I am a black woman."

Jonathan laughed. "You think they don't know that already. The most famous black model on the planet in the last decade and they're shocked that you're "Black"?! Come on, they are so excited about having you in the family that they are the ones tied in knots with nerves." Jonathan smirked. "Trust me, they are really happy for us." He smiled reassuringly, and then his eyes sparkled at a second thought.

460

"Mind you," he grinned. "We may have to pay <u>my</u> grandchildren extra for babysitting," he nodded to Andrea, "... babysitting -- their Aunt!"

Danielle looked at him with mocked distain. "Humph." She gave him a resigning grunt that the topic had come to an end.

"What's in the pack?" Jonathan asked.

"The usual," she reached into the bundle she had carried on her head. "Beach towels, a sun hat for Andrea, roasted peanuts, a basket of fresh mangoes from our tree ... <u>and</u> ..." She paused, letting her words hang to build anticipation... '<u>AND THIS!</u>" And she jerked out a tan manila envelope and waved it excitedly in front of him.

Jonathan's heart sank. He recognised the self-addressed envelope that he'd sent to a publisher in Barbados that produced an annual compendium of top Caribbean literature. By the fact they'd returned the manuscript, Jonathan knew it was his <u>first</u> rejection slip.

"Well, open it!" Danielle demanded.

Reluctantly, he slit open the envelope and began to read, keeping a stoic demure to the last -- looking up defeated!

Then, he let out an uncharacteristic yell. "They're taking it!!" He yelled. They are going to publish it in next year's anthropology!"

Infected by her parents' excitement ... their hugging and laughing, Andrea too laughed with glee and clapped her sandy hands.

" See, I told you all long, you're going to be a writer. What did you send them? ' May I see?" Danielle grabbed the manuscript from his grasp and began to read while Jonathan took a ripe mango from the full basket and began to peel it for Andrea.

CALVIN and ALPHONSO.
By. Jon Douglas

"I just came back from a hike with two ancient neighbours. It is our custom, and like Carnival, each year we go through the same ritual of walking our shared fence line, which takes fifteen minutes if you're under fifty, an hour if your eighty-something and prone to visiting... as are my two companions.   Still, though our corner bounds are marked by four-hundred-year-old gumtrees, and unlikely to be altered, I look forward to the experience with great anticipation.

Our mutual land boundaries sit on a ridge shouldering off a jungled volcano, the consequence of a crack in the earth's mantle midway along the Caribbean fault --through which molten-magma once surged up for ten miles across and three thousand feet above the ocean.

The trade winds brought soil, seeds, birds, reptiles, and a working jungle complete with life zones of birds, bugs, exotic trees, all carried on the wind's currents from Africa and the Amazon. Arawak Indians from South America, Carib Indians after them. Plantations, slaves, freemen and finally down to the present owners-- to Calvin and Alphonse and my land between them.

Calvin Webbe and Alphonso Liburg are friends. They have been since birth, eighty years plus. Calvin lives at the top of the ghaut with a view clear to Saba Island, while Alphonso resides down in the ghaut, on a garden plot of rich bottom soil. Calvin has to walk to his garden, Alphonso likes to have his near so he can talk to it -- hear it's reply.

Calvin wears a flat English roadster hat and a Howdy-Dowdy wide grin that stretches his cheeks chipmunk fat. His pupils are worn to ebony that's been lacquered with polished humour. The whites of his eyes are marbled with coffee-colored tracks -- trails from squinting at sun-soaked fields. The bridge of his broad nose arcs back exposing two wide, open, tunnels into his soul it seems, and I feel embarrassed to stare too long. But Calvin doesn't care if you see his soul, all is in order.

Alphonso wears a baseball cap from a long time back, before plastic snaps made one size fit all. Back when the hat you picked out at the store had to fit you for the rest of your life. And it seems that Alphonso either didn't spend enough time shopping, or maybe he just hadn't stopped growing when he bought it, because it sits high on his round breadfruit head like a dried leaf.

His most prominent feature, however, is a great upper lip which hangs like a curtaining over his protruding teeth. Sometimes the lip drapes down with heavy shyness, but when it lifts, it exposes a stage full of grinning teeth caught up in a gentle comedy that seems to follow Alphonso like a stray carnival. It's no secret that Alphonso is different. His eyes are too innocent for an adult, they are Christmas-child eyes of wonderment and beatitude for even the common things. And though his hands show the wear of two lifetimes, his soul is uncalloused.

Alphonso is a "Yep, das so" sort of man -- even when his answer doesn't make sense. "Will it rain or not today, Alphonso?" One asks, and "Yep das so," he'll say emphatically. With Alphonso, you're not completely sure if he's shy, slow, deaf, all three, or -- none of them, for he might just as well, possess the wisdom of Saul and the inner peace of Christ.

"Who makes you gates?" Calvin inquires, as we begin our hike at my gate posts.

"Sam Webbe. Any relation?" I inquire assuming everyone on Island is related.

"None a-tall. He be de boy o' de Zion Webbes. He fodder's name be Abrohom -- Abrohom Webbe from Brown Hill.

Alphonso frowns. "Who dat be?"

"Abrohom Webbe? You don't know Abrohom Webbe? Mon, you's trick'n me." Calvin stares astonished at Alphonso, and suddenly I see by his look that whether Alphonso is shy, slow, deaf or all of them, or none of them and the incarnate of Buddha, Calvin' contribution to their friendship is infinite patience.

"You <u>know</u> de mon," Calvin argues. "Dey calls he 'Mongoose'. He's de mon whot morried de Liburg girl from Hardtimes. He mudder be Lindicea Freemon. Me wife calls she Auntie."

"<u>I</u> had an Auntie Freeman." Alphonso says. ".... but she longtime-now be dead."

463

"Mon!" Calvin wags his head sadly with frustration "... Everybody on St. Augustine gots an Auntie Freeman!

"No, de one what's I speak of worked the land down by 'Remember Me ...'"

And so it goes, back and forth, for the two old men are as familiar with each other as two mango trees growing old, side by side, their lives are so intertwined that their conversations are like limbs rubbing against each other in the winds of December. And should one die, the living one would surely hold him up, until death would eventually topple both.

And, as we hack our way through the year's growth of vines, the two old friends work their way through their private jungle of distant Island genealogy. Diligently, sorting through common friends and relatives' lives, exploring one by one in search of Mister 'Abrohom Webbe'.

Then... just when it seems that in fact Alphonso does <u>not</u> know the man, he blurts out, "I know'd de mon!" Two egrets exploded in startled flight from a corner gumtree. "Chure, chure, I does know'd de mon. He be a friend to me."

"Well," Calvin sighs with finality. But then he adds with sobriety, "I hope you wasn't too attached ... cuz he dead!"

"Yea so?!" The curtain drops and Alphonso grabs for a tree trunk, clearly stunned. "When dat be."

"A year ago come June, mon! Where you be all dat time dat you don't hear so?"

"Den!" Alphonso exclaims. "He a jumbie -- or a zombie be!" His big walnut eyes expand even wider than usual, "cuz me jus see'd d'mon yesterday morn heggling fish from Miss Brown."

"Oh mon!" Calvin snaps, suddenly realising that after all their laborious travels through Alfonso's memory, they are <u>still</u> not talking about the same man.

"Abrohom Webbe!" He barks, "Mon, I knows you know'd de mon."

"Abrohom Webbe!" Alphonse exclaims. "Mon ... I tout you mean de odder <u>Alfonso</u> Webbe!" Then he pauses in thought for a moment, "but he ain't dead ... then he shakes his great head, "sides he ain't got no Auntie Freeman. And he ain't from Brown Pasture."

"Brown Hill." Sighed Calvin.

The hike around the circumference of the fence-line takes exactly the same amount of time as the conversation, and one hour to the mark, we are back where we began, at my gates. Alphonso, this time, looks around closely and sees afresh the familiar terrain.

"Dem's fine gates. Who'd makes dem?" He asks.

"A man named Sam Webbe made them?" I say, understanding full well that I have just stepped onto a merry-go-round, and that we will never reach anywhere that we haven't been before. "

"Do you know the man?" I ask.

"Now tell me'gin what mon dat be?" Alphonso smiles and looks at Calvin.

The End.

Danielle lifted her eyes from the manuscript. They were full of emotion. "You <u>will</u> write... and it <u>will</u> be read because you see with your heart, and not just with your eyes!"

She turned to the child. "Andrea, I told you your Daddy would be a writer."

She spoke... then turned to the sea, and then him. There were tears in her eyes! "You write with your heart.

He thought about her words for a long time. Still the question loomed, "About <u>what</u> would he write if he did decide to do it seriously." His eyes fell upon the fresh mango in his daughter's sandy hands, and then the basket beside her... brimming with them, <u>all</u> off the ancient mango tree in their backyard.

He remembered when he first saw the great, ancient Buddha tree, how one of the work crew would in passing, strike it with a machete, and grudgingly the tree would produce a single mango, maybe out of habit, or just to prove it could.

Then came the "Hurricane of the Century" stripping it to a barren trunk! Surely it would die or be the last thing to recover. But suddenly, it too tapped into an ancient elan vital and like the Island itself, against all odds, not only did it withstand the storm, it produced mangoes by the bushel. That is what he'd write about.

Made in the USA
Middletown, DE
03 September 2024

60232479R00258